Kingmaker

by

Alexey Braguine

First Edition

Edited by:
Daniel Godfrey
Nancy C. Lepri

Formatted by:
Laurie Christopherson

Cover design:
Sean Dickey

ISBN 10: 0-9800733-4-0

ISBN 13: 978-0-9800733-4-8

PUBLISHED BY Artistic Endeavors Publishing, LLC

www.artisticendeavorspublishing.com

Dedication

To Barry and Linda Piper:
Friends everyone should have.

Acknowledgements

No book is the creation of one single person. In writing *Kingmaker*, I had the help of many. Eugenia Arensburger edited the first draft and pointed out inconsistencies. Leslie Kellas Payne taught me a lot about writing suspense. A virus in the computer is also to be thanked as it forced me to rewrite the whole story from memory.

I must also thank the members of Brenda Hyat's online critique group for invaluable comments that improved the work.

Sher Hames Torres, Charlotte Parker, June Phyllis Baker, Pamela Reese, Nancy C. Lepri, and Neva Franks participated in finding fault with the manuscript until it was suitable to submit to a publisher. My thanks to all.

Last but not least, I thank the wonderful staff at Light Sword Publishing: Linda Daly, who runs a publishing house the old-fashioned way; Daniel Godfrey and Nancy Lepri edited the final draft.

All errors and omissions are my own.

Prologue

Impatiently, she glanced over her shoulder at the door to the parking apron and freedom. Her last obstacle stood across the counter, meticulously droning his weather briefing. "The Intertropical Convergence Zone is well south of us." The African meteorologist tapped the weather chart with the eraser side of his pencil. "You should have a pleasant flight."

Anna Karolenko smiled back. "The winds pushing it back will slow me down over the Sahara."

"C'est la vie, mademoiselle. There's always reason to complain about the weather."

"I never complain when the news is delivered by charming people." Anna gathered the charts and shoved them into her flight bag.

"I hope your visit to our country has been rewarding."

"I'll be back." She lied.

"We are always at your service."

"Aurevoir, monsieur, and thank you." Anna turned and tried not to make her departure seem too hasty.

Expecting Longo or his minions to appear at any moment, she stepped out into the overheated tarmac. After the hum and rattle of air conditioners inside the airport offices, the silence on the parking apron was almost eerie. Controlling her urge to run, she strode toward the twin-engine Aerostar on loan from the CIA. It was a beautiful, fast airplane, a pleasure to fly. With refueling stops in Khartoum and Cairo, she would land in Crete in ten hours.

Her CIA contact was an urbane gentleman of the old school and she was guaranteed an excellent dinner while he debriefed her.

Going against normal preflight routine, she climbed in without inspecting the airplane.

It didn't matter that she was going to fly over some of the most desolate geography on earth. She had to get out!

Without using the checklist, she fired up the engines and taxied at high speed. Skipping a run-up check, she called on the radio, "Aerostar alpha-victor-bravo is ready for takeoff."

To her relief, the tower answered. "Wind is calm, cleared for takeoff, contact departure control on one-two-two-seven."

Anna smiled. Tower, Departure, and Approach Controls were the same guy talking into three different radios.

Oil pressure, oil temperature, all gauges indicated normal. The airplane gained speed and soon was airborne. "Gear up, flaps up," she said as if she was flying a large transport airplane.

The city of Turako vanished under the wings. Anna turned north. She loosened her seat belt, shifted in her seat, and engaged the autopilot at five-thousand feet. The thought that in a few minutes she would be out of Zengawali airspace almost made her dizzy and her legs began to shake.

Anna lit a cigarette, reclined the back of her chair and propped her feet on the instrument panel. That prevented her legs from shaking. She thought about her arrival in Crete. Free of fear, she would treat herself to two glasses of wine.

The terrain ahead was becoming arid, rolling plains sparsely covered with scrub and crisscrossed by dry riverbeds.

Passing seven-thousand feet, a sharp bang on the port side rattled the airplane. Anna's heart made a double beat and her skin felt as if a thousand ants crawled over her.

A thin veil of gray smoke poured out of the left engine's cowling.

"Damn." Her facial muscles sagged. Turako was only twenty minutes away. She didn't want to go back there. There was an airstrip in Wow. That was an hour-and-a-half away--but in the Sudan. She would go there.

The oil pressure gauge had fallen into the red.

Anna punched the feathering button and watched the propeller come to a stop. The airplane could maintain five- thousand feet with one engine out. She watched the airspeed bleed to a hundred-and-sixty knots. She re-estimated her ETA. Two hours to Wow.

Smoke stopped coming out of the engine.

Anna trimmed the rudder to help her keep a straight course.

She wondered who was in control of Wow--the Sudanese government, some local warlord, or one of several rebel groups? For all she knew, she could end up in a harem.

Movement of the wing drew her attention. The damn thing was wobbly. "Damn, damn, damn." She pulled the throttle of the good engine back a little to reduce speed and stress on the wing, and scanned for an open field where she could make an emergency landing. "Longo, you bastard!" That hadn't been a cylinder swallowing a valve or tie rod busting. The son of a whore had placed a bomb!

The airplane was getting difficult to control and developed a nasty vibration. Anna eased the wounded machine to the left a little, aiming for an area free of huts. She hoped the fences were not stone. All the cultivated fields were too small to land at and the non-farmed areas had scattered trees.

Going through four-thousand feet, she saw it--a school with a soccer field next to it, good enough for a belly landing.

Turbulence rocked the plane. Now, the wing was actually flapping and the nose corkscrewing. The engine cowling separated from the wing and flew off. Anna battled the controls. The airplane no longer flew. It swayed through the air. "Keep flying!" she hollered.

About five-hundred meters to go. "We're going to make it."

The turbulence increased as she got closer to the ground. She had the yoke twisted all the way to the right and her right foot fully depressed on the rudder pedal.

Another bump rattled the plane. The wing separated, the airplane flipped and entered a into a graveyard spiral. "Longo, you bastard!" was the last thing Anna said.

∼

The children in the school scrambled outside. Several goats, their hair aflame, ran from the ball of fire on the ground.

Part I
Dead on Departure

Chapter 1

"Enough!" John Trager growled through clenched teeth. He wanted to spit on the note and jam it down Blanky's throat.

Lunch at the Frog place, noon.

Closing his hand into a fist, he scrunched the arrogant communication. "Enough," he repeated to the walls of the austere office in the attic of his Georgetown townhouse. With a growing sense of bravado, he fed the note together with an incriminating copy of the ISAS--Institute for Strategic Advanced Studies--report to the shredder.

The voracious machine buzzed, a happy vandal, singing a song of rebellion.

Humming along, Trager hit send on his computer. The newsletter, a paraphrased version of the ISAS report, was on its circuitous way. Seventy-three clients in the White House, Pentagon and Senate would eat it up. Though he hated himself for doing it, Trager slanted the report to what the White House wanted to hear. At two-hundred bucks a pop, today's issue would bring the Merril kids' trust fund up to the level required to see them through college.

Free of his moral obligation, he was unfettered to move on. Blankenship--Blanky behind his back--would shit when he heard what Trager had to say.

Thinking of the upcoming change in his life, he gazed at the framed photographs on the wall, all of them fifteen years or older, as if his life had stopped when he left the Marine Corps. Trager shook his head. Fifteen years of drifting from mission to mission with brief interludes in between. Like an avaricious collector, every time he returned to Washington, he bought a piece of fine furniture or a painting to plush up his house. *What in the hell for?* To impress cockroaches and Norwegian rats who proliferated during his absences? He swiveled his chair and his gaze rested on the neatly made-up bunk, which could pass boot camp inspection. That was all he needed, a place to lay his head. In the rest of the house, he felt like a visitor from his earlier life of genteel poverty. Were his parents still alive, he would have given the house to them. They would have liked it.

Trager sighed. Time to go see Blanky, the gourmet prick.

~

Ignoring the muggy July heat, Trager strode down M Street toward La Cigalle. Elation, doubt, fear spun in his mind, accelerating his heartbeat. After all the years of working with Blanky, Trager knew the old spook's reaction would not be a pat on the back and a good luck speech. He pushed the restaurant's frosted glass door open. A shock of cold air made his light gray tropical suit cling like a leech. Like aliens from another world, the denizens of the nation's capital lived much of their lives in artificial environments shielding them from the realities of the planet. Trager waited for the *maitre d'* to emerge.

"*Bonjour Monsieur.*"

"*Bonjour Etienne, il fait froid ici.*"

Etienne smiled and winked. "Shortly, when our clientele arrives, we'll enjoy plenty of hot air."

Trager followed Etienne to the plush corner booth Blankenship always reserved. For an experienced case officer, it was bad tradecraft. Or maybe Blankenship had the booth bugged. Next time, he would refuse to sit there. Next time? Trager reminded himself he and Blankenship were finished. Severing a relationship with the CIA was final and total. Trager would instantly become an outsider to be warily observed from a distance. The few friends Trager had would vanish from his map.

A fanatic for psychological advantage, Blankenship never arrived early to a meeting with an agent. He always gave the poor wretch at least ten minutes to feel nervous and insecure. He probably lurked in the lobby of the building across the street, watching the restaurant to see if anyone followed Trager. Even in DC, Blankenship acted as if he were in Moscow at the height of the Cold War.

The old spook would make it difficult for Trager to quit. Wishing he were in Arles or Aix en Provence, or anywhere out of Blanky's reach, Trager poured water into his Ricard and swirled the drink, watching it turn from clear amber into milky vanilla.

To Trager's surprise, only two minutes late, Blankenship huffed up the steps to the dining room. He bulldozed past Etienne and slid his bulk into the booth. Ignoring Trager, he let out a grunt and turned to the waiter, who rushed over as if his life depended on swift action. "*Martini, Monsieur?*"

"*Oui, comme toujour,*" Blankenship growled.

Trager sipped his drink while he studied his boss. The carefully trimmed, ash-colored beard gave Blankenship a sinister appearance. He no longer wore comfortably shabby but well-tailored suits. His almost new seersucker, already too tight, barely hid the Colt .45 in a shoulder holster.

Except when inside the Pickle Factory, Blankenship and his pistol never parted company.

In less than a minute, the waiter returned with the martini.

Blankenship raised his glass. "It's good to see you, Johnny."

Surprised at Blanky's bonhomie, Trager chuckled, trying to disguise his anxiety. "This is our farewell lunch," he blurted.

Blankenship tilted his head to one side. "What do you think about the elections in Kenya?"

Trager wondered why Blankenship bothered to ask such a banal question--compared to Trager's--Blanky's expertise of African politics was encyclopedic. "My parting pearls of wisdom--about time they got rid of Moi--but I doubt Kibaki can clean up the mess."

The waiter returned.

Finished ordering, Trager turned to Blankenship with a wicked smile. "And a bottle of the best Burgundy in the house."

Blankenship frowned as the waiter left. "Isn't that extravagant?"

"My last chance to skin the poor, meek tax-paying stiffs."

Blankenship shook his head and launched a startling bomb. "Remember Dankov?"

Trager swallowed the wrong way. He jerked the blue decorative handkerchief from his outside breast pocket and coughed into it.

Blankenship seemed amused as he watched Trager's distress.

Recovered from his coughing fit, Trager gave Blankenship a hard look, took a sip of his drink. When the tickling in his throat stopped, he said, "I came here to gracefully--"

"Remember Dankov?"

"Who?" Trager answered as if interrogated by a foreign security service.

"Dankov. Your *compadre*."

"He always gave me indigestion." Trager didn't know whether to blame Dankov, Blankenship, or himself for what happened in Bratislava. But that was ancient history.

"I want you to find him."

Trager laughed. "That's a good one. You gave him such an effective new identity you lost him?"

"This isn't funny. Your show of amusement is impolite."

"You've screwed up. Now you want me to wash your dirty skivvies--the answer is *no*. Would you like me to spell it?"

Blankenship's face reddened. He opened his mouth as if to say something, but the food arrived.

"*Bon appetit,*" the waiter said as he withdrew.

"Listen to me. I'll spell out a couple of things for you." Blankenship's face returned to its normal gray. "Rosemarie Merrill. Would you like to see the nice lady go to jail?"

Trager fought to control himself, put down his fork. Rosemarie provided him with copies of the ISAS reports, which helped him make the newsletter such a success. "You're talking gibberish."

"I can also give the IRS your list of subscribers. They'll find it fascinating."

Trager wondered how Blankenship found out about his newsletter, which was re-transmitted from an Internet café in Barcelona. Threatening Rosemarie was incredibly low. What made it more galling was that during the Gulf War an American plane had drilled her husband. With Chuck in a wheelchair and two kids to raise, she had a hard time. Intelligence officers like Blankenship were sewer rats with good table manners. "Are you willing to admit to engaging in domestic spying?"

Without looking up, Blankenship answered. "Haven't you heard of anonymous tips?"

"Can't you find something pleasant to say? After all, this is an expensive lunch. I'd like to finish it."

"Dankov left his suburban Iowa house, deserted his American wife, and reverted to his real identity."

This wasn't surprising. Trager couldn't imagine the outrageous Dankov happy as a suburbanite. "So what? The Cold War is over. Defector goes home. It's not even newsworthy."

"He's morphed into a troublemaker."

"He was always a troublemaker, always caused problems." Trager tasted his crepe. It was superb.

"He's now working against U.S. interests."

"I have trouble believing that."

"I want you to find him."

"Okay, I'll go to Russia tomorrow and whack him. This is back in fashion, I hear."

Blankenship sighed loudly and rolled his eyes, looking at the ceiling as if seeking divine inspiration. His gaze returned to Trager. "You'll find him in Africa." After delivering this last bit of information, he got busy harpooning snails.

Trager's stomach knotted. After two more bites of his crepe, he felt full.

"Eat," Blankenship said. "The worst sin is the waste of taxpayer's money." With a piece of bread Blankenship sopped the last of the garlic oil, shrugged, took Trager's crepe, and ate it, too.

Trager toyed with his fork, wanting to twist it inside Blanky's gut.

Blankenship daubed his lips with a napkin. "You have two weeks to find Dankov."

"Send someone else."

"I have. They failed. I want you to ask him what the fuck he's up to--and give him my personal, warmest regards." Blankenship smiled. "He used to call me Uncle Dougie."

"How touching."

"You lack understanding of warmth in human relations."

"Uncle Dougie--this side of you I've never seen."

"You don't deserve it."

"I'm tired. I want a fresh start. I want to have long-term human contact in my real identity. I'm searching for a polite way to tell you to go fuck yourself."

"Johnny, you are impulsive. Don't burn the house that sheltered you just because it's ugly."

"It stinks."

"You have two weeks to find out what Dankov is up to. By then, you will have found a way to express your feelings of abhorrence or reconsider." Blankenship's expression softened. "One last favor for Uncle Doug."

Trager took a deep breath. Two more weeks under Blanky's thumb wasn't the end of the world. He always knew severing his ties to the Agency would be difficult. "Where in Africa is he?"

"Zengawal. He's running a bunch of mercs. And I'm getting bad vibes." Blankenship took an envelope out of his pocket and slid it across the table. "You fly to Brussels tonight, connect with Sabena for your flight to Kinshasa. You'll probably need to bribe someone there to get you a seat on Air Zengawal. I need the info *pronto*."

"Okay, I'm giving you two week's notice *now*."

Blankenship nodded. His eyes narrowed and the corners of his mouth sagged.

"Who's my contact?"

"Nobody. We don't have an embassy in Turako and no station."

"I don't believe it."

"You don't have to. Fact--no local contact." Blankenship shook his head and sighed. "We don't even have a consulate there."

"Come on." Trager was sure Blankenship was lying. "Not even one guy under commercial cover?"

"You know perfectly well that in the last few years we've been decapitated. On 9/11, the FBI had more agents in New York City alone than we had case officers worldwide."

Trager hated to agree with Blanky. Inept foreign policy, politics, turf wars and bureaucracy had dramatically eroded the CIA's human intelligence collection capabilities.

Blankenship placed his elbows on the table and leaned forward. "You're flying solo. Commercial cover."

Trager lifted the envelope. "Pretty thin briefing."

"One sheet, one mug shot. The expense money is in your account."

Trager opened the envelope and inspected the photograph of a brunette. The fourth-generation copy of the passport photo couldn't hide a striking face. "Who is she?"

"Mademoiselle Simone Loriot. Dankov was last seen in her company." Blankenship grinned. "A pretty woman, a lead."

"Who is she?"

"That's what you'll find out and report."

"I thought you were interested in Dankov."

"Yeah, and his Axis of Evil."

Trager wanted to smile but didn't. Blankenship's contempt for politicians was well known in the Agency. After President Bush's Axis of Evil speech, Blankenship took to carrying a roll of duct tape when walking the Pickle Factory's corridors and asking for volunteers to wrap tape around Bush's mouth. It was rumored the director had Blankenship on the carpet over it.

Trager slid the photograph back into the envelope.

"If I accept this assignment, will you destroy whatever evidence you have on Mrs. Merrill?"

"If? Dear boy, you misread me again." Blankenship touched his beard. "You have no choice."

"I asked you a question."

"Extortionists *never* destroy the goods."

"Driven by desperation, after lunch, I'll go to the Dupont Metro station and jump in front of a train," he said only half-joking, worried about Rosemarie.

"I wish I could go with you and watch."

"Give me your word you'll destroy the evidence."

Blankenship sighed. "Okay, you have my word."

Without illusions about Blankenship's sense of honor, Trager pulled out the rest of the contents of the envelope--airline tickets and some pocket litter. "You call this a briefing?"

"Mademoiselle Loriot works in the Ministry of Education."

"A white woman in an African government?"

"Interesting, isn't it?"

"Is she with the UN?"

The question brought a grin to Blankenship's face. "Supposedly she's a French national. But the French claim to have zero on her. A Simone Loriot worked for the UN refugee organization in Bosnia." He reached over. "Now give me the picture back. You don't want to be caught carrying it."

"Since I'm not the first assigned to this job, what happened to the others?"

"They failed to contact Dankov."

"That's obvious--why did they fail?"

Blankenship shifted in his seat. "You have access to Dankov, you and he were buddies."

"What happened to them?" Trager tapped the table with his fingers.

Blankenship's expression grew dark. "You're good at finding the truth. When you return, *you'll* let me know." He reached inside his jacket and drew out an American passport. "Use the Davenport identity."

Chapter 2

After lunch with Blanky, Trager ran a quick computer scan on Zengawal before having to leave for the airport. He found nothing he didn't already know. Two years earlier, Pierre Bamondo returned from exile. In a bloody coup, he overthrew dictator Mbaya. He then nationalized the diamond mines. The U.S. and most other countries withdrew their diplomatic personnel. Like the rest of the world, Africa was becoming less secure. Marco Polo, Livingstone, Baker and others would have not been able to carry out their expeditions in the twenty-first century. Some progress, Trager thought.

Not far south of the equator, the old Fokker F-27 turboprop shook and rattled as it banked, dodging tall columns of vapor flashing with lightning. His attention outside the airplane, Trager tried to ignore the stench caused by airsick passengers.

Most operations took days, if not weeks, of preparation and study. Never in his life had he launched into a mission with such haste. In a way, he was flattered. It showed the CIA had confidence in him. Trager reminded himself he had to shake out old mental habits. Who cared if they had confidence in him or not? On the other hand, one had to rely on the survival habits formed by experience. He was still the best and had one more job to do. His disenchantment would have to wait 'til he got back.

As Blankenship predicted, Trager bribed a ticket agent to get a seat on Air Zengawal's flight 202.

With nothing better to do, when clouds permitted, he searched the ground below for some hint on their position. Memorizing land features not only relaxed him, but also might be useful in the future.

Blankenship could stoop pretty damn low, but he didn't send agents on kamikaze missions. Was this a first, or had Trager's status changed to expendable? He brushed the bothersome question aside. He suspected two dead agents had paved the way to this mission. Like a drug, finding the truth was addictive. Damn the gourmet prick, he knew how to manipulate people.

Beyond the line of thunderstorms, the air smoothed. Forest gave way to cleared fields and scattered arid villages, thirsty for the rains the airplane had encountered.

White mercenaries kept a low profile, and Trager was convinced his only lead was a weak one. Since European nations first established colonies, adventurers, fortune hunters, fugitives, exiles and family black sheep had flocked to this alluring continent. Since decolonization, new types of expatriates appeared on the scene, so-called experts, and the rip-off artists. Trager wondered into what category Simone Loriot fell, and more importantly, Dankov. He chuckled silently. Dankov had a talent for disturbing governments. In the past, he shook the Kremlin. Now Washington was rattled.

With a soft thunk, wheels hit concrete.

The plane taxied past rusting metal hangars and turned onto the apron in front of a terminal with peeling paint.

The well over twenty-four hours in airplanes and airports hadn't done Trager's leg any good. It ached more than usual. The rare parachute failure had not only ruined his military career, but had also intensified his fear of heights into full-fledged acrophobia. Trager retrieved his briefcase from under the seat. His grip tightened around the handle as he got up to begin his *last* fucking mission.

Going down the short steps to the tarmac, he ignored a menacing group of sloppy-looking soldiers aboard an open Land Rover.

From Tangiers to Cape Town, Africa was a land of wonders and contrasts. Below the wonder, one didn't need to dig deep to find government sponsored danger and brutality.

Doing his best to appear disoriented and lost, Trager followed the neatly-uniformed female ramp agent into the terminal building.

Momentarily blinded by the dimness inside, he almost bumped into the man in front of him as the ramp agent stopped abruptly, swung her arm out, and said, "Zengawali citizens this way."

A burly African in a black safari suit held a 35-mm camera against his face, aimed at Trager. The shutter zinged three times. Trager wondered if the local service's clumsiness was a warning or ineptitude.

The black suit nodded at the ramp agent who put her arm down and turned smiling. "Welcome to Zengawal."

~

"Reason for your visit?" The white-uniformed immigration officer inspected Trager's passport identifying him as John Davenport.

"I sell textbooks. I'll be visiting the Ministry of Education." Trager pulled out a business card that reinforced his cover.

The immigration officer glanced at it. "How long do you stay?"

"A few days."

"Going to sell American textbooks in a French speaking country?"

"I represent a Canadian publisher."

The man with the camera bothered him. If things got ticklish, his only emergency contact was a fax machine in an Atlanta lawyer's office.

The immigration officer nodded. "A fifteen-day tourist visa costs thirty dollars." Trager handed over the money. The immigration officer stamped his passport and landing card. "Welcome to the Republic of Zengawal." He pointed at a black-and-white portrait of president Bamondo that hung behind him. "*We* wish you a pleasant stay."

As he headed for the customs hall, Trager reviewed his meticulously selected pocket litter of an innocuous businessman from Cleveland--an address book with names and addresses of Cleveland residents, a restaurant receipt, ticket stubs from a concert. He carried nothing that would tie him to Washington. So they photographed him. Big deal. His cover would stand scrutiny. After all, this wasn't Czechoslovakia during the Cold War.

A Hindi couple looked on despairingly as a customs inspector dumped out the contents of their luggage.

Trager studied the faces peering through the glass door leading to the Arrivals Hall. Several men held out signs with passengers' names on them. Everything looked normal.

"Anything to declare?"

"No."

The customs man made a chalk mark on Trager's gray Samsonite and waved him through.

Piece of cake. Davenport, watch yourself.

Harsh sunlight struck Trager outside the terminal building. He donned Ray-Ban aviator sunglasses. His forehead burned.

A policeman wearing a kepi waved his white baton at a battered-looking taxi. "Where to, *Monsieur?*"

"Hotel Metropole."

The policeman nodded. "Don't pay more than seventy-five zee-franks. Taxi drivers are crooks."

"Thank you." Trager moved toward the yellow-and-black taxis lined up at the curb.

The constable's baton across his chest made him stop.

Now what?

The policeman waved to an African couple who got into the first taxi. A cab that had not been queuing pulled up against the curb.

Trager had no choice but to get in or make a scene.

Cooling wind from open windows hit Trager's sweaty chest. The driver wove around potholes and groups of oblivious men standing and talking in the middle of the road. Women wore colorful towel-size cotton tangas wrapped over dowdy dresses. Most of them carried heavy loads strapped to their backs.

The taxi driver barely missed a man coifed in a pink plastic shower cap, pushing a bicycle loaded with sacks of charcoal.

Shantytowns gave way to solid buildings with stores attended by Hindis.

The taxi turned from the airport road and entered a wide park-divided boulevard. Except for a tall modern apartment building with laundry sprouting from its balconies, two- and three-story buildings of the colonial era lined the well-kept boulevard.

With a squeal of brakes, the taxi stopped in front of a four-story beige building. An elevated terrace with tables and bright parasols gave the otherwise stolid edifice a festive appearance. The terrace was already half full with the pre-lunch drinks crowd. As the driver removed his suitcase, Trager studied the clientele. Of course, there was no sign of Dankov.

~

Light filtered through slats of the shuttered window. An overhead fan rotated slowly, giving the dark room a soporific quality. Trager fought a strong desire to stretch out on the bed. He was glad he had chosen the old hotel. Even with the paint beginning to peel, it had style. He picked up the phone and dialed the number of the Ministry of Education, got Simone Loriot's secretary, and made an appointment for the following day. If the local security service was interested in him, the call served to reinforce his cover as well as to start his search.

He got out of his sticky clothes, took a cold shower and dressed in a cool, tailor-made safari suit that would blend with the attire of resident whites.

The hotel verandah was obviously a popular lunch place. European businessmen jovially mingled with Africans and Hindis. The number of bottles of Jumbo Lager on the tables and bar indicated it was a popular beer. Trager sidled up to the bar and ordered one. The barman poured it into a glass mug. Through the babble of French, English and German, he detected a conversation in Russian; two engineers discussed the repair of a power plant. Again, he wondered what he would do if la Loriot did not furnish him with a lead to find Dankov. He could hang out at this bar hoping for Dankov to make an appearance or start scouring a country half the size of France. If Dankov were with a bunch of mercenaries, he would be in the jungle or in the mountains. As at the beginning of all missions, a depressing loneliness crept in. Trager's chances of success looked minimal. He cursed Blankenship, wondered about the man's real motives. He looked around, trying to spot Americans, but didn't see any.

~

In the afternoon, as suggested by a hotel brochure, Trager walked past Flamingo House, the presidential palace. It was a pleasant white, neoclassical building surrounded by a park. In sharp contrast to the slovenly soldiers at the airport, the palace guards were neatly turned out in well-fitting, starched camouflage uniforms and carried new-looking Kalashnikovs.

The cooler air coming from the palace's park brought relief from the overheated breath of the city center.

Trager continued downhill past the palace and strolled around a lake dotted with flamingoes. The sight was beautiful, but Trager's thoughts kept wandering back to the cameraman at the airport. The unspeakable had happened. The local security service had been informed of *his* arrival. That info could have only come from Washington.

A gaudily painted bus left a black cloud as it roared by. Trager pretended to cough, using the distraction to look around for a tail. There were enough pedestrians on the lakeshore boulevard. Any one of them could be tailing him.

Decaying pastel-colored villas nestled under a cliff lined the wide street. Corn grew in some of the front gardens. In the colonial era, before Zengawal's secession from the Congo, comfortable Belgians probably inhabited the street. Villas perched on top of the hill appeared better kept. From studying the city map, he knew the area was called Flamingo Heights.

Back on the main boulevard, he still hadn't spotted anyone shadowing. The smell of freshly roasted coffee drew him to a Lebanese café with sidewalk tables. He ordered Turkish coffee. The sweet mud-like drink restored his energy.

Sunset neared. Under a large gazebo in the park, a military band tuned up and a crowd began to gather. The aroma of roasting corn competed with that of coriander, turmeric and hot curry coming from Indian restaurants. Trager listened to the overture from *Man of La Mancha* and resumed his tour.

The park was now full of people. African ladies in long colorful dresses and tall turbans, Indian women in saris promenaded in a show of elegance. Using steel rollers similar to wringers in early washing machines, street vendors squeezed sugar cane juice. Children ran here and there, chewing on sugar cane sticks. A blind beggar jumped to the side to avoid a collision with a running boy.

Trager pretended to be window shopping and watched the beggar's reflection on shop windows.

The quantities of goods in the shops and the number of people buying, suggested a thriving economy. A store advertised duty-free diamonds. Trager knew Zengawal exported tea and that there was a boycott on Zengawali diamonds since the mines were nationalized after the coup.

Daylight faded. Shops began to close. The beggar talked with two men and shuffled off into the crowd in the park.

Observed or not, it was time to begin his round of local bars. Working under the noses of the local service was part of the game. If lucky, he would run into Dankov. At least if there were any mercs around, Trager was sure he would recognize them.

After he left the second bar, he was sure the two men in Hawaiian-style shirts and sunglasses who had talked with the beggar tailed him.

Trager entered the Okapi Bar, a large, long room paneled in dark wood. A mean-looking Cape buffalo head with spectacular curving horns mounted behind the bar dominated less impressive hunting trophies hung on the walls. Trager noted the head of a Bongo, the most elusive of forest antelopes. The place bespoke an era when Africa was the playground of the well to do.

He ordered another Campari and soda, studied the crowd by looking in the large mirror behind the bar, mostly men, probably business people. Three heavily made-up African hookers wearing blond wigs sat on the far end of the bar eyeballing him. No one in the room looked the type Trager was interested in. At least his shadows stayed outside, giving him an opportunity to shake them off. Trager ambled down a dimly-lit corridor past the restrooms, looking for a rear exit. A closed grille with a sign *Access interdit* barred his way. He pressed the door handle and went through.

The unmistakable snap stopped him. A big bruiser with a shaved head materialized from the darkness, aiming a sawed-off shotgun at Trager. "*Peut pas entrer.*"

"*Pardon.*" Whatever the bruiser guarded, he was serious about it. Trager shrugged and turned around. He had to learn the city. A feeling of inadequacy oppressed him.

In front of the Okapi, his two shadows stood next to a street vendor eating barbecued green corn.

Avoiding eye contact, Trager stepped briskly past and looked for a taxi. The street was empty of traffic. Ahead, where a streetlight had gone out, there was a dark patch. Entering it, Trager looked back. His two shadows followed. One carried a stick with a bulbous end.

Oh, shit. Muggers.

Trager ran.

The damn leg hurt. Behind him, soles slapping on pavement drew closer. He tried to run faster. The chance of outrunning them was nil. Better to face them sooner rather than later, his energy spent.

Trager stopped and turned. Screaming like a maniac, he charged his pursuers.

To his chagrin, he now counted three.

In the dim light, the bludgeon swung toward him. He ducked to the side, cannonballed into the second man and knocked him down. The bludgeon swished past his shoulder. To his amazement, two men tussled with each other.

Trager kicked the stick-wielder in the crotch.

The man groaned and fell to his knees.

"Jolly nice foot work," Trager's rescuer said.

"Thanks." Trager studied the man who had come to his assistance. Tall, white, a mop of wavy brown hair and an aristocratic nose.

The man extended his hand. "Bond, Tony Bond."

Trager chuckled. "You certainly live up to your literary namesake."

"Cinematic, dear chap, cinematic. I could have avoided this--"

The man who had wielded the bludgeon started to get up. Bond turned and slammed his knee into the man's chin, causing him to fall backward and roll on the ground.

Bond continued as if nothing had happened. "If I had known you fight so well, I would have stayed away from this drama. The poor blokes never had a chance."

"I'm grateful." Trager really was. In all his years in the intelligence business, violence had been a threat if he was caught, arrested and tossed into jail. This was a new, bothersome development. The guys who had followed him were not regular muggers. Bond's appearance at the scene was providential.

"I'll walk you to your hotel--safer that way. And you can stand me a beer."

Glad of the extra security, Trager would be happy to buy several drinks. "Live here?" he asked as they started across the park.

"Most of the time. The tea, you know."

"Do you deal with the Zengawalis in their local language?"

"Mostly French, sometimes Swahili."

Trager recognized Bond's accent as Sandhurst. At age thirty plus, a bit early for a career officer to be out of the army. "I saw lots of police during the day. Where are they when one needs them?"

"At night, the streets belong to Colonel Longo."

"Who's he?"

"A charming fellow. The director of ZSS, Zengawal Service de Securité."

Trager cursed for allowing himself to be rushed without an adequate briefing or time to research the local security apparatus. "Were you military?"

"Long time ago. Royal Hussars. I'm better known for my agricultural work in Wye College."

"There's a pub in Wye, The Green Man," Trager said with regret, remembering Margaret, the horse-mad girl he had met in Vienna while at a performance of the Spanish Riding School. Later, he visited her in Wye. He liked her enough to request a background check. It revealed she was a vociferous activist for the Palestinian cause. To marry her, he would have had to resign from the CIA. At that time, he'd been sure he had an interesting, possibly brilliant, career with the Agency.

"I'm surprised a Yank would know where Wye is."

"Selling textbooks, I get around a bit."

"You don't act like a book peddler in a fight."

"I learned a couple of things in the Marines."

Bond chuckled. "I thought Yanks were only good with large weapons systems."

The hotel bar was almost empty. They sat at a table, and Bond ordered beers in Swahili. "So what brings you to this charming locale?"

"Developing new markets. Venturing where no American enterprise has gone before. I've a meeting at the Ministry of Education tomorrow."

"To see Mademoiselle Loriot perchance?"

Trager's pulse quickened at the connection. "Matter of fact, yes."

"Good luck, old boy. She's the most sought after woman in this country."

"I'm going to sell her books."

"You should ask her out, wine and dine her. Bring her here for lunch, then step aside and let me move in. Remember, you owe me a bit of a favor."

"You don't want much," Trager said, chuckling.

"If you succeed, I'll treat you to a champagne dinner."

Spurred by Bond's interest in the woman, Trager said, "Maybe you could give me a bit of background on her."

"She appeared here shortly before the coup, is very active in matters of conservation. She also works for the Ministry of Natural Resources. They call her the Pygmy Lady. If you tell her your company is considering a grant for her Pygmies, she'll agree to lunch, at least."

"In that case, why don't you pitch her yourself?"

Bond looked wistfully into the distance. "She's beautiful, sparkling, hard, cut in a unique way. A priceless diamond."

Trager chuckled. "You seem smitten."

"Hardly. A woman like that is a challenge to one's manhood. A precious trophy among life experiences."

When Trager returned to his room, his briefcase on top of the dresser was a quarter of an inch off from where he had left it. A hair he had placed inside his address book was missing. Whoever had gone through his things had done a nearly world-class job. *In Africa?*

Chapter 3

After an uneasy night's sleep, the appearance of the muggers still gnawed at the pit of Trager's stomach. Even after a second cup of strong coffee in the Terrace Bar, he felt groggy. His mind wandered from *L'ajourdui*, the local French language newspaper.

If the meeting with Mademoiselle Loriot didn't produce a lead, Trager considered an alternative approach to finding a band of mercenaries. Any military unit needed a base, supplies, and a reason to exist. In the rest of Central Africa, the main reason for rebel groups and peacekeeping foreign armies was diamonds. Likely, the local government used mercs to protect the diamond mines in the Mountains of the Moon bordering Uganda.

Trager went to the travel agency next door to the hotel. The office looked surprisingly modern. Travel posters decorated the walls, Muzak blended with the hum of air-conditioning. An African lady in a blue business suit accented by a pink Hermes scarf sat behind a desk. She smiled at Trager motioning him to sit in an art deco chair in front of her desk. "I'm Madame Kanzo. Welcome to our wonderful country," she said in slightly accented English.

Trager sat. "I would like to rent a four-wheel drive vehicle."

Her smile broadened. "We can provide you with a car and driver."

"I prefer to drive myself."

She shook her head. "We don't rent cars in this country. Where would you like to go?"

"I'd like to see some tea farms." Trager tried to disguise his interest in the Mountains of the Moon.

"Oh, are you a buyer?"

"No, Madame, just an aficionado. I particularly like the champagne teas grown at high altitudes."

Madame Kanzo turned and took a brochure from a rack. "I have a wonderful tea tour, very popular with buyers from Europe."

"I think that would be too specialized for me. I'm also interested in other high-altitude plants like the giant heather and lobelia."

I will be happy to plan a personalized tour for you. Mister . . .?"

"Davenport."

Madame Kanzo spread a map on her desk.

"Are you sure I can't just rent a vehicle? I'm willing to pay top price."

"It is against government regulations. Only permanent residents are allowed to drive cars. A licensed guide must escort all tours. It is for your own safety."

Madame Kanzo pointed with a pencil and described a one-week tour. "You will stay in guest houses, and we will show you the tea, some wildlife, high-altitude forest elephant, the magnificent flora. And, of course, you shouldn't miss a gorilla tour. Silverback sightings are guaranteed."

Trager was pleased his ruse had worked. Madame Kanzo had suggested a route close to where he wanted to go. He would need to make only small detours. Bribing the driver shouldn't be a problem.

"If you fill out this form, we will obtain a travel permit for you from the ZSS."

Trager thought of the burly cameraman at the airport, his searched room. The way Bond had said, *The night belongs to Colonel Longo.* "The ZSS?"

"Zengawal Service of Security. It is strictly a formality. We'll have it ready by tomorrow."

This was a dream of Eastern Europe in the bad old days. With resignation, he filled out the form that would make it easy for the ZSS to check on his movements. Madame Kanzo made photocopies of some of his passport pages.

She returned the passport. "For your delight and comfort, in the city we can provide charming escorts."

"Very thoughtful of you, but no thanks."

"If you worry about AIDS--"

"Tomorrow morning?"

"Is six o'clock convenient? It avoids travel during the hottest--"

"Perfect." Trager had enough of the excessively charming lady who wanted to control his movements. He stood. "I feel I'm in competent hands." His mission was going down the tubes before he had even started. No wonder those who preceded him had failed.

~

At three o'clock sharp, Trager entered the Office of Procurement located on the fifth floor of the building housing the Ministry of Education. He leaned on the counter, fascinated by the clack-clack and bell of a manual typewriter, the sound of another era. The typist looked up. "Monsieur Davenport?"

"*Oui, Mademoiselle.*"

She smiled, got up, and stuck her head through an open doorway. "*Monsieur Davenport est ici.*" She approached the counter, opened a flap at its end and ushered Trager into a cramped office.

For a moment Trager stopped, as if a glass door had slammed in front of him.

Neither photograph, nor Bond's description, did justice to Simone Loriot in the flesh. A face with high cheekbones and a wide, full mouth framed widely-set dark eyes. He liked the tan, indicating time spent outdoors. Shiny, long black hair was gathered tightly at the back and held by a red scarf. Trager was glad she was writing something in a file and hadn't noticed his admiration.

A military-style shirt with epaulets gave her an air of severity. She looked up and removed horn-rimmed glasses. "Have a seat. You have five minutes."

Trager gave her his best smile. "Thank you for seeing me." He sat and opened his briefcase.

"I apologize, our budget for this year is already exhausted, but I am curious about what sort of textbooks are produced in North America. It is never too late to learn something new, no?"

Trager nodded and smiled in agreement as he handed her a catalogue. His heart beat faster as he watched her flip through the pages. The buttonholes over her chest strained from the pressure of her breasts.

After a few minutes, she looked up and shook her head. "Quite unsuitable for us, or for any African nation I know of. Your employers are wasting time and money sending you here."

Ignoring her abrupt manner, Trager gave her his shy smile, the one designed to melt icebergs. "It is a form of speculation on my part. I'm really on vacation. If I make a sale, my company pays for the trip."

She responded with a smile capable of knocking men off their feet. "So you're a passing cloud, a fleeting shadow over the savanna?"

"And you must write poetry."

Her smile vanished. "Only for myself." She recovered from her momentary lapse. "I hope you enjoy your vacation."

Trager desperately sought a way to extend the interview. "I understand you are quite knowledgeable about Pygmies."

She nodded slightly. "If you want to see Pygmies, Madame Kanzo of Tours Paradis can arrange a safari to the Loldawa Reserve. The accommodations are still primitive, but the experience is unique. I recommend it." She took a file out of the wire basket. "I have work to do."

"Can we meet for a drink this evening?"

"Thank you, my calendar is quite full."

"Not meeting with my friend Igor Dankov?"

"No, Monsieur." She shook her head. "Good day."

"I heard he works here."

"Ask the receptionist downstairs. If he is a government employee, he'd be listed in the directory."

"If you see Igor, tell him Johnny would like to meet with him."

Simone Loriot put her glasses on, opened the file, and began making notes.

For an awkward moment, Trager stood like an idiot. "It was kind of you to see me."

Her expression softened, but her gaze stayed on her work. She nodded slightly.

Trager shrugged and left the office.

Blankenship's great lead turned out to be a dead end. He drew comfort from the idea that this was the last mission. On the other hand, it was a matter of professional pride. His last mission could not end in failure. If Simone Loriot knew Dankov, she wasn't talking. Maybe Dankov was using another name. Just for the hell of it, when he got downstairs, he asked the receptionist to look at the government directory. Dankov's name, of course, did not appear.

~

When Trager returned to the hotel, Tony Bond sat at a table on the verandah. He motioned for Trager to join him.

"From the look on your face, you didn't succeed with *la belle* Loriot."

Trager dropped onto a chair. "She's as cold as a Salvation Army bell-ringer around Christmas."

Bond chuckled. "My dear chap, in a moment of disappointment, it is time to show transatlantic solidarity. I'll still treat you to a meal at the Cellar Club, known by the locals as Hell's Basement."

Trager ordered a Jumbo Beer from a waiter.

"What are your plans now?"

"I'm going on a tour tomorrow, to get my picture taken while being stomped by a gorilla."

"If you want to visit tea estates, I have connections."

"Does everyone need a travel permit?"

"Yes, old chap. At least foreigners do. If you go missing, like old time Bolshies, they quickly start a search. Colonel Longo learned his trade in East Germany."

~

In the dim light of the Cellar Club, one couldn't really see what one ate. Trager's steak *maitre d'hotel* was a stringy lump of mystery meat and the wine an Italian atrocity. A sextet played reasonably good music. Trager liked the African numbers best.

On his way to the bathroom, he took a closer look at the clientele. No sign of Dankov or anyone who looked a likely merc. As he returned to his table, a pair of gold pantaloons on the dance floor drew his attention. Simone Loriot danced with a tall African man in a navy blue suit, white shirt and regimental tie. Trager suppressed a pang of envy.

"Do you see what I see?" Bond asked.

Loath to remove his gaze from la Loriot's graceful posterior, Trager nodded.

"The chappie with her is Colonel Longo."

The words hit like an electric shock. Trager had certainly blabbed about his objective to the wrong person. He wondered when Longo's people would grab him for questioning. The memory of last night's thugs surged in his mind's eye and brought out a shiver. He looked around searching for security goons, didn't spot any.

The music stopped.

Followed by Longo, la Loriot headed toward their table. Trager's heartbeat accelerated as they approached. *Shit, shit, shit.* Holding a deep breath, he lowered his head and raised the wine glass trying to cover his face. Everything he'd done so far had been wrong.

With a swish of pantaloons, she passed by without a glance, and made her way toward the bar.

Trager exhaled, took another deep breath, and made a show of looking at his watch. "Time to go to bed. I have an early start tomorrow," he said, trying to sound casual.

"You should ask her for a dance."

"I remember you saying the night belongs to Longo."

"You're a fast learner, old boy."

At the bar, three men in dark suits joined Colonel Longo. He seemed to be giving instructions. La Loriot sipped a pink cocktail from a tall glass.

Bond said, "You leave first. I'll take care of the bill."

Trager made it out as far away from the bar as possible. On the stairs leading to ground level, he controlled his urge to run.

Outside, a black Mercedes was parked in front of the door. Two men dressed in identical black safari suits stood nearby cradling MP-50 submachine guns.

Trager turned away. With his legs stiff as logs, he headed toward a taxi.

"*Monsieur*," stinging like the lash of a whip, a voice called from behind.

Trager stopped, turned slowly.

One of the men had backed against the wall with his weapon pointing at Trager.

The other approached and slowly inspected him then grinned. "Do you have a match?"

Out of habit Trager patted his pockets. "I don't smoke."

The man nodded, turned, and rejoined his comrade.

Wanting to puke, Trager got into a waiting taxi and leaned back on the seat. After a deep breath, he was able to say calmly, "Hotel Metropole." As the taxi pulled away, he waved at the security goons.

~

The sight of la Loriot with Longo had been disturbing. The now-familiar surroundings of the hotel gave Trager what he knew was a false sense of security. Driven by the need to relax and pretend he lived in a normal world, he decided to have a nightcap.

A sleepy waiter slid off a barstool as Trager headed toward the terrace and the table he already thought of as his. A group of five men sat in a corner speaking Russian. They lowered their voices as Trager ordered a cognac.

The Russians, all in their late twenties or early thirties, looked athletic. Trager tried to listen to their conversation. He understood the word *burduk*, a Chechen cape.

". . . and then he begins sewing. Everyone hits the ground. They're shitting in their pants. You understand, the guy's crazy. So Kolbasin yells, 'don't shoot, we surrender'. The guy yells back, 'you're too many'." Laughter rolled from the table.

If that wasn't soldier talk, nothing was. Trager considered approaching them and asking if they knew Dankov, but being grabbed and questioned by these characters had the same appeal as being interviewed by Longo's goons.

Nevertheless, he screwed up his courage, got up and approached the men. "Good evening," he said in Russian.

The conversation stopped and they glared at him.

"Has any of you gentlemen seen Igor Dankov lately?"

"Never heard of him," said a man with a massive chest. He asked his buddies, "Any of you?"

The others shook their heads.

Pretty sure the guys were lying, Trager returned to his table.

Five minutes later, one of the Russians said, "*Noo, para.*"

They finished their beers and trooped out of the bar. A moment later they reappeared on the street and climbed into a minibus. Trager wished he had the means to follow. After the minibus disappeared, he called the waiter. "Who were those people?"

The waiter shrugged. "They come sometimes."

Considering his first day on the mission a total loss and expecting a midnight knock on the door, Trager went to his room.

Chapter 4

It was still dark. Sleep had been elusive, and Trager felt as if his eyeballs had retreated into his head. A beat-up Land Rover with a *Tours Paradis* sign attached to the door with duct tape, waited in front of the hotel, its engine running.

Trager opened the door, saw khaki trousers tucked into paratrooper boots. He threw his duffel in the back, got in, and closed the door. "*Bonjour*," he said to the driver.

"*Bonjour Monsieur*," Simone Loriot greeted him, engaged the clutch and the car surged forward.

Stunned, Trager said, "You . . . you . . ."

"I also work for *Tours Paradis*. It gives me more opportunities to get out of the city." Her khaki shirt with epaulets gave her a crisp professional look.

Images of her with Colonel Longo made Trager think of beaters driving prey to its doom. He had been mistaken in his assessment yesterday. Operating here was more difficult than in Eastern Europe during the Cold War.

Simone drove around the park and headed in the direction of the airport. "I'm stuck with budgets and other administrative work, but my interests remain with nature and cultural anthropology."

Trager was fully awake, wishing he were asleep, dreaming. "It must be convenient to be able to flip-flop jobs."

"Flip-flop?"

"Change overnight."

She laughed. "This is Africa."

Approaching the bazaar, she turned right and leaned on the horn. In the tropics, life starts early. Groups of people, probably exchanging news or discussing trade, stood on the street in the dim light of dawn.

Simone slammed the brakes, shouted something out her window. A man in a long robe and turban ran up to the car and handed her a parcel wrapped in newspaper. She tossed the package on Trager's lap. It was warm and the car soon filled with the scent of cinnamon.

"Breakfast. It's called *mandazi*."

Trager unwrapped a stack of thick, golden brown pancakes. La Loriot reached over, took one and bit into it.

The taste reminded him of doughnuts, but did nothing to relieve his gloom. The more he thought of it, the less he liked having Miss Loriot as his driver. She would be a lot more difficult to handle than a semi-literate African. Then, there was her Longo connection. Had she seen him at the club? Was she aware he knew who her companion was? Trager decided to probe. "You dance very well."

"I told you my calendar was full."

"Your boyfriend?"

"An acquaintance."

The car bumped its way out of town. Sisal plantations replaced shantytowns. Rows of what resembled giant pineapple tops with long spear-like stalks extended into infinity. The road, a straight, red strip, cut through a sea of orderly green.

She pointed outside. "Sisal, one of our exports. Manila rope is made out of it. You want some facts and figures?"

"Spare me."

"It's nice to be out of the madness of the city, no?"

She played her role well, was almost believable. Trager inhaled the fresh cool air that held that certain magic of Africa. "Very nice."

"Mind if I smoke?"

"No, go ahead."

Her hand searched the tray under the windshield and produced a thin cigar. She tossed him a box of matches. "Light it up please."

When you're taken for a ride, enjoy it. He had to develop some sort of trust with this woman if he was to have any hope of success. "I used to smoke. Now my stress level has increased to the American average."

To his surprise, la Loriot laughed.

He lit her cigar.

"In an hour, we'll reach the Majidogo River. From there, as the terrain begins to rise, we'll enter Bassi country. For the moment, there's peace. No fighting with the Wussi. We're still cursed with tribal animosity, a legacy of the colonial administration, but our president is working on that. People are learning that, as in the kingdoms of pre-colonial times, different tribes can work together."

Trager wanted to groan.

She drove well, working the gearshift like a pro. Maybe this wasn't such a bad deal after all. In his bag he had a bottle of Scotch. With time, she would loosen up.

Extended fields of agro-industry gave way to small, irregular plots and scattered wattle huts with thatched roofs. Mostly women tended the fields. Pyrethrum, maize, and papayas grew in cheerful disorder.

A great red sun drifted across mid-heaven, rapidly transforming the beautiful morning warmth into a brain-cooking furnace. Glad the Land

Rover was an ancient Model II, Trager opened the flap in front of him and let the air-blast cool him. "I didn't think any model twos were still around."

She patted the glare shield. "Old but reliable Schnookie. My own vehicle."

Schnookie? Miss Frigid Tundra with a car called Schnookie? The interior of the old vehicle had been repainted recently, and clean olive-drab canvas covered the seats. A magnetic compass was screwed on top of the glare shield.

"We'll have a picnic lunch and arrive at the Talawa guest house in time for tea. There's a spring nearby where you can swim. Monkeys congregate there in the evening."

If she was trying to put him at ease, it was almost working. She did sound like a tour guide. He got the impression she looked forward to the swim and seeing the monkeys.

The terrain changed from flat to rolling, but the road remained straight. On top of a hill, spiked boards barred the way. A policeman approached with an FN assault rifle cradled in his arm.

Simone handed him the safari permit Trager had signed yesterday. The policeman walked to Trager's side, bringing with him a strong whiff of sour armpits. "Passport."

Trager produced it.

The cop compared the names on the permit and passport, gave Trager a close look. "*Ça va.*" He returned the passport and signaled his partner to move the spikes aside.

Simone drove off. "That . . ." she swung her thumb back, "reminds me. Just as you don't care where you eat, you lack prudence in with whom you associate."

"I don't understand."

"Colonel Longo doesn't like Tony Bond."

Her statement surprised Trager. "The man you were with last night?"

"Yes, he's the head of Internal Security. He asked me to point you out."

Ah, confession. "Do you work for the police, too?"

"Sometimes," she said in a flippant tone and smiled brilliantly.

"Are you assigned to watch me?"

"Is that what you think?"

"I don't know. You brought up the subject of State Security. Since you didn't buy any books, I'm on vacation, a tourist."

"And I'm your tour guide."

Approaching a village, Simone slowed the car giving some chickens time to flap out of the way. Unpainted clapboard shacks with corrugated tin roofs lined the road. A group of men stood in front of a ramshackle building plastered with tin signs advertising Afri-Cola, Agip Gas, Guiness, Jumbo beer.

Many of the people waved. Aware of the Africans' sensitivity about having their pictures taken, Trager shot a few photos without bringing the camera to his eye. He'd made his preferred cover of photojournalist honest over the years. Without her noticing, Trager had taken la Loriot's picture, too.

Since he asked before, no harm would come by asking again. This time he distanced himself from his objective. "There is a fellow I used to know; someone told me he works in Zengawal. His name is Igor Dankov. Do you happen to know him?"

"Didn't you ask me that yesterday?"

"You seemed busy."

"Yes, I had to finish today's work, too."

Interesting, she'd already known she would be leaving town before he showed up at her office. Of course, Madame Kanzo would have lined up a guide the moment he made the booking. But too many coincidences had piled up: the photographer at the airport, the muggers, Tony Bond and Longo's interest. "Why is Longo interested in a publisher's rep?"

She shrugged. "Who knows why he takes an interest in people. I certainly don't recommend encouraging his attention."

Trager took some comfort in the indication she didn't like Longo.

The road snaked alongside a dark strip of forest that bisected a valley.

After negotiating a sharp turn, Simone brought the vehicle to a stop and switched off the engine. Ahead, a rickety bridge crossed the placid Majidogo River. A sign read *Five Tons Max*.

On the other side, a tall minaret rose above huge mango and tamarind trees shading a village. Trager noted a couple of white structures among the trees, thought he could distinguish a fort. There was no question that-- unlike everything so far--this was a pre-colonial village. The tamarind trees gave him an idea. Where tamarinds grew, there had to be tamarind pods. If he could get some pods, he'd be able to put la Loriot out of action with diarrhea. "This looks more like the traditional Africa."

La Loriot gave him a quizzical look. "Not your first time in Africa?"

"I've been to Tanzania and Kenya." He didn't mention Uganda. One of the twists he liked about Africa was that it always presented interesting opportunities. "I'd like to walk through the village. By myself." He gave la Loriot his most shy, endearing smile. "I'd like to make at least one discovery on my own."

"Our time *is* limited," she said. A frown crossed her face, and then she smiled. "First, let's absorb some atmosphere."

Women washed clothing in the slow, green water, slapping their laundry against huge boulders. Dense riverine forest with intertwining skirts of creepers created solid green walls on both riverbanks. Monkeys screeched in the distance.

"I like stopping here and watching Bassis and Wussis do their wash together. They used to shoot poisoned arrows at each other."

Two African policemen armed with bolt-action Mauser carbines stood idly on the other side of the bridge.

Simone got out of the car. Trager stepped out and stretched.

Laughter of children playing caught his attention. He walked to the other side of the road. About forty naked kids splashed in the water.

"School break," la Loriot said. "Since President Bamondo took over, Wussi and Bassi children go to school together in the border areas."

Trager admired her politics, almost had second thoughts about his nasty little plan.

"This used to be an Arab trading post. They exchanged spices, cloth, and trinkets for slaves, diamonds and ivory." She looked at him with that quizzical look of hers. "We still have diamonds and everyone wants them. That wouldn't be too bad, except they still want to give us trinkets in return. Are you interested in diamonds, Mr. Davenport?"

"Not particularly."

"You should buy some at the duty-free shop when you leave. We sell them cheap."

"I didn't realize Arabs got this far west," he lied.

"They had trade routes all the way to the west coast, long before European explorers discovered the interior of this continent. Of course, a lot of history predating the Arabs was lost in the fire of the Alexandria Library."

"That was more than sixteen-hundred years ago. Surely, nothing much was happening here prior to the Alexandria catastrophe."

She tilted her head slightly, said as if teasing, "You think not?"

Her question sounded like a challenge.

"You're not going to tell me about the Maasai being descendants of the Romans?"

Simone laughed. "I have more interesting theories."

A woman called the children out of the water. The kids stampeded ashore toward two rows of little bundles. They dressed in white shirts, blue shorts or skirts, and formed two orderly lines behind the teacher. Singing, they marched back to the village.

Trager and his guide returned to the car, and drove across the bridge, loose planks rattling under the wheels.

"That's the old Arab fort. At least five hundred years old, it's now used as a police station."

With white crenellated walls, the fort looked like something out of *Beau Geste*. Simone stopped in the shade of a tree. "The market is behind the fort. Go ahead and make your discoveries."

Trager got out. Crossing the street, he noticed a vaguely familiar man in civvies watching him from just inside the fort's gate. Trager turned the fort's corner and connected the man as the one who had photographed him at the airport. He forced himself to amble away without looking back.

Behind the fort, women sat cross-legged on the ground with their wares displayed on top of gunnysacks or sheets of plastic. Trager stood at the edge of the square, framed by the fort and rectangular wattle houses. It was a slow day at the market, no chance of getting lost in a crowd. The smell of dung wafted from somewhere.

Trager scanned the offerings on sale and planned his approach to check if anyone followed. The presence of Cameraman was no coincidence. He, and probably others, was Simone's backup. His gaze roved over piles of corn, yams, bags of beans, spices. Live goats and chickens clustered in a corner. Shirts and cuts of brightly patterned *mericani* hung from a line strung between trees.

Several men jabbered words he did not understand and wanted to shake his hand. Trager smiled, shook hands and moved forward. A little crowd followed him with curiosity as he searched for tamarind pods. His gaze settled on a dark-brown pile on top of a red-checkered cloth.

The square came alive as women shouted to get Trager's attention. As he approached the woman with the pile of bean-like pods, she jumped up and stuck two handfuls in front of his nose. He took a ten zee-frank note--two dollars--and handed it to her. She wrapped the pods in newspaper and handed him the parcel, giving a toothy smile.

Now Trager was able to turn naturally. Sure enough, leaning on the fort's wall and chewing on a toothbrush stick, Cameraman watched.

Trager considered his options. There were none. He had to keep acting like a tourist and be able to protest his innocence if they grabbed him for interrogation. To disguise his purchase, he bought four mangoes.

An old man wearing an ancient, badly frayed safari jacket tightened at the waist with a military leather belt approached Trager, saluted. "*Mon cher Monsieur*," he said, in well-accented French. "We are honored and delighted by the visit of such a distinguished, noble gentleman. May God bless you and give you good health. With the Monsieur's magnanimous consent, please honor the invitation of the worthless chief of this insignificant village for a humble cup of tea." He waved a carved walking stick. The market exploded with a cheer. Cameraman didn't join in, but continued with his tooth cleaning exercise.

"Come." The old man strode toward a doorway with two tables and some stools set in front. He gestured for Trager to sit.

A teenage girl brought out a tray with small porcelain cups and a teapot. The crowd opened and Simone joined them, beaming her captivating smile.

Trager couldn't help but stare.

"So much for your own discovery. One can't turn down the chief's invitation, no?" She glanced at Trager's newspaper parcels. "I've heard Americans love to shop. What did you buy?"

"Fruit," Trager said, feeling guilty over the effects of the laxative he planned to administer to her.

The chief leaned forward toward Simone and spoke rapidly in a low tone. Simone answered in the same dialect, quietly, as if not wanting to be overheard. The word *utabu* came up several times. Then they switched to French. After ten minutes of exchanging florid Gallic platitudes with the chief, Simone said abruptly, "It's time to go."

~

The road wound into the hills. With engine whining, the Land Rover labored at twenty kilometers an hour. Parcels of tea bushes grew on the gentler slopes. Thick jungle covered the steeper ones. The road offered plenty of ambush possibilities. Maybe Cameraman's job was to radio ahead Trager was on his way.

Simone drove across a concrete ford and stopped on the other side of a fast flowing stream. "Lunch time," she said cheerfully.

Trager looked around for possible escape routes. Going downstream from the ford presented the best chance of escape if this was an ambush. The smell of rotting vegetation was strong and the jungle quiet.

She hung a leather satchel across her shoulder then slung across her back a little knapsack with a baguette sticking out.

"Follow me." Simone jumped from stone to stone and climbed up the streambed. Impressed by her agility, Trager followed, unable to match her speed. He knew he made a perfect target for a sniper.

The narrow ravine, shaded by tall trees on both sides, felt pleasantly cool. After ten minutes of rigorous climbing, the ravine opened, and Trager caught up. With hands on her hips, la Loriot stood before a clear pool with a ten-foot waterfall on the far end.

"Does this meet with your approval?"

"Yes." His fear of an ambush diminished, Trager admired the orchids growing out of old tree trunks.

"We can have a swim before lunch."

"My trunks are in the car."

She laughed, flinging her arms into the air. "Wearing clothes in paradise? That's almost obscene."

Simone sat on a rock, began undoing her boots.

Incredulous, Trager took his clothes off, trying not to stare at Simone. Of course, with a French education, she wouldn't think anything of nudity.

She stood, stretched, and gracefully dove into the clear pool.

Trager followed. Cool water caressed his skin, soothed his burning ankle. Simone swam under the waterfall. The cool cascade pummeled his back and gave immediate relief to his frayed nerves. Trager wanted to laugh and yell like a kid.

"This is a fairy-tale place, a stage set for a magic show," he said as they clambered out of the water.

Simone looked at him as she wrung her black hair, breasts raised and firm. "You don't look like a romantic." She smiled. "This country is full of magic places."She put on black panties and passed Trager a thermos. "Lemonade."

Simone laid out a piece of checkered cloth and placed a variety of sausages and cheeses on it. "Too bad we forgot to bring the fruit you bought. What did you get?"

"Mangoes."

"Tuck in, I'm starved." She broke the baguette in two, handed Trager half. "Eat well. We still have a long way to go."

Trager calculated that, in two hours or less, they should reach Talawa. But in Africa one never knew. "How did you end up in this country?"

"I'm an anthropologist, a very logical place for me to be."

To Trager, there was nothing logical about the woman. She was a maze of contrasts. He had the urge to reach out and touch her.

She must have noticed his yearning look. "Remember I'm your tour guide. If my breasts bother you . . ." She reached for her shirt.

"No, no. I was admiring you, a natural work of art. Stay still." He pointed his camera at her. "Venus in Paradise."

Simone arched her spine, threw her head back and smiled at the lens. Click. The light was too harsh, but otherwise he had captured a wonderful photo.

~

On the way back to the car, Simone walked slowly. In sandy and muddy spots, she paused to inspect animal tracks, mostly dik-dik, an antelope the size of a large hare and beaver-like hyrax. About fifty meters short of reaching the road, his sixth sense announced danger. Trager stopped, instinctively crouched. Simone was a few feet behind him. He signaled for her to do the same.

"Don't move," she said softly.

"Yeah, someone's out there," he whispered.

"Put your hands up and stand. Slowly."

"Huh?" Trager turned his head.

Simone held a pistol aimed at him.

Chapter 5

For its size and caliber, the compact Tokarev in Simone's hand would deliver one hell of a wallop.

Trager obeyed, stood facing her, and raised his arms.

Despite his suspicions, he had not expected la Loriot to pack a gun and use it on him. With a steady hand, she aimed at his chest. Her distance was also perfect--too far for him to reach and disarm her--yet close enough she couldn't miss. He wished she'd aim at his head. A shot between the eyes was instant oblivion.

Oblivion was something he didn't fear.

"Do I get a cigar before the execution? It lasts longer than the proverbial cigarette."

A faint smile appeared on her face. She looked like a teacher pleased with her student.

The rustle of brush behind him sent a current down Trager's spine.

La Loriot nodded. "Turn around."

A tall African with a neatly clipped moustache, wearing a black beret and camouflage uniform stood ten feet away, his hands on his hips as if inspecting a disgusting sight.

Two soldiers emerged from the brush, with Kalashnikovs leveled on Trager. They had him perfectly boxed in.

"I'm Major Kisima," the moustached man said. "At the least sign of resistance, I have orders to shoot."

"*Mimi nafikiria yeye hakuna silaa.*" I don't think he's armed, la Loriot said in Swahili.

"*Msuri.*" Good. Kisima smiled.

"Am I under arrest?"

"Worse, my friend. Much worse." Kisima gestured with his head.

One of the soldiers propped his rifle against a rock, approached Trager like a cat. He took Trager's hands and tied them with wire behind his back, then looped piano wire around Trager's neck.

Kisima said, "I imagine you can visualize what will happen if you try to escape?"

Trager nodded.

The soldier held Trager by the elbow and helped him negotiate the last few meters to the road. A minute later, an open Land Rover with a machine gun mounted on a pedestal, arrived from up-hill. The driver had to to turn the truck several times to face the same way Schnookie did. La Loriot and Kisima talked in low voices.

"*Alons-y*," Kisima ordered.

La Loriot told Trager, "You're coming with me." She held the wooden handle of the piano wire garrote while his minder clambered in Schnookie's back.

When Trager settled in his seat, the guard slipped a black hood over Trager's head.

"I didn't book a mystery tour."

"I suggest you keep quiet." Simone started the engine.

It didn't take long for Trager's hands to go numb. He knew his sense of time would be way off, but he tried to imagine the car's progress on his memorized map of Zengawal. The road led to a plateau four-thousand feet high. East of the plateau was the Sheba Range, part of the Mountains of the Moon. To the west was the now extinct Matukumba volcano.

From the cooler air and the car's acceleration, Trager knew they had reached the plateau. To successfully escape, he had to have some better idea of where he was. "I have to pee."

La Loriot laughed. "If you hope to have your hands untied, forget it." She then spoke with the soldier in the back. To Trager she said, "Umangi says he doesn't mind undoing and dropping your trousers. You still want to go?"

"I could ruin your seat covers if I don't."

La Loriot stopped.

Umangi led Trager outside.

The ground was slippery. Trager heard bee-eaters chirping and smelled recent rain. From the heat of the sun, he could tell they faced northeast. The wind told him they were in an open space. After Umangi pulled Trager's jockeys and trousers back up, Trager returned to his seat. Having achieved relief and gained information, his resentment ebbed. His brain concentrated on ways to escape.

But that would probably not be necessary. If they wanted to kill him, his corpse would have already been feeding forest scavengers. The hood gave him comfort. People were blindfolded so they would be not able to tell where they'd been.

"*Merde*," la Loriot muttered and came to a quick stop.

"Step outside, with your hands up," an amplified voice boomed in French.

Trager almost grinned at the sudden turn of events. He'd like to see Simone's face and strangely felt sorry for her.

The noise of a Land Rover engine drew alongside. "Get out of the way, this is Army business."

Behind Trager, Umangi cocked his rifle.

"Surrender the American."

"He's our prisoner. If you don't move, we'll blow you out of the way. *Move*." Major Kisima's parade-ground voice didn't need a loudhailer.

Trager thought of opening the door with his elbow and rolling out of the vehicle while the rifle occupied Umangi's hands. He leaned forward and the piano wire tightened around his neck. The bastard had it secured to something.

After a minute, la Loriot placed the car in gear and drove on.

Trager's spirits took a dive.

Maybe half-an-hour later, the car slowed. Trager heard people talking, the ringing of a bicycle bell. They were going through a town. Probably Fort de la Porte.

They must have reached a checkpoint--the car stopped, but this time-- to Trager's disappointment, there wasn't an altercation. After a brief banter-like exchange with someone outside, la Loriot drove on. The car dipped sharply, rattled over a bridge and began climbing. They were heading toward Uganda.

Trager's arms had grown numb and his shoulders and neck ached. The car must have left the main road. It crept at a steep angle in low range.

Reaching level ground, the car stopped.

"I hope to God you are who you've said you are," la Loriot said.

Trager heard the driver's door open and slam closed.

Umangi removed the garrote from Trager's neck. "Outside."

Someone opened the door. This was the decisive moment. Hoping that his hood theory was correct, Trager staggered out. By the heat on his back, he knew he faced east and the sun was about to set.

"*Otkroi*," a voice said. Open, in Russian.

The hood came off and Trager blinked at sunlight reflected off a white wall. Someone stood in front of him.

"Mmm, *da*."

Trager thought he was dreaming as his eyes adjusted to the glare.

"Confess, why you use the name Davenport?"

The man in front of him had a large, blond, waxed handlebar moustache. On his head, a blue cap with a small shiny peak sat at a ridiculously sharp angle. A tunic-like shirt, a *gimnastiorka*, with gold epaulettes covered his torso. A number of medals graced his chest. On his side hung a *shashka*, a curved Cossack sword similar to the Sword of Mameluke worn by USMC officers on ceremonial occasions. Baggy blue trousers inserted into soft, tall riding boots completed the picture of a nineteenth-century Cossack officer.

"Did you lose your speech, Johnny?"

Behind the impressive moustache, Trager recognized Dankov. The face was now lined, but the eyes livelier, younger. His barrel chest and slim waistline looked as they had when he was thirty.

"Untie him." Dankov stepped aside and hugged la Loriot.

While someone loosened the wire around his wrists, Trager gawked at the tall white walls of an Arab Fort standing like a stage set in front of a rocky cliff. On top of the cliff, like an eagle's nest on a rocky pinnacle, sat a modern concrete blockhouse. Under camouflage netting behind the blockhouse were a number of antennae that would have made NASA proud.

"Eh, Johnny, how many summers? How many winters?" Dankov gave him a crushing hug. Releasing Trager, he turned. "Present arms." His command repeated itself in an echo.

At the slapping of rifles, Trager turned. A platoon of Cossacks stood at attention and presented arms in front of a row of Land Rovers bristling with machine guns and smooth-bore antitank cannon. Next to the Cossacks stood a platoon of African soldiers in camouflage dress and black berets.

"Let's inspect the guard of honor."

Not knowing whether to feel like an idiot or a visiting dignitary, Trager followed Dankov and inspected the guard. The expressions on the soldiers' faces were different from what Trager was used to seeing in Americans. These guys almost smiled with a kind of cheerful arrogance. Their gray karakul *papahas* worn at a jaunty angle looked out of place in time and Africa--especially with the black-and-gold Romanoff cockades.

The African soldiers were as sharply turned out as the Russians. Their weapons looked new and well cared for. The eyes of the soldiers shone with admiration as they followed Dankov.

Trager was more than glad to be on the right side of this lot. He had had a glimpse at their performance in the ambush. Their parade ground sharpness confirmed this was superior to any African mercenary force Trager had ever seen.

Circulation was returning. His arms and hands hurt like hell.

Finished with the inspection, Dankov faced the formation. "If it wasn't for this man, the Bolshevik *svolochi* would have caught me. I owe him my life."

Trager almost squirmed with embarrassment.

In un-military fashion, Dankov slapped Trager in the back. "They're all good lads, but now we use vehicles as our cavalry to spread terror to our enemies. The Africans like our traditions. We're very tribal."

Two African soldiers brought out and set up a folding table, spread a white cloth on top. An elderly Orthodox priest in a white cassock and a blue surplice decorated with gold crosses followed them and placed a large silver cross on top of the field altar.

"When friends meet, it should be properly celebrated. We'll have a small service of thanksgiving." Dankov turned to his troops and bellowed. "For prayers, caps-off."

In a rich baritone, the priest intoned a prayer. Cossacks answered the chant while a deep throaty hum came from the Africans.

To Trager, attending Russian Orthodox mass was like going to a concert. He didn't understand old-church Slavonic, but the melodies were beautiful. Today, they were moving. After the darkness and uncertainty of the black hood he felt delivered and a deep sense of gratitude enveloped him.

Ten minutes later, after a lusty rendition of *Mnogoe Leta*--Many Years-- the service was over.

Dankov dismissed the formation and led the way to the Arab fort, which had an air of mystery after the sunset. Trager looked for Simone, but she had vanished.

Chapter 6

In the ancient Arab bathroom, Tragger dipped water from a cistern with a plastic jug, careful not to scoop the small mosquito-eating fish. He doused himself washing off the odor of fear, soothing his nerves. He strangely missed having Simone next to him and regretted his earlier suspicions. Had he used his real identity he could have avoided a lot of trouble. Once he finished this mission, never again would he pretend to be someone else.

He found his objective. Now, to uncover what Dankov was doing. And what about the Dankov-Loriot connection? No stranger to weapons, she and Kisima had acted as a team.

Trager toweled himself dry and returned to his cell-like room, furnished with a military cot and ammunition crate that doubled as nightstand. Dankov had said dinner would be a gala occasion. The best Trager could do was a safari suit and a silk paisley scarf.

An African guard, armed with a compact Bizon-2 machine pistol, stood outside the officers' mess. He came to attention and opened the door for Trager.

Stepping into the austere whitewashed room, Trager thought he had entered a Kipling scene. Dankov, Simone, Kisima, two other African officers, and two Russians stood in a group. The soldiers wore high-collared white tunics and black trousers. It surprised him to see this level of military decorum among mercenaries in such a remote outpost. In his safari suit, he was under-dressed, out of place. Long ago, he had also worn a uniform. If not for that stupid parachute accident, he'd probably be a lieutenant colonel in line for eagles on his shoulders. The partial disability pension from the Marine Corps did little to assuage the deep bitterness that surfaced from time to time.

In an effort to show he harbored no hard feelings, Trager smiled at Simone.

Fetchingly clad in red pantaloons and white blouse, she nodded back, a curious expression on her face. A black sash accentuated her slim waist and the curve of her hips.

"Ah, our guest of honor." Dankov handed Trager a champagne glass.

"We should drink to Mister Davenport's *sange froid*," Simone said. "He's a real comedian when guns point at him."

"The more the merrier, eh, Johnny?" Dankov said, raising his glass.

Pleasure surged through Trager. He clicked his heels and drank. "I'd like to return fire. The lady is an extraordinarily believable adversary, I was secretly disgracing myself."

The door opened and Father Alexey walked in. "Children, champagne helps the work of the devil."

"Here, *Batiushka*," Vadim, the young lieutenant said, pouring the priest a shot of vodka.

Father Alexey nodded at Trager, "May God protect you from these scoundrels. Are you an Orthodox American?"

"No, I learned about orthodoxy while studying Russian culture."

The priest turned to Simone. "And you, the wicked city hasn't swallowed you yet?"

"Coming here is so revitalizing, seeing how the forest is regenerating--"

"Shame on you for hooding your guest and robbing him of visual pleasure."

Simone said to Trager, as if atoning for her sins, "Would you like to see gorillas tomorrow?"

"Thanks, but I think Colonel Dankov and I have some matters to discuss."

"It is really worth seeing the impact Colonel Dankov's management has had on the forest."

Trager glanced at Dankov. *Now what? Ecological mercenaries?*

Dankov chuckled. "The forest is part of the border security zone. We have kicked out the charcoal burners and scared the poachers. When you do a job well, other benefits come automatically. Call it collateral repair."

"The colonel is modest," Simone said.

Major Kisima grinned widely, eyes sparkling with mischief. "And intimidating."

Trager wondered how loyal the African troops were to Dankov. He would love to have a private chat with Kisima.

Simone said, "It will not be long before we have a thriving, responsible tourist industry. The elephants are having an unusually high birth rate."

Dankov laughed. "If Simone had her way, this whole country would be a nature reserve."

Simone gave Dankov a withering look. "A balanced ecosystem, where people and nature live in harmony."

Blankenship hadn't sent him to investigate tourism development and the protection of wildlife. These people were staging a show for his benefit. Trager wondered what they were hiding.

"A table," Vadim said.

Dankov laughed. "We must obey the *Tamadá*, the president of the mess." He gestured toward the damask covered table.

The five-course dinner was a lively affair full of banter and private jokes. Before offering a toast, one had to ask permission from the *Tamadá*. Vadim ruled the table, a humorous, benign autocrat. At one moment he said, "Colonel, for neglecting our guest, I fine you one vodka."

Dankov made a face and pleaded, "But I'm tired."

Vadim gestured at the steward. "Carry out the sentence with a double."

The steward poured Dankov a large vodka.

"May God have mercy on young officers who try to get their commander drunk." Dankov raised his glass and dumped the vodka with one swallow.

After dessert of fresh fruit cocktail in triple sec, Dankov said, "*Ma chere* Simone, shall we introduce our guest to the grenade game?"

"Yes, yes," chorused the others.

Simone tilted her head, looking at Trager as if sizing him up. "I don't know."

"Please," Vadim begged.

"It may not be appropriate." Simone appeared embarrassed.

"Roll up the carpets, bring the grenades." Dankov ordered.

"Good night, my children. Don't kill yourselves." Father Alexey, who had only eaten two boiled potatoes, blessed everyone and left.

Trager helped the others roll up Oriental rugs, exposing black and white tiles. Vadim brought in a carton containing twelve glass jars, each with a hand grenade inside, and placed it on the table.

"If you insist." Simone sighed, gave each grenade a twist and removed the pins.

Intrigued, Trager watched, shifting his weight from one foot to the other. If one of the jars broke, the free spindle would release and the grenade explode. Nervous sweat gathered on his upper lip.

Simone closed her eyes and took several deep breaths. "Ready?"

"Fire at will." Dankov waved a five-hundred Z-frank note.

Simone unfastened two buttons of her blouse, revealing the tops of a lacy black bra.

Trager cringed as she took a jar and tossed it high in the air. He held his breath. The jar almost touched the ceiling and came down. Simone caught it with one hand. She tossed it up again, turned, and caught the jar behind her back.

Trager let out his breath.

Dankov said, "Three-second fuses. If she breaks a glass, the last man out of the room wins."

This was crazy, worse than Russian roulette.

"Open your wallet. The winner gets to remove the money she'll have in her bra, and Simone will pay him three times the amount she has taken. If she doesn't have enough money . . . well, it's up to her to settle in any way she can. So it pays to be generous."

The men laughed. They all held money. Trager took some bills out, wondering what would follow, calculating how he would get out of the room. Jumping out the second-story window was out of the question. He imagined a traffic jam at the door as the grenade exploded.

Simone took another deep breath. "Now, we begin." She gave the jar a twist and spun it like a top on her index finger as she approached Trager. His eyes locked on the jar wobbling in front of his nose. Behind it, out of focus, Simone smiled at him.

"Oopla." The jar flew up. Simone twirled, picked up another jar and sent it flying.

As she juggled the two jars, Dankov said, "Voila," and handed her his money.

Simone stuck it into her bra. "The next one is for you, *mon cher.*" Simone blew Trager a kiss, picked up another jar. She now had three grenades in the air.

Extending his hand with a twenty-dollar bill, Trager cautiously approached Simone, trying not to interfere with her juggling.

"*Merci.*" She snatched the bill from his hand and stuck it into her bra.

She now had four jars working. This was crazier than he could have envisioned. The way the men handed her bills, she would have quite a take. Five jars, her juggling was flawless. Trager took out a fifty and handed it over.

The men clapped wildly.

Six jars.

The sound of broken glass made Trager blink and stiffen his muscles. *One thousand.* Trager held his place, glanced at Dankov who had dropped a wine glass on the floor.

"Your sense of humor, sometimes . . ." Simone glared at Dankov as she recovered the jars and returned them to the carton.

With relief, Trager watched Vadim insert the pins where they belonged.

Simone wiped perspiration from her face with a napkin and buttoned her blouse.

Trager's tension receded and was replaced by fascination. He had to control his impulse to wrap his arms around Simone. When she caught him staring at her, he said, "That was a marvelous act."

"Pshaw. It's like sex, demeaning when you don't want to do it." Simone wandered off to the sideboard, poured a cognac and lit a cigar. With her elbows resting on the sideboard, she said, "I hope your visitor was suitably amused. He called it an act. What do you call it, Colonel? A game?"

With her rebuff, like a kid, Trager wanted out of the room.

To his relief, Dankov handed him a snifter of cognac. "A desperate madness that reflects the stakes of the game being played in this country." He chuckled. "Tomorrow, Johnny will explain his presence here."

"You'll have a more enjoyable time tracking gorillas." Simone finished her cognac. "Good night, I have an early start tomorrow." She left the room.

Dankov touched Trager's shoulder. "Quite a woman, don't you think?"

"Your girlfriend?"

Dankov shook his head. "A fascinating, very complex person. Like the lady said, tomorrow will be a long day." He went to the sideboard took a half-empty bottle of champagne, two glasses, and headed for the door.

"Igor, what happened to the CIA people who were looking for you?"

"That question is in bad taste." Dankov frowned and left the room.

Chapter 7

The clatter of boots on the staircase and Russian curses mingled with the aroma of coffee and fresh bread. Emerging from a surprisingly deep sleep, Trager rubbed his eyes and jumped out of bed. It was still dark. He peered out a narrow window. In the courtyard below, soldiers formed a line outside a cookhouse.

Jet lag gone, his objective within easy reach, Trager hummed as he shaved. Interview Dankov, return to Turako, get on an airplane, say good-bye to Blankenship. Life seemed simple. He still had to decide where he would live as the new and free Trager. Cyprus, Greece and Spain were high on the list because of the weather, the number of interesting expatriates, and social opportunities.

Outside his room, Trager peered into an open doorway. A set of ladders spiraled the walls of the fort's tower-like scaffolding. He looked up as if hypnotized.

"Forget it," he said softly.

The next thing he knew, he was five rungs up. Looking straight in front of him, he climbed to where the ladder changed direction, pressed his back against the corner, and looked down. *Not bad.* He ascended rapidly to the next corner. When he looked down, a tremor ran through his body. *Get back down before you turn to jelly.* He was almost halfway. If he did this often enough, fear would leave. Staying close to the wall, he clambered to the next corner.

The light streaming through the door at the top was a lot closer. Forcing himself one step at a time, Trager continued. On the last flight, he pressed his back against the wall and took two steps sideways. This made it worse. He closed his eyes and wiped sweat off his brow. His legs shook. The door at the top offered escape. He negotiated the last flight, thinking only of that.

The opening was a trap door and Trager staggered out of the tower feeling dizzy.

Two soldiers, an African and a Russian, leaned on the crenellated parapet looking out. The chest-high rampart gave Trager a feeling of security. He grabbed it and breathed deeply.

"*Privet*," the Russian said.

Trager nodded, hoping his fear did not show.

"Look." The Russian offered binoculars.

Trager peered in the direction the soldier pointed. A group of five elephants stood on the side of the mountain, ripping off tree branches with their trunks.

"Guard duty is a pleasure here."

His legs still felt weak, but Trager appreciated the spectacular view. A huge, red sun climbed over the ridge-tops and wisps of fog drifted up from the forest.

"Thanks." Trager returned the glasses. If he lingered, he would never muster the courage to get down from the tower. Trying to look nonchalant, he ambled toward the trap door.

With his eyes closed, he made his way down, one step at a time. *Never again*, he promised when he reached bottom.

Trager was surprised to see only Simone in the officers' mess. Dressed in camouflage, she sat at the long table, spooning a soft-boiled egg. "Sleep well?" She indicated a place in front of her and poured red wine from a carafe. "You look pale."

"I feel fine."

"Want to see gorillas?"

"Not today, thanks."

Her mouth formed an exaggerated pout. "You're not angry at me?"

"No." Trager sat down.

"You see, we had to make sure you weren't an impostor. And Longo was about to arrest you. Actually, Major Kisima had to be quite forceful at the roadblock the ZSS had set up." She tilted her head slightly while looking him in the eye. "I don't know what you've done to draw Longo's attention. When he grabs people outside the capital, they're never seen again."

Trager thought of Cameraman, his unofficial greeter. "When did Longo contact you to point me out?"

For a moment, Simone looked uncomfortable. "You called to make an appointment just before lunch, what, about quarter to twelve?"

Trager nodded.

"When I returned from lunch, I had a note to call Longo."

Trager summarized. They knew he was coming, but relied on a phone tap to learn where he was going. Someone had been listening live to inform the head of security. In that case, Blankenship was not the leak.

Trager added milk and sugar to his coffee. A nasty picture was forming in his mind.

Simone continued. "When I gave Igor your message, I told him of Longo's interest." She smiled. "Igor must value you. He sent some of his boys to the hotel."

The guys drinking at the bar. "Where is he?"

"When in the fort, the officers eat breakfast with the troops. Are you sure you don't want to see the gorillas? I'd like to complete my promise as tour guide. I have the impression you like nature."

A feeling of affinity came over Trager. "I love being out."

"But you have to follow your ulterior motives for being here. That's too bad." She stood and slung her leather satchel over her shoulder. "I'll see you this evening."

"I'll walk you outside."

When they stepped beyond the fort's gate, Simone sat on a large square stone at the side of the entrance and lit a cigar. She patted the space next to her. "Sit down, this stone is one of the oldest man-made objects in this country."

Trager sat almost touching her.

In the forest, colubus monkeys roared, sounding like motorcycles cranking up.

"This fort is nearly four-hundred years old, built over a man-made terrace that is much older. Feel the stone."

Trager ran his palm over the smooth surface. The edge of his hand touched Simone's hip, giving him a pleasant little jolt.

"Nobody knows who the stone workers were. I wish Igor would let me excavate. But, the moron soldier doesn't appreciate the value of archeology."

"I thought you were an anthropologist."

"The world is too fascinating to limit interests to one's profession, no?"

Trager chuckled. "And today you'll practice zoology."

"Zoologists dissect animals, I think."

Trager laughed, delighted with Simone's girl-like freshness.

"*Bonjour, Mademoiselle.*" A man in a green uniform, wide-brimmed canvas hat, and a .375 Winchester slung over a shoulder came out of the gate.

Simone rose. "Too bad you don't want to come. Bouduin would have enjoyed showing off his tracking skills."

Trager watched Simone and her ranger climb the path behind the fort and vanish into the forest. Somewhere near, an elephant trumpeted.

~

While waiting for Dankov to make an appearance, Trager sat on a hard, wooden bench in the fort's orderly room. Sergeant Kuzma, a tall, middle-aged Cossack, ruled the office like a patient uncle. Two harassed clerks completed duty rosters and inventories as soldiers complained or petitioned.

Trager thought, *all armies are the same, and soldiers are the biggest moaners in the world.* Kuzma, dressed in traditional Cossack garb with an ancient Nagant revolver strapped to his waist, was the epitome of the NCO who held a troop together. When he snapped a riding crop on his desk, it signaled an interview was over.

For an hour, Trager watched the routine. In his head, he filed away pay-rates, quantities of ammunition spent in training, family allowances for African soldiers. He learned about the acute shortage of officers and NCO's. It appeared the fort was an NCO training school.

Everyone leaped to attention when, wearing a khaki shirt, camouflage riding breeches, and tall boots, Dankov entered like a cyclone. He paused at the swinging door of the rail dividing the room and glanced at Trager. "Come." He hurried toward a door at the back.

Intrigued by the urgency in Dankov's manner, Trager followed.

In what looked like a front-line command center, a Russian and an African sat in front of field radio consoles. Dankov strode to a large- scale map of Zengawal pinned on the wall. Animated chatter blared from one of the speakers. The African soldier wrote in shorthand on a pad. Trager stood quietly without interrupting.

Dankov's finger hovered for a few seconds and landed on the map. "Right here." He pointed near Lake Kachimba, close to the Congo border. "We had a successful ambush. Killed two rebels and captured a truckload of weapons and ammo." He grinned. "Maybe you brought us luck."

"You seem to cover a wide area."

Dankov made a sharp about face. "Good intelligence, ambush, and mobility."

The African soldier said in French, "Roll call is complete, all units reporting operations normal."

"Thank you, corporal," Dankov said, inspecting a message clipboard. "Send a signal to Kachaev--issue two-hundred-and-fifty thousand rounds of rifle ammunition to the Simbas. I want their marksmanship training completed by the end of the month."

Returning the clipboard to the table, he said to Trager, "Time for a drink and lunch."

In the small adjacent dining room with two corner windows, Dankov switched gears. An affable smile replaced his thunder-and-lightning scowl. He gestured toward a sideboard and a silver tray with a bottle of

Stolychnaya was surrounded by shot glasses. Another tray held an assortment of Russian appetizers. "We're very lucky. Father Alexey's wife organized the ladies in my village. They think we're suffering from lack of good things to eat."

Trager admired the marinated mushrooms, little caviar sandwiches, and herring sprinkled with thin onion rings.

"You like to live dangerously and deserve a drink." Dankov poured vodka. "To life and beautiful women."

Like Dankov, Trager tossed the shot down his throat and chased it with a square of herring with onion.

Dankov said, "It is great to meet a good and true friend, but I hate to see the mess you've gotten yourself into. You have angered the wrong crowd. Longo loves people with assumed identities. The penalty for spying is death. Arrest, interrogation, trial, execution--all in one night."

He poured another shot. "You're okay in my protection, but the airport is not under my control. So you wanted to see me. Here I am. What can I do for you?"

"To quote Blankenship, 'Ask him what the fuck he's doing'."

Dankov chuckled. "Is the old goat still around?"

"He's fat now."

"I'll never forget Blanky's face at the Austrian border." Dankov slapped Trager on the back and broke out laughing. "Remember the filing cabinet?"

Trager remembered it all too well. "Tell me what you're up to."

"I won't tell you--I've become allergic to interrogations--but to a friend, I'll provide access to the best source in the country. If you manage to avoid Longo, you'll return to Washington with a flaming report. How would you like to have a tete-a-tete with the president of Zengawal?"

"I want it from the horse's mouth. You owe me."

"Not any longer. If it wasn't for my intervention, you would have been sitting in Longo's basement. Good thing Simone contacted me the moment you left the ministry. Do you like her?"

"I love women who point guns at me."

"A remarkable woman. Shoots well, too."

The same orderly who had served breakfast entered the room. "Lunch is ready, Atamán."

Dankov crossed himself as he sat at the table. "*Bon apetit*, as they used to say in Imperial Russia."

"Yesterday, you wore Imperial medals."

"In honor of my grandfather. He earned them in the Russo-Japanese and First World wars. My family kept them buried during the Soviet era.

The orderly served borscht.

"So how did you end up in this exotic situation?"

"You like it?" Dankov made a wide gesture with both hands.

"The borscht is very good." Trager said, meaning it. The rich broth had the right combination of meat and vegetables and wasn't too heavy with beets. It was at least as good as in the best Russian restaurants in Paris.

"I mean my situation."

"You seem happy. But why did you leave the States?"

"Hell is Fort Wayne, Indiana. That's where the CIA installed me after pumping me dry. Suburbia, Lazy Boy, TV, dumb wife, a stupid lawn to mow. My neighbors were dead baseball zombies."

Trager added sour cream to his soup. It appeared he had touched the right button to get Dankov talking.

"I escaped to Bosnia for a bit of fighting. After that fiasco, I went to Greece to rest. There, I met Bamondo, who had escaped here with a sizeable stash of diamonds. He lived on a yacht with his wife, the former Miss Belgium. We made a few plans to liberate Zengawal from the dictator Mbaya." Dankov looked like a satisfied cat. His hands, open flat, tapped the table lightly. "I recruited my Cossacks in Russia, and here we are."

Dankov was capable of great daring-do. Stealing the complete Soviet battle plans for the Southern Front had been an act of incredible recklessness. "You mean you staged the coup here?"

Dankov shrugged. "Somebody had to do it. Actually, it was quite easy. We arrived as a group of tourists. An airplane dropped us weapons. Within two hours we had secured the palace, restored electricity to the capital, and President Bamondo made his acceptance speech."

"So Bamondo depends on foreign mercenaries to prop up his government."

Dankov looked irritated. "We're training the Army, have a pre-revolutionary Russian-style cadet school that will produce honest, honorable officers. It all takes time. The president needs us to protect him from the machinations of external forces that want to steal this country's wealth." Dankov's eyes flashed with a fiery passion that surprised Trager.

With the Cold War over, Dankov's activities didn't seem to conflict with American interests. Why had Blankenship called Dankov a troublemaker? Although no longer a superpower, Russia was still a country with worldwide interests. If the Russian government was involved in this, it certainly behooved the U.S. to be alert. "Do you work for the Russian government?"

"Do you take me for a moron? No! No one with brains works for the Russian government. Free enterprise is the keyword in Russia, and you know I've always been an independent thinker." He laughed. "If Putin knew what was going inside my brain, he would get a touch upset."

"Would he?"

"If he chose to believe it." Dankov gave Trager an enigmatic smile and got busy with his soup.

"Now tell me something." Dankov pointed his spoon at Trager. "I'm just a stupid soldier and you are a veteran intelligence officer."

"Ex-intelligence officer."

"If you didn't tell Simone over the telephone you were traveling under an assumed identity, how did Longo know?"

A knot formed in Trager's stomach. "I don't know. Does Simone work for the ZSS?"

"She lives in the capital. A dangerous place if you don't cooperate with Longo." Dankov paused and shook his head. "She insists on playing politics. That can be fatal."

"I gather you and Longo are not the best of buddies."

"Part of the daily court intrigues and turf fights." Finished with his soup, Dankov let his spoon clang into his bowl.

A delicious aroma preceded the return of the orderly.

"*Beuof* Stroganoff." Dankov rubbed his palms together.

"How do you get sour cream here?"

"Canned. Once a month a supply plane brings us the goodies and picks up our stuff."

"Your what?"

"Diamonds. DeVries and their cohorts have an embargo on Zengawali gems. So we launder them through Russia. Another reason for my being here. Enjoy. We make Stroganoff properly, shave the beef while it is still frozen. Then it just melts in your mouth. American barbarians give you chunks of beef and call it Stroganoff."

"Superb." Trager said after the first bite. This was ridiculous. He was inside an old Arab fort with a man who paraded in a uniform of an army that on another continent ceased to exist in 1921. Trager's gaze wandered out the window across a steep forested slope. Bright red wings of turakos flashed between the treetops adding to the surreal feel of the place.

"God loves the Trinity," Dankov said with a chuckle. He poured the traditional third round of vodka and raised his glass. "To the souls of the late martyred Czar Nicholas II and his family, may they rest in peace."

Feeling like a dimwitted character in a Chekhov play, Trager clinked glasses with Dankov. Surreal, but Dankov was real and so were his men and weapons.

"Why are you in *this* fort?"

"Don't you think it's quaint?"

"A perfect setting for a Hollywood production. A film about a mad Russian general."

Dankov chuckled. "I like your description. Men of genius are often described as mad because they dare to think differently and big. When I was a little boy, my grandfather used to show me a French pictorial magazine with engravings of Czar Nicholas II and the Czarina during their state visit to France." Dankov's eyes gazed upward and his expression became wistful. "I loved those pictures--stately, regal, beautiful people. It was a time when Russia was respected for its grandeur and its culture. I was a kid living up to his eyeballs in cow manure and Communist party hacks. You know why I joined the Army? Because, in the mess, officers still called each other '*gospoda*'."

"Gentlemen don't bring rocket launchers into cafes."

Dankov was crazy. Nearly twenty years ago, Trager first saw him in Vienna. Dankov wore a Soviet Major's uniform and on top of a café table he had an antitank RPG-7 launcher. Had Trager been more experienced, he would have backed off, but instead, he went ahead with the meeting triggered by an anonymous phone call to the embassy. Dankov demanded five-hundred dollars, arranged for a second meeting, swung a bag with four RPG projectiles into Trager's lap, and left the café. That event altered Trager's life and eventually ruined his career with the CIA.

Dankov laughed. "You and I changed the history of the twentieth century, prevented World War Three, and fought the decisive battle that ended the Cold War. Did anyone say 'thank you'?"

Trager shrugged. Dankov had given him the complete battle plans of the Soviet Army for the Southern Front, revealing the intended dash through the Austrian Muhlviertel area to deliver a crushing flank blow against the Americans in Fulda. Once the Americans knew about it, a quick Soviet victory in Europe became much more difficult. Trager had delivered the plans to Blankenship.

"You could join me in another great enterprise."

"Tell me."

Dankov made a sly face. "First, you must quit the CIA."

"I quit twelve years ago. I'm only an outside consultant."

"Really quit."

Trager smiled. "I told Blanky to go fuck himself."

"But you're still working."

"This is it, my last mission. I need to make a life for myself."

Dankov appeared to mull over what Trager had said, then suddenly asked, "How did you meet Tony Bond?"

"He helped me sort out some muggers. I thought he was a nice fellow."

"Dangerous."

"Why?"

Dankov frowned. "We don't really know who he works for. Unlike you, he has an impeccable cover, buys tea."

Chapter 8

Trager learned dinner at the fort was always a dress affair. The same group from last night sat drinking coffee and cognac. Simone talked about her excursion. "We have failed to catch up with the gorilla group, but I was pleased with what I've seen. Once our security situation gets stabilized, we should import and re-introduce rhinos. Mr. Davenport, what do you think it would take to attract American tourists?"

"Luxury lodges, hot running water. Roads so they don't have to walk. The major problem is Americans are afraid to travel. I would concentrate on French and Italians, they're adventurous." To Trager's amusement, Simone took notes while he spoke.

"Simone, you're going to drive everyone crazy with your tourism projects," Dankov said.

"This fort could be converted into a luxury lodge. All we need to do is install modern plumbing."

"I spoke with the president this afternoon. He's having one of his intimate soirees tomorrow. Johnny will be your escort, do you mind?"

Simone made a sour face. "It sounds like an order." She then smiled at Trager. "Not that I would mind if *you* had asked."

Dankov said, "Ah, noblesse oblige. That's what I like about the aristocracy. They are so polite. Did you know Simone is a princess?"

"Colonel," Simone protested.

"Simone El Oriot, the rightful queen of the Atlas."

"Again, you exaggerate."

"Her father was the famous Kasim El Oriot, leader of the Berber rising against the French. Quite a fellow; kidnapped Simone's mother."

"They eloped."

"Same thing." Dankov continued with an amused expression on his face. "Simone's grandfather, General Duplesis, was upset. Went after Simone's father with five-thousand legionnaires."

"He was a colonel and took fifty paratroopers with him," Simone corrected.

"You tell it then."

Simone took a deep drag of her cigar and blew a line of smoke rings toward Trager. His attention on Simone had been so intense he didn't notice the others had left the room. Now he saw her face at the end of a tunnel of smoke. He hardly dared to breathe so as not to disturb the rings that seemed to unite them.

"On the southern slopes of the Atlas there is a stone-strewn gorge. About halfway up sits a huge rock. From the top of the rock, you have a magnificent view of the Sahara that gives the illusion you have the whole world at your feet. We call it Inspiration Stone. If you sit on top of it long enough, you will be inspired to great deeds. My father invited Colonel Duplesis to meet him there.

"As the French troops surrounded the area, they heard the clatter of hooves. Kasim El Oriot appeared on top of the rock mounted on a white stallion. Behind him sat my mother.

"Colonel Duplesis yelled, 'Kasim El Oriot, return my daughter unscathed and I will spare your life'.

"My mother's voice echoed through the canyon. 'Papa, if you won't let us marry, we will jump off the cliff'."

Trager imagined the scene, the tenseness of the drama, as if he had been there. A jumble of stone, the pink colors of the desert; a suitable place of origin for the extraordinary woman in front of him. "Quite a story," he said just above a whisper.

"Not a story, a heroic event. They were all brave people. When the troubles with Algeria started, my father sent my mother and me to France. Neglected by the King of Morocco, he died defending his mountain fortress. He was the last of the Lords of the Atlas."

Simone's eyes shone. Trager couldn't tell if it was from bitterness, pride, or sorrow.

"We have an early start tomorrow. *Bon nuit.*" She got up and left the room.

"Another cognac," Dankov said.

Trager pushed his glass forward. "Igor, what happened to the CIA people who were looking for you?"

Dankov finished pouring and raised an eyebrow. "You won't give up, will you?"

Trager chuckled. "Of all people, you should know."

"When it comes to people who don't know when to let go, you are like those foolish English dogs. They are so stupid that they even have a man's name. Jack Russell."

"Remove your boot, so I can lock my jaws on your ankle."

Dankov nodded, sipped his cognac, his gaze on Trager. "The first was a man, got mugged in Turako, died of concussion. The second was a Ukrainian gunrunner. A pretty lady with good bed manners, at least that's what Longo told me. She flew her own airplane. It crashed shortly after takeoff."

"I don't think you keep good company."

Dankov chuckled. "Tomorrow you'll see what kind of company I keep."

~

As a counter to possible foul play by Longo, Vadim, with his face and hands painted black, and two heavily-armed African soldiers rode in Schnookie's back. The return drive had been uneventful, but tiring. In his hotel room, Trager transferred his exposed rolls of film and the camera from the duffel to his briefcase and locked it. He then ran a bath as hot as he could stand and got into the tub with a bottle of Perrier. He let out a groan as the kinks from the rough ride began to unknot. On the way back, Simone had said little, asked if he had a tuxedo. On hearing he didn't, she told him a dark blue suit would be acceptable for the party at the presidential palace and that she would pick him up at nineteen-hundred hours--exactly. She also advised him not to use the telephone. Longo didn't expect him back for a couple of days. If she needed to contact him, she would let the telephone ring twice, hang up and call again.

When he could no longer stand the heat, Trager got up and let cold water cool his body. No sooner had he dried then he was sweating again. Trager sat on a towel at the edge of his bed and let sweat drip off him, remembering Simone by the natural pool. Had the moment not been marred by ambush, it would have been magical.

Reluctantly, he erased Simone's image. He had learned enough to consider his mission a success. Now he had to reckon how to get out of the country. Simone had said she had a couple of ideas.

The telephone rang. Trager held his breath. One ring, two rings, three. It wasn't Simone. The phone kept ringing. Trager restrained the urge to find out who would be calling. After ten rings, the phone went mute. Maybe the hotel operator could tell him who had called. Trager discarded the idea. Hotel operators usually worked for the security services.

Who would be calling? The question drove him nuts.

Trager waited until he stopped perspiring and went back into the shower. When he came out, the phone was ringing again. The persistence indicated it had to be someone who knew he had returned. Ignorance was not an option. He had to know who it was and be ready to escape via the back door.

Ready to jump into some clothes and bolt, he picked up the phone.

"Bond here. You're back early. How about a spot of wompo at the bar?"

How did Bond know he had returned? Once again, Trager speculated who Bond was and whom he represented. Maybe *he* was the backup Blankenship denied Trager had. "Come up to my room," he said, trying to reduce the risk of being seen by some security snoop.

"That won't do, old boy. Remember the saying about walls?"

Trager wanted to say something about telephone taps. He might as well act like an innocent tourist and accept the invitation.

As he entered the Terrace bar, Trager noticed one of the Russian soldiers he had seen a few nights before. Dressed in a loose sport shirt, he sat at a corner table from where he had a complete view of the terrace and the hotel entrance. His glass was half full, the beer flat.

Bond sat at the opposite end of the terrace with two bottles of Jumbo in front of him. He waved.

"Hullo, old bean. With Mademoiselle Loriot as guide, I would have stayed for weeks in the bush. Ah, Nirvana."

"Not many secrets around this place," Trager grumbled as he sat.

"People talk about people. It's called 'gossip'. The manager of Talawa farm says you never showed up. Enjoy love under the stars?"

"I'll write you a full memorandum." Trager didn't bother hiding his irritation.

"The area east of La Porte is a closed zone. Was it interesting?"

"I think we went north. I'm not good with directions. We saw some elephants but failed to find gorillas."

"Good chap. Did she mention the Utabu?"

"Huh?" The word sounded faintly familiar, but Trager couldn't remember where he'd heard it.

"Let's have dinner tonight."

Trager pulled at his beer. After all the sweating he'd done, it tasted wonderful. "Sorry, I have a prior engagement."

"Dinner with the fabled mademoiselle?"

"I understand it's traditional to treat your guide after a safari."

"And a heavenly night in her apartment." Bond took a box of Silk Cut cigarettes out of his pocketa and lit one.

"Is that where she lives, in an apartment?"

"I don't know, dear chap. Just a manner of speech."

Trager thought Bond was lying. "How about you?"

"Oh, I rent a villa on the outskirts, very suitable for entertaining lovelies. I'm sure Mademoiselle Loriot will love it."

"Remember, she doesn't like you."

"One never knows. Things may change."

Trager would be leaving soon, while Simone and Bond would stay. The thought that something could develop between them bothered him. "Well, ta-ta. I have to make myself presentable for dinner."

"Where are you taking *la belle*?"

"She's the local. I let her choose." Trager gulped the last of his beer and rose.

Bond grinned. "Be careful. Remember who the night belongs to."

Heading out, Trager glanced at the Russian in the corner following him with his eyes, beer glass still half full.

As he opened the door to his room, Trager had a jolt.

No sign that the maid had been in, but someone had moved his briefcase.

He unlocked it. All his exposed film was gone, including the film inside the camera. *Tony Bond, you devil.*

Chapter 9

If Bond knew he was back in town, so would Longo, and Longo wanted to arrest him. To reduce his chances of getting picked up, he had to minimize his exposure. Trager checked his watch; 18:57:32. He waited ten seconds, stepped outside his room, and closed the deadbolt with his key. He took the stairs instead of the elevator, descended at a moderate pace, and paused at the door until his watch read 18:59:45. Cracking the door, he scanned the lobby. No obvious ZSS people. The Russian he had seen on the terrace now sat in the lobby with a newspaper on his lap. Though his presence was reassuring, Trager had no clue of the man's role. He marched past the man and nodded at the desk clerk. The distinctive purr of a Land Rover engine approached as he descended the front steps.

He glanced at the terrace bar. Still there, Bond gave him a slight wave. The doorman held the car door open. Trager tipped him and got inside.

Simone wore black pantaloons with a gold sash. Obviously, she liked white blouses. A lacy, white mantilla covered her shoulders. "I like men who are punctual," she said as she tore away from the hotel.

"And we didn't synchronize our watches."

"No need to among people in the know." She gave him a quick, brilliant smile. Instead of heading for the palace, she turned right in the direction of the ministry building.

"Where are we going?"

"We'll make a few twists and turns in case someone is following. No need to advertise the president is seeing a high-ranking U.S. government official."

"But I'm not--"

"You *are* a high ranking official. If you want to get out of here alive, just follow my cues and Igor's."

"Is Igor going to be there, too?" Silently, Trager cursed Dankov. For an old friend, he had been too reticent in sharing information.

"He never misses a chance to visit the palace." Simone made a turn into a litter-strewn street. Away from the main boulevard, the city looked empty. Trager wondered if she still carried her pistol.

She continued. "He doesn't need an invitation."

"It looks like Bamondo trusts him."

"He does, he does." She sped up. Tires squealed as she turned a corner.

Trager's heart pounded an extra beat. Blocking the street was a row of steel drums painted white. "Not again."

"Don't be silly. You're quite safe with me."

Two soldiers in olive green berets emerged from behind the barricade. One directed a light beam at Trager's face, forcing him to squint.

"*Bon soit, Mademoiselle, ça va?*"

"*Ça marche, merci.*"

Trager let out his breath when the soldier waved them through.

"The Simba Guards, our best regiment." Simone snaked her way around the barrels. Beyond the checkpoint, the street inclined sharply until they came to the lake road.

"What does '*utabu*' mean in Zengawali?"

She gave him a sharp look. "It's a rarely-used, ambiguous word. It could mean 'thing' or 'sacred'. Where did you hear it?"

"You and that village chief used it a lot."

Simone laughed. "The old boy speaks in an archaic way." She slowed as they approached the palace. "You don't mind the back door?"

"Never," Trager said, thinking of Simone's delicious rump.

A wrought-iron gate opened. Simone stopped. A soldier came forward, checked a card Simone handed him and made a note on a clipboard. Another soldier, by the looks of him, an officer, approached Simone's door. "Hello, Simone," he said, leaning an arm on the window that framed his Caucasian face painted black. He looked at Trager closely. "Okay." He stepped back and saluted.

"That's Genadiy. His last job was advising Americans in Afghanistan." She drove up an inclined circular driveway and stopped under a striped canopy. Guards in white uniforms with red sashes under leather belts opened the car doors. Simone waited for Trager to come around and took his arm. One of the guards drove off with the Land Rover.

Double white doors opened. A short man in a tuxedo greeted them with a bow each. "*Monsieur, Mademoiselle, souyes les bienvenues.*" Gesturing in a grand manner, he turned to lead the way.

A festive riot of white, Trager thought. Inside a white corridor with a row of sparkling crystal chandeliers, two Cossacks stood in white silk *cherkeska* coats that fell to their knees. On their chests, ammunition pockets held silver cartridge cases. Each had a long *kinzhal*, the dagger hanging across the stomach. Modern pistol holsters at their hips broke with tradition. Both men saluted as Trager and Simone went past. Though dressed in a plain blue suit, with Simone at his side, Trager thought he was making a grand entrance, but the idea of impersonating a U.S. government official bothered him.

Toward the front of the palace, they reached a large foyer. The sound of a piano and conversation came from a set of open doors.

"*Monsieur Davenport et Mademoiselle Loriot,*" the majordomo announced.

In his various assignments, Trager had socialized with ambassadors, ministers and other high-ranking people. He had never met a head of state and reminded himself to act naturally.

A tall, athletic-looking man strode forward. Trager recognized President Bamondo.

"Simone, what a pleasure to see you." He hugged her. "And *Monsieur . . .*" He stretched a hand and gave Trager a firm handshake. "Welcome. I'm delighted to meet you."

There was something likeable about the man. "Excellency, the pleasure is all mine," Trager said.

"Come in, meet some of the people." He took Trager by the arm.

The large room had tables scattered along the edges with the center left open as if for a dance floor. French doors on two sides remained closed. In the dim light, about fifty guests stood in small groups, drinks in hand, while waiters floated among them with trays of canapés.

A redhead wearing a clingy imitation snakeskin dress detached herself from the buffet where she had been conferring with a cook.

"Ah, Leonora. Meet Mr. Davenport. My wife, Leonora."

Up close, it was easy to see how she had captured the Miss Belgium title. The woman had a superb, full body that moved with fluid grace. Her dress concealed little. It even clung to her navel.

Trager forced himself to keep his eyes above her shoulder-level.

Leonora and Simone hugged and traded kisses on the cheeks. Leonora then shook Trager's hand. "So good of you to come. I'm going to steal Simone for a moment so that we can exchange news. Feel right at home."

Bamondo led Trager toward the grand piano. "I would like to introduce you to Professor Wimbo. He teaches at our conservatory."

The pianist stopped playing while Bamondo made introductions.

Bamondo said, "Professor Wimbo helps me keep my sanity with his music."

Wimbo made a mischievous face. "The Prez has a dual personality; on nights like these, when he pretends he's running Rick's Bar in Casablanca, he secretly calls me Sam."

"How true. We have so many ceremonial occasions with drums; I thirst for soft music. Have you seen Casablanca?"

"Both the film and the city, Excellency."

"Once was enough; no need to remind me of my status. Call me 'Pierre'."

A waiter approached with a tray.

"I hear you drink scotch on the rocks."

Where did Bamondo hear this? "On the rocks or any other place I find myself."

Bamondo laughed. "Splendid sense of humor." He turned slightly. "Ah, here comes Madame. If you will excuse me, I must attend to my ministers. They get nervous if they think they are in disfavor."

As Bamondo strode toward a group of men huddled in the middle of the room, Leonora took Trager's arm and led him away from the piano. "Actually, it's Pierre who gets nervous when more than five men congregate and give the appearance of reaching an agreement."

Trying to imagine what sorts of court politics a head of state had to deal with, Trager chuckled politely.

"From what Igor tells me, you're a brave man. You saved his life."

"He exaggerates."

"Igor is flamboyant, bold, a darling, but he doesn't exaggerate."

"Is he coming tonight?"

"It's such a comfort having the dear man around. He's checking the palace security, should be down any minute." Leonora glanced toward the door. "And here comes Colonel Longo."

Trager's gut tightened as Longo materialized from within the crowd. He approached as if unsure he would be welcome. In The Cellar Club, Trager hadn't noticed the ugly scar from a cut on the side of his face.

"*Bon soir, Madame, Monsieur.*" In a most un-African manner, Longo clicked his heels and bowed slightly. "I presume you are the famous Mr. Davenport?"

"Nothing famous about me."

Leonora seemed to be searching the room with her gaze.

"I'm thinking of certain newspaper headlines."

"I don't understand."

"In the world of security, one is encouraged to think about, and predict, the future."

American Spy Executed At Dawn came to Trager's mind. "Do you sell securities?"

"I'm afraid you misunderstood me." Longo's scar twisted, made his black face look like two-mismatched puzzle pieces. "I'm responsible for the well being and security of the people of Zengawal. Isn't that right, Madame?"

"Yes, of course."

Trager thought he detected nervousness in Leonora's voice.

Longo smiled. "Though I don't believe Madame likes it, my men provide security for Madame when she visits town and her favorite charities."

"You are diligent."

"Thank you. I'm flattered to be complimented by a foreign spy."

"He's not--"

"Well, well. I'm glad you two have met." Simone came to Trager's side. "Mr. Davenport is a special envoy from the president of the United States."

"Envoys travel with official passports."

"Haven't you heard of confidential envoys? He has just delivered a private letter to our president. The day after tomorrow he will be taking a reply to the White House."

"I see," Longo said. "I'm sure we'll meet again." He clicked his heels and walked off.

"The poor man is a loathsome paranoid," Leonora said.

Simone added. "A peeping Tom, a corrupt ghoul."

Trying to exploit the expressed dislike, Trager said, "He seems quite well educated."

"In the wrong places. He trained in East Germany," Simone said.

"And here comes Igor." Leonora brightened.

Dankov wasn't exactly coming. He stood by the doors in a badly fit tuxedo that failed to hide the bulk under his arm. He took a cigarette from a silver case, lit it and surveyed the crowd, like a teacher supervising a yard full of mischievous children. After a moment, he ambled to the piano, leaned on it, and spoke to Wimbo. He motioned toward Trager's group.

Leonora laughed. "Excuse me. As a child, I always wanted to be a chanteuse. Pierre will not let me sing at a karaoke bar, so this is my chance."

As Wimbo broke into *J'atends*, Leonora strode forward and sang. She had a pleasant if not commanding voice.

The room grew silent.

Trager was glad of the interruption. Longo's remarks and Simone's outrageous fabrications bothered him. The worst was Longo hadn't seemed impressed.

When Leonora finished, the crowd broke into applause. She deserved it.

Simone said, "I wish Igor would invent a different song request. Someday, he will anger Bamondo."

Dankov talked with an obese man in a white tunic, red sash, and chest full of medals.

"That's General Mawingi, Commander of the Army."

Trager was beginning to familiarize himself with faces, which, on the surface, looked like a herd of herbivores peacefully grazing on a plain. He wondered who, besides Longo, was a predator. "He looks like a jolly fellow."

"He hates Igor."

"They seem to get along."

"That's because he still remembers what happened to General Mbaya." Simone inclined her head to one side and gestured with her eyes.

Trager's gaze rested on a man sitting in a chair in a corner of the room, smiling.

"He's as gentle as lamb now."

The man didn't look at all like the newspaper photographs Trager had seen of the former dictator. "I'm surprised to see him here."

"Bamondo keeps him around as a sort of pet."

Mbaya, it had been reported at the time, was overthrown after a fierce fight in the palace. Of course, nothing had appeared in the press about white mercenaries. Trager wondered what this room had looked like after Dankov's invasion of the palace, presumably the bloodiest piece of real estate in the country.

Out of the corner of his eyes, Trager saw Longo approaching a group of people. As if by magic, the group dissolved. Longo caught a gray-haired man by the elbow and started telling him something, getting vigorous nods in return.

One of the few people not wearing a tuxedo said hello to Simone. She introduced him. "Professor Najua, the Minister of Education. The most important man in this country."

Najua took an unlit pipe out of his mouth, smiled shyly and shook Trager's hand. "Mademoiselle Loriot doesn't understand politics. I'm a simple school teacher who ended up at a level above his competence."

"The next generation will remember Minister Najua as the man who brought enlightenment to Zengawal."

"My dear Simone, please don't magnify my humble effort," Najua said while scrutinizing Trager. "Not a treasure hunter?"

"An American diplomat," Simone interjected.

"Will Mr. Davenport come to the recital on Friday?"

Simone said, "He's leaving the day after tomorrow."

"Pity, we need fresh minds in this country. I'd better rejoin my wife. She doesn't like being left alone in this . . . this . . ."

"Nest of ruffians?" Simone finished for him.

Najua looked around. "You're too harsh in your judgments. Everyone here is trying to do their best."

"We still haven't wiped out all corruption."

"The task of nation building is a long cultural process." With a friendly wave, Najua headed for the other end of the room.

Trager asked Simone, "What's this about my leaving day after tomorrow?"

"I've made a booking for you on Sabena through Madame Kanzo--but you'll be leaving tonight, while Longo and the President discuss business. You'll fly out on a Panafrique 707. No pretty stewardesses. It's a cargo flight, I'm afraid. I'll take care of your luggage and hotel bill tomorrow."

"I'm not trying to escape. I haven't--"

"Oh, don't argue. Just enjoy the party. Igor told you he doesn't control the airport and that your predecessors were killed."

"But you've said yourself I'm a special envoy. Surely the President . . ." The way Simone inclined her head to one side, and her smile stopped him.

"Yes, just stick to your story while Longo beats you with a rubber hose. You can also ask him for a *jeton* to make a call to your lawyer."

"The puzzle left to solve is why my predecessors died. That takes time."

"You may find out sooner than you expect, but it won't do you or anybody else any good. Corpses don't report their findings."

Trager gritted his teeth. It appeared Blankenship sent him on a suicide mission, but why? On an impulse, he took Simone's hand. "Simone, will you come with me?"

She squeezed his hand. "Nice of you to ask, but I'm busy this week."

People were gathering around the tables, looking for their place cards.

"Time to eat, we'll leave the palace a two-thirty."

As she stepped away, he took her wrist lightly, she his. Their hands slid and parted like a broken cable.

For dinner, Trager got stuck at a table with the Minister of Posts and Telecommunications, and two African businessmen and their wives.

Dankov, Simone, General Mawingi, and Longo sat together. Bamondo had nothing but men at his table, and Leonora presided at a table for women. Trager presumed these were the senior ministers and their wives.

The Minister of Posts and Telecommunications was holding forth about methods of sorting mail and how important mail was in the modern world. Trager nodded politely without really listening. It was ten-fifteen. If he went along with Simone's plan, he had only a few hours to complete his mission. If this place was as dangerous as Simone and Dankov implied, he hated the idea of leaving her behind. He was also curious what she was up to. There was more to her than model civil servant.

A young blonde with strong facial features and a red rose pinned to the shoulder of her badly-fitting black dress entered the room leading a tall man in dark glasses who held onto her shoulder. They raised their violins and began scratching *Dinah*. For no reason at all, Trager felt sorry for them. Maybe it was the quality of their playing.

Finished with *Dinah*, which seemed to be their theme song, they played some Django Reindhardt tunes. For this, a guitar was missing. Trager realized he was getting depressed. When they finished strolling around the tables, Leonora stood to applaud and made a big fuss about their music. She led them to the table where General Mbaya sat alone, still smiling.

One of the businessmen said, "They are refugees from Croatia. Good thing Zoltan is blind; he only heard his wife being raped. His daughter saw it all."

As soon as dinner was over, Trager went to the bar, asked for a cognac and picked up a panatela from a selection of cigars. The atmosphere in the room had become too oppressive. He opened one of the French doors and stepped out on a terrace.

The air had cooled and the scent of jasmine was strong. A half moon gave the terrace a soft glow that soothed Trager's frustration. There was something going on here he didn't understand. A lone motorcycle roared in the distance then became quiet. Trager leaned over the balustrade, looked at the garden and lights reflecting in the lake. So far, the evening had been a complete flop. He hadn't learned much. He was skulking out of the country, his work only partially done.

Trager's gaze rested on the trees in the garden and his mind searched for an earlier time he could hardly remember. There were trees around the house they had lived in. He imagined the sound of his mother playing the piano. He knew his early childhood had been a happy one. Whenever he felt sad, he searched for that vague picture in his mind, trying to remember more. A little boy and his dog in the garden, his mother playing Tchaikovski's *First Piano Concerto*.

Another scent overpowered the jasmine. Perfume. Trager turned, expecting to see Simone.

Leonora stood not two feet away from him. Her cleavage reflected moonlight.

"Hello," Trager said.

She stepped forward and the tips of her breasts touched Trager's chest. "Kiss me," she said in a low voice.

Chapter 10

Leonora's hands pressed against Trager's cheeks, lips touched, and her tongue flicked inside his mouth. Before he had time to recover, she stepped back and smiled at him. "Let me have a puff of your cigar." Without waiting for an answer, she took the cigar out of his hand. "I like cigars." She brought it to her mouth and ran her tongue around it. "Too bad we don't have time to enjoy yours." She took a puff and blew smoke into Trager's face. "These make me cough."

Trager stood like a stupefied dummy.

She handed him back the cigar. "The President would like to have a word with you later, so don't leave. Do you dance?"

"Yes."

"Good, we will dance shortly." She turned and walked to the door. As she opened it, light from inside silhouetted shapely legs.

Trager took a deep breath then inhaled cigar smoke, something he hadn't done in years. His heart had been racing. *Cock teaser.* He erased her image from his mind. At least he would have a conversation with Bamondo. That would look good in his report. He shook his head and forced a small chuckle. *This is my last report. It doesn't matter at all whether it looks good or bad--or does it?*

He remembered Simone by the pool, and the photograph he would never see. After he quit, he would be denied access to the secret world. His capability of finding out the truth would be diminished. He'd never discover who stole his film, and more important, who had warned Longo of his arrival. The thought that a traitor sat in Washington made his hands tremble from rage. That sonofabitch had to be uncovered and brought to trial.

Back in the room, the crowd had thinned. Quadraphonic sound came from everywhere--Glen Miller. Seeing Trager, Bamondo gestured for him to come over. He stood next to a thin African woman with fine facial features. A long, light-blue print dress with a flared skirt and a tall turban on her head gave her an exotic, regal appearance. The effect was diminished by a large wrap of the same material as the dress. She wore it as if dying from cold.

"John, I would like you to meet my wife, Tissu."

Smoke and mirrors. What? Trager tried not to show confusion.

Tissu extended her hand from under the wrap. *"Tres horeuse de faire votre connaisanse,"* she said in schoolgirl French.

"Mr. Davenport comes from the United States."

Tissu smiled. "When you go back, tell the President we are a peaceful country and will be delighted if he would visit us."

Inwardly, Trager cursed Simone's fabrication. "I will tell him that," he said out of kindness for her naiveté.

Bamondo smiled, seemingly pleased with Trager's words. "I will be back, so please stay." He took Tissu by the hand and led her out of the room.

Trager checked his watch. Ten to twelve. Two hours and forty minutes to make the most out of his mission.

General Mbaya still sat at his table, smiling. Excessively loud laughter drifted from the foyer. It appeared Longo had told a joke to a group of cigar-smoking men. Simone was leaning back, her elbows on the bar, smoking a cigar and blowing smoke rings. Trager marched toward her.

"Hey, you clumsy oaf. Look out."

Four feet short of Simone, Trager froze in his tracks, trying to understand.

Simone laughed. "I was going for nine rings. Look what you have done by displacing air around you."

"I'll take lesser displacement training. Next time we meet, you won't recognize me."

"No need to--we won't meet again--but if this was a paying bar, I would let you buy me a farewell drink." She smiled. "You have a confused air about you."

"I thought Leonora was Bamondo's wife."

"He has two. His ceremonial wife, who is a Wussi, and his private wife he can't show in public. The Bassi-Wussi marriage also helps keep the peace." She nodded to the side. "Leonora doesn't take too kindly to this."

Leonora and Dankov sat together at a table. They appeared to be in a heated discussion.

Simone chuckled. "You could ask *her* if she would like to leave with you."

"You're full of brilliant ideas. How am I going to get aboard this famous freighter of yours?"

"On the way to the airport, we'll pick up an ID card that will make you an employee of Panafrique. You'll walk through the cargo terminal. On the other side, you'll find your airplane. It will be easy to recognize, it has two wings and four engines."

"Ach." The exclamation drew Trager's attention to Dankov's table. Dankov shook his hand, a pained expression on his face. Leonora was slipping a shoe back on her foot. She got up and came toward Trager. "Care to invite me to dance?"

Trager took her arm and led to the center of the room. Several other couples followed suit.

Leonora pulled him close and he felt the softness of her breasts. Trager looked around, but no one appeared to be paying attention to them. At the bar, Dankov held a snifter and talked with Simone. Leonora's warm cheek rested against his. She said, "Are you the forerunner to diplomatic recognition by the United States?"

"I just came to see an old friend."

"Igor is such a wonderful man."

"Why did you hit him with your shoe?"

"For making a joke in bad taste. We are old friends, too."

"You've hit him on his shooting hand. It seems that's not a good idea here."

Leonora moved her head back and looked into Trager's eyes. "Although Igor plays an important role in keeping the political balance, it is Pierre who builds consensus and keeps the peace. This will be a wonderful country when Pierre's reforms take hold."

Longo, who was leading the ever-smiling Mbaya out of the room, distracted Trager's attention. "What happened to Mbaya?"

Leonora gave Trager an amused look. "He's now a firm supporter of Pierre's reforms."

The music stopped. Trager led Leonora back to the bar. She said, "Soon, Pierre will be back from his pedophiliac session, and will see you in private." She stopped, suddenly forcing Trager to half-turn. "I had my doctor check the poor girl for HIV."

"It must be hard on you."

She smiled. "The situation has its rewards."

Whatever it was Dankov and Simone were discussing, must have been serious. As Trager and Leonora approached, their intense expressions changed to smiles. Dankov's backhand was turning blue.

Simone said, "You two looked good on the dance floor."

"I can't wait 'til we get to the tangos. Did you learn to tango in Buenos Aires?" Leonora's remark hit Trager like a wet towel across the back. How in the hell did she know he'd been to BA?

They spent some time chatting about the climatic differences in Zengawal and about Simone's work with the Pygmies in the swampy lowlands. Simone said the area had an incredible tourism potential.

"*Monsieur Davenport, le president vous atend.*"

Trager followed the majordomo out of the room, through the foyer and down a corridor. A soldier with a submachine gun stood in front of a door. The majordomo ushered Trager into a small sitting room furnished in French Provençal.

"Good morning," Colonel Longo said.

Trager halted, looked at his watch--01:14. "I guess it is morning already."

Longo nodded. "Enjoying yourself?"

"Fascinating."

"I'm pleased to hear it. You *will* tell me about it later."

The majordomo opened another door. "Monsieur Davenport." He turned and gestured for Trager to go through.

A desk lamp and a corner lamp dimly illuminated the spacious presidential office. Wearing a terrycloth robe, Bamondo sat behind a large desk. On seeing Trager, he put down a sheaf of papers, stood, and extended an arm toward a set of sofas in a corner of the room.

"How high in the CIA do you report?" Bamondo asked as they sat facing each other.

"With the CIA, it is the value of the information that decides what level of attention it will receive. The reporter could be a thief or an inconsequential beggar."

"I see you are modest. I will go straight to the most significant problem our country faces. It is the lack of diplomatic recognition and a *de facto* trade embargo. I now realize nationalizing the diamond mines was a tactical error. The former owners of the mines have strong allies and have formed a consortium dedicated to destabilize the country."

Trager's throat felt dry and he wished Bamondo had offered coffee.

"Thanks to your friend, Colonel Dankov, the looters of our natural resources find it more profitable to rob the Congo. I'm trying to create a sort of Switzerland of Africa, a politically stable and prosperous nation that will attract legitimate foreign investment, tourism and trade. For this, we need time. We are also working very hard to eliminate tribal animosity. To that end, Mademoiselle Loriot is making a great contribution."

Trager's curiosity about Simone had been roused the moment he first saw her. "She has led me to believe she is a low ranking civil servant."

Bamondo smiled. "A low profile lady who has her own way of getting things done. She never claims credit for her achievements."

"So what does she really do?"

Bamondo laughed, shaking his head. "It is difficult to keep track of her activities. Tourism infrastructure development, conservation, school curriculums. She's one of my most valuable advisors, full of creative initiative."

She gave me the impression that history was her forte."

"Anthropology, history, archeology. She's a Renaissance woman."

"I understand Dankov helps in laundering diamonds in Russia."

"That's perfectly legal under international law. DeVries and other private enterprises control the world diamond market. Colonel Dankov is honest but expensive. Not only are we forced to sell our diamonds cheaply, but he keeps a thirty-percent commission."

For a second, Trager's mind froze with astonishment. If this was true, Dankov was probably one of the richest men on the planet. Trager had trouble believing this. It didn't square with Dankov's personality. "So you're no better off than before nationalization."

Bamondo shook his head. "Our income has almost doubled. If the diamond consortium, they informally call themselves *Asociacion de Sureté Sociale*, ASS for short, settled on doing proper business or at least stopped trying to subvert our government, we would quickly become a prosperous nation."

The subject of subversion brought Longo to mind, the man waiting for him on the other side of the door. "What kind of subversion are you faced with?"

"The ZDRP, Zengawal Democratic Reform Party for one. The syndicate finances it. Colonel Longo raided one of their houses a month ago and found a cache of weapons. The Tradition and Drums Party wants to do away with government and re-instate the witch doctors. Witchcraft is illegal. We call them opposition in hope they will enter and respect the political process once we're ready for elections."

Trager had heard this pap before, but Bamondo seemed to understand the outside world, and had a grasp of statesmanship. Too many African rulers only understood raw power and were moved by greed.

"Another danger comes from the Zengawal Army of Liberation. It consists mainly of Hutu and Katanguese mercenaries. Though largely ineffective, it forces us to spend money that otherwise would have been earmarked for education and medical services."

Bamondo opened his arms in a gesture of hopelessness and shook his head. "Though their acronym sounds comical in English--I understand that on your side of the Atlantic, the word generally refers to a part of the human anatomy--The ASS poses a serious threat to our country. Although, the expression originates in Greek myth, you Americans have a splendid way to describe our situation. We find ourselves between a rock and a hard spot. I need help but I can't use African military experts because of their venality. The use of Europeans is restricted by political considerations. This results in the slow growth of our defense capability."

Bamondo reached for a silver box on the coffee table and offered cigarettes.

"Thank you, I quit some years ago."

"During the Cold War, it was easy to get economic and military assistance. All one needed to do was yell 'Communists'! Americans would arrive in force. Now, for reasons I find hard to understand, my unofficial representative in the U.S. informs me that the State Department is considering labeling us a terrorist state. These misunderstandings could be avoided if the United States reopened a diplomatic mission. It needn't be at ambassadorial level. A low profile charge would be adequate."

"I doubt the U.S. government would do it. They would demand elections."

"Our tribal elders elect the chiefs. We need the U.S. to understand that their system might be wonderful for Americans, but, in other cultures, other systems work just as well."

Lots of luck. One needed powerful lobbyists to get the U.S. government to consider anything. Bamondo appeared to be as naïve as his young African wife. The only other powerful force was the news media, but no one in the States, even those capable of finding it on the map, was interested in Africa. If DeVries or ASS wanted to sink Zengawal, they could do it with impunity. Why was Blankenship interested enough to send another agent after two had died?

"Your Colonel Longo makes me nervous."

"I will have a word with him about that, but had you come officially, we would have welcomed you warmly, the way we did tonight."

"Is Longo a Wussi?" Trager asked, considering that Bamondo possibly had to make major concessions to the rival tribe.

"We don't consider tribal origins in selecting government officials." Bamondo stood. "I'm glad you came. I sincerely hope that our meeting will lead to further contacts with your government."

Trager felt sorry for Bamondo, a well-meaning leader of a beautiful country with great potential. Zengawal was in the situation of a gorgeous woman walking the slums while wearing gems. "Excellency, thank you for seeing me." He headed for the door. Beyond it, he had to face Longo, the other side of the coin of recent African history.

Chapter 11

The ugly bastard was still there. He stopped writing in a notebook, slid it into a pocket, and stood blocking Trager's way.

"Nice meeting you. Good night," Trager said.

Longo handed Trager a card. "Will eleven o'clock be convenient for you?"

"A bit early for lunch."

"For your convenience, a car will pick you up at your hotel." Longo smiled and walked by Trager. He entered the president's office without knocking.

Relieved to be past Longo, Trager hurried down the corridor, his heels clacking on the pink-and-white marble tiles. He considered the interview with Bamondo satisfactory, but Longo's apparent awareness of the purpose of his visit to Zengawal and the fate of his predecessors disturbing.

Simone was right. With Longo's invitation, he had to get out of the country--quickly!

The foyer was no longer brightly lit. Trager opened one of the reception room doors and peered inside. The lights were off, moonlight filtered through the French doors. He looked at his watch, almost two thirty. Where was Simone?

He headed down the corridor toward the back of the palace. A few wall lights made the corridor look like a subway tunnel. The ceremonial Cossacks were gone, replaced by a Russian in camouflage uniform, a Kalashnikov slung from his neck.

"Did Mademoiselle Loriot leave?" Trager asked the guard.

The soldier pointed at a door.

Trager knocked.

The door opened, a face painted black stuck out. The door opened wider, allowing Trager to see inside. Simone sat at a table, playing cards with several Russian soldiers in what looked like a guardroom. On seeing Trager, she picked up a telephone and punched three numbers. After a moment, she said, "He's out," and hung up.

"Well, boys, I must go." She stood, picked up some money from the table, and stuck it into her little handbag. With a swishing of pantaloons, she stepped past Trager and out the back door.

The beat-up Land Rover stood in the driveway, its engine running. It looked odd amidst the luxurious palace surroundings.

Inside the car, Trager asked, "Did Igor leave? I haven't said good bye."

Simone gestured with her thumb. "He's upstairs putting his trousers back on."

"What?"

"I just called him. Pierre could be returning to the boudoir soon."

She drove out the gate and through a checkpoint with white barrels, and they were soon on the main boulevard.

"You mean Dankov and Leonora . . . ?"

"Yes."

Trager had trouble believing Dankov was that crazy. No wonder he carried a gun in the palace. Uncontrolled laughter rose in Trager's chest. "Imagine that. Only Dankov would screw a president's wife in the presidential bedroom," he said, annoyed at his own touch of envy.

"They use the linen room. Leonora complains the ironing table is too hard."

Trager wiped tears from his eyes.

"Get what you want?" Simone asked.

"No, just propaganda."

"You go through a lot of trouble to get nothing."

"That's the story of my life."

"I'm sure."

As they drove past the spot where he had met Bond, Trager said, "Why would professor Najua ask if I was a treasure hunter?"

"Some people say King Solomon's mines were located in Zengawal. Odd people come here trying to talk Pierre into crazy joint ventures. Najua has a subtle sense of humor."

Instead of heading to the airport, Simone turned at the market onto the same road they had driven that first morning of the safari. Two blocks further, she stopped the car. "You get off here."

Surprised by her abruptness, Trager looked around with a sense of alarm.

"Get off. There's a taxi in the alley. He'll stop to pick up your ID then take you to the airport."

"Thanks." Trager reached to kiss Simone. She pushed him off with the flat of her hand. "Get out and good luck."

He clambered out and watched the Land Rover vanish down the road. The city was deathly quiet. Light tap-scratching of claws on pavement made him turn. A stray dog scurried down the street. Oppressive loneliness squeezed his chest. *Good luck to you, Simone.*

In the dark alley, Trager moved forward, careful not to stumble. An engine roared to life. Headlights blinded him. There was no way he could get out of the alley before being run over.

Frantically, he searched for a doorway. There was none. Trager pressed himself against a wall next to a drainpipe. The taxi stopped, a door opened.

Feeling like a fool, Trager got in.

The driver zoomed out of the alley, raced past the market and across the boulevard. Trager recognized the illuminated door to Hell's Basement, which seemed to be still open. The streets on the north side of town were narrow, dark, and empty. Soon they left pavement and bumped down a deeply rutted country lane.

Through the open window, Trager kept track of the general direction of travel by watching the stars. He wished he had confidence in the driver but kept a hand on the door handle, ready to jump out if this was a trap.

The driver slowed as they descended into a hollow and stopped in front of a shack silhouetted against the pink glare of city lights.

"*Alez dedans*," the driver said as he switched off his lights and engine.

Starlight reflected from a small pond. A dog barked beyond the noise of crickets and whistling frogs.

Trager got out, found a door. He listened for a moment. Hearing nothing alarming, he knocked.

"Come in," a voice answered inside.

The door squeaked as he pushed it open. A strong smell of dust tickled Trager's nostrils. The uneven dirt floor seemed to heave as bumps and ridges cast moving shadows from flickering candlelight.

"Spot of wompo?" A glass in hand, Tony Bond sat on a crate.

"What are you doing here?"

"Abetting a fugitive, so it seems. Have a seat and a spot of whisky. Your plane is running a bit late."

Trager found another crate and sat down. On top of a third crate stood a bottle of Bell's Scotch and a glass. The crates were boxes of ammunition. By shifting his weight, he could tell the crate he sat on was full. "I like your furniture."

"Birth control pills." Bond handed Trager a laminated ID card. Trager recognized his own photograph from a batch he carried in his briefcase. "How did you get my picture? He asked as if unaware his briefcase had been ransacked.

"La Belle Loriot sent it to me this evening."

"I thought you didn't know her."

"Just met her this afternoon. She came to my office, seems quite concerned about your welfare, old chap." Bond grinned. "She promised to bestow me with a favor or two if I got you out of the country." He lifted his glass. "Cheers. Sometimes we do foolish things, but helping a friend has its rewards. She's a delightful piece of crumpet."

Trager's hand tightened on his glass. He took a good swig of Scotch to wash away the jealousy that gripped him like an ugly claw. To distract himself, he counted the crates stacked against a wall, if each box contained one thousand, there were fifty-thousand rounds in the shack.

"Ah, I hear it."

"What?"

"Your airplane."

Trager listened, heard a slight rumble above the chirping of crickets; jet engines reversing on a runway.

"I hope your visit was a profitable one."

"A flop." Finding Bond with a stash of ammo was one hell of a bonus. It made Trager wonder why Bond didn't worry about Trager discovering it.

"Don't despair, old chap. Life is full of disappointments. In a country like this, it takes time to learn how to operate. Divide and conquer. That was the strategy of the British Empire. It still works today."

If Bond's conceit was real, he was a stupid man. The damn airplane was waiting just as things were getting interesting. "You're not afraid your medical supplies will get ripped off? This shack seems awfully fragile to me."

Bond chuckled. "This consignment won't stay long."

"I guess I should head for the airport."

Bond looked at his watch. "No rush, you should arrive as they get ready to leave. They're loading twenty tons of tea. One thing you should remember, never carry oranges and tea in the same freight. It ruins the tea."

"Any other pearls of wisdom?"

Bond appeared to be taking him seriously. "You're a charming fellow, count your blessings."

Trager finished his scotch and stood up. "Thanks for everything."

"It is I who thank you." Bond's face widened in a sly grin. "*Bon voyage.*"

The taxi drove down the back roads. They came to a rise. In the distance, red lights marked obstructions near the airport. The green-and- white rotating beacon on top of the control tower, flicked like the proverbial light at the end of the tunnel. The place where the journey ends. As the cab drew closer, emptiness inside Trager stirred and grew. The thought of Bond with Simone bothered him. What sort of favors had she promised? It didn't matter, he would never see her again.

The bumpy road became asphalt. As they drove along the airport perimeter fence, they passed a couple of dilapidated and apparently abandoned hangars. The driver turned the vehicle onto a well-lit gateway with a guard booth. "*Taxi peut pas entrer*," he said.

Beyond the gate, a parking lot and a building separated Trager from the aircraft apron.

Trager sat as if nailed to the seat, remembering Schnookie's vanishing taillights. *Sentimental drivel.* It required a mental effort to go with the next step. He handed the driver a five-hundred Z-frank note, got out of the cab, and forced himself to stride to the guard booth. Trying to muster an air of authority, he hoped the card would do the trick. In some places, one needed two IDs, one from the employer, and one issued by the airport.

A policeman stepped outside. "*Oui?*"

"I'm with Panafrique." Trager presented his ID.

The policeman looked at the card then at Trager. "Not a pilot?"

Trager laughed. "No, cargo inspector."

The policeman gave him a long look. In his blue suit, Trager was probably an unusual sight.

"Cargo inspector, that's a new one."

As the policeman turned away and stepped into his booth, Trager moved forward, raised his arm to give him a karate chop.

The cop turned.

Trager pretended to scratch his head.

"Sign here."

Trager took the clipboard and signed his name.

Beyond the gate and parking lot, several trucks were backed against loading bays of a building. The throb of an auxiliary power unit came from the other side. A second chain-link fence barred the way to the apron. Trager spotted a set of metal stairs leading to a yellow door. He went up and pulled the door open.

Inside the cavernous building, somehow avoiding collision, forklifts raced back and forth amid a labyrinth of stacked cargo pallets and containers. Beyond huge roll-up doors, an all white Boeing 707 was starting engines. Trager hurried across the terminal and stepped outside.

The rear cargo door was closing. Turbine noise increased as an engine fired. Looking at an aluminum ladder propped against the forward cargo door, he took a deep breath. *It isn't that high.* He forced himself up the rickety ladder, with relief spotted a rope hanging alongside. With one hand on the rope and the other grabbing the rungs above, he broke into a sweat and climbed. The rope helped him get on solid footing inside the plane.

"Pull the ladder up and stow the rope." A thin man in a white shirt with two stripes on his epaulettes came forward. He pressed a switch and the door began to lower. Gingerly, Trager turned to face the ledge, pulled the ladder up then tossed it in the opening between cargo pallets and the bulkhead. He gathered the rope and stuffed it into a bag attached to the bulkhead next to the door.

The flight engineer slammed locking bars, shutting out the noise of the engines. Trager swallowed as air pressure increased. The heavy, pungent smell of tea almost made him gag.

"Come, take a seat." The engineer went into the flight deck.

In the cramped gray space full of switches, dials and circuit breakers, the pilots were finishing engine start. "Rotation, oil pressure, fuel, ignition, EGT temperature normal . . . good start."

Trager settled on the seat behind the captain and struggled with the unfamiliar shoulder harness.

The airplane lined up on the runway, a vee of yellow lights that began to move. Lights flashed by faster and faster. The cockpit lifted and the lights were no longer visible. The thumping of wheels stopped. Like the sound of rushing water, the noise of the slipstream increased.

Turako's lights blinked below. Trager could make out Flamingo House, the boulevard, the blackness of the lake. Instead of relief, he felt something akin to shame. He was running away.

The lights faded and the sensation of movement stopped. Caught between stars and the darkness of Africa, Trager thought of limbo. He was alone in the world, an orphan.

Chapter 12

In the dark hour before dawn, his Georgetown kitchen looked strangely familiar, yet different, as if he had been gone years instead of less than a fortnight. Trager raised the window and let the aroma of sumac growing in his back yard enter the townhouse. The gentle velvet breeze did nothing to relieve his dissatisfaction. He padded to the stove and put the kettle on.

With the taste of good coffee in his mouth, he placed his report-writing typewriter on the kitchen table. Work was the antidote to post-mission doldrums. On a scratchpad, he wrote a column of key points he would cover and began pounding keys.

The juiciest bit of information he had, if he was to believe Simone, was Dankov's affair with the president's wife. Even in these days of peeping-Tom spies, where satellites and other surveillance equipment did most of the work, the CIA still loved smut. It would go to great lengths to obtain control over a compromised individual. Trager decided not to include this in the report. He wrote about Dankov's stabilizing influence in Zengawal and reported his own conversation with Bamondo almost verbatim. In his conclusion, he stated the present government was better than most African regimes. It seemed to be heading in the right direction and was worthy of support. To avoid alerting a traitor, he omitted that his mission had been compromised from the very beginning. Instead, he wrote in a few red herrings.

By noon, he was finished. Trager counted the single-spaced pages. Ten. No one would read anything longer than that. For a moment, he felt dizzy, and remembered he'd hardly touched food since leaving Zengawal.

Out on Wisconsin Avenue, he bought a pastrami sandwich at a deli and munched on it while looking for a payphone. He punched the numbers to Blankenship's office. To his surprise, Blankenship was not out to lunch.

"About time you called."

"Got your report ready."

"Give it to the hippie in the bookstore."

"There aren't any hippies left."

"At four-thirty, that's sixteen-thirty real time." Blankenship hung up.

Trager slammed the phone back on its cradle. Blankenship would get the report, study it then arrange for a debriefing. It would take several days before he would get to see the inconsiderate old goat. He picked up the phone and dialed Sabena's airport office. A pleasant female voice told him that yes, his unaccompanied luggage had arrived and, if he brought identification, he could have it today.

Driving along the George Washington Parkway, Trager passed CIA headquarters. As he always did, he gave the woods surrounding the Pickle Factory the finger. He hated the place and the bureaucracy it spawned. His disenchantment started with one of the greatest intelligence successes of the Cold War. Crazy Dankov and his filing cabinet containing the Soviet Southern Front's battle plans. But instead of giving Trager accolades, Blankenship, then the Vienna station chief, questioned Trager's judgment and wrote a caustic fitness report that scuttled Trager's career as a case officer. He wound up working as an analyst in headquarters. After two years, he'd had enough of the bureaucracy and resigned. Now, he was quitting again, but under the most unsatisfactory circumstances. The bastard who had compromised his mission made it a job unfinished.

Trager hadn't been sent to get a job done, but simply to be killed like his predecessors.

He almost jammed his foot on the brakes at the sudden realization.

Blankenship had been under pressure to send someone to Zengawal in a hurry. Why keep sending agents to have them killed? It made little sense. Blankenship did mention two predecessors failing. *That* had been a warning.

Inside the Dulles International terminal, he identified himself to the pretty Sabena representative who led him to a small office and handed him his briefcase and suitcase. In checking the contents, he found nothing new missing. A small envelope held a note written with a childish scrawl in Russian. It told him that, if he sent Simone his address, she would return his films after they'd been processed. The return address was the Ministry of Education. He pocketed the note, disappointed it wasn't more personal.

Back in Georgetown, Trager entered the bookstore with only seconds to spare. In the crime section, a young man dressed like a bozo in shorts with the crotch around his knees and a baseball cap facing backward leafed through a novel--Blankenship's *hippie*. Trager checked that no one was observing them, went past him, and slipped the envelope into one of the bozo's huge pockets.

"See ya, man," the bozo said in a low tone.

Trager wondered if the young man dressed like that as a disguise or if the dumb shit was for real.

~

Feeling somewhat more settled, the following morning, Trager sat in the kitchen with a mug of strong coffee in front of him. The telephone rang. It was a surprise to hear Blankenship's voice. Trager checked his watch--07:49. The old spook was ahead of schedule.

"Yeah, I'm awake," Trager grumbled.

"See me in the downtown office in an hour."

Blankenship was still in a hurry. He usually dilly-dallied when it was time to pay for a job. "I'll be there by nine."

"Your version of an hour seems longer than mine." Blankenship hung up.

~

On the third floor of a grubby building on 20th Street, a cheap plastic plaque on the door read: *Army Psychological Welfare Dept.* Trager hated the musty place with its strong smell of disinfectant coming from the toilets across the hall.

He pressed the buzzer, heard it chirp inside.

Bolts slid, the door cracked open the length of a chain. Someone peered through the door, slammed it shut, then reopened.

"*Entrez*," Blankenship growled. "You have just witnessed the latest procedure suggested by the Department of Homeland Security."

"Very impressive." Trager waited for Blankenship to move aside.

"A majestic layer of Byzantine bureaucracy added to the national security cake." Blankenship led the way to the back of the suite of offices, and entered the windowless, soundproof conference room. On one end of the large table sat two coolers and a large thermos. Blankenship pointed to them. "Make yourself comfortable. We have food and drink."

"Expect a siege?" Uncomfortable with the presence of the picnic lunch, Trager unbuttoned his suit jacket and took a seat.

"I expect work from you."

"You got my report yesterday. I expect my money."

Blankenship squeezed into a chair in front of Trager. "Report? All we need is a song writer and a happy ending." He opened his briefcase and waved the report in front of Trager's nose. "It'll be Broadway's next smash hit. Scene one: Dancing Cossacks enter stage left. African chorus stage right, sing *Happy to See You*. Get my drift?"

Puzzled, Trager stared at Blankenship. "So what's wrong with my report?"

"*Hombre*, this report is headed for the White House. Haven't you been reading the papers? Don't you know what they want to hear?"

"It's the value of the information inside the report that decides what level of distribution it will reach."

"The White House wants a report on Zengawal. That's why you were picked for the mission."

"Yeah, and two of my predecessors didn't make it." Trager made a stern face. "You didn't warn me."

"I told you they've failed."

"You told me I didn't need to know."

"I had confidence in you. Besides, third time's a charm." Blankenship laughed. "I liked the way you stole the ID from the Panafrique employee."

Trager watched Blankenship closely. His report was full of red herrings. Whoever had leaked the information to Longo would probably also read his report and react to his bits of fiction. Trager was quite sure that for the moment Blankenship was playing it straight. That meant Bond was not CIA.

"I also calculated that Dankov wouldn't let his *compadre* die."

"You seem to know more about Zengawal and Dankov's role there than you pretended."

Blankenship banged his fist on the table. "You're damn right. What I want is your take, the list of characters and their agendas."

"My report does that. And you asked me a specific question, 'What the fuck was Dankov up to?' It says in my report, he's making lots of money. Now quit bitching and let me have my legal tender."

"Want some coffee?" Blankenship reached into his briefcase and pushed a yellow legal pad at Trager. "Here, rewrite the report. We have a bunch of Russians in Africa creating trouble."

"The Cold War is over, haven't you heard?"

"Not only Russians but reactionary Cossacks who support a dictator who has not been elected."

"In Afghanistan, the ruler has been selected by a tribal council. We provide Green Berets for his bodyguard. There's no difference between what we do and what Dankov does."

"Now you're cutting close to the bone. Afghanistan and the War on Terror. Operational nightmares created by political fuck-ups. Give the boy in the White House a break. He can easily form a coalition to sort out Zengawal. This would stop the defection of our allies because of disagreements over how to deal with Sadam's Iraq. All we need to do is provide logistical support. No casualties, presidential approval ratings up, and once again the U.S. will lead the world in its struggle for the democratic ideals on which this country was founded." Blankenship entwined his fingers over his growing belly.

"Bravo, Uncle Duggie. Do you wear star-spangled underwear?"

"You should have more respect for our national symbols."

Trager walked over to the thermos and poured coffee into a paper cup. Few things irritated him more than misguided or blind patriotism--the sort of craze that brought and kept Hitler in power.

"Dankov has always had a bad influence on you."

"Stamp 'Secret' on the report and forward it."

"I can't do that. This report contradicts other extremely reliable sources."

"You sent me to confirm someone else's bullshit?"

"CASC has a firm grip on African affairs, their information and evaluations have been impeccable."

"Cask?" What the hell is that?" Trager asked with genuine interest.

"Coordinated African Security Committee. It's composed of members of American, British and other European intelligence agencies. Because of the European commercial ties with Africa, this committee has been very effective in getting information, avoiding red tape and delivering it to the customer quickly." Blankenship smiled. "Now, the CIA was able to outdo them and interview Bamondo. That's a coup. My boy, you did it. Now write a suitable report."

The CASC had Trager intrigued; he thought of Bond and his ammunition. "I get it. CASC obtains its product and sends it directly to the White House."

With a sour grimace, Blankenship said, "The National Security Council."

Trager put his coffee down. "And you've told the NSC I was going to Zengawal." Trager grabbed the edge of the table to keep his hands from forming fists.

Blankenship's face remained impassive, but his eyes glared back defiantly. Trager knew it would be fruitless to ask who Blankenship's NSC contact was. He steered away from his target. "Where is CASC based?"

"London."

Trager nodded. "Embarrassing the Agency, and someone is making the Agency pay back for disagreeing with the White House's rush to war."

"Just change the report."

"What does CASC say about Simone Loriot?"

"That's part of the mystery, she appears out of nowhere. CASC says she's a high ranking member of Al Qaeda."

Shocked, Trager sat down and stared at the blank yellow pad. The image of Simone blowing smoke rings at him clouded his vision. Dankov and his silly medals, Longo, Bond. The thin African girl, Tissu. He had trouble reconciling to the idea Simone was a terrorist. "Al Qaeda is an Islamic fundamentalist network. It is highly unlikely they would use women, even as low ranking soldiers. Arrange for some State Department undersecretary or special envoy to visit Zengawal and meet Bamondo. They'll find a kindred soul and gain a new ally for the United States."

Blankenship made a sour face. "The U.S. doesn't need African allies. We have enough problems with the allies we already have."

"I'm surprised they haven't retired you."

"You told me you wanted to quit. Write a good report and I can get you a cushy spot with the present administration."

Trager rolled his eyes. "Have you gone bananas?" Just the idea of associating with political toadies disgusted him.

Blankenship rumbled something while he seemed to think. "When the carrot is abhorrent, the stick may appear more palatable, at least for the stick user. Remember the IRS? Once they check on your newsletter subscriber list, they'll lock you up."

Trager was fed up with Blankenship's threats. Anger rose in his chest. He placed his hands on the table to keep them from shaking. "This is the last time you threaten me, you piece of shit."

Blankenship paled as Trager stood.

"Pay up the money you owe me."

"Don't be hasty."

"Pay up!"

For the first time in his life, Trager saw Blankenship at his wit's end. This gave Trager a perverse pleasure. He watched Blankenship shrug, dig into his briefcase and count out twenty thousand dollars.

Trager distributed the hundred-dollar bills into various pockets of his suit. "Thank you, and I wish you luck."

"You're the one who'll need it."

Trager left the room. Behind him, he heard the soft thud of a chair hitting the carpeted floor.

"Wait." Blankenship huffed right behind him.

Trager reached the outer door, and Blankenship grabbed him by the shoulder. "I'm serious about the IRS. I can't risk sending another agent."

Trager turned, throwing off Blankenship's arm. "Open up an embassy and get a true picture of what's going on. That's what civilized nations do."

Red in the face, Blankenship shook his head. "You've got a bad case of something."

Trager grabbed the doorknob and flung the door open.

"You'll be sorry." Blankenship's shout echoed in the corridor.

Chapter 13

The clock on the townhouse sitting-room's mantel ticked loudly. Trager sat in a wing chair, a notepad on his knee. He studied the page where he had written *MR. X* in big, bold letters. Mr. X was the bastard in the NSC who had shopped him. An arrow led to a circle with *CASC* written inside. From CASC, an arrow pointed at *Bond* and *Longo*. On the margin of the sheet he listed a column with names: Blankenship, Dankov, Loriot, Bamondo, Leonora.

The rough schematic helped Trager compartmentalize his thoughts. The NSC was getting information from CASC, but for some reason wanted the CIA to send agents to Zengawal. Objective: One, two, three agents dead. Where was the gain?

Blankenship had mentioned about the U.S. leading a coalition. Tick-tock, tick-tock--the clock was telling him something. The answer to the question was simple--a matter of adding two and two. But Trager's head was clouded by the thought. *No one shops Trager and gets away with it. Don't hate, think.* What happens when one CIA agent gets killed? The CIA gets pissed off. Bingo! *Casus beli*, reason for war. Trager jumped out of his chair. Bond and his crates of ammunition. The diamond syndicate wanted to oust Bamondo. No one else gave a shit. With two agents dead, the CIA would not object if Bamondo was overthrown. *Murderous greedy bastards*, Trager almost shouted. He went to the liquor cabinet, poured himself a cognac to calm his agitation.

As he sniffed the cognac, a plan of action began to gel. The only way to fight someone high in government was through the news media. But Trager was not a whistle blower. Even if he was, he didn't have any evidence or political allies. Having used the cover of travel writer, he did have a few contacts. He needed to find an angle to interest the American press before the body count demanded headlines.

Blankenship. The old goat had been warning him. *Change the report or they'll lock you up.* No wonder they sent him. They hadn't been planning to kill him. Maybe Longo would have had him roughed up a bit. They wanted a shitty report and had been sure they would get it from him.

He had already screwed up Mr. X's plan and X would be pissed. Pissed royally enough to have Trager killed? Maybe. Going to jail for tax evasion was not an acceptable alternative. Trager had a job to do. He had to unmask a traitor who had exposed an undercover CIA agent to a foreign government. Realizing his commitment and the danger he was in, he put the cognac down and ran upstairs. Trager added a tuxedo to his still-packed suitcase then threw a few additional items into a ditty bag. On his way out, he stopped by the door and took his Glock from under the umbrella stand, racked the slide and stuck the pistol into his waistband leaving the safety off.

~

He spent the night in a motel in Fairfax. The following morning, Trager left early to make arrangements to leave the country before the IRS or others got their hooks into him. His first stop was Office Max, where ordered a rubber stamp. Then, using a telephone card, he made a number of calls from different locations. The first call was to the Chilean Embassy that had recently expanded its personnel. Fernando Marticorena, the embassy's Minister, quickly agreed to rent Trager's house. The rent would be paid into Trager's account in the Bahamas.

The next call was to the editor of *Far Away Places,* a glossy magazine specializing in off-the-beaten-path travel. No, they wouldn't give him an advance, but, if he wanted, they would give him a letter of assignment to facilitate with visas. Trager gave a tobacco shop in Geneva as his address. *Barricade Press* was interested in an article on how to avoid taxes. No, they wouldn't deposit money in an offshore account, but would mail him a check anywhere in the world.

On the other end of the line, Bernie Hull of the *Morning Star* said, "Why should I care about Zengawal?"

"My feeling is there's going to be action there. In the meantime, I can fill you in on background. A beautiful lady that works with Pygmies. I can get an interview with President Bamondo. There's more stuff that so far is off the record. I can get you a scoop on the diamond trade."

"Diamonds are no longer news."

"Buy me lunch, I'll come to New York for that."

"I'm busy, BEEZE. Now what about the Pygmy lady?"

"She's beautiful, a princess, juggles hand-grenades, smokes cigars and wears colorful pantaloons. Real human interest stuff."

"Yeah, if she gets murdered, you've got a story."

"I come cheap, I'll work for the per diem."

"If you write something worth printing, you'll get paid. Keep me posted on your whereabouts, should we need to follow up on something."

"Right," Trager said. Bernie had already hung up.

It was almost noon. Trager looked around the mall. So far, he hadn't spotted a tail. He went into a bookstore and bought a book thick enough to hide the slide of his pistol. The plastic frame he would carry in his suitcase, and he would send the slide and ammo by DHL to Turako. He stuck a small metal brush into the barrel, the thing would look like a battery-operated brush if it was X-rayed. The two magazines with the ammo fit inside a lead-lined container that looked like a power pack, compliments of the CIA's TSD. Trager loved the Technical Services Department.

~

In the office he rented inside a warehouse in the rough Anacostia section of Washington, Trager went through his mail. Sure enough, there was a letter from the IRS. Trager let out a devilish chuckle, took his new rubber stamp, stamped:

Deceased: Return to sender

Unseen, and two months behind on his rent, Trager walked out of the warehouse into his new life, a life where, guarded by Longo's evil spirit, Simone stood as a shining beacon.

Part II
The Kingmaker

Chapter 14

Busara, Congo.

Gunfire came from his right. In the moonless night, Marcel Payot peered over the slit trench. He had no recollection of how he ended up here, but it had been good reflex action. The MP-50 submachine gun was in his hands. He thumbed the safety off.

He recognized the authoritative barks of Kalashnikovs. A long, panicky burst from a Belgian FN ripped a little closer. Payot rubbed his eyes and swore under his breath. Why had there been no warning? The Kalashnikovs fired well inside the camp's perimeter and drew closer.

Several dark shadows ran through the clearing in front of his tent. "Cowards," Payot muttered.

His long experience fighting in Africa told him the battle was lost. If he tried to rally his troops, he would end up getting killed, possibly by one of his panicked men. At least he had had the good sense to pitch his tent well away from the main camp.

An explosion boomed from the direction of the ammo dump. Payot tried to figure out the safest route of escape. The light of a fuel fire followed a muffled crump. The attackers had reached the motor pool.

Payot didn't like the light. It made his getaway that much more difficult. Out of the relative safety of the trench, he crawled toward the nearest thicket, about thirty meters away. If anyone came close he would pretend to be dead. Mosquitoes buzzed his head, bit into his back. He was almost completely naked and thorns cut into his belly and chest.

A voice shouted not far away, "*Na levo.*"

Russian. A Russian giving orders to another Russian.

A burst of fire, very close.

Payot was completely in the open, undershorts probably glowing like a neon sign. He forced himself to crawl slowly. When the bastards came, he would see them first, take out a few.

He reached the thicket. Light footsteps approached. A slight rustle of brush. A man crouched less than five meters away.

This is it, I'm dead. Payot tried to make himself smaller, held his breath.

The man swung his arm. Another figure ran across the clearing, hit the ground and fired at the clump of trees where Payot's tent stood.

The man close to Payot got up and went into the clump of trees.

Payot breathed easier. He could see quite well, the blaze from the motor pool provided a lot of light. In the pink twilight, the attackers walked about as if promenading on the streets of Brussels. They wore black jogging shorts and lightweight running shoes. Cammo jackets covered their torsos. Payot was reminded of the Zealous Scouts during the Rhodesian war.

It looked like his tent was the assembly point for the attackers. The cocky bastards were lighting cigarettes. The ground shook as something else, possibly the mortar shell bunker, exploded.

Payot's heart almost stopped as he heard a loud crunch just behind him. Someone stood urinating not two meters away. The man must have had a radio; in a low voice he said, "*quarante ei un, reçu.*"

In the clearing, the men formed two files and trotted off. Payot also heard the man who had urinated trot away. He surmised this was a flank guard.

"*Merde,*" Payot muttered under his breath. If what he had seen was the main assault force, it was no more than twenty men. One-tenth the size of Payot's Hutu mercenary battalion. Disgusted, he wondered who the other people were. His ammunition was gone. His transport was gone. Food probably gone. Weapons surely gone. It would take months to recover from this fiasco. His dumb shit employers would blame it all on him. How many times had he requested more European officers and NCOs? Payot swiped at the mosquitoes torturing his back.

Shortly after dawn, the vultures were already landing. Payot considered it was safe to emerge from his hideout. He walked toward his tent, careful not to step on thorns that could go right through his foot.

The tent and all his belongings had been burned. The only thing that survived was a kerosene lamp that had been emptied and tossed aside. With a stick, Payot stirred the ashy debris. There was no sign of his leather mapcase with all his documents, passport, money and the almost completed report for the next courier.

Standing nearly naked and barefoot in the middle of Africa, Payot thought his troops would soon straggle back. Food was the great African magnet. But he didn't have any. He had no transport, no radio, no boots, no shoes--nothing! For the first time since he became an adult, he wanted to cry.

~

Langley, Virginia

The only good thing about his windowless office was he didn't have to share it with anyone. As was his daily habit, Blankenship scanned the newswire services feeds. His attention was drawn by a Reuters report filed in Kinshasa of an attack on a refugee camp in the Congo not far from the border of Zengawal. The reporter cited up-country sources.

Blankenship rang the West Africa desk duty officer. "What do you have about cross-border raids from Zengawal?"

"Just a Reuters' item on a refugee camp. We've queried Kinshasa station. They're sending a man to the area. We had no reports of raids from Zengawal. Do you know something I don't?"

"Yeah, I need a station in Turako."

"Once a station is closed, it's closed. Budgets and all that."

Blankenship hung up, gritting his teeth. He had an office but no responsibilities, just weird assignments, crumbs to an officer close to retirement--and retirement scared the bejesus out of him. What would he do, become a useless old man and watch television? He wondered where Trager vanished to. The poor guy's report on Zengawal was a masterpiece. Too bad it was badly received by the White House.

His phone rang. "T.A. Schmutz," Blankenship answered, using his work pseudonym. The director of intelligence was on the line. Blankenship braced himself. Calls from the top always meant trouble.

"Winton Alberg wants another briefing on Zengawal. Get A.C. Shoe and trot him over to the White House."

His breakfast made a spin inside his stomach. Blankenship groaned. "A.C. Shoe has vanished."

"Find him," the director demanded in his most unreasonable manner. "After he briefs the Security Council twit, send him to Turako."

"They'll kill him there."

"You're just confirming the CASC reports. You and I know Zengawal poses no threat to the U.S. For Christ's sake, prove it. This whole thing is a political embarrassment to the Agency."

"Political embarrassment?" Blankenship remembered Anna, the pretty Ukrainian gunrunner he had recruited in Malta. "They've killed two of my agents."

"That's why I wanted an American on the job. A.C. Shoe got back alright."

"American or not, the CASC people will try to kill him."

"If that's how you feel, get him a diplomatic passport, bodyguards. The works."

Blankenship put the phone down as if it was made of delicate porcelain. He vented to the wall, "Trager, you dumb, stubborn shit."

A minute later he had calmed down. Blankenship dreaded going to the White House. The last time he had been there was to brief President Reagan on how the entire battle plans of the Soviet Southern Front had ended in American hands. The way the files were taken out of Czechoslovakia into

Austria was so outlandish, the authenticity of the documents was in doubt for a long time.

Johnny Trager had recently arrived in Vienna on his first foreign posting. It was quite an accident that he got assigned to handle a Soviet agent, a task usually given to a seasoned case officer. The Soviet was a major, Igor Dankov, who provided some low-grade material, mainly army training manuals.

On one occasion, he indicated he had important information and a meeting in Bratislava was arranged. Blankenship was suspicious of a trap for Trager, so he covered the meeting with two surveillance teams.

A few minutes before the meeting was to take place, Team A observed a Soviet Army GAZ jeep pull up in front of the address where the brush contact meeting was to occur. Two soldiers unloaded a filing cabinet and pulled away. Dankov, armed with a Kalashnikov, stayed behind smoking a cigarette.

Quickly passing an envelope, a roll of film, or even a file was one thing. Transferring a whole filing cabinet during rush hour in downtown was simply ludicrous. The surveillance team leader radioed Team B to put out the signal to abort.

Driving a rented Opel Kapitan, Trager acknowledged the signal. Nevertheless, he stopped where Dankov waited. They loaded the filing cabinet into Trager's car, and tore off toward the Austrian Border.

When Blankenship, who was watching with binoculars, saw Trager with Dankov in uniform approach the border checkpoint, he almost had a heart attack, but Dankov had fake documents and the two bluffed their way across.

Safe in Austria, Blankenship chased after the two lunatics and caught up with them in a bar in Schwehat, near the airport. Neither Dankov nor Trager deserved to be alive. Blankenship had no alternative but to write a fitness report stating Trager lacked the judgment suitable for covert operations.

Blankenship groaned thinking of that decision. Trager had been a lousy spy handler, but with Blankenship's guidance and grooming, he had become a first-class operative, troubleshooter and analyst--a self-contained cell. He also became a master of telling people what they wanted to hear. Blankenship wondered what had caused Trager to suddenly stand on principle. He shook his head in admiration, then grumbled, "Trager, you dumb, stubborn shit."

Chapter 15

Trager had finished a satisfying breakfast of croissants, cold cuts and cheese when the Sabena jet began its descent. While in Switzerland, he had gone to the Zengawali embassy in Bern, presented his letters of introduction and applied for a visa under his real name, giving his profession as journalist. He now had a multiple entry visa valid for two years.

Across the apron, the old Air Zengawal Fokker was taxiing out when Trager stepped off his airplane ready to take on the world. The last time he'd come, even though he'd sniffed a bad smell before leaving Washington, he had arrived like some stupid innocent kid, ignoring the alarm bells that kept going off in his head. Now, he had no one to answer to. No one could betray him.

At the foot of the airstairs, the same neatly uniformed lady of his first trip waited to lead the passengers into the terminal.

The critical moment would be going through immigration and customs, but as soon as he was out of customs he would call Simone from a payphone. That would alert Dankov, and neutralize Longo.

No photographer waited in ambush. Trager smiled. Whoever had shopped him on the last trip hadn't had a chance to warn Longo this time.

"Bonjour," Trager said as he handed his passport to a white-uniformed immigration official. The man leafed through Trager's real passport and studied the page with the visa. He looked at Trager's face as if trying to memorize it, stamped the passport and made a couple of hand-written entries. Handing Trager's passport back, he smiled. "Journalist?"

Trager nodded.

"Bienvenue a la republique de Zengawal." He waved Trager through and picked up the telephone.

"Shit," Trager muttered. Surely the official was telephoning either Longo or one of his men. A tingling sensation traveled along Trager's neck, but the reassuring payphones were just on the other side of customs. In a few minutes he would be talking to Simone. A lightness of movement stayed with him and his heartbeat remained normal as he moved toward the next hurdle. A smile crept on his face as he thought of the pleasure he would have in hearing Simone's voice. *You're back, no?*

Trager controlled his impatience while the inspector searched the suitcase of a Belgian businessman who, with old colonial arrogance, kept asking the customs inspector whether he hadn't seen men's underwear before. Finally, the inspector said, "Sa va."

The Belgian closed his suitcase muttering something.

Trager approached the counter.

"Where do you come from?"

"New York."

"Anything to declare?"

"No."

"May I see your passport, please."

Imperceptibly, Trager shifted his weight from foot to foot while the man meticulously leafed through the passport. When he got to the last page, he smiled and handed the passport back. "Very good, open your briefcase."

Trager placed the case on the counter, opened it. "*Voila*." He glanced at the cop standing by the exit, hands behind his back, looking bored.

The customs man finished looking through the briefcase and snapped it closed. "Very good." Snap, he had the case open again. He then clicked it closed. "Very nice click-clack." A big grin appeared on his face.

Trager grinned back, picked up his suitcase and started to go.

"Your suitcase, please."

Trager heaved the suitcase on the counter. If the inspector found the frame of the pistol--by itself it did not constitute a firearm--but it could raise uncomfortable questions.

"Nice suit." The inspector held the unfolded tuxedo by the hanger, showed it to Trager as if trying to sell it.

"Yes, to visit with President Bamondo." Impatiently, Trager fingered the *jettons*, telephone tokens, in his pocket.

The short-wave radio also held the customs man's interest. For a few seconds he listened to the BBC news. "Very good."

He must have gotten bored, started putting things back, making a mess.

"Let me help you," Trager volunteered. In a minute, he had the case repacked.

The bank of payphones was on the right-hand side of the Arrivals Hall. In a few seconds, he would be past the officious klutz and safe. Briskly, Trager headed for the exit.

Shit.

Two men in black safari suits stepped out from the waiting crowd. As he strode past, one of them said, "*Bonjour, Monsieur. Venez avec nous.*" They came up on both sides.

Trager smiled, kept going as if he hadn't heard.

The crowd's chatter died. People stepped aside, giving ample space for Trager and his escorts to pass through.

Past the crowd, Trager turned right, toward the payphones.

A black suit yanked him by the arm, firmly pushing forward toward the exit.

"No taxi for you," one of the black suits said and pointed at a black Mercedes sedan waiting at the curb. The second man took Trager's suitcase, shoved it into the trunk. "Journalists get VIP car."

As he slid into the cool interior of the sinister vehicle, Trager cursed his impulsiveness. He had made a big mistake coming back. His mind screamed at him, asking how could have he been so stupid.

The car sped, its two-tone siren blaring.

A familiar calm returned. *The present situation is called, Get Trager Part Two.* But he had initiated it. The enemy was only reacting. Therefore, *he* was calling the shots.

Groups of men chatting on the road scattered and traffic pulled off to the side at the approach of the ZSS car. They entered town in half the time it had taken Trager on his previous arrival.

"Where are we going?" Trager asked the somber looking man sitting next to him.

The man didn't answer.

On passing the Central Market, instead of going down the familiar Boulevard de la Liberte, the car turned right and the driver switched the siren off. One positive aspect, they didn't have him handcuffed.

People on the sidewalks stopped and stared as the car passed. Another right turn and they entered an industrial area of small, dilapidated factories, workshops and warehouses. A few pedestrians wore mainly coveralls and, in contrast with the people downtown, studiously ignored the black Mercedes. The Jumbo Beer Brewery bustled with activity; trucks lined the street waiting to get in.

The Mercedes came alongside a tall brick wall, half a block from the brewery. A man in black, submachine gun hanging from his shoulder, stood outside a wrought iron gate covered with corrugated metal sheets to block the view. The guard turned and spoke into a hole cut through the sheeting.

The gate opened, revealing a courtyard and a three-story building with bars on all windows. Several men in civilian clothes watched a group of people disembark from a van and shoved them into a side door. A woman clambered off and tripped. A ZSS agent's kick sent her sprawling on the pavement.

Trager controlled his indignation.

The Mercedes pulled up to the front entrance of the foreboding building. Trager took a deep breath of the malty humid air as his escort got out and held the door open for him. The man reached for Trager's briefcase. "I keep."

With a shrug, Trager let go of the briefcase and followed the other black suit into the building. *Keep your cool.* The secret of resisting interrogation was to keep terror at bay.

Another black suit sat at a desk reading a newspaper. Trager's escort said something to him, led the way up a set of concrete stairs with metal railings painted green. Their footsteps echoed off bare walls. Trager was glad they were taking him upstairs instead of down to a dungeon.

On the second-floor landing, a black suit stood waiting. He looked Trager over, nodded at the escort. *"Bien,"* he said, and turned, leading the way down a dark corridor.

He stopped at a gray metal door, opened it with a key and nodded for Trager to step in.

It was obviously an interrogation room. In the center stood a stained wooden table and two straight-backed chairs. Cigarette buts littered the floor.

The door slammed shut. Trager heard the lock turn.

This is it. You'll see Longo again. And that's it. End of story. Trager wondered what madness had possessed him to make such stupid move as to come back. The search for truth, a job unfinished. A quest to find and meet himself. It was odd to see how his spirits rose in this dark moment. He had heard and read accounts of victims of the KGB, how they had found their ordeals an uplifting experience. It was all a matter of holding the moral high ground. Trager lit a cigarette. He wondered if he would live long enough to finish the pack.

An hour went by. Tired of pacing the room, Trager sat on one of the chairs. If he'd had a knife he would have carved his initials on the desk. The last chance of leaving a memorial before they buried him in an unmarked grave. From time to time, he heard footsteps outside and doors slamming shut.

Even though he tried to control it, his anxiety grew by the minute. The room was five-by-five paces. That meant a lap around the room was approximately sixteen meters. Trager imagined he was on the Champs Elyses walking from the Place de la Concorde to the Arc de Triomphe. That would be approximately one-hundred-and-fifty laps. As he went past his imaginary Fouquet's, he felt thirsty.

At two-fifteen, he was a block away of L'Etoile, totally relaxed in his imaginary world. Footsteps stopped in front of the door. With a mixture of relief, dread and self-control, he stopped his pacing when he heard the lock turn.

"Good afternoon. Mr. Trager, is it?" Longo wore a white, double-breasted suit, light blue shirt and regimental tie. Except for the ugly scar on his face, he looked like a prosperous businessman.

"It's a pleasure, Colonel."

"Journalist?" A baffled expression on his face, Longo studied Trager. "Sit down, feel at home." He gestured to the chair Trager had occupied earlier. With a handkerchief, he fastidiously wiped the chair facing Trager before sitting down, taking his time.

Trager realized Longo was trying to put his thoughts together. He hadn't expected to see Trager.

"I apologize for the minimal comforts of this reception room. My men must have misunderstood my instructions."

"No need to apologize. I have simple tastes."

Longo chuckled. "Pity you left in such a hurry. I was disappointed you didn't drop in to say good-bye."

"I apologize."

"Why?" Longo shook his head as if amazed. "Why are you back?"

Trager smiled. "It's a beautiful country, now I have time to see it at my leisure."

"Leisure. You amaze me. And now you're a journalist. A journalist with leisure." Longo's voice had a soft, almost whispering quality. "Let me see your passport."

Trager passed it across the table.

"It looks genuine."

"It is."

Longo slapped the passport on the table. "Due to the unusual circumstances, we will keep this passport while your case is reviewed. You will report to our business offices in the Biashara Building next to the Metropole Hotel tomorrow morning. In the meantime, consider yourself under house arrest in your hotel."

~

The same black suits who had greeted him at the airport drove Trager to the Metropole and escorted him to the reception desk. "He doesn't have a passport," one of them said to the desk clerk.

The clerk looked puzzled when Trager handed him the completed registration card. "Ah, Mr. Trager, we have a--" He stopped on seeing Trager's slight negative shake of the head.

Trager's expectations were dashed when the black suits followed him and the bellman up to his room. One of them took the room key from the bellman and locked the door from the outside.

Trager took the card Longo had given him and dialed the number for the ZSS downtown office. Instead of ringing on the other end, he got a dial tone. Trager tried room service and got an answer. He ordered his first prison meal and a bottle of burgundy.

~

Out of the shower, Trager put on a terrycloth robe provided by the hotel and lit his second cigarette of the day. There was a knock on the door before it opened and a waiter entered with a tray. Trager glimpsed a chair in the corridor. The waiter left. A black suit closed the door and re-locked it.

While he ate his dinner, Trager thought of the baffled expression on Longo's face when the ZSS chief saw him, as if the man had expected to see someone else. There was no doubt Longo was confused and didn't know what to do with Trager. It would have been interesting to know whom he had to consult with. Trager doubted it would be Bamondo.

The hotel windows didn't have bars. Trager looked at the hotel courtyard three floors below. The idea of stepping off the ledge and sliding down a drainpipe made him dizzy. Breathing heavily, he turned and leaned against the wall. What in the hell was he going to do?

Chapter 16

Trager knew dark patches under his eyes betrayed lack of sleep. Two new guards escorted him the half-block to the Biashara Building. A brass plaque by the door stated the building housed the Office of Immigration.

Inside the lobby, people queued up in front of little windows. His wardens led him to an elevator and got off on the fifth floor. Two black suits with submachine guns on their laps lounged in a couple of chairs. This floor had the ambiance of a company gone into receivership. At the end of a hall, a scalloped glass door had *Public Relations* written on it. Trager was ushered through.

A chubby man with thick spectacles sat behind a desk. "Have a seat and fill this out," he said in an offhand way.

This was becoming weird. Trager filled out an application for press credentials.

Finished, he handed it to the heavy man, who held the sheet so close to his face, it looked as if he was using it as a towel. "Very good, come back in three days."

Trager's relief was short lived.

"Venez," one of the black suits said.

They took him back down the elevator to the rear of the building and into a black Mercedes; like the one he had ridden in the day before, but it had different license plates.

Oppressive deja-vue. As they drove past the brewery, Trager felt he was having an out-of-body experience.

Inside the ZSS building, the suits led him to an open freight elevator that slowly rumbled up to the third floor.

At first, red wall-to-wall carpeting, potted plants, and two ticket booths made Trager think of a cinema. But these ticket booths sprouted machine guns. Grim faced gunners sat behind bulletproof glass. Two men in white safari suits stood guard by a set of white doors. Was the setup an ostentatious show of power or an indication of fear?

One of the white suits opened the white doors.

With newfound confidence, Trager marched through them like a conquering general about to demand unconditional surrender.

In shirtsleeves, Longo stood in the middle of a huge room, coffee cup in one hand, saucer in another, dictating to a secretary. On seeing Trager, he dismissed the secretary. A nickel-plated pistol butt stuck out of a shoulder holster.

Not waiting to be invited, Trager sat on a plush chair in front of Longo's desk.

"Had a comfortable night, I trust?" Longo placed the coffee cup on the desk, next to an MP-50 submachine gun, and sat down.

"Quite."

"Since you have used different identities to enter the country, we can safely assume that they are false. People do that when they engage in criminal activities or espionage." Longo smiled slightly. "I certainly would never believe you were a criminal."

"Thank you."

"I'm thinking of convening a summary court tonight and trying you on espionage charges. What do you think of that?"

"I haven't given it a thought, but you should be aware of the existence of the World Court in The Hague."

Longo chuckled and said mockingly, "Mr. Trager had our fullest cooperation, he arrived in the country, requested press credentials, which we were happy to issue. I don't know what happened to the gentleman, he never returned to pick them up."

Trager said, "And Colonel Longo looked foolish as the investigator read the credentials application of John *Tirger*." Trager spelled out the wrong name he had written in the application.

"Ah, we're still playing games." Longo rested his chin on clasped hands.

"Naturally, otherwise life would be dull."

"You don't seem to grasp the seriousness of your situation."

"On the contrary, my dear Colonel. Those little ticket booths won't help one bit when my employers send a Predator drone to fire missiles through your window."

"I like the way you bluff, Mr. Trager." Longo rose from his chair, his face twisted in a wicked grin. "You no longer enjoy the protection of the CIA."

Trager was amazed at the ease he had elicited what Longo knew. "That's what your friend in Washington thinks. The stupid jerk fell for it." Trager stood and leaned over Longo's desk. "The reason I came back was to provoke you into calling him. Now we know who's been leaking information to you."

Longo's calculating eyes settled on Trager. "You do lead a dangerous life."

"Not as dangerous as your dealing with rogue elements." Trager warmed to his subject. "Maybe it's time for you to re-think your position. As a practical man, you should consider buying insurance."

"Insurance? Mr. Trager, let me remind you, it is I who runs this organization and *you* are under arrest."

Trager smiled. "But you are connected to the wrong people in Washington--people who are about to become have beens. When my government establishes relations with yours, there might be some demands difficult not to accept. Colonel Longo, to put it bluntly--you don't want to piss me off."

Longo blinked rapidly.

Believing he had the upper hand, Trager moved in for the kill. "The CIA has a long memory. With your friend in Washington under observation, all he can do is dig his own grave. I believe you are a practical man. Would the CIA have sent me back if we didn't have a winning hand?"

Longo leaned back on his chair as if considering Trager's words. After a long silence, he said. "Let me give you a tour." He got up and took the jacket that hung on the back of his chair.

The elevator ground its way to the basement. Beyond a barred door opened by a black suit, was a foyer with two metal doors painted green. Another guard unlocked one of the doors, held it open. They went through into a corridor smelling of feces and urine. An inhuman scream made Trager wince.

"The piano man likes to work with the entrance to his studio open," Longo said as he stopped and unlocked a door. "This is my night office."

The room was furnished with metal folding chairs and a folding table. The walls were bare.

"Difficult to install listening devices here." Longo took a seat and gestured for Trager to follow suit.

"What kind of insurance are you talking about?"

Trager lit a cigarette and blew smoke in Longo's direction. "My good will."

Longo grinned. "You are fishing."

Trager shrugged. "Governments change, some people get support in the process and others fall. I'll be around for a while."

Longo nodded. "I'll give you the benefit of the doubt. You'll have to come up with something more tangible than talk."

"What? A written contract?"

"I have an account in Switzerland."

"For that you'll have to do better than issue press credentials."

Longo chuckled. "I'm loaning you your life."

"I'm not impressed."

Longo stood, went to the door and opened it. Inhuman screams entered the room. "You know why we call him the piano man?" Longo didn't wait for an answer. "He uses a piano leg. He's been working on that woman for a week."

"What has she done?"

"It was reported she knows where the Utabu is."

Trager remembered Simone and the old village chief using the word "utabu". His heart pounded so hard it seemed to beat in his head. "Utabu a thing or something sacred. Worth torturing people for it?"

"If one is to believe the witch doctors, it is a matter of national security. The Utabu. It is an allegoric legend. Whoever holds the ancient kings' Utabu rules Zengawal. I don't know what the Utabu is. It could be a sword or a necklace. Lately there have been rumors the Utabu, after being lost for hundreds of years, has been found and is in the possession of a witch doctor." Longo gave Trager his crooked smile. "If the Utabu falls into the wrong hands, it will be disaster for this country."

Longo slammed the door.

"Don't forget the piano man. I will keep your passport and wait for your bona fides." Longo chuckled. If you've been lying to me . . .'"

~

Noonday sun baked the ZSS courtyard when Trager walked out of the building. A taxi waited in front and a black suit held the door open for him. Glad to still be alive, Trager took a deep breath. Soon, he'd be at the terrace bar having a beer. How long could he play Longo? This Utabu business sounded intriguing, along with Blankenship's outrageous comment that Simone was a suspected member of Al Qaeda. Something was going on here that defied common sense.

The taxi drove around the building into a courtyard at the rear, through a narrow gate into a sausage factory then out the back into the street. The driver looked vaguely familiar. It took Trager some minutes to recognize the man who had driven him on his first arrival to Turako.

At the Metropole, Trager studied the crowd sitting on the terrace. Glad he didn't see Tony Bond, he hoped one of Dankov's soldiers was there.

At the reception desk, the clerk gave him a questioning look. Trager responded with a reassuring smile. "Now, I can accept the parcel you have for me."

"Of course." The clerk went into the office. A minute later he returned with a DHL package.

Back in his room, Trager's legs felt weak and his eyes wanted to close. He undid the ball of socks and removed the pistol frame from his suitcase. Inside the book, the slide and ammunition were intact. Trager put the pistol together, twisted the power pack and removed loaded magazines. With a sense of relief he slapped a magazine into the pistol grip and let the slide slam forward.

The accumulated nervous tension was draining. To hell with the beer. Trager hung a "Do Not Disturb" sign on the door, slipped the Glock into his waistband and gratefully let himself drop on the bed.

~

The following morning, Trager wrote an Email on his laptop, consisting of meaningless five-number groups, and sent it to the CIA. This would keep Longo off his back for a little while. Longo's men obviously watched the hotel closely. The best thing was to stay somewhere else. He decided to rent a villa.

Madame Kanzo looked at Trager's temporary resident document issued by Longo, gave him a questioning look and said, "Mr. Trager, well, well. I have a nice selection of villas with excellent service staff suitable to a distinguished gentleman." She pulled out a binder and handed it to him.

Each page had a photograph of a house, a floor plan, and location map. After looking through several, Trager found one he liked on Flamingo Heights overlooking the lake. "What's the rent on this one?"

"You have excellent taste, Mr. Trager. This villa is *tres mignon*. It comes with gardener and manservant/cook. It's one-thousand dollars a month, utilities included."

Trager liked the location, it was walking distance from the city center, and it would be difficult for someone to watch without drawing attention. Madame Kanzo handed him a card. "Please fill out the police registration card. We'll take care of delivering it to the police station."

~

Trager checked out of the hotel, studied the drivers waiting on the taxi rank. He waited for the one up front to pick up a fare, got into the second cab.

The ride was short. Right turn by the presidential palace. Left up the hill on a residential street with bougainvillea spilling over fences in a riot of pinks and purples.

A driveway went downhill through a garden. Two huge fig trees gave the place an air of mystery and kept the garden cool. Best of all, the villa could not be seen from the street.

Trager cringed when he saw the pretentious and ugly portico, two pink spiraling columns supporting a Roman style overhang. Wangohi, the portly manservant, stood waiting by the front door. "Welcome, Monsieur." He hoisted Trager's suitcase from the trunk of the cab and gestured toward the door. "Tea is ready on the terrace."

With the villa perched on the side of the hill, the entrance was on the top floor. Liking the unusual layout, Trager entered the house and descended the three steps into a spacious sitting room. A throne-like chair that sat inside accentuated the uselessness of a huge fireplace. Trager chuckled. Somebody had a sense of humor. The place had a friendly feel, somehow made Longo seem less threatening.

Trager walked through French doors onto a balcony wide enough that he didn't need to approach the edge. On a table with a parasol, Wangohi had laid out a tea service and a plate with sandwiches.

The view was spectacular. A parade of pink flamingoes crowded the edge of the lake, marching back and forth. Trager looked toward the presidential palace. A number of people played croquet on the lawn. From the distance, he couldn't tell who they were. He thought he recognized Leonora, but a wide-brimmed hat made identification difficult.

The house pretty much met the expectations he had for his life after spooking, and wondered how Simone would like it. The thought surprised him. The image of them together was an appealing one. Trager smiled. Instead of calling her, he would surprise her by going to the ministry.

~

With their weird croaking song, turakos woke him shortly after dawn. The green plumed birds, the size of small chickens, clambered on vines growing on the side of the cliff. Now he understood where the name of the city originated.

While he showered and shaved, he heard Wangohi pottering about upstairs. The spiral staircase with a strong rail connecting the two floors was another oddity of the house that Trager liked. He climbed it, taking three rungs at a time. "Good morning, Van Gogh."

"Good morning, *Monsieur*." Wangohi stopped dusting and smiled widely. "What would you like for breakfast? I got nice papayas and bought eggs."

Trager was pleased with Wangohi's efficiency. He had thought there wasn't any food in the house after he finished all the sandwiches at teatime.

"I spent one-thousand-five-hundred franks."

Trager dug for his wallet.

"You make list. I go shopping today and fix good food. Yesterday I borrow sandwiches from neighbor. I also borrow coffee, it's ready." Wangohi marched off to the kitchen and returned with a pot of coffee he set on the balcony table.

The mundane housekeeping details gave Trager a sense of ironic amusement. He thought of telephoning Bamondo to set up an interview. But Longo would have his telephone tapped, and Trager had to be honest with the president.

After breakfast, Trager went to the small study adjacent to the sitting room, opened his laptop and began writing an article on Turako.

~

His plan was simple: Show up at the ministry at about four o'clock, hand Simone a bouquet of flowers, and invite her for dinner. Of course, she would be surprised but delighted to see him. He had wanted roses, but carnations were all he could find.

Just like the previous time, the lady in the front office clacked away on the manual typewriter. "*Oui, Monsieur?*"

"I came to see Mademoiselle Loriot."

"Do you have an appointment?"

"No, please tell her it's Johnny." Trager said loud enough so he would be heard inside Simone's office.

"You must make an appointment. Mademoiselle Loriot is not available today."

Trager smiled. "Mind if I wait?"

The secretary pointed at a sign on the wall saying "No loitering". "If you have business, make an appointment. If it's personal . . ." she paused looking at the flowers, "you should contact her residence."

"Could you give her these flowers?"

"Monsieur, giving gifts to a government official is illegal." She pointed at the door. "Please. We have work to do."

Outside the building, he looked at his watch. It was four-fifteen. He had only forty-five minutes to wait.

The street was crowded with pedestrians, and people turned to look at him. A white man with a bouquet was not a usual sight. Trager craved a cigarette, but he had left his pack behind. He went to a bar at the corner and bought a pack of Roosters made in Uganda. Outside, he lit one of the small, unfiltered cigarettes. The taste was harsh, but it assuaged his unease.

At fifteen to five, people began to trickle out of the building. The stream increased until five when a bell rang inside the ministry. A sea of people poured out. Trager had trouble keeping his place next to the door as people rushed by him. Five minutes later, the flood ebbed to a trickle.

Simone's secretary walked out carrying a plastic shopping bag, gave him a quick glance, and hurried down the street.

The sidewalk emptied of people. A cool breeze blew from the direction of the lake. Trager lit another Rooster. Laughter and chatter from the corner bar drifted out to the street. At six o'clock, a uniformed janitor pulled a sliding grille across the ministry entrance and snapped a padlock shut.

Trager stuck the flowers into the grille and headed for the Metropole. A black Mercedes with smoked windows cruised down the street. Trager's life depended on Simone. Without her, he couldn't contact Dankov, nor Bamondo. As the equatorial night approached, he was alone, and the night belonged to Longo.

His life on "loan" by Longo, made him wonder when the ugly bastard would move to foreclose.

Chapter 17

The coffee tasted good and began to dissipate Trager's headache. He had drunk too much at the Metropole, waiting for someone to show up. No one did, not even Bond.

Trager sat at the desk in the study and penned a letter to Simone. If she didn't want to see him, it was her right. The least she could do was meet him once and tell him that. He closed the envelope, wrote the address of the ministry. "Van Gogh," he called.

Wangohi noiselessly materialized. "*Oui, Monsieur?*"

Trager handed him the envelope. "Can you deliver this?"

Wangohi read the address and smiled brightly. "Ah, the Pygmy lady. She's very beautiful. You want to invite?"

"Yes," Trager said, mystified at Wangohi's sudden enthusiasm.

"She's very good. I go buy champagne, fix a beautiful dinner. She likes leg of lamb."

"You know her?"

"Oh yes. She's the best of Madame Kanzo's ladies."

Like a broken glass brick, Trager's heart seemed to have dropped and scratched its way to his stomach.

"Very expensive." Wangohi bunched his fingers in front of his mouth and kissed them. "I hear, worth every last frank."

Trager recovered from the blow. *Let's hope she's a whore with a heart of gold.* He then wondered how much she charged. What else did she sell? Was she dangerous? Of course she was. Was she dangerous to him? Trager stopped speculating. He would soon find out.

He was finishing the article on Turako when Wangohi returned with a note from Simone:

> *Sorry about yesterday. You write compelling letters. I'll stop by tonight at seven.*
> *S.*

~

From the darkness of the terrace, Trager watched Wangohi potter around inside. He was dressed in a white Eton jacket, black trousers and bow tie. The manservant turned on the stereo and the voices of Nat King Cole and his daughter filled the house with *Unforgettable*. Trager thought this was a bit much, but Wangohi did things his way. The old boy had placed flowers on the coffee table, the sideboard, and the half table with mirror by the front entrance. There was no question he enjoyed his role of evening orchestrator.

Trager put his cigarette out and instinctively pulled back into the shadows of the terrace as he saw Wangohi rush to the front door, which he opened. He stood aside, beaming a huge grin.

Like a magic vision, Simone materialized out of the darkness. Trager's heart took a leap. She regally paused, acknowledging Wangohi. Pantaloons, a high-collared, white silk, Russian peasant shirt, gathered at the waist with a red sash, gave her an aspect of severe elegance. She held a large rectangular handbag, big enough to carry a pistol. After taking in the room, she said something to Wangohi, gave him a smile of approval.

Trager stepped into the room.

"Ah, the man who won't go away." She came down the steps and extended her hand, stepped back, sighed and shook her head. "With some people, to help them is a waste of time. I may as well take advantage of the opportunity and ask you to fix me an American martini cocktail. I've never had one."

Trager easily fell into the role of gracious host. "A pleasure, and prepare yourself to be spoiled. I make the best martini in the world."

"Better than James Bond?"

The question brought unpleasant implications. He remembered Tony Bond's sly smile, wondered what sort of favors Simone had promised him. "Van Gogh, bring the martini things." He turned back to Simone. "James Bond doesn't know a thing about martinis."

"Van Gogh? That's funny."

Wangohi returned, placing a tray with gin, vermouth and two martini glasses on a sideboard.

"First of all," Trager said, "you keep the gin, vermouth and the glasses in the freezer. Plop a drop of vermouth into the glass and shake it out. Then pour gin and swirl gently. Ice ruins a cocktail." He handed Simone a glass.

"Hmm." Simone tasted her martini. "Superb, let's step out on the terrace. This cocktail warrants the magnificent view."

"You know this house?"

"I've been here before."

Unpleasant jealousy gripped Trager. Though he knew it was a mistake, he couldn't resist saying. "Business? Van Gogh hinted you're a businesswoman."

She gave him an enigmatic smile. "I'm different things to different people."

Trager stood back as she approached the railing. She pointed at the palace. "The Bamondo's are having another intimate soiree. I chose to come here instead."

"I'm flattered."

"You shouldn't be. How did you get past Longo?"

Trager considered what line to offer. "I gave him a rather tall story. He's waiting for confirmation. When he doesn't get it, he'll be upset."

"And you objected to my little white lie. I thought you were a Boy Scout or a knight in shining armor. No?"

Trager looked at the lake to hide the unexpected shiver of pleasure her words gave him.

Two Land Rovers drove up to the palace rear entrance.

"That's Igor. He brought some extra boys in case of trouble."

"What sort of trouble?"

The Land Rovers stopped. Soldiers clambered out.

"When I told him you were back, he almost had a fit. He said if Longo didn't have you yet, he would arrest you and hand you to Longo himself. But what he really meant was he feared Longo had nailed you."

"What's he doing in the palace?"

Simone sneered. "What do you think?" She laughed. "I sent him on a fool's errand, told him you were staying at the hotel. He's probably frustrated--look at him."

A man in a dark suit strode away from the Land Rovers. By his walk, Trager recognized Dankov. In one hand, he held what looked like a pair of boots. Guards presented arms and he vanished through the door.

"I don't understand you."

"Nobody does. Except maybe Igor." She raised her glass toward the palace. "I love you, Igor."

Her words slammed Trager as if he'd been hit in the gut.

Simone turned to face him. "That's right. I love the rascal. He used and humiliated me. But he does this to everyone."

Not knowing whether he admired, hated or was jealous of Dankov, Trager said hopefully. "You need a distraction from him."

She nodded thoughtfully and sipped her martini. Her face was half- lit by the lights from inside; the lit part showed anger. The half that remained in shadow appeared serene. The effect of the light accentuated the complexity of the woman. She looked Trager in the eye. "The letter you wrote was beautiful, the sort of missive a young girl dreams of getting. Then you made a not so tactful remark about me and this house. Coming from you, it hurt."

Simone moved closer. "Yes, I sell my body," she spat out. Just as suddenly, her face calmed and she smiled. "Just often enough to finance my project."

Confused, Trager didn't know what to say. A mixture of anger, pity, curiosity and pain stirred inside him.

"Let's have another one. No?"

While Trager mixed fresh drinks, Simone leaned on the sideboard and took a cigarillo out of her bag. "Johnny, tell me the truth. Why did you return?" There was warmth in her voice.

Trager kept looking at the glass he was swirling. He wondered at the madness that had come over him. "Too many questions, too many loose ends." He handed her the glass and for a moment felt lost in her eyes. "And you?"

She raised an eyebrow. "Me?"

"Yeah. Remember when I asked you to come with me? I meant it. With Longo around, this isn't a healthy place."

"That's chivalrous. But the damsel is not in distress. And it's better you found your windmills elsewhere."

"Windmills." Trager chuckled. "I guess that's what I'm after."

She nodded as if understanding. "Johnny, your business here was finished on your last trip. But you're a stubborn man. I'm not going to ask what your real reason is, but if it is because of me . . ." She blew smoke into his face. "I will tell you what I am." Simone gestured at the fireplace. "It was my idea to put the chair inside the fireplace. Men love to abase women. He sits on that chair facing a woman on her knees. It makes him think he has power over her." She let out a small laugh. "Do you know what I'm talking about?"

"I think so," he said, hating himself for having brought the subject up.

"Do you really? I doubt it. You know what brings the most money?"

Trager shook his head as he put his glass down. His hands began to tremble. He didn't want to hear more.

"Oh darling," she said in an exaggerated, sexy voice. "How I wish I was still a virgin. I have only one place no man has been before. Do you want it, my darling?" Simone let out a small chuckle. "That's how I've milked an elderly gentleman out of an extra thousand dollars." She paused and gave him a bitter smile. "I offered him my . . . my. Pshaw, never mind."

"Why do you tell me this?"

"Because you asked. And I'm honest with you. *Go home.*"

Trager nodded. "How much do you charge a night?"

"None of your business."

"I want you to stay the night."

Simone gave him a flashing smile. "But I *am* staying the night. Longo will think I'm selling my favors and extracting your secrets."

Trager reached for her waist.

Simone twirled away. "Hands off," she snapped.

Her sharp rebuttal hurt.

She smiled as if apologizing. "You *are* a nice man. Although it was stupid, thanks for coming for me. I have things to do. If I would have known . . ." she shook her head, "that you were interested in me. I would have told you that it wouldn't work." She moved closer to him, touched his cheek. "I'll never take money from you."

She raised her glass against the light, looked at it. "These martinis should be called 'true confessions'." She downed her drink. "Let's have dinner. I'm hungry."

During dinner, they acted as very polite acquaintances. Simone did most of the talking, went through a variety of innocuous subjects including her work with the Pygmies. She thought tourism should be carefully developed not to interfere with the cultures of the tribes. That the income derived should be used to provide health services. Trager expressed interest in going to Pygmy country. Simone said this could be arranged.

Wangohi brought out a cheese board.

Simone said to him. "Thank you, that will be all for tonight."

Wangohi left, closing the kitchen door behind him.

Trager said, "You seem pretty knowledgeable about Zengawali history, what's the story about the Utabu?"

She gave him a curious look. "Have you heard about it? It's something that's been buzzing through the bush telegraph and whispered in the bazaars, a sort of mysterious prophesy."

"But what is it?"

Simone shrugged. "I don't really know much about it. You should ask Professor Najua. On Friday afternoons, he attends the Zengawal Women's League teas. That's a good place for you to meet people."

Simone had skillfully deflected the question. Trager remembered the Minister of Education and his unlit pipe.

"Did Longo ask you to find out about the Utabu?"

The inhuman screams in Longo's basement rang inside Trager's head. "He was asking someone else." The Utabu, whatever it was, grew in significance in Trager's mind.

Simone smiled knowingly. "Give me a snippet of information I can pass to the dear colonel."

"You're his informer?"

"He pesters, doesn't dare touch me." She appeared to think. "If something premature happened to Igor, we'd all be cooked." After a sigh, she added. "So I play along with Longo. He thinks he has a handle on me. The devil thinks I'm Igor's girlfriend and threatens to tell Igor about my infidelities."

"Infidelities?"

Simone gave out a little laugh. "If he knew I charged for my services, he'd demand a cut."

"I see." Simone's situation appeared to be even more precarious than he had imagined.

"Tell the ugly bastard I'm also investigating human rights abuses for the World Court."

Simone let out another one of her little laughs while spreading brie on a cracker. "Should I add that commandos will rescue you if anything happens?"

"I've already tried. I don't think he's convinced."

She gave him a long look. "Yes, no one would believe it. By wanting to be exempt from the jurisdiction of the World Court, the United States is quickly becoming a pariah state. Or at the very least, the most hypocritical empire the world has ever seen."

"You don't like the United States?"

Her mouth twisted into an expression of disgust. "I'm disappointed. America, freedom, equality under the law. But only for Americans. If you are a foreigner, you get put away without trial, you have no access to lawyers. But war criminals like Ariel Sharon are supported. I can give you a long list of genocidal criminals the U.S. has backed. We used to think Americans were naïve. That notion is wearing thin."

Trager remembered Blankenship saying Simone was suspected of being a member of Al Qaeda. But she had helped an American agent, *him*. Because she shared a widely accepted view of the States, it didn't make her a terrorist. Trager smiled. "What am I, naïve or evil?"

She reached across the table and patted Trager's hand. With a tender expression on her face, she said, "So far you have proven to be the stupidest man in the world." The tenderness vanished as suddenly as it had appeared. "Let's have a cognac before I go to bed in the guest room."

Trager rose from the table, helped Simone with her chair. He took a good sniff of her light floral scent and kissed her neck as she got up.

"Don't get naughty." She turned around and pushed him off. "I'm staying the night for the benefit of Longo. He thinks if you screw me, it will create a rift between you and Igor. But we're not going to let that happen in real life. Are we?"

"I guess not," Trager said, thinking that, by going along with Simone, he was getting further involved in a dangerous game he didn't yet understand.

Chapter 18

London.

The Sabena flight from Brussels had been only ten minutes late. Traffic along Cromwell Road was heavy as usual, but not snarled. Tony Bond had made allowances for this and instructed the driver to stop at the Tara to drop off his suitcase. Standard modern, barely comfortable, but the hotel offered anonymity.

He picked up a *London Times* and scanned through it as the taxi crawled across Kensington. On the second page, he found the article with details on the refugee camp massacre in the Congo. He liked the photograph of an emaciated African child crying. A picture *was* worth a thousand words.

At Marble Arch, the taxi turned left in the direction of Haymarket. Bond had to give directions to the driver to reach the quiet mews where the damn meeting was about to take place. Although it wasn't his fault, Bond knew that part of the blame for the disaster at Payot's camp in Busara would be his. Even though he managed to introduce a couple of spies into Bamondo's Special Operations Group and his source at the palace was impeccable, his agents had been able to provide information only after the fact. Dankov had fooled everyone by his preoccupation with Uganda.

Knowing that Cruizet would be present at the meeting made Bond nervous. The Belgian tycoon was the most unforgiving, ruthless bastard he had ever known, and the man had made it his personal crusade to depose Bamondo.

Bond paid the driver and watched him turn the corner before entering the mews where old coach houses had been converted into fashionable living spaces. With a bit of caution and envy, Bond studied the alley. It was empty of movement. A Jaguar and a Bentley stood parked on the back alley for the very rich and privileged.

Christopher Baker kept his mistress here. Bond had never met the reportedly dazzling lady. Baker sent her off to the country whenever meetings took place. In a way, Bond thought himself superior to Baker, who claimed a nebulous family connection to Samuel Baker, the famous nineteenth century African explorer, and later governor of Sudan. Like the old Baker, Bond's African experience was with boots on the ground, and he expected to be generously rewarded for his work.

Shrugging off the lingering damp morning chill, Bond strode into the mews, approached number five, and looked around again. He gave the green velvet cord hanging from the side of the door a pull and heard the cowbell clank inside.

Dressed in a tweed jacket and wearing a paisley cravat, Baker opened the door. He looked like a gentleman farmer ready to jump into his Bentley the moment the meeting was over. "Your punctuality is simply amazing." He stepped aside to let Bond in.

The sitting room looked like a used furniture display room. Almost lost in the clutter sat the fat little Belgian, Cruizet, a butterball poured into a pin-striped suit.

Baker said, "How about some sherry while we wait for Van Flotten. My merchant got hold of a splendid amontillado."

Bond smiled, took a seat in an ugly Victorian chair. Even with Cruizet's pig eyes staring at him, it was good to be in England where sherry went well midmorning.

It was obvious Cruizet was angry. In response to his miscalculation of financing the then playboy Bamondo, the Zengawal Army of Liberation had been his idea. After the raid on Payot's battalion, the ZAL was in disarray. It couldn't be reorganized before the rains came.

Baker served glasses filled with rich amber liquid.

"Thanks, old love." Bond sipped sherry, closing his eyes. "Lustrous nectar, suitable for a meeting of God's chosen few."

Bond knew it galled Cruizet when a hireling considered himself equal to him, but Bond's position was secure. He was now indispensable, his bonus sitting in an escrow account in Luxembourg as safe as houses.

Baker left to answer the cowbell and returned pushing Van Flotten by the elbow.

One thing Van Flotten had was presence. Despite his immaculately tailored blue suit, a red beard and unruly hair made him look like the pirate he was. He tapped Bond on the shoulder, bowed to Cruizet and sprawled on the sofa. On average, his Moluccan crews hijacked two tankers or copper carriers a month and sold the cargo in China. Though less profitable, Africa was his true love. He owned a game ranch bordering Kruger Park in South Africa and a twenty percent share of Miniere du Zengawal. Bamondo had no idea what sort of people he had angered when he nationalized the Shabaka mine.

Van Flotten asked Cruizet, "What sort of delay can we expect after the Busara disaster?"

Cruizet wiggled in his chair, folded his fat little hands on his lap. "Sometimes, with careful calculation, one can snatch victory from the claws of adversity. I think our plans can actually be accelerated."

His head cocked to one side, Van Flotten looked amused. "Bond, as usual, saves the day?"

Cruizet said. "Our work force has not been completely decimated, and we have reinforced Payot with a South African, Markus Pirz. Lots of experience in Angola, and Claude Poletti recently retired from the Foreign Legion. We're beefing up lower management with experienced Zimbabwean personnel. I had to give the Zimbabwe minister of defense a half a percent share in our enterprise." The lumpy Belgian held his glass with two fingers as he drank. He put his glass down and gave Van Flotten his nasty-pig look.

"Find out yet who is cutting the diamonds?"

Van Flotten shook his head. He had good reason to be annoyed with the Belgian, who was trying to squirm out of an uncomfortable situation. "None of the experts who have inspected the work have been able to recognize the cutters, but there are at least six different patterns detected. The Shabaka vein stones, as we know, are cut in Russia."

Baker said, "Even Bond's agents are in the dark. The other source is still a total mystery."

"The only reason the gem market is holding its own is due to the American accounting scandals and stock market decline," Van Flotten added.

Baker refilled Bond's glass. "Tony, would you kindly brief our associates on your new plan?"

Bond sipped the sherry. What he was about to propose made him feel sick. He swished the sherry inside his mouth and let the spasm ease before swallowing. "The air gets ghastlier by the day. Gives a bad taste to one's mouth." He took another sip.

Baker, who was highly placed in MI-6 and sat on the CASC acting as chairman, looked like the cat who had a mouse by the tail. Cruizet tapped his fingers against each other. Van Flotten waited patiently.

"Are any of you Catholics?" Bond waited and after the three shook their heads, he said, "Good. That raid on your camp," he waved a finger at Cruizet, "was a wonderful prelude for things to come.

"Forty kilometers north of Busara, there is an orphanage. It is run by a group of nuns, the Sisters of Mercy." Bond forced a smile. "Raped nuns with their throats slit from ear to ear is bound not only to make headlines but create world-wide indignation. What is more important, it will create unrest in Zengawal. If I whisper a few things into the right people's ears, students will protest the presence of murderous white mercenaries. We would have a nasty little riot or two."

Cruizet said, "Do you have the resources to do it from *inside* Zengawal?"

"Certainly. Once the riots start, you can march your Zengawal Army of Liberation to Turako. It will be a promenade."

"A battalion of Zimbawean peacekeeping paratroopers would ensure success," Cruizet said just above a whisper.

Baker added. "I'm sure the Americans would not want to be left behind. A couple of cruise missiles against that Tartar fort--"

"Cossack," Bond interjected.

"Nun-raping Cossack barbarians. Pogrom in Central Africa. Tony, you do write a good script."

"Divide and conquer. Out of the ashes of gloom and defeat, Tony Bond does rise to save the day. I presume, gentlemen, there will be a generous bonus in my bank account?"

Cruizet glared at Bond. "Do you have a concrete plan?"

Bond reached inside his jacket and produced a number of folded pages. He couldn't keep himself from saying, "*Voila, mon vieux.*"

Since his feet barely touched the floor, Cruizet had to slide off his chair to take Bond's papers.

This was probably the first time in his life that Cruizet was addressed so intimately by hired help.

While everyone waited for Cruizet to finish reading, Baker brought out a picnic hamper. After moving a vase, a porcelain figurine, and a lacquered box aside, he placed the hamper on top of a massive buffet. "We have *pate de foi grass*, roast duck, *terrine* with truffles, potted salmon."

Bond stood. "Mind if I start?" He undid his shirt collar, loosened his tie and stuffed a napkin into his collar. "Be a dear, bring out some champagne, old chap," he said waving a duck leg.

Seeming amused by Bond's outrageous behavior, Baker left the room and returned with a bottle of champagne. "Now, what is the mumbo jumbo about the Utabu?"

"I was afraid you were going to ask," Bond said, his mouth half-full. "I don't have a clear answer."

Cruizet said, "Narrow it down to the succession. How will this rumor affect the new government?"

"Quite simply, the effect today is that it has robbed President Bamondo of whatever shreds of legitimacy he had. His successor will be at least equally, though probably more handicapped."

"Assuming the rumor is true, that the Utabu really exists, how would it affect the succession?"

"*Mon vieux*, our operation would go down the tubes." Bond grinned. "Unless we had the Utabu. Then we could crown any beggar as King of Zengawal."

"So, in your judgement, if the Utabu did exist, we should Focus maximum effort on obtaining it?"

"I've been working on that assumption. I believe Bamondo's people are doing the same." He was sure Trager was in hot pursuit of the Utabu. Why else would the man have quit the CIA and returned to Zengawal? He turned to Baker. "How about the Americans?"

"As long as they get to dismantle the terrorist support infrastructure, they're happy. I don't think they are aware of the Utabu rumor."

By terrorist infrastructure, you mean Mademoiselle Loriot?"

Van Flotten said, "The money going through her account and transferred to funny destinations is enough to nail anybody."

If it wasn't the same two–hundred-and-fifty-thousand dollars that shifted back and forth, Bond would have been tempted to tell la belle Loriot about the account opened in her name. Perhaps she would again regal him with a night of incredible delight.

Croizet said, "Judging from your reports, I would call the Utabu more than rumor. It is beginning to take the shape of a movement. Maybe you should arrange for reliable people to lead it."

"None of my people will dare. Everyone is afraid of the witch doctors."

"Are you?"

Bond swallowed. "When you've been in Africa long enough, you don't take them lightly." Although the power of a witch doctor's curse was mainly effective on those who believed in witchcraft, he had seen enough to think that non-believers were affected, too.

Van Flotten said, "I think we should focus in obtaining the Utabu, if it does exist."

Cruizet leaned back and seemed to relax. "What is Bamondo doing about it?"

"He personally doesn't believe in it."

"Are you certain?"

"Absolutely." Before leaving Turako, Bond had had a meeting with his source in Flamingo House. It confirmed that Bamondo was as confident of his ship as the captain of the Titanic.

Chapter 19

As noon approached, the temperature in the little study grew uncomfortable. Trager read the background article he was writing for the *Christian Science Monitor*, one of the best papers in the States. The request had come as a surprise, but the *Monitor* was often ahead in sniffing out places that would be in the news. To conclude the article, he wrote: *In Africa, one seldom sees political leaders with a balanced world view. Urbane and moderate, President Bamondo deserves support in creating what he sees as the Switzerland . . .*

A commotion outside made him stop. Trager jumped out of his chair, reached into the drawer and pulled out the Glock. He stepped forward and peered over the doorsill. Quickly, he pulled his head back. His hands high in the air, Wangohi stood looking ashen-faced and perplexed. An African soldier in camouflage uniform crouched by the front door pointing a rifle at him.

What? Looters?

A clatter of boots indicated two people running down the spiral staircase.

Trager's pistol rested against his leg. In this situation, being armed wasn't profitable. He stepped back, replaced the pistol, and slid the drawer shut.

"*Sa va*," a voice yelled from the bottom floor.

"*Sa va, Ataman*." Someone repeated in the sitting room.

Furious, Trager went out of the study. The soldier now had his folding stock Kalashnikov pointing at the ceiling.

Wearing a light gray suit and carrying a Bizon II machine pistol in his hand, Dankov entered through the front door. "Am I in time for lunch?"

"What sort of crap is this? You scared the shit out of me."

Dankov stood aside to let the soldiers file out of the house. "Security, get the vodka out of the freezer, it's almost noon."

Wangohi's facial color returned to its usual rich chocolate. He glanced at Trager questioningly.

Trager gave him a smile of reassurance. "Open a can of crab meat and salmon to go with the vodka and slice up some bread."

Wangohi returned a slight smile, nodded and marched out of the room.

Dankov tossed his Bizon on the sofa, took his jacket off, and loosened his blue tie. "What are you doing here?"

"Writing articles for newspapers."

Dankov shook his head. "You dull-witted peasant, you're adding to my headaches. Had a busy morning figuring out where you were. One of my men got your address from the taxi driver who brought you here. After the song and dance I got from Longo, had to make sure it wasn't an ambush."

"I thought this was a haven of peace and stability."

"A tea cup floating in a storm." Dankov chuckled. He looked for something in his jacket pocket, tossed a booklet at Trager.

Trager leafed through the Belgian passport issued to a Marcel Payot.

"Former Belgian paratrooper, been training the Zengawal Army of Liberation. They're actually a bunch of Hutus led by Zimbabwean officers and NCOs. They are mustering a force of almost two thousand. I paid them a visit a few nights ago. Hopefully, we've delayed their plans." Dankov grinned as he sprawled on the sofa. "You can pass that information to your CIA bosses."

"I have nothing to do with the CIA."

Dankov gave Trager a strange look. "Longo told me he let you go--"

"I bullshitted my way out."

Dankov leaned forward, propped his elbows on his knees and covered his head with his hands. "*Yob tvoyu mats.*" He shook his head. "When Longo was training in East Berlin, he actually worked for the Americans. He has contacts in the CIA. It won't take long for him to--"

"Bamondo told me--"

"Bamondo can tell you anything he wants. Longo is pretty much out of control." Dankov sighed. "And I told Bamondo . . . give me that passport back. I presented this guy's boots to Bamondo." Dankov pulled out a newspaper clipping. "This comes from *The Daily Mirror.*"

Trager read the five-hundred-word article about an attack on a refugee camp in the Congo, sources saying the raid originated in Zengawal.

Dankov said, "These refugees were very well taken care off. Had plenty of rifles, ammunition, eighty-millimeter mortars, rocket-propelled grenades. It looked like New Year in Saint Petersburg when their ammo bunkers went up."

Wangohi returned, placed vodka, little crab and salmon sandwiches on the coffee table. "For lunch, I can heat up the leg of lamb."

"That will be fine."

"Leg of Lamb?" Dankov said, "It's Simone's favorite. Too bad she isn't here."

Trager wondered if he should mention Simone had dined here the night before, decided against it. He didn't know what sort of fires he might light.

Dankov rubbed his hands. "Though a patented moron, you're one American who knows how to serve vodka."

Trager sat on the sofa, poured the liquor into shot glasses. "Have a happy war."

"To old friendships." Dankov belted down the shot. Dankov shoved a couple of the little sandwiches into his mouth. He appeared to be hungry. After pouring himself another shot, he said, "War on two fronts has always been the strategist's nightmare. The Ugandans increased their military activities on our eastern border. We are training a new regiment--the Simba guards--but it won't be ready for nearly a year. The goal is to give these people a backbone of national unity and purpose, but they don't seem to be able to rise above petty tribal self-interest. The Simbas are intertribal, a template of the future army."

Drinking vodka Russian style always gave Trager a sense of well-being. Dankov's troops outside added a sense of security. Trager relaxed, tossed a shot of vodka down his throat, ate a salmon sandwich. "If Longo was an American agent in East Germany, he's probably still--"

"Aha." Dankov waved a cigarette he was about to light.

"Only now you tell me."

"Then you were the CIA and God only knows what part you played in their intrigues. Now, you're an orphan. If you join my force, you'll be out of Longo's reach. I'm short of officers."

The security it offered made the proposition tempting, but the proverbial pen was mightier than a Kalashnikov and he was making good headway in screwing Mr. "X's" plans. With Dankov aware of his presence, the risk factor had diminished considerably. "Thanks, Igor. I have a few things going."

"It's your ass. This evening we're loading the monthly stash of diamonds on my plane. Then I'm off to stiffen our defenses on the Eastern Front." Dankov pushed off brightly-polished loafers and stretched out on the sofa. Trager moved to a chair across the table.

"A soldier's work is never done. I need to get some sleep one of these days."

Wangohi announced lunch was served.

Before sitting down at the table, Dankov picked up the bottle of Bordeaux and inspected the label. "We didn't use to drink much wine in Russia. Just the ladies. Travel does expand one's drinking habits."

For a second, Trager was simply amused by Dankov's remark. Then it dawned on him the great changes in Dankov since he defected from the Soviet Army--from sort of country bumpkin to swashbuckling soldier/philosopher. At that moment, Trager realized he envied Dankov. When Dankov defected, he had felt sorry for the Russian who had given up a military career Trager had failed to achieve. Whatever happened while Dankov lived in the Midwest, exile had not softened his mind, nor his zest for life.

Wangohi served fresh mint sauce, over which Simone had raved the night before, and horseradish. Dankov helped himself to a slab of lamb, smeared it with horseradish, and heaped rice on his plate. "I like your hospitality, you're living beyond your means."

"I have a bit of private income. The rent is cheap."

"You've said you're writing for newspapers?"

"Yeah, there's a rising interest on Zengawal."

After emptying his plate, Dankov lit a cigarette. "I'll provide you with opportunities to get great stories, but don't mention anything about me or my boys." Dankov stood up from the table as Wangohi entered carrying a dessert tray. "Take that back. I don't want dessert."

Wanhogi stopped, looked at Trager.

"Thank you, we'll skip dessert."

"A good lunch consists of two glasses of vodka, one glass of wine and one of cognac," Dankov said as he descended the steps to the sitting room. "Dessert in the middle of the day encourages slovenly thinking."

Trager poured cognac. Dankov again sprawled on the sofa. Wangohi re-entered bringing cups of Turkish coffee.

Dankov said, "You may as well give your man the afternoon off. We won't return 'til late."

"Where are we going?" Trager asked after dismissing Wangohi.

"Didn't you hear me say, tonight we ship diamonds?"

Trager made a show of looking at his watch. "As far as I can tell, it's still early afternoon."

"Illusions take time to prepare."

~

The second long-wheelbase Land Rover kept a good distance away from the red dust cloud raised by Dankov's vehicle. Trager rode on the front passenger seat. Four soldiers sat in the back and one stood braced against the machine gun mount, gun at the ready.

Adding to Trager's curiosity, Dankov had refused to explain further where they were going or what they were going to do. For the moment, they headed south on the same road Simone had first driven him.

The vehicles did not slow down passing villages. A few people about in the afternoon heat waved and exchanged shouts with the soldiers.

Isolated huts dotted the parched, undulating landscape. Dankov's plume of dust turned off the main road, rolled up a hill, and vanished behind a ridgeline.

The driver, a sergeant, grinned widely. "Chai, you like?"

Trager nodded.

An uneven track dropped steeply into a little wooded valley with tall, yellow swamp grass growing below the trees. Women walked up the track carrying five-gallon tin cans of water on their heads. Inside the little forest, cooler air touched Trager like a gentle hand. A herd of goats lazily gave way to the Land Rover.

Dankov's vehicle had stopped next to a pool of water. His soldiers busied themselves brewing tea in billycans, using collapsible Sterno stoves. Disregarding a group of women washing clothes some distance away, Dankov undressed down to his shorts. One of the soldiers held a camouflage uniform on a hanger.

Glad they had arrived somewhere, Trager got out of the Land Rover and stretched. The soldiers in his truck clambered out, billycans in hand, and went to a woman holding a long reddish gourd. She poured milk into the billycans.

"Napoleon said, 'An army travels on its stomach.' In Africa, all armies stop for tea." Dankov approached, buckling a leather pistol belt over a starched uniform jacket without rank insignia.

A soldier handed Trager a can with milky tea. *Chai*, the almost universal name for tea.

"Goat milk is good for you."

Trager took a long pull of the hot, sweet brew.

"After this refreshing pause," Dankov said, "we'll go back to Turako the long way, and escort the diamond convoy past Longo's thugs."

"Would Longo highjack the diamonds?" Trager asked, hoping he would get his comeuppance in the attempt.

"Maybe, but what drives him crazy is the provenance of our best quality diamonds." Dankov chuckled. "Tonight, you will see a somewhat unusual procedure and a bit of sleight of hand. You'll ride with me the rest of the way."

"You and your mystery are driving *me* nuts."

Dankov finished his tea and looked around. *"Ingia kwa gari,"* he ordered.

Trager asked, "How come you use Swahili here?"

"A few people speak it. We're making Swahili the language of the army. For Africans, it's easier to learn than French. It minimizes tribal differences."

Dankov got into the driver's seat. "You hold this." He handed Trager the Bizon II, put the truck in gear and waded to a little stream trickling out of the pool.

"We will cross over to the Maridani Road and arrive in Turako from the west. That keeps Longo, Mawingi and others confused. On diamond day, I have vehicles coming from all points of the compass."

Out of the valley, Dankov downshifted to negotiate a steep slope. Upon reaching the top, the terrain was almost flat. Boys with long sticks drove small herds of cattle home. Trager was impressed by the huge arched horns resembling inverted elephant tusks.

Driving in Africa was like dealing with an indefinite obstacle course. Frequently, Dankov had to slow down to negotiate a gully created by rain and flash floods. Speed up, slow down, creep and eat dust.

"Airplane," the machine gunner shouted.

Coming out of a semi-stupor, Trager looked back. An airplane was diving for them. "He's attacking."

Dankov glanced over his shoulder, said nothing.

The plane passed overhead, maybe five-hundred feet above, a MIG-17.

"Today is no-fly day over Zengawal," Dankov explained. "I don't want anyone watching us from the air. The plane also takes care of any tails on the ground. One of Bond's cronies got his car scorched a few months ago."

Trager was getting tired of all the bumping around. From what he could tell, they had described a huge semi-circle around Turako. Because of the dust, sunglasses were useless and he had to squint against the setting sun.

Abruptly, they were inside a sisal plantation and the track became smooth.

Dankov said, "Excellent place for an ambush, and it's easy to plant mines in this type of dirt."

"Thanks for telling me."

"In a few minutes, we'll make a rest stop. How does a steak and a beer sound?"

His throat filled with dust, Trager thought a beer would be marvelous.

They were coming to an intersection. A five-ton truck with people sitting on top of cargo rumbled on the main road.

"Eight kilometers to Maridani," Dankov said, tuning onto the highway.

A water tower gleamed pink in the sunset. The road became asphalt with huge potholes, which required a zigzag course.

Maridani's main street was a wide boulevard bordered with alternating tall jacaranda and colorful flame trees. In the past, someone had tried to make this a pleasant place to live.

Dankov stopped in front of a well-kept white building with a sign proclaiming it to be the Grand Hotel. Across the street stood what looked like the town hall with a clock tower indicating ten past twelve.

"We get off here. My boys will eat at the market."

The hotel bar was paneled in dark wood and full of noisy Africans drinking beer. A chubby man in a checkered shirt said, *"Bienvenue,"* and pushed his drinking companions aside to make room for the new arrivals.

The barman placed a saucer with cheese cut into cubes, smothered in Maggi sauce and sprinkled with ground chili peppers. Without asking, he slammed a couple of half-liter Jumbo beers on the counter along with two glasses.

Trager poured his beer too fast and ended with a glassful of froth. He slurped the somewhat cool beer with pleasure.

Dankov said in Russian, "Tomorrow, our comrade of security will learn we were here. But I like this hotel. It has a nice garden in the back and a swimming pool."

Trager speared a cheese cube with a toothpick. It went well with the beer. He wondered what Africa would be like had it not been colonized. It was difficult to imagine. There would be fewer cities, but the buildings would be new, maybe promising a brighter future.

Finished with their beer, they went across the hall to eat.

The dining room was almost empty. Dankov chose a table in the corner, away from a European, French-speaking couple that kept giving them curious looks. The only things on the menu were soup and the *grill d'hote* with *frittes*. Wine came in a carafe and wasn't bad.

The soup was excellent and the grill consisted of a large steak and a spicy sausage, a surprisingly good meal. Trager was beginning to like Zengawal. Without Longo, one could lead a pleasant life here. This place wasn't far from Turako. He could come down for a weekend, hopefully with Simone.

~

It was only fifty kilometers from Maridani to Turako. On the well-paved road, it took them less than an hour to roll along Flamingo Lake and the illuminated presidential palace.

Dankov drove behind the central market.

Backed by other sentries on the sidewalks, a soldier stood in the middle of the street with his arm extended in the signal to halt.

The soldier recognized Dankov, saluted smartly, and waved them on. In a parking lot strewn with garbage, several five-ton Isuzu trucks stood with a mob of soldiers milling about.

Feeling tired, Trager got off, wishing he could have a cup of coffee.

Dankov went to where the trucks stood.

Another detail of two Land Rovers arrived. Though his face was painted black, Trager recognized Genadiy, whom he had seen guarding the palace. While Dankov went from truck to truck, conferring with and slapping soldiers on the shoulder, Trager felt foolish and out of place, wondering what was going on. After fifteen minutes, a white van with Boulangerie Mikate written on its sides entered the parking lot. Soldiers opened the doors and loaded small ammunition crates into the van, two from each waiting vehicle.

Dankov returned. "Now you can tell which vehicle has the diamonds."

Understanding dawned on Trager.

A whistle blew, soldiers quickly climbed into their trucks. Sentries came running in. Genadiy's Land Rover headed the convoy with the bakery van in the middle. They rolled toward the airport.

The nearly one-hundred soldiers was more than an escort. They were a show of force.

At the cargo terminal entrance, the convoy turned left, went through a second gate, and headed for the dilapidated hangars. Next to the line of MIG-17 fighters stood a Tupolev 154 jet.

The convoy stopped. Soldiers scattered, forming a defensive perimeter, some occupying sandbagged positions. Trager noticed several Mercedes parked on the side of the hangar.

"Now you will see the show of your lifetime," Dankov said.

A file or soldiers formed, each holding an ammo crate. A sergeant gave an order, and they marched into the hangar.

Trager followed Dankov inside.

Under the glare of halogen lights illuminating the center of the hangar, Bamondo, Longo, Mawingi, and two other men Trager didn't know stood by a long table, on which the soldiers placed the ammunition crates.

With a pair of pliers, Longo broke the seal of the first crate, opened it, and pulled out a bag of sand. "Empty."

He opened two more crates repeating. "Empty."

On opening the fourth, he said, "Inventory."

A diminutive European came forward out of the darkness with a set of jeweler's scales. He inspected the rough diamonds, weighed each, made an entry into a ledger and ticked off a list that had come with the crate.

An hour later, he was finished.

"Empty." Longo discarded a crate. He opened another one. His mouth dropped a little and he gave the impression he was about to drool.

Bamondo and the others crowded toward the crate.

"Keep your distance, gentlemen," Dankov bellowed.

"Inventory," Longo finally said.

From where he was, Trager could see the little man was handling cut stones that sparkled like stars. It was well past midnight and the little man kept inspecting stones. Some were the size of his thumb.

When he finished, four Europeans in blue jumpsuits, flack jackets, and armed with MP-50 submachine guns escorted a forklift loaded with a large safe.

Dankov's men placed the newly sealed ammo boxes into the safe. Dankov closed the safe door and twirled a combination lock. He then turned and shook hands with Bamondo and the others. Hangar doors opened to the sound of jet engines spooling up. The forklift raised the safe and loaded it into the airplane. Blue suits clambered up a ladder similar to the one Trager had used the last time he left. The cargo door closed.

Bamondo and his companions walked out of the hangar to watch the airplane taxi out.

When the airplane lined up on the runway, it disappeared from view as its lights went off. Only the rumble of engines indicated its position. Yellow runway lights came on and engines screamed. A shadow lifted from the ground, and the runway lights went off. Trager noticed the airport's rotating beacon wasn't on. The rumble became faint as millions and millions vanished into the night.

Trager looked at the starry sky and thought of the constellation of shiny, cut diamonds he had just seen. Where did they come from?

As they drove back into town, Trager posed the question to Dankov.

"That's the high-grade product we keep everyone confused with." Dankov chuckled. "It even confuses the dealers at the major diamond exchanges."

"You must be extremely wealthy now. What keeps you playing soldier in the jungle? You should be enjoying life in the Riviera, rubbing elbows with the world's wealthiest."

"What is money? Nothing but a tool." Dankov slowed as they passed a group of dark figures pushing bicycles loaded with heavy sacks. "The only way a man surpasses in greatness the sum of his deeds is by working for the benefit of his people. In this last century, the Russian people have been reviled, laughed at, murdered, and oppressed. When you are planting a garden, you go to the store to buy seeds. That's what I'm doing now. Our Cossack traditions have survived through the cultural vacuum of the Soviet era. We are the bridge that will bring greatness back to the Russian community."

Driving through the dark streets where miserable people scurried through the shadows, digging through piles of garbage in the hope of finding God knows what and listening to Dankov speak as if he were addressing a crowd, Trager felt he was watching a play centered on the absurd. He looked at Dankov. In the faint light, with his chiseled face and remarkable moustache, he did look like a bust of a past hero. What sort of greatness was he talking about? In the chaotic months after the fall of the soviets, in many provincial areas, armed Cossacks emerged as the force that maintained order. Their political views were sometimes extreme, ranging from monarchist to ultra nationalist.

A sudden thought occurred. Blankenship was an expert on Russia. Why would he be concerned with the little goings on in an obscure African country?

Trager asked, "What's your vision of Russian greatness?"

Dankov gave him a quick look, slowed the truck and waved for the rest of the convoy to go ahead. He pulled to the side of the road and let the convoy roar past. "The answer to that question deserves a toast." He produced a pocket flask. "To the Czar of all the Russias." He took a swig and passed the flask to Trager.

The enormity of Dankov's toast stunned Trager. This was not some old Russian émigré of the last century dreaming. This was a soldier with real troops, guns, and a source of incredible wealth. An airplane loaded with diamonds was headed toward Russia right then. It would be received there, the diamonds sold. Dankov was only part of a larger organization.

"To your dream," Trager answered Dankov's toast. The vodka burned its way down and settled with a warm afterglow in his stomach.

Trager didn't know much about diamonds, but he knew enough to know diamonds were rarely cut in Africa. "Those sparklers, where do they come from?"

Dankov chuckled. "People, powerful people, are willing to kill for that information."

Chapter 20

Even though he had been busy, the previous night's spectacle at the airport and Dankov's revelation kept replaying in Trager's mind. He tried to find out more, but Dankov wouldn't add anything else. He dropped Trager off at the villa and left, refusing to say where he was going.

To get hooked up to the Internet, Trager had to personally go to a villa in the outskirts that sported a large parabolic antenna on its roof. The Hindi proprietor of the Internet server company accepted Trager's cash and wrote the phone number to call along with a password on a slip of paper.

Five minutes after he sent his new e-mail address to his newspaper contacts, the editor of the *Christian Science Monitor* was asking for news on the refugee camp raid.

Trager replied that he didn't have specific information but one reliable source indicated no refugee camps existed in the area controlled by Hutu mercenaries.

Less than an hour later, the telephone rang. It was Longo. "Who is the source that gave you information on the Hutu mercenaries?"

Did the bastard need to be so blatant about having his phone tapped? Or was he simply trying to scare him? Trager said, "Reliable source means I'm guessing."

"You should be careful with wrong guesses. We don't want adverse publicity. You should check article seventeen of the National Security Code. It deals with the spreading of false rumors." Longo hung up.

Trager hadn't forgotten it was Friday, and Simone's suggestion he'd go to the Women's League tea. The memory of Longo's near-mad expression when he had talked about the Utabu and the inhuman screams echoing through the basement kept popping up. Maybe Najua would be more informative. Trager also hoped Simone would be there.

~

The Women's League was headquartered in the mansion of the provincial governor in colonial times. A large gray house, walls splotched with mildew, sat on several acres of parkland. Squeals, laughter and yells from a playground nestled in one of the corners of the property gave the place a peaceful atmosphere. One of Longo's black suits stood by the open wrought iron gate, ruining it all.

Trager's taxi drove past the goon into an uneven paved driveway with weeds growing through the cracks. His heart beat faster when he saw

Schnookie parked amid a number of Peugeots, Volvos, and Mercedes in front of the house. More black suits loitered on opposite sides of the lawn.

Inside the house, someone played Chopin on a piano. For a fleeting moment, Trager saw a boy and his dog running through a garden.

He entered a large hall separating the two-storied house into wings. Except for a folding table staffed by two African women in long cotton dresses and turbans, the hall was bare of furniture.

Under a cupola where once must have hung a grand chandelier, a lone naked bulb dangled like the victim of an execution.

"Bonjour, Monsieur," the welcoming ladies chorused. They smiled happily and gestured for Trager to come in.

"Welcome, how nice to see you. First time here?"

Trager signed his name on a clipboard; paid fifteen-hundred Z-franks, three dollars, for the tea, and donated ten dollars that went into a glass jar labeled Kabura Elementary School Library.

Passing potted palms decorating the entrance to a large room filled with folding tables, Trager immediately spotted Simone. He swallowed, trying to suppress his excitement. She stood talking to a group of high school boys in blue trousers, white shirts, and blue ties, and held their undivided attention.

Wimbo was playing the piano. Trager recognized several women he had seen at the palace party.

As he strode toward Simone, to his annoyance, Madame Kanzo intercepted him. "Is everything satisfactory at your villa?"

Trager smiled. "Wangohi is a real jewel. Everything's perfect."

"How good of you to come. Can I sell you some raffle tickets?"

Trager stuck raffle tickets into his pocket as Madame Kanzo pounced on her next victim.

On one side of the room, three tables loaded with trays piled with sandwiches and pastries formed a bar. Leonora was among volunteers serving tea. In a simple print dress with short sleeves, she was less blatantly sexy than at the palace, yet her figure showed well.

She waved at Trager, making him feel uneasy as every head turned toward him. He was forced to change course and approach the tea bar.

"I was delighted to hear you were back in town. It is wonderful to see you giving support to our charities. Do come for dinner some night. Pierre will be pleased." Leonora handed Trager a cup of tea.

Trager waved at the minister of posts and telecommunications and quickly sidestepped, trying to avoid getting stuck with the fabulous bore. He looked for Simone but couldn't find her. Professor Najua, pipe in mouth, was talking to the students now.

Frustrated, Trager went through one of the open French doors and took a deep breath of the cooler air outside. A group of nannies with white scarves on their heads sat on the lawn chatting.

What an idyllic setting, Trager mused. Everyone was having a good time--except of course, the black suits patrolling the grounds.

He went around the building. Schnookie was still there, but no sign of Simone.

The piano music stopped and was replaced by a scraping of chairs. Trager returned to the building, hunting for Najua. Schoolboys marched up to a small stage and began singing. The choir was quite good. Trager stood by the door, searching the crowd. Someone tapped him on the shoulder.

Professor Najua was offering him a cup.

"Thank you," Trager whispered, and showed Najua his own cup.

"Come, this is *real* tea." Najua winked.

Trager followed the minister of education. They settled on a park bench facing a set of croquet hoops.

"Cheers," Najua said, a mischievous smile on his face.

Trager sipped from his new cup. *Scotch, neat.*

"I hear you're interested in the legend of the Utabu."

"I still don't know what it is."

"A very exciting rumor, gaining strength with each passing day." Najua's eyes gleamed. "It is said the Utabu has been found and that soon we will have a new king."

"What is the Utabu?"

"Ah, my dear fellow, nobody knows. Our history is mostly oral, so things get distorted. The Bassis say it's a crown. The Wussis say it is a sword. The Pygmies call it The Sacred Thing. Some of our witch doctors argue with the tribal keepers of the word. What everyone agrees on is that all will recognize the Utabu when they see it."

"I'm still in a fog, Professor."

"The fog and darkness of the ages." Najua chuckled. "Generally, the story goes like this. Long, long ago, wise King Bomoto was the last wearer of the Utabu. His two sons, Bologo and Keimati, quarreled and started a war. The old king was so saddened he buried the Utabu. That's how the Bassi and the Wussi tribes were born and the ancient Kingdom of Zengawal died."

"I see, so whoever gets the Utabu will reestablish this ancient kingdom?"

"Very exciting, don't you think? He will be accepted by all tribes."

The screams in the basement gave the story an awful ring of truth.

Trager had thought, like most torturers, Longo was a little mad. He now realized the man was power-mad. Trager accepted the story as truth. He had to. Whoever got his meat hooks on the thing could also grab absolute power. "Does Bamondo worry about this?"

Najua's eyes sparkled. "Bamondo is a good ruler. It is said when the witch doctors are ready, they will parade the Utabu through Turako and hand it to Bamondo. He is a descendant of Bomoto."

"So Bamondo's enemies would want to prevent this from happening."

"That's why he very wisely chose a Wussi as chief of security."

"You mean Longo?"

"Yes. His loyalty to Bamondo is well proven."

If it seemed like a sure thing Bamondo would get the Utabu, why would Longo be torturing someone to find its location? Trager took a cigarette out and lit it.

"My friend, those Roosters will kill you."

The choir stopped singing. Someone inside scratched a violin, making the sinking sun look sadder.

"From what I hear, you can't leave this life alive."

Najua let out a laugh. "Very true. I hear you have a different name."

"We Americans do this all the time. Go see a judge and change our name into something more exciting."

"I'm glad you came. This country needs new, outside blood. It stimulates the flow of ideas." Najua stood up. "It was nice chatting with you."

Trager turned to watch Najua amble back to the house and noticed a man in a brown suit a teacup in his hand, watching.

Trager got up and headed for the house. The man turned and went around the corner.

The scotch hadn't gone down well. Trager felt thirsty. At the bar, he got tea with lemon. The refugee girl stopped playing for a moment and the room broke into applause. It wasn't for the girl, but for Leonora, who stood, a hand leaning on the piano.

The refugee girl opened with *La Vie En Rose*. Leonora's voice was sure, and the violin accompaniment seemed to improve. Trager swallowed the last of his tea and wanted to get another cup. No one paid any attention to him while Leonora sang. He searched the room for Simone. No luck.

Great applause followed the end of the song. Leonora and the girl curtsied then hugged. As Leonora walked away, the violin girl reached inside the piano and took out what looked like a piece of paper. She slid it under the violin resting under her arm. Had it not been for her quick, furtive glance before taking the paper, Trager would not have noticed.

It was already completely dark and people were leaving.

Disappointment filled Trager when he went outside. Schnookie was gone. His gaze searched for his cab. Neither cab nor driver was anywhere to be seen.

From the far end of the driveway, he watched Leonora get into a white Mercedes. The black suit who held her door open got into the front seat. A black Mercedes followed as hers sped away.

To Trager's surprise, a black suit was still around. The man approached him. "You go outside, turn right," the black suit said and kept walking past Trager.

Shit, Trager almost said out loud. He was sure Longo was playing silly games. Missing the company of Dankov's soldiers, Trager strode out of the property and turned right. The other side of the street was lined with small, fenced-in bungalows. There were few lights burning. The feel of the pistol in his waistband was comforting. Reaching the corner, he stopped. By then, all the cars had left the Women's League house and the street was empty.

A black Mercedes approached slowly and stopped. A door opened. Trager got in, noticing two thugs in the front seats. Dressed in a tuxedo, Longo sat in the back. He pressed a switch and the glass partition between back and front seats slid up.

"Where did you go yesterday?" Longo asked.

"To the airport to check on your security upgrades."

"Don't try to be funny. You've lied to me about your status with the CIA, but I don't thrive on vengeance. Success comes to those who recognize and grasp opportunity." Longo crossed his legs, took out a cigarette case, offered it to Trager.

"Thanks." Trager pulled Roosters out of his pocket.

Longo flicked a gold lighter, lit Trager's cigarette then his own. "Your account in my ledger is heavy on the debit side, but foreclosing is not always good business. So let's see a token of good will from your part. I want your whereabouts between three o'clock in the afternoon to ten o'clock in the evening yesterday."

Trager thought about lying but decided to tell the truth. He would need his maximum ability to dissemble later.

"So Dankov did not carry the diamonds?"

"I don't know, he had a pair of boxes in his car."

"He didn't stop and pick up anything anywhere?"

"Nope."

"You will find it beneficial for your health to discover from where he gets the cut diamonds."

"You want me to become your asset?"

"You speak like a true professional."

In the darkness, Trager could see only Longo's profile. The heavy odor of 411 Cologne overpowered the cheap smell of Trager's cigarette.

"Did you have an interesting conversation with Professor Najua?"

"He's a cultivated gentleman."

"Cultivated." Longo chuckled. "The term makes me think of people plowed under. Learn anything about the Utabu?"

"The what?"

Longo extended his arm, placing his cigarette close to Trager's cheek. "Recently, Najua spoke to a gathering of teachers and wrote a memorandum that went to all school principals. The Utabu is his subject of the moment. Don't tell me he didn't mention it to you."

"Ah, that thing. You also mentioned it during our last meeting. Najua told me the story of King Bomoto."

"Patience is the ally of the security officer." Longo took an envelope out of his pocket and tossed it on Trager's lap. "We have a tradition in our service. We call it the Judas money."

Trager tossed the envelope back to Longo.

"My friend, you either take the Judas money or by morning you will hang from a tree, slowly, slowly turning in the wind." Longo slid the envelope into Trager's jacket. "You're a professional, find the Utabu."

"Be reasonable; it's only a legend."

Longo turned, his eyes shining like beacons in a dark sea. He stuck a finger under Trager's jaw. "You think this is the black man's silly superstition?" he spat out.

Trager tried to move his head out of the way of Longo's finger and the pain it brought.

"You think you may come to my country and laugh at us? When I say find out about the Utabu, you get the information." Longo pulled his finger away; he seemed to be calming down. He picked up a handset, said something to the driver. The car began moving.

"What did you and Najua talk about?"

Trager repeated what he had already told.

"Did he mention Babaku?"

"No, what's that?"

"Babaku is said to be the chief witch doctor. You Europeans are immune to witchcraft. Find Babaku."

"Your shopping list is expanding."

Longo looked pensive. "Mademoiselle Loriot spent the night with you."

"So?"

"Colonel Dankov would be upset if he found out. I hope you realize he's dangerous. I'd hate to lose you."

"I'm grateful for your concern."

Longo smiled. "It would also distress me if anything happened to Mademoiselle Loriot. Don't you find her charming?"

The veiled threats were becoming annoying.

Longo said casually, "Mademoiselle Loriot and Professor Najua spend an unhealthy amount of time together. Why do they seek your company?"

"My magnetic personality, obviously."

"That's not the way I see it. This woman of loose morals is using you for something."

Trager held his temper. He felt like pulling out his pistol and pressing it against Longo's temple.

"The night you left for the United States, she slept in Tony Bond's villa."

"I'm not interested in smut." A picture of him strangling Longo replaced Trager's pistol against the temple.

"I'm looking after your welfare. Being aware of who you're dealing with will help you keep a clear perspective on your objectives and loyalties. Connected to the right people, you can carve yourself a comfortable niche in this country. Find out where the Utabu is and the origin of the cut diamonds and you will be generously rewarded."

Trager had trouble imagining Longo rewarding anyone.

The car entered Lakeshore Boulevard.

"I would like to have a longer chat with you, but I have to be in the palace shortly. Will you be there?"

"I wasn't invited."

"Too bad, I'm looking forward to dancing with Mademoiselle Loriot."

He had never met a more loathsome person in his life. Trager's hatred for Longo increased along with his heartbeat. "I thought you said she had loose morals."

Longo laughed. "That's what I find charming."

The bastard was teasing. Worst of all, he was succeeding in getting to Trager.

For a moment, Longo hummed some undistinguishable tune then stopped abruptly. "I'll drop you off a couple of blocks from your house. Should the president not invite you soon, I shall encourage him to do so. I want you to gain his confidence."

"He won't confide in me."

"Oh, but he will. You are white."

~

Walking the two blocks uphill made Trager break into a sweat. Though Longo had him by the short hairs, Trager had room to wiggle. He was concerned with having come close to losing his temper.

Trager took a deep breath. The night watchman sat by the gate already asleep.

"*Reveilles toi,*" Trager growled.

Startled, the watchman jumped up, dropping the baseball bat that had been resting on his lap. "*Bon soir, Monsieur.*" He grinned sheepishly, showing missing teeth, and opened the gate.

Inside the house, Wangohi came out of the kitchen carrying a small silver tray with a square white envelope on it.

Trager opened the unsealed envelope and pulled out a card embossed with the Zengawali coat of arms. In elegant handwriting, it said: *We expect you for a family dinner tomorrow. We hope you can come.* It was signed, Leonora and a telephone number followed.

"When did this arrive?"

"Maybe half an hour ago."

Leonora hadn't wasted time inviting him over. She hardly had time to consult with Bamondo. Without an RSVP, Trager assumed the phone number was there only to convey his regrets. He checked in the telephone directory; that particular number was unlisted.

He poured a scotch and went out on the terrace. Cars were entering through the palace back gate. This appeared to be the norm for unofficial functions.

He was about to go inside for a second drink when the roar of an exhaust drew his attention. Schnookie had arrived. Simone obviously needed a new muffler. Squeezing his glass, he watched her, in black pantaloons, red sash and white blouse, saunter into the palace.

What was it that attracted him so strongly to that exotic woman who wouldn't give him her phone number, never mind her address?

Chapter 21

He had heard it from three different individuals in government, but what did the common folk say? When Wangohi brought breakfast out on the terrace, Trager asked, "What's this thing about the Utabu?"

"Has Monsieur heard about it?" Wangohi smiled, holding the tray flat against his chest.

"Yes, a tale about a king and his two sons."

"That's the old story. Some witchdoctor of powerful medicine say, somebody found the Utabu. Now in sacred place waiting for prophesy to come true."

Trager put his coffee cup down and leaned forward. "And what's the prophesy?"

"Long, long time ago, before Arabu come, white magic people live in Zamani. They make swords for king's army and make Zengawal strong. Before they leave, they make king a gift, the Utabu. If magic of Utabu work no more, king must bury it and wait for son of magic people to bring the Utabu. Everybody talk the son of magic people is back and he will give our president the Utabu."

"Why the president?"

Wangohi gestured toward the palace. "He good man of king blood."

"Interesting. And you think this will happen soon?"

Wangohi nodded energetically. "Very soon. Everybody get very excited." He gestured toward the park beyond the palace. "Hear the drums?"

"Yes." Trager listened to faint drumming mixed with the noise of Saturday morning traffic.

"People drum and dance to make prophesy good. Tonight big *ngoma*. *Everybody* come."

After breakfast, Trager studied a map of Zengawal and found Zamani at the foot of the extinct Matukumba volcano. It was marked as an archeological site. In the *Discover Zengawal* booklet, a bad black-and-white photo showed a square column and was captioned, Tomb of the Wizard. The booklet claimed the Zamani ruins were the oldest in sub-Saharan Africa. Trager shook his head. If that demented Longo wasn't so powerful, his obsession with the mythical object would have been pathetically funny.

~

Throughout the afternoon, the sound of drums gained depth, making the air feel heavier, as if a storm were approaching. Shortly after sunset, Trager walked down the hill toward the center of town. The park was crowded with people and the drumming reverberated throughout the city.

At the head of Avenue de la Liberte, in front of Flamingo House, a line of buses parked bumper to bumper acted as a dam to the sea of humanity in the park spilling into the thoroughfare where vendors' stalls and carts had replaced vehicular traffic.

So as not to be seen, Trager gave a wide berth to the Metropole and moved along the edge of the crowded park. About twenty policemen in riot gear stood in front of the hotel, their transparent shields resting against the wall.

Like racetrack attendees in the member's enclosure, people on the terrace bar crowded the rail, watching the spectacle in the park.

Approximately every fifty yards, a group of drummers and dancers attracted dense crowds swaying and clapping to the rhythm of the drums. As usual, the air was thick with the aroma of roasting corn. Trager tried to get a closer look at one of the dancing groups, but was unable to push his way through without running the risk of ruining his clothes. Though he was in sports coat and tie, not to speak of the difference in color, no one paid attention to him. From a distance, he could see the heads of leaping dancers rise above the onlookers.

Trager estimated the crowd to be nearly a hundred thousand. If this was a sort of political demonstration, the movement was a powerful one.

Sidewalk tables were piled inside the Lebanese café that remained open despite the lack of clients. Trager went in and ordered a Turkish coffee. Though the café was stuffy and hot, it was a relief to get away from the drumming. The only way the Utabu business made any sense was as a political movement. Not only African politics relied heavily on symbols. Here you had a mythical object, witch doctors and peaceful drummers conveying a strong message, while the people leading remained in the shadows. Longo was scared shitless. Finished with his coffee, Trager turned the cup over to let the sediment form a mosaic forecasting the future. He knew in advance what he would read. Revolution.

Trager had to detour to reach the lakeshore road, eerily empty of traffic or pedestrians. The throb of drums competed here with the cackling voices of flamingoes on their evening parade.

The rear gate to the palace remained closed as he approached.

"*Oui, Monsieur?*" A soldier in camouflage asked from behind the gate.

"John Trager to see the president."

The soldier appeared perplexed. "*Caporal de Garde,*" he shouted.

A somewhat older soldier emerged from a white bunker at the side of the gate. Trager repeated he was to see the president. Looking puzzled, the corporal demanded Trager's passport. After leafing through the passport, he asked, "No car?"

"I'm on foot."

There was some shouting as the first soldier opened the gate. A white uniformed soldier came running down the driveway. He saluted Trager, led the way up the incline.

At the door, a Russian with a blackened face stood grinning. He saluted and said, "Please follow me."

Only a few lights were lit on the ground floor.

As they emerged out of the long corridor into the foyer, the incongruous sight of a wooden kitchen table in the center of the room startled Trager. On top of it, a 7.2 millimeter Dektarev machine gun rested on a bipod, its ammo belt ready to feed. Two soldiers jumped up. They had been sitting on the marble floor, their backs against the wall.

The Russian explained, "The crowd in the park is thicker than usual. One must take precautions. This Utabu business has everyone on edge."

"You believe in the Utabu?"

"It doesn't matter what we believe. It's those people out there who are going crazy."

They went up a circular red-carpeted staircase, past a balcony, down a wide corridor in front of the palace. A bunker-like outgrowth with firing ports protruded from the wall. Trager thought this probably wasn't part of the original architectural plan. Anyone coming down the corridor with hostile intentions would have a hell of a time taking the strongpoint.

Two guards in white uniforms stood in front of a set of doors with peepholes. The Russian returned the guard's salute, pressed a buzzer, and stood back. A chambermaid in a black dress and white apron opened the door and invited Trager to enter.

To his astonishment, Trager found himself in a stodgy, middle class apartment. The furniture in the living room was the sort one could find in any department store. Bamondo got up from an overstuffed chair. "How good to see you again." He wore a sport jacket and cravat. Trager's fear of being underdressed vanished, but his heartbeat accelerated as he caught sight of black boots and red pantaloons.

"Remember Mademoiselle Loriot?" Bamondo guided Trager toward a chair facing the sofa occupied by the ladies. Leonora looked elegant and comfortable in a blue silk caftan.

"It was a pleasant surprise to hear you were coming," Simone said. She sat in the corner of the sofa, relaxed, as if that was her usual place.

"The ladies were all going crazy over him yesterday," Leonora added.

Bamondo laughed. "These silly girls are trying to cover up *their* excitement of being in your company. How about a snort? Still on scotch?"

"Thanks, the excitement seems to be out in the park. I guess it has to do with the Utabu thing."

Bamondo handed Trager a glass. "I wish those foolish rumors would end. It is difficult to govern under such circumstances. At the moment, we can't even promise elections. The people are in a daze, as if waiting for the Second Coming of Christ."

"Let them have their fun," Leonora said.

"There is a collective wisdom when the masses rally to an idea. There's probably something to be learned from that. No?" Simone took a sip from a sherry glass, lit a small cigar. It seemed her thinking paralleled Trager's.

"We work hard trying to rid the people of superstition, to help them take on modern ideas. Then this crops up." Bamondo hit his broad forehead with the palm of his hand. "Sensibly, witchcraft had been outlawed in this country during the Belgian period, but it is difficult to enforce the law when thousands violate it."

The drumming outside, like the distant throb of a far thunderstorm, could only be felt. Or maybe it was Trager's imagination the building vibrated slightly.

"Tell us about the outside world," Leonora said. "What are the movies, the plays?"

The shelf under the glass-topped coffee table was loaded with a disorderly pile of European news and women's magazines that gave the room a lived in feel. Trager told about a couple of film reviews he had read. Leonora appeared to be avidly hanging onto every word he said. The isolated life in the palace must been weighing on her. Regardless of status, life in a foreign culture was usually hard for women with a liberal Western upbringing. Trager thought of Longo's goons escorting her when out of the palace.

He glanced at Simone, who seemed adept at navigating dangerous waters, always appearing nonchalant. He tried to understand what created his powerful attraction for her. Sitting quietly next to Leonora, she looked almost plain but not overshadowed by the former Miss Belgium. Maybe after dinner she would accept an invitation for a drink.

"I hear you're writing for a newspaper now," Bamondo said.

"Freelancing, newspapers and travel magazines." He noticed Simone staring at him. "Spending some time up country, I could write some articles that would attract tourism."

Bamondo chuckled. "Based on your previous travels through our country, that would make my director of security nervous. Are you still with the CIA?"

"No, I have severed my affiliations with that club."

"Severed? It sounds drastic."

Simone said, "He *is* extreme."

"That's too bad. I would like to have a line of communications with the United States. At the moment, we have only five embassies; only one in Europe--Switzerland."

Leonora said, "He will write wonderful things about our country." She gave Trager a coquettish smile. "Won't you?"

"I write about wonderful things when I see them."

"Plenty of opportunities for that," Simone said. "You could start with the ruins of Zamani."

"The grave of the wizard," Trager said.

Simone shot Trager a smile. "You've been doing homework. No one knows who built it. Some speculate it was one of King Solomon's outposts."

It was unfortunate that very few records of the Arab period in Africa survived. Trager thought if records existed, a lot of mysteries would have had simple explanations. One of the most widely spread African myths was King Solomon's mines. People still searched for them.

"A very mysterious place." Leonora hugged her shoulders, imitating a shiver. "We camped there once." She chortled. "Imagine, me in a tent."

"Next year's budget will allow us to build a lodge there," Bamondo said. "But that will remove some of the mystery."

"It's a deliciously spooky place." Leonora imitated a shiver.

"Pshaw, you should spend more time outdoors," Simone said to Leonora. She then turned to Trager. "The most interesting parts of the country are away from the capital, in the wilderness."

The maid came in and announced dinner was served.

The dining room reminded Trager of the furnished apartment when he lived in Vienna. The round table, comfortable for four, would have been cramped with six persons. A stodgy, tall china cabinet held a number of souvenir plates from cities in Europe. Impressionistic paintings of Brussels street scenes, and a corner cupboard with a collection of ceramic dolls conveyed a stuffy middle-class ambiance.

The first course was palm hearts wrapped in thin slices of ham and topped with a delicate mayonnaise.

"I'm sure, in ancient times, travel through Africa was easier than it is today," Simone said. "If one considers the quantity of ivory artifacts remaining from the classical Greek period, it is evident trade existed beyond the Sahara."

"A lot came from India," Bamondo said.

Under the table, an ankle brushed against his. At first Trager thought it was Simone's. As it wrapped around his leg, however, there was no doubt it was Leonora who was sending shivers up his spine.

"And when we examine the Maasai tribe, their toga-like dress and simis, their short swords, and their war formations, bear great resemblance to the Roman legions. It has now been firmly established the Roman city of Raphta did exist south of the Equator." Simone gave Trager a mischievous look. "One of my little secrets is I know the location of this lost city. It is on the Kenya coast. I even have a Roman brick to prove it."

Bamondo said, "Our dear Simone knows more about our continent than most Africans."

"But I am African," Simone protested.

Trager tried to concentrate on what Simone said and ignore Leonora's leg rubbing against his. He hoped Bamondo would not notice his discomfort. Sweat began to drip at the back of his neck.

"The trade route to Central Africa was along the Nile," Simone continued, "which I don't think was as choked with reeds in ancient times as the Sudd is today. I think the Zamani ruins pre-date the Roman period. Johnny, you should visit them, write about it."

"Yes," Trager said.

Conversation stopped when the maid brought a soup tureen. The aroma of leeks made Trager think of a European country kitchen.

As they were finishing the main course of wonderfully tender lamb chops, Bamondo looked at his watch. "You will excuse me, I never have a complete weekend off." He smiled at Trager. "You will take care of the ladies, won't you?"

Trager wondered if Bamondo said the same thing to Dankov.

Leonora's leg was still messing with his. "We'll miss you, darling."

Bamondo left the room. Simone lit a small cigar, and Leonora's hand rested on Trager's thigh, squeezing gently. "Another meeting with his security chief. I don't know how they find so much to talk about. The man simply lacks charm."

"How did he get that scar?" Trager asked.

Simone answered. "Igor did it with his sword." Noticing Trager's stupefied look, she smiled her Do-I-need-to-explain-everything-to-you? smile. "When they stormed the palace, Igor carried a sword. Longo was the commander of the Palace Guard. He barricaded himself on the stairs to the roof, refused to surrender even when out of ammunition. Igor went after him, spared his life."

Incredulously Trager said, "And now he is . . ."

"Pierre is an angel, in a gesture of reconciliation, he gave Longo a medal," Leonora said. "He can be altruistic to the point of naivete."

"Igor and Pierre are great men," Simone added.

Leonora's hand edged to the inside of his thigh. She said, "I find powerful men fascinating; today's world leaders are so drab."

"Arafat stands out," Simone said.

"But he's so unsightly. I can't imagine him sitting at my dinner table."

"Should we have coffee in the sitting room? Or remain at the table Italian style?" Simone asked.

"Let's go to the sitting room," Trager suggested. "I'm beginning to get a cramp."

"A cramp?" Leonora released his leg, ran her hand down his cheek. "A cramp, he says. Poor darling." She stood and rang a little silver bell.

In the living room, Trager was more comfortable as he alternated between sipping coffee and cognac and munching mango strudel with a delicate crust. "That was a wonderful dinner. You have an excellent cook."

Leonora gave him a flashing smile. "Darling, on Saturdays, I cook myself." She sighed. "It is my only opportunity to shine in this universe."

"Don't despair," Simone said, "soon things will change."

"Sure, they will get worse for me."

"Don't be such a pessimist. Soon, Johnny will become weary of this place and he'll take you to America."

Trager's jolt made both women look at him.

Simone said, "You two can discuss that while lunching on Monday."

"What a wonderful idea."

"Ladies--"

"Shush, before you say something you'll regret." Simone stood, towered over Trager. "Tell Wangohi to make lamb couscous the way I like it."

Leonora joined in. "And we'll sit on the floor and eat out of a big tray with our hands and drink mint tea."

"It will be a pleasure," Trager said as Simone's light scent dissipated his anger. He could almost feel the heat of her body.

She handed him her brandy snifter. "Will you be so kind?"

As he refilled drinks at the sideboard, Trager thought there was a lot more going on in this palace than he had imagined. He was being swept right into the middle of some soap opera drama he wanted no part of. Simone. The damn woman was pushing him not only away from her but also into big trouble.

They had been sitting and listening to excerpts from *La Boheme* when Bamondo returned and headed straight for the drinks cabinet.

"Worrisome news, darling?"

Bamondo laughed. "The trouble with security people, they always make you feel insecure. I guess it has to do with *their* job security. The mob in the park is peaceful and self-absorbed. The only thing I don't like is that Bassis are on this end of the park and Wussis have gathered on the far end. Let's hope nothing sparks animosity. In Mbaya's days, the police would have mustered out in force and dispersed the crowds." Bamondo dropped into a chair.

"Darling, John has invited us to lunch on Monday. Would you like to come?"

"Sorry, I'm having lunch with the Chamber of Commerce, giving another blessed speech."

Trager jumped at the opportunity Bamondo gave him. "That's too bad, we'll cancel, make it on another date."

Simone gave him a withering look.

Leonora said, "No need to cancel. Simone and I will be happy to come." She smiled at Bamondo. "He's making couscous."

"What a pity I'll miss it. I like eating out of a communal tray; it brings people together."

Being together with these two women, Trager knew, would lead him further into trouble.

Chapter 22

Reaching maximum intensity sometime after midnight, the drumming spilled into Sunday, gradually easing until crowds, like a tired, defeated army, straggled toward the shantytowns ringing the city.

The aroma of lamb and spices had been permeating the house since Trager became aware he was awake. Fortunately, he didn't have time to worry about the accursed lunch. He had a busy morning going to the Ministry of Interior to get a press card, and to Madame Kanzo's to arrange a safari to the Zamani ruins. Once there, he would gather material for the dynamite article he had in mind, forecasting a revolution.

The visit to the Bamondos had ended when Simone offered Trager a ride back. He invited her for a nightcap, but she turned him down, saying she had work to do. He had wanted to raise the subject of the forced lunch but thought better of it. The damn thing was inevitable, and he would see Simone only on her terms.

In the intelligence business, he had learned the value of patience and knowing when to flow with the current. One gained nothing by trying to crash the gate. If you stood near the door, someone would eventually open it.

Finished with Madame Kanzo, it was a few minutes before noon when he arrived home.

Wangohi handed him a note with a telephone number. "Urgent you call now."

"Who is it?"

Wangohi shrugged.

Trager dialed.

"Ah. Mr. Trager. I'm glad you did not delay my departure for lunch."

Trager recognized Longo's voice. "Why are you going to Zamani?"

That damn Madame Kanzo must have been on the phone to Longo the moment Trager left her office. "It's a place of interest. I will take photographs. Possibly write about it. I hear it's one of Africa's oldest archeological sites."

"The pyramids are in Africa, also. They are much older. Zamani is an insignificant abandoned village. Next time, before you travel, clear your plans with me. I'm concerned about your personal safety."

Trager clenched his fist, imagined hitting Longo in the face. "Right now is still *before* I travel. I applied for a travel permit."

"You and I have a special relationship. You clear with me when you *think* about travel. Who suggested you go there?"

"There's a booklet called *Welcome to Zengawal*. On page three, it suggest places to visit. The booklet also says Zengawalis are friendly and polite."

"It also warns that people should be cautious when in the backcountry. I certainly wouldn't want anything to happen to you."

Trager was honing a sarcastic response, when Longo asked. "Where were you on Saturday?"

Maybe Longo didn't have him under constant surveillance. Or maybe he was testing him. Trager decided to lie, do his own testing. "I was in the park watching the dancers. Had a sugar cane juice and two brochettes, a bottle of warm beer. Didn't see any of your black suits lurking around."

"Our presence was discreet. As one professional to another, you would appreciate our ability to disguise ourselves. I must remember to invite you to the carnival we hold on Security Day. I give generous prizes for the best disguises."

Longo's sudden chattiness surprised Trager.

"Anyway, don't forget what I told you." Longo hung up.

It appeared Longo was unaware of Trager's visit to the palace. Thank God for small blessings.

~

Out of the shower, wearing fresh trousers and a sport shirt, Trager was ready to receive his guests. He was finishing a scotch on the rocks when tires scrunched on the driveway.

A white Mercedes followed by a Land Rover loaded with presidential guard soldiers pulled in. Two black suits jumped out of the front of the Mercedes and opened both passenger doors.

Leonora's shapely legs swung out first. She emerged with a radiant smile, wearing a beige linen suit with a short skirt. Simone came around the car in her military-style ministerial clothes--khaki shirt and a skirt that revealed very nice legs.

Leonora planted a hot, wet kiss on his cheek. Simone's greeting was a firm handshake.

"I'm happy you could make it." Trager led the way inside.

"How delightful," Leonora said, as she inspected the room. Wangohi had laid out a carpet to the side of the living room furniture and spread out cushions. For effect, he dug out a hookah pipe from somewhere and had it standing to the side.

Trager fixed Cinzanos and tonic and decided he would have one, too.

"All set for your safari?" Simone asked.

"Yes, but I have the wrong guide."

"Daniel is very good," she said, surprising Trager with her knowledge of the safari details. It seemed everyone was keeping track of his movements.

"I wish I was going," Leonora said. "Imagine, you and me in a tent."

Trager felt hemmed against the sideboard as the two women crowded him. Leonora, her bust pushing a pale blue blouse, smelled of Eau de Printemps. Simone's was a more exotic fragrance Trager could not identify.

Simone said, "When in Zamani, make sure to see Funga da Milango. He's the caretaker. Have him show you the Waze cave."

Leonora added. "There's a wonderful spring there, surrounded by a grove of giant sacred fig trees."

"You might run into one of Igor's patrols."

This was a surprise. Though Zamani was not too far from Dankov's fort, it was at least a hundred kilometers to the west, away from the Ugandan border. Trager remembered Longo opening the box with the cut diamonds. An odd idea struck him, too wild to take seriously. "And where is Igor?"

Leonora shrugged. "Who knows. The dear is such a busy man."

"Probably destroying the Hutu mercenary army gathering near our border with the Congo," Simone said.

Wangohi came in and placed a huge tray on the middle of the carpet. "*Bon appetit*," he said.

The meal was worthy of a sultan in *A Thousand and One Arabian Nights*. It certainly wasn't just couscous. The aroma made Trager's mouth water.

Like harem queens, Simone and Leonora stretched out on the carpet, leaning on cushions. Leonora's skirt had slid dangerously high. Simone looked strange without pantaloons.

Trager's concerns dissipated completely. Eating Arab food while sprawled like Romans was fun, and the women were in good humor. The strong, sweet tea with fresh mint was the perfect drink to go with the lamb, quail and tilapia, accompanied by handfuls of delicate rice and couscous. Leonora talked enthusiastically about cruising the Greek islands on a yacht. Even Simone, who seldom laughed, was in good spirits. By the time Wangohi served baklava, Trager considered lunch a complete success.

His feeling of well-being took a nosedive when Simone said, looking at her watch, "Boys and girls, I am off to a little *sieste*. Ta-ta." She leaped to her feet, slung her bag over her shoulder and headed downstairs for the bedrooms.

"Darling, will you get me a little kirsch?" Leonora asked, running her hand up her thigh. Her skirt hem was at nearly hip level. Trager could see a hint of white between her legs.

"Sure," he said, thinking of the black suits and soldiers outside his door.

Trager poured kirsch into a liqueur glass and cognac into a snifter. He almost dropped the glasses when he turned. Leonora had unbuttoned her blouse and unsnapped the front of her white bra.

"Darling, do you like what you see?"

Trager swallowed, lowered himself slowly, handed Leonora her drink.

Resting on an elbow, Leonora stroked one of her breasts, a virtual goddess of temptation. "Do you like what you see?" She repeated, an amused expression on her face.

Trager cleared his throat, took out a cigarette and lit it.

Leonora stopped massaging her breast, pulled the cup away revealing a wide, pink aureole and a semi-erect nipple. "They are still quite firm," she said looking down at her breast. "Nature has been good to me." She then picked up her glass and raised it. "Here's to us, John."

As an erection pushed, Trager crossed his legs, checking his impulse to leap on the luscious woman and pull her panties down. "You'd better re-do your bra and button up. You can't tell who could walk in."

"You have a cool head, but darling, you haven't answered my question."

"Yes, I find you very attractive."

She smiled, pleased with herself. "Do you like to live dangerously?"

Trager tried to control his breathing. He thought of Simone downstairs, the guards outside the house, Wangohi in the kitchen. The situation was preposterous. "No. I think it would be prudent for you to button up."

"Prudent?" She sat, cross-legged, showing white panties. Her hands pulled both bra cups aside. Trager swallowed. He had to admit, in front of him sat the sexiest woman he had ever seen. His body vibrating with desire, he again thought of Simone. *Screw the stuck-up bitch who fucked everyone but him.* He placed his drink on the side table and started to get up.

"Don't move, I could scream." Still smiling, Leonora snapped the bra together and buttoned her blouse.

Remembering the time on the balcony, Trager thought, *She's the biggest cock-teaser I've ever seen.* "I'm afraid you're abusing my hospitality."

"Really?"

"You're a cruel tease." He wanted to say she was abusing her position of power but decided to limit his comment. The damn woman was dangerous. Really dangerous.

She laughed. "Call it a generous display of what could be yours."

"You're beautiful and charming, and I'm flattered, but I don't think I could perform under the circumstances. You would be terribly disappointed."

"You think I want an affair? My darling John, I want more than that. I want you to take me out of my prison." She gestured toward the door. "I'm guarded all the time. I need to get out."

"Can't you get a divorce?"

She shook her head. "Not in this country."

Trager frowned. "What you're asking is simple. I'll kill a dozen guards, make reservations, then we fly out of here. First class, of course."

"I love your sense of humor, darling. You've been a spy. You'll concoct a delicious scheme, a diversion. You'll find a way."

Trager shook his head.

Leonora dug a little suede drawstring purse out of her handbag, and dangled it in front of her. "This may add motivation, I'm not a beggar, you know." She spilled diamonds into the palm of her hand, got on her knees and extended it toward Trager as if to feed him. "These can be yours, too. I'll be generous with more than my body."

Trager chuckled. "It would be easier to kill you and grab the diamonds."

Leonora got up and moved to the sofa, where she sat looking prim. "Oh, you do wonders to a woman's self esteem. But in Switzerland, I have more diamonds and a sizeable bank account. It would be stupid to kill me enroute."

"Have Dankov get you out. He has the troops, the resources."

"Igor will never do it." She let out a small, bitter laugh. "He limits his double dealing to the bedroom. Actually, the dear is an honorable man who couldn't resist my advances. If it weren't for me, he would never have helped Pierre liberate this country from General Mbaya."

"So you dump Pierre and Igor, then my turn will come. I'm not interested."

Leonora's expression changed to one of anger. "Think about it. Although I'm not official, I *am* the most powerful woman in this country."

She walked up to Trager and slapped him in the face. "Remember the woman scorned? Do you think I offer myself to a man lightly?" Her voice rose in pitch. "I offered myself to you because you're decent, unassuming, courageous. You have no right to insult me."

His cheek burning, Trager leaned back.

"There," she said, now smiling, her hand reaching out and caressing his cheek. "I could have called my babysitters. Can you imagine what would have happened to you?"

Trager fought the shiver creeping up his back, the image of soldiers grabbing and delivering him to Longo's basement, all too vivid. He was only one scream away from this nightmare to turn into reality.

"But all you get is a slap."

"Thank you."

She nodded, acknowledging his remark, stepped back, and sat on the sofa patting the space next to her. "Sit next to me and be less adversarial."

"Or you'll scream?"

"And pull my panties down to my knees. Sit."

Trager sat next to her. She moved closer to where their hips touched and placed her hand on his thigh. "That's better, don't you agree?"

Looking straight ahead, Trager nodded. "Threats are not conducive to seduction."

Her breath tickled his ear as she whispered into it. "All I'm doing is trying to convince you I need to get out of here. I need a man who will help me get out and protect me once I'm free. Lucky for me I find you attractive." She gave his ear a slow lick. Her tongue sent a current straight to his crotch.

"Would Pierre seek revenge if you left him?"

"No, not him."

"Dankov?"

"He kills only men." Her hand moved to Trager's crotch. "Let's think positive, darling. You'll be rich, able to pursue whatever interests you have--think of us in the Riviera with a view of the sparkling Mediterranean. Me in your bed, submissive to your demands, ready to fulfill your fantasies."

The conjured image was tempting. "Will you excuse me for a second?" Trager stood, wishing his erection down, and went to the booze cabinet. "Another drink?"

"Thank you, no."

Trager poured another cognac and sensed Leonora come from behind. Her chin rested on his shoulder, her hands encircled his waist. "I'll buy Simone's Land Rover. During one of the teas, I'll sneak inside and cover myself with a tarp. Then you drive to Uganda. Don't you think that's quite clever, darling?"

Trager placed his glass on top of the cabinet. The feel of her breasts rubbing against his back was clouding his mind. His earlier fear had evaporated. Her fingers slid down and stroked him.

"That's nice, he feels good waking up. I want him."

He turned. Her arm wrapped his neck and pulled him closer against swaying hips, an open mouth and searching tongue. Trager's hand went under the skirt up a leg, inside silk.

"Yoo-hoo." Simone's voice rang from downstairs.

Trager realized he had two handfuls of buttocks, that somehow he had turned around and was pressing Leonora against the wall. He let go of her. She remained leaning against the wall, her eyes closed and breathing heavily.

"Yoo-hoo," Simone repeated.

Leonora opened her eyes. "You may come up."

Simone emerged, placed her head over her arms on top of the stairway rail. "I hope I'm not interrupting, but I must return to the office."

"And I can't be late for the tea at the Children's Hospital."

To Trager, Leonora said, "Darling, see you at the Women's League tea on Friday. Thank you very much for a wonderful lunch."

Simone stepped out of the spiral staircase well. "Have a safe trip." She waved and went out.

Engines started in front of the house. Trager took a deep breath. His legs felt weak. He leaned on the buffet.

Diamonds scattered on the carpet gave him a jolt.

He leaped, scooped the sparklers, returned them to the little sack, and rushed outside. His jaw sagged as the tail of the escorting Land Rover vanished behind the fence.

He stuck the bag into his trouser pocket. He had no safe place to keep the small fortune. What would he do? He couldn't telephone Leonora. Keeping the diamonds until Friday was a risky proposition.

Chapter 23

A slight chill lingered in the air. The sun was about to come up when a new-looking, green Toyota Land Cruiser pulled into the driveway. The truck certainly appeared trustworthier than Simone's beat up heap. The pickup was modified for hunting with a bench seat in the back and an empty rifle rack bolted to the back of the cab.

The driver, wearing a drill bush jacket, got out. "Good morning, Mr. Trager," he said in English and picked up Trager's duffel. He placed it into a cage-like storage compartment in the rear of the truck.

Trager also wore a bush jacket, which hid the Glock very nicely. The bag of diamonds fit easily in one of the ample pockets.

There was something shifty about the driver, who seemed to avoid making eye contact. Maybe Longo had placed his own man to keep track of Trager's movements. He remembered Simone saying that Daniel was a good guide. "What happened to Daniel?"

The driver moved a tent bag to the side to make room for the duffel.

"He got sick."

"And your name?"

"Komora, sir." He covered everything with a tarp and closed the rear doors. "We are ready to go."

Trager didn't like the substitution. It could well be innocent. Komora looked competent. Trager placed his bag with camera, binoculars and a few practical odds and ends in the cab and got in.

~

The first part of the road was familiar. Trager had driven it with Simone and then with Dankov. He remembered Dankov's turnoff and said, "Turn right on that track."

Komora gave him a strange look, not showing any intent of following Trager's instructions.

"Go ahead, turn. There's a good view from the top of the hill, and I have a thermos in my bag."

Komora eased the accelerator and veered into the track.

"Keep your speed down. Bumps do terrible things to my back," Trager said. He wanted to keep their dust down. If anyone was following, they might not see where they had turned off. Halfway up the hill, Trager glanced in the direction from which they had come. A red plume of dust rose about two miles behind.

"Here nice view." Komora stopped.

Trager pulled his pistol out. "Keep going. Remember I'm the boss."

Komora gave him an alarmed look then drove on.

Once over the ridgeline, Trager said, "Stop here, get out of the truck and lie on the ground."

Komora opened the door, glanced back at Trager's Glock. Trager slid across the seat. "No sudden moves, I'm a nervous customer."

Out of the cab, Komora lowered himself carefully and stretched out on the ground, his arms extended forward. Trager took spare bootlaces out of the handbag. He patted Komora for weapons, found a nine-millimeter Beretta. "Nice. Hands behind your back."

He tied Komora's thumbs together. "Get up and sit on the bumper." With the other lace, Trager secured Komora's hands to the bumper. "You try anything funny, I'll drive the truck forward. You can imagine what'll happen to you."

Although it was still relatively cool, Komora had broken into a sweat.

Trager took binoculars and crept up the ridgeline.

The other vehicle, a long wheelbase passenger Land Rover with four or five men inside, had almost reached the turnoff with no sign of slowing. The white license plate indicated a government vehicle.

His worst fears confirmed, Trager returned to the truck.

Komora still sat tied to the bumper, sweating. Trager removed his wallet and spread the contents on top of the hood. Five dollars worth of Z-franks, a posed photo of Komora and a woman staring at the camera with a boy and a girl smiling. A driver's license issued to Albert Matungi and a ZSS ID in the same name. "Well, Mr. Matungi, how nice to meet you."

Matungi twisted his head, his face showing fear or desperation. "This is a fabulous photo op." Trager took his camera out, snapped several shots of the documents. He then took a picture of Matungi sitting on the bumper. "Colonel Longo will love seeing one of his men in action."

Matungi lowered his head. His body shook.

"Not having a good day, are we? You cooperate with me and things may turn out okay for you."

Matungi looked up.

"Is that Land Rover following us?"

Matungi nodded. "To protect you."

Trager laughed. He was sure Matungi was lying. "Why?"

"I don't know."

Trager sighed theatrically. "Your operation has failed. We'll return to Turako, and I'll personally deliver you to Longo. Perhaps *he* will explain things to me."

Matungi gave him a pleading look. "They won't hurt you, but if you pull a gun on them, they'll shoot."

"Why would I pull a gun on my protectors?"

Lines of concentration formed on Matungi's forehead. "What happens if I tell you the truth?"

Trager gave him his best smile. "You'll work for me, you'll become a CIA agent. If you doublecross us, we hand the photos over to Longo. If you're loyal, you'll be rewarded. You have to decide *now*." In getting to the truth, the carrot worked better than the stick. "Tell me, what's the real reason for those men following us?"

"To commit a robbery."

Shit. Trager thought of the diamonds in his pocket. How in the hell had Longo found out about them?

No way unless Leonora had . . . "When is the robbery going to take place?"

"After we finish visit to Zamani."

"What will they rob me of?"

"Everything."

"Why wait until after Zamani. Why not today?"

Matungi shrugged. "I don't know. All I know is they take everything to a safe house to give to the chief."

"Who's in charge of the operation?"

"Captain Kongoni."

"Kongoni? That's an antelope."

"That is his working name. He is the boss of surveillance."

If the man in charge of surveillance was messing about with him, and Longo himself wanted the robbery loot, the trip to Zamani took a significance that escaped Trager. Something was about to happen there, so Trager decided to continue the safari.

~

At first, Matungi's nerves showed; he stalled the engine then ground the gears. But, after two hours of driving, he seemed settled in his new situation. The road kept reminding Trager of Simone. The way she looked at him from time to time made him think she liked him.

They drove across the Majidogo bridge. On the main street of the village where Trager bought the tamarind seeds, a Land Rover was parked in front of the police station. Two men lounged nearby.

"Is that them?" Trager asked, studying the men.

"Yes, Captain Kongoni must be inside the police station." Matungi smiled faintly. "He must be telephoning and going crazy."

One of the loungers on the street ran inside the police station.

Trager chuckled. "His mind is being put to rest."

About two-hundred meters beyond the village, a rusting yellow sign with fading black letters showed an arrow to the right. It read: Mazuri 47km, Zamani 65km.

Matungi turned into the narrow road with a light down-slope that wound through dense forest. Often, the tops of the trees created a shady canopy. After passing a sawmill, the road became a little-used track wide enough for one vehicle.

Matungi said, "Someplace here, they stop us and do the robbery."

"Any specific place?"

"No, plenty of good places."

If he turned around now, he would still be able to surprise the ambushers and get back to Turako safely, but curiosity drove him on. He observed the thick underbrush on both sides of the road favoring the hunted. Satisfied with how he would deal with the ambush, Trager hummed a silly song about bears going on a picnic.

The road kept going downhill. The air became muggier. A group of men in raggedy shorts and carrying adzes stood aside and waved as they drove by.

"Years ago, when Europeans came to hunt, there was a hunting camp not far from here. They got very good leopard trophies. I worked as a gun-bearer. That's how I learned English."

Trager was pleased with Matungi's emergence from his state of shock. By evening, maybe with the help of a little whiskey, he would hopefully become garrulous.

An ox cart loaded with timber blocked the track.

Matungi had to go back about a hundred meters to a place where he was able to give way. While waiting for the oxen to pass, Trager asked, "Is there another road out of Zamani?"

"Long time ago, there was a ferry across the river. Now it is abandoned."

Trager filed this information and remembered a track shown on the map with a notation, *no longer in use*. He could probably swim across the river and walk the track on the other side. He hadn't spent time in Recon School for nothing. He discarded that option. Longo wasn't after him but after something he carried or would carry. Trager wondered where in the truck he could hide the diamonds.

The creak of the cart's huge wheels had a soothing effect. If it weren't for the knowledge he had walked into a trap, he would be enjoying this trip.

Matungi and the cart driver, who walked next to the oxen prodding them with a stick, exchanged a few words in Wussi.

"Did you tell him to pass a message to your friends?"

"No. Honestly. I asked him if he had seen any big cats." Matungi smiled. "Old habit. I like the hunt. That is what drew me to the security service."

"You like your work?"

"I'm assigned to watch foreigners. It is easy work. I spend time in hotels."

"Ever watch Tony Bond?"

"Now maybe six months, we don't watch him."

"Why is that?"

"He buys tea, is strictly commercial."

"But why were you watching him in the first place?"

"He used to have contacts with suspect politicians from the past government. Somebody reported he offered to give arms."

"As a hunter, you must have a good sense of smell. What does your instinct tell you?"

Matungi gave him a long stare. "Like you, he is a hunter. A treacherous hunter."

About an hour later, they began to hear the sound of rushing water, which gradually increased. Matungi said, "Shaitani falls. Biggest waterfall in the country."

Without warning, the nature of the terrain changed from sandy to rocky. The forest ended abruptly. Matungi put the four wheel drive into low gear. The truck crawled up a steep incline of loose rock. It looked like a volcanic dike protruding from the side of the mountain. Matungi stopped at the top of the dike. They were at the edge of a precipice. Turbulent water rushed several hundred feet below. With awe, Trager watched the waterfall slightly behind him. Roaring brown water turned white as it tumbled off a black basalt shelf.

He studied the river. Swimmable. Turbulent water near the falls would keep crocks away.

Ahead, the track hewn out of rock dropped abruptly. Trager wondered how the truck would negotiate the steep descent.

Matungi eased the clutch and let the truck roll over the edge. The vehicle lurched and jolted as tires hit loose rock. At one point, it appeared they were going to tip over and fall into the river. Trager had trouble visualizing Leonora taking a trip like this. Maybe she and Bamondo came to Zamani by helicopter. Simone would have said, "Perfect place for ambush, no?" With an inner chuckle, Trager agreed.

The truck bumped to the bottom of the dike. Matungi let out a loud sigh. "Could I have a cigarette?"

Trager lit a cigarette for himself as well.

"The Valley of the Sorcerers. Neither Bassis nor the Wussis across the river come here."

Slowly, Matungi drove into the shade of giant fig trees.

Zamani was a triangular lip of flat land covered by fig trees. To call it a valley was an exaggeration. It was maybe a hundred meters wide at the bottom end.

Throughout Africa, fig trees were closely associated with magic and often were sacred. Trager felt as if he had entered an enormous cathedral.

The roots of the trees made him think of pews.

A row of square columns, each about three-foot square and six feet tall, drew his attention. "What's that?"

Matungi answered gravely. "The tombs of the wizards."

Trager got off the truck and inspected the first column. It was made of dark red brick, almost brown. He had seen brick like that in the ruins of Moejandaro on the mouth of the Indus River, a city that predated Alexander's conquest.

Simone's words during dinner with the Bamondos came to mind: *"One of my little secrets is that I know the location of this lost city. It is on the Kenya coast. I even have a Roman brick to prove it."* This was far from the coast, but he would like to compare Simone's brick with what he was looking at. Simone had mentioned something about this possibly being one of King Solomon's outposts. He thought of Longo's greedy expression when he opened the box with the cut diamonds.

"For the moment, you are safe. Nobody will dare do anything here." Matungi said, interrupting Trager's train of thought. "This is the place where the ancient kings of Zengawal came to be blessed by the wizards."

Trager took some pictures. With the roll finished, he put it in the pocket with the diamonds. Carrying a fortune with him and knowing he was going to be robbed, drained the magic from his surroundings, which had taken a sinister aspect.

Matungi pointed at a huge boulder, the size of a small house, that must have rolled off the mountain. "There's a small spring on the other side. I will pitch your tent there."

"Okay."

"*Bouge pas,*" a voice said.

Trager didn't move. The expression on Matungi's face indicated this was not in his program.

Chapter 24

A tube-like leopard skin hat made the tall man look towering. A leopard skin wrapped around his midriff. A black and white colubus monkey cape hung from his shoulders. His regal appearance was enhanced by a heavy gold chain around his neck. He stepped from behind a tree with a finger pointing up. Trager looked in the direction the man pointed. Pygmies stood on tree branches holding large bows with arrows pointing at him.

"*C'est pas possible*," Matungi said in astonishment.

"The little people have come," the man in the hat said. He said something to the Pygmies, who returned the arrows to their quivers and clambered to the ground. A half-dozen elderly Pygmies surrounded Trager and inspected him with curiosity.

The man in the hat said, "Follow me."

"How did the Pygmies get here?" Matungi asked in a low tone.

As they followed the man in the hat, the aroma of roasting meat reached Trager's nostrils.

They entered a street with crumbling adobe walls. Once upon a time, this had been a sizeable village. The street ended in a square at the foot of a cliff overgrown with vines. Two Pygmies roasted a warthog over a heap of charcoal. On one side of the square, surrounded by a pile of stone debris, stood what might have been a tall tower. It made Trager think of Mayan pyramids.

"The little people are honoring us," the man in the hat said. He sat on a log. With a gesture, he invited Trager and Matungi to sit, too.

One of the Pygmies handed out cheap plastic mugs, another poured a whitish liquid out of a gourd.

"Welcome to Zamani," the man in the hat said.

Trager asked, "Are you Funga da Milango?"

On hearing this, the Pygmies gathered and prostrated themselves in front of Trager. "Funga da milango, funga da milango." They repeated several times. Then they got up and danced around the roasting pig, chanting funga da milango.

Totally puzzled, Trager asked Matungi. "What's going on?"

"I don't know. From what little I understand, they are saying it's true, it's true."

Trager raised his voice above the din of the Pygmies. "What is your name?"

The man in the hat laughed. "I have no name, but everyone knows me."

Trager heard a strange noise next to him. His eyes bulging, Matungi had turned ashen. "The Ngoloko." He made choking sounds, swayed and fell to the ground, spilling his drink. Had the man drunk from his cup, Trager would have thought he had been poisoned.

Trager felt surrounded by people gone mad.

The man in the hat got up and came to where Matungi had fallen. Like a doctor, he lifted Matungi's eyelids. "In about an hour, he will recover. Let us feast." He yelled something at the Pygmies, who stopped dancing and began carving large pieces of pig.

One of the Pygmies impaled a chunk of meat on a stick and handed it to Trager. "Chamwanamuma," he said.

"Eat, drink, be happy," the man in the hat said.

"Who's the Ngoloko?" Trager asked.

The man laughed in his basso profundo voice. "Shaitani, the devil, but not as high up. Everyone fears the Ngoloko, especially in this most sacred of places."

Trager was sure he was in the presence of a witch doctor. Judging by his dress, a powerful and prosperous one. To show respect, and that he was not afraid, he took a swig from his mug. The drink was refreshingly bittersweet.

The witch doctor nodded, his face expressing satisfaction. "Palm beer. It is good for you, takes away the heat."

Tentatively, Trager asked, "May I take photographs?"

To his surprise, the witch doctor answered, "Yes."

Trager took pictures of Pygmies gorging themselves and of the regal man in the hat.

Matungi came to, shaking his head.

The witch doctor asked something in Wussi.

Matungi got on his knees, his hands clasped in a gesture of pleading.

The man in the hat went into a long speech. Matungi listened and nodded frequently.

The man in the hat turned to Trager. "I have suspended his curse, but if he gets more evil ideas, he dies, and his children will die. Now *you* have the *dawa*, the power over him. Through your eyes, the curse will strike him."

Now Trager understood what had happened to Matungi. Realizing he was in the presence of a powerful witch doctor, he must have believed the witch doctor could read his mind. The power of witchcraft was in the recipient's belief of its power. In Africa, if a man thought he was under a curse of death, it didn't take long for him to die.

The witch doctor told Matungi, "Take picture of me and my guest."

Matungi took pictures of them standing together and shaking hands.

Trager found the warthog to his liking. It tasted like strong pork. He washed it down with palm brew the Pygmies kept topping up.

Maybe it was the beer or the atmosphere in the sacred grove, but Trager felt as safe and secure as he did surrounded by Dankov's soldiers. Nothing would happen to him while in this sanctuary. Tomorrow, on his return, would be another matter. He would worry about it when the time came.

When the warthog was nothing but bones smoldering on top of the charcoal, the witch doctor said, "You will now wash in the sacred spring."

The spring was behind the ruined tower. Water came out of the rocks and collected into a bamboo pipe. The stream flowed into a shallow basin carved in stone.

The witch doctor took Trager's head and made him bow into the stream of water that was warm as it wet his hair and ran down his back.

After chanting a few words, the witch doctor let go of Trager's head. "Your soul is now clean. After your death, your soul will come to live in this sacred place."

For a moment, Trager felt giddy, had to grab a vine that came down from the cliff not to fall. The spell of dizziness must have lasted longer than he thought. When he regained his balance, the witch doctor was gone.

Trager spent about an hour looking for him but couldn't find him anywhere.

Only the pygmies remained. Silent like statues, they sat on tree branches seemingly oblivious to the activity going on beneath them.

By nightfall, Matungi had completely recovered from his fit. With professional efficiency, he had erected a tent with ample headroom and comfortable camp bed for Trager. For himself, Matungi pitched a small tent next to the truck, and vanished into it as soon as he was done.

After twilight, fruit bats came out, darting between tree branches and pinging in the darkness. Trager sat in a camp chair outside his tent

Between the branches of the trees, a new moon headed for an early rest while the sun washed itself in the rivers to come out the next morning bright and powerful. Or so believed most African tribes.

Trager was absorbed by the magic of the place. He sipped his whiskey, feeling almost happy. Each trip to Africa was an unforgettable experience. This time, he may have come to die. He touched the bag of diamonds in his pocket. Even if they weren't his, he wouldn't give them up. The pseudo-robbers had no idea of the fierce resistance they would encounter. *Funga da milango.* If he made it back to Turako, Simone had some explaining to do. Trager watched a Pygmy silhouetted by the moon. Simone, the Pygmy lady, was thick with the little guys. She had given him a password that had thrown them into a frenzy.

~

Shortly before dawn, Trager got up and quietly left his tent. Sacred place or not, dawn was a favorite time to strike. Under concealment of darkness, the hunter moved into position. With first light, the fear of night gone, the prey presented a good target.

There was no sign of the Pygmies.

From behind a ruined wall, Trager watched Matungi emerge from his tent and brew tea on a camp stove.

Night was completely gone when Matungi, tea mug in hand, headed for Trager's tent.

Trager came out of his hide. "Where are the Pygmies?"

Matungi stopped, startled. "Then it was not a dream?"

"No."

"I think we saw spirits of the ancients."

After accepting the tea, Trager went into the ruins. No sign of a fire. No footprints. The logs they had sat on were rolled to the sides of the square.

The only evidence of yesterday's event was the rancid aftertaste of palm brew in his mouth. When Trager returned to the truck, Matungi was already striking camp.

Trager poured himself another mug-full of sweet tea with condensed milk. At the first sign of ambush, he would jump out of the truck into the jungle. He would be in sight of the ambushers for a couple of seconds max. Longo's goons would have a hell of a time finding him. If he was quiet, they would have to spread out. He'd shoot the first to come close to him, then move, hide, shoot. He'd get them one at a time.

~

The roar of the waterfall grew louder as they emerged from the sacred grove. Matungi slammed on the brakes. Trager grabbed Matungi by his jacket before he could jump out of the truck and aimed the Glock at the terrified driver.

Matungi pointed at the top of the rocky track. *"Askari."*

Trager didn't see a soldier. He peered through binoculars. Behind a reddish rock, a bit of green protruded. That was all.

"Reverse," Trager ordered.

Tires spun, throwing a shower of pebbles forward.

"Easy."

Back under the cover of trees, Trager got out of the truck. So much for jumping into the jungle. He looked at the cliff he would have to climb if he was to outflank the ambush. Forget it, he'd rather die. "I'll swim the river. Good luck with your buddies."

Matungi grabbed Trager by the sleeve. "Askari, not ZSS."

A soldier in green camouflage appeared at the top of the rock dike, waving a rifle. An amplified voice boomed, *"Idi siuda,"* come here in Russian.

Trager took a deep breath of relief, climbed back into the truck. His luck was holding.

You may run into one of Igor's patrols. Trager wondered what else was included in Simone's script.

Vadim, the lieutenant he had met at the fort, and five African soldiers waited at the top. Trager dismounted and shook hands with the young Russian officer.

Vadim said, "We saw fresh track going to the magic place, came to take a look. Now I'll put two soldiers on your truck but you'll have to eat my dust. *Haraka endelea.*"

Two soldiers with a radio got into the rear seat of the Land Cruiser.

The military Land Rover started moving, barely giving time for the machine gun crew to hop on board.

Thank you, Simone. Trager chuckled. He would like to see the expressions on the ZSS men's faces when they saw the Land Rover crammed with heavily armed soldiers.

Vadim had told Matungi to drive no slower than thirty-five kilometers an hour. Not half an hour had passed when the soldiers in the back rapped on the cab's roof. One of them spoke through the rear window. *Iko matata kidogo mbele."* Small problem ahead. *"Endelea pole-pole."* Go slow.

Trager heard bolts sliding and the soldiers chambering ammunition.

Two minutes later, they came to the Land Rover stopped at a curve. The truck was empty, the machinegun gone.

The soldiers jumped off the truck and vanished in the jungle on both sides of the road. Trager opened the door and rolled into cover.

There was thrashing in the undergrowth some distance ahead.

Trager seethed with frustration. He wanted to be out there with the soldiers flushing out the ambushers, but not having trained with them, he'd only be a hindrance.

Several minutes passed.

Somebody broke a twig. There was the sound of a large animal crashing through the bush.

"*Arretes toi, zimama.*"

A short burst of automatic fire ripped the quiet of the forest.

It sounded like the soldiers found someone.

Carefully, Trager crept forward until he was beyond the Land Rover.

About thirty meters ahead, several logs that had apparently fallen off an ox cart, blocked the road. Not a bad idea. The scene would not seem alarming to an ambush candidate.

A man emerged from the forest and stood in the middle of the road, his hands on the back of his head. A few minutes later, another man came out, stumbling as if pushed.

An engine started somewhere in the distance.

Shortly after, the government Land Rover came into view, driving slowly. It had three bullet holes through its windshield. Vadim got out. "City slickers in the forest make big mistake."

A soldier came up with the two prisoners. *"Watu he sema iko serkali."* These people say they are government.

Vadim inspected their wallets. "Have them clear the road." He then opened the hood and removed the distributor cap, and tossed it inside his vehicle. "They can walk back."

Trager put his hand into his pocket and fingered the diamond bag. His chances of returning them to Leonora had improved. His fingers touched the rolls of exposed film. The only thing he had acquired was pictures. Did Longo want pictures of Zamani?

Of course. Bingo. He wanted photographs of the witch doctor. The answer was too simplistic, but Trager thought he was getting close to something.

Longo would not be pleased with this outcome and would react. Whatever it was he wanted, he could just as easily take it in the city where the night belonged to him.

Chapter 25

The return to Turako was uneventful. Dankov's patrol escorted them to the Majidogo Bridge and returned to the fort. During the drive, Matungi was in a somber mood. Longo, he insisted, would want to know why the ambush had failed and would suspect Matungi of treason. Trager told him to stick to the truth as much as possible, but skip the events of the first detour. Falling back on old agent handling habits, he lied. He told Matungi the CIA, which was more powerful than the ZSS, would protect him. They made arrangements for meeting places and danger signals. Matungi gave him the addresses of several safe houses, an organizational chart of the ZSS, and the names of some of the officers. As far as he knew, Madame Kanzo was not a member of the organization but a co-optee. It was not a good idea to say "no" to the ZSS.

Not too bad for a couple of days work. What the hell was he doing? He had begun a penetration of a hostile service, but on whose behalf? The question came to Trager as a shocking self-discovery. He was still an intelligence operative, but one without a country, an agency or an assignment.

The villa had the feel of home. Trager lifted the floor of the ugly armoire in his bedroom and placed his exposed films inside the empty space below. He then took a couple of fresh spools and wound the tails of the film in, making them look like exposed film, and left the rolls in the bag with the camera.

As Trager was checking his e-mail, Wangohi brought in a sealed envelope and placed it on his desk.

Inside was a note in Russian. Trager recognized Simone's child-like Cyrillic script.

> *Dear Johnny*
>
> *I check parking lot. When your truck return I know you come back. Go to hotel Metropole at seven have drink in terrace. Take taxi to market. Walk into small alley and go to rear entrance of Okapi Bar. We have drink together. Tell watchman you come see Ishtar.*
>
> *Hugs,*
> *Simone*

Hugs? That didn't sound like Simone, but the rest of the note did. Fatigue dissipated. Trager looked at his watch, 5:37. He had a bit over an hour to wash off the dust, get rid of the kinks of the road, get out and make sure he wasn't followed. Not much time at all.

In the shower, he thought of the muggers outside the Okapi and meeting Tony Bond. He was pretty sure now, this had been a staged farce.

This time he was carrying a pistol.

Trager went downtown on foot, detoured a couple of blocks, entered a bookstore, and bought *Time* magazine. He went into a bar, had a beer and bought a pack of Roosters. So far, he saw no sign of a tail.

By seven o'clock, it was already dark and he sat in the Metropole's Terrace Bar.

Less than five minutes went by. He saw Simone's Land Rover drive past in the lane nearest the park. After finishing his beer, he took a taxi and got off in the parking lot behind the Central Market, which was still open.

Inside the cavernous pavilion, the smell of spices mixed with that of rotting produce. Wickerwork and other stands dealing in non-perishables were closing for the night. Sweepers pushed piles of garbage down the aisles. Some vendors were already asleep, sharing their display tables with unsold products covered with gunnysacks.

Anyone following him would have stood out like a wart in a beauty pageant. Trager stopped and turned while lighting a cigarette. No warts. Reasonably sure he was clean, Trager went out through a different door, crossed the street and entered the back alley. He wondered how he would recognize the entrance to the Okapi.

He needn't have worried. A stack of empty beer crates stood next to a metal door.

Trager twisted the door handle and pushed the door open. The same shaved-head bruiser who had greeted him that first night in Turako pointed his shotgun at Trager. "*Peut pas entrer par ici.*"

"*Je cherche Ishtar.*"

The giant stepped aside and pointed the shotgun at a narrow stairway. "Welcome, first door to the left."

Trager went up the ill-lit stairs. He stood aside and let a waiter with a tray of empty beer bottles pass. On the second floor, a hotel-like corridor gave access to a number of doors. From an open door came the unmistakable clack of mahjong tiles.

As instructed, Trager opened the first door to the left and found himself in a little sitting room furnished in standard safe-house style. A red sofa and chairs with wide, curving wooden arms looked well worn, not quite threadbare. A corner table with an oriental vase stuffed with foxtails gave the room a minimal touch of homey comfort. On a lacquered coffee table sporting numerous chips stood a tray with a bottle of Bell's Scotch, two glasses, an ice bucket and two bottles of Perrier.

Looking for a possible escape route, Trager tried a door by the far corner. He entered a minimally furnished bedroom with a double bed. Another door led into a tiny bathroom with a shower stall. With some bitterness, Trager thought about Simone's intimate confessions. *Lots of wasted space for an efficient whorehouse. Maybe not for a high-class hooker.*

Back in the sitting room, he poured himself a scotch, added a splash of Perrier. The windowless room was uncomfortably stuffy. If he had not seen Simone drive by in front of the hotel, Trager would have been getting nervous. If this was a trap, he had no avenues of escape. He sat on the sofa, his pistol between two cushions, just in case.

He was half way through his scotch when the door opened.

"You're clean. No one followed you," Simone said. Instead of wearing her habitual pantaloons, she looked chic in an exquisitely tailored black silk safari suit. The collar showed a modest hint of cleavage. Trager's heart accelerated as he stood.

"You're the most beautiful thing I've seen in ages."

Simone tossed her shoulder bag on one of the chairs and sat on the other. "Save your compliments and be a *real* gentleman. Pour me a drink."

"Ishtar, the Summerian goddess of love and war. Is that what you are?"

"I like the sound of it." She made herself comfortable in the chair, crossed her legs, revealing sensible shoes. She accepted the drink and took a sip. "How was your trip?"

"Funga da Milango," Trager muttered sarcastically. "You really set me up."

Simone smiled. "I wanted to make it simple, without the drama of passwords."

"Longo wanted to know who gave me the idea of going there."

"Did you tell him?"

"Yeah, a guidebook."

Her businesslike face for a second melted into that of warm affection. "I'm happy to see you back. I hear the ZSS tried to ambush you."

"Yeah, good thing Dankov's cavalry showed up."

Simone nodded. "Why would Longo do that? Any idea?"

Trager looked Simone in the eye. "You need to ask?"

Simone looked amused. "But do *you* know?"

"I have a dear female friend who has successfully bamboozled me a couple of times and never gives a straight answer. She generally avoids my company, but tonight she invited me for a debriefing. I enjoy your company, it's a pleasure having a drink with you. I would like to see you more often. But I'm not paying by being the fool."

She tilted her head to one side. "Running out of patience with me?" A light chirpy laugh and a quick smile made Trager feel like telling her anything she wanted to know.

He lit a cigarette.

"Longo thinks you have returned to the country to steal the Utabu."

"Sure, I just bought a treasure map in the market."

"And you went to the valley of the wizards."

"Where I was met by your Pygmies and honored by the man in the hat."

Simone suppressed a guffaw. "Man in the hat, that's funny. What name did he use?"

"Ngoloko."

"Quite suitable. Longo will torture and kill to find out Ngoloko's identity. The man you have met is Babaku, the country's chief witch doctor. Someone tipped off Longo that you two were going to meet. Neither Longo nor anyone in the ZSS would dare to interfere in Zamani. Longo is after your film."

"And you tipped off Longo."

"Johnny. You don't think much of me."

"Who, then?"

"Someone in the chain of messengers." Her amused smile returned. "Longo's men are presently searching your house."

That didn't surprise Trager. He let out a bitter chuckle. "So you are the distraction."

She shook her head. "Longo won't find anything. I removed the film ten minutes after you left the house. I almost fell for your decoy rolls. It took me less than two minutes to find them. As I was going out the door, I remembered the expression on your face when I pointed the pistol at you. A sort of curious expression, and then you smiled, saying, 'Do I get a cigarette before the execution?' I told myself, Johnny is a pro. Now the films are safe. We'll keep them in Fort Chaipangani."

"Dankov's place?"

She nodded. "Do you still have Leonora's diamonds?"

"In my pocket. Can you give them back to her?"

"You take care of your own business with that woman," Simone said with surprising venom.

"I thought you were the best of chums."

"Sisters in misery." She gulped her drink and extended her glass toward Trager. "May I have a refill?"

While Trager plunked ice cubes into the glass, she said, "Sometimes, I have trouble not being bitchy. The stress of the situation gets on my nerves."

Trager handed her the refill. As she took it, he clasped her hand with both of his. "If you'd quit playing with me and be straightforward, I might be able to help you in a more intelligent way. I am on your side--I think."

Simone smiled, leaned forward, and kissed the tips of Trager's fingers. She smelled of honeysuckle. "I know, but too much is at stake. If Longo grabs you--and there are others, too--you will talk." She tugged her hand free, sat back in her chair.

To slow down his pounding heart, Trager lit a cigarette. Simone was driving him crazy. The little rewards she gave him were the same as drops of water to someone dying of thirst, or maybe just meager crumbs to a beggar.

"Why did you arrange the Zamani theater?"

"You needed a starting point. You've met Longo's enemy, hopefully got an ally. Johnny, I don't know what you're doing, but you can't go at it alone."

"You could have told me."

"You didn't need to know."

All his life, he'd been hearing that crap. Her words triggered a furious reaction. Trager felt he was about to explode. He got up with the intention of leaving.

Simone sprung up and blocked his exit. "Don't be rash and stupid." Her expression made another turn into softness. She smiled. "You were going to leave your pistol behind."

Trager felt like a fool. "You drive me nuts."

She pushed him back gently. "Sit down and let me fix you a drink." The touch of her hand on his chest had a surprisingly calming effect. Trager sat down, stuck the pistol into his waistband.

She handed him a drink and sat on the other end of the sofa. "I wish you would trust me. I feel I need to explain things to you and end up talking too much. Let's be friends for a moment. They have a decent Wienerschnitzel here and I'm hungry."

"Okay," Trager said with resignation.

Simone pressed a button on the wall. A few minutes later, a waiter came in. Simone ordered. When the waiter left, she said, "You'll see--everything looks brighter after you have eaten. No?"

"There were Pygmies in Zamani. That's not their area."

"It's a sacred place for them, too. Later, you should visit the Loldawa Pygmy country.

"Supposedly, you are *the* authority on Pygmies, will you show it to me?"

Simone gave him her rare flashing smile. "But of course, *mon cher*. One of the reasons I wanted to meet with you was to talk about that."

Trager's mood lightened. The idea of spending several days with Simone was a happy one.

"I have to go to Loldawa in two weeks. If you make arrangements with Madame Kanzo, we could meet there. Give yourself at least a week. You'll be in for a fascinating experience."

The waiter brought in the food and a bottle of Rhine wine.

Trager squeezed lime juice on his schnitzel. "Where did you learn to write Russian?"

Simone jerked her thumb backward. "In Russia. You had no problem reading my writing? I write secret messages in Russian. It stumps Longo."

"How did you and Igor meet?"

"That's a romantic story."

Trager had trouble seeing Simone as romantic. She was attractive, sexy, fascinating, and outrageous, but certainly not romantic.

"I was studying in Bosnia. When war broke out, I volunteered with the Red Crescent as a nurse. I was in an ambulance and suddenly my driver was shot dead. We had driven into the middle of a battle in a narrow gorge. Igor came out of nowhere and pulled me out of the overturned ambulance. Shells were exploding everywhere. He carried me down to a brook and covered me with his body. I felt safe and grateful and . . . we made love."

That damn Dankov.

"Though he was fighting on the Serb side, he protected Muslim civilians. The man who shot up our ambulance was later executed."

It was a bitch competing with someone like that. Trager wondered what sort of power Dankov had over women. How did he get away with bedding Leonora and having Simone, who was obviously in love with him, cover for him?

"I don't understand how you put up with Igor's behavior toward you."

Simone stopped eating and gave him a bitter smile. "What other choice do I have? I want him to succeed. He helps me succeed. It's love and hate. It's symbiosis. But we do have magical moments."

"You seem surrendered to fate."

"When you abandon the mediocre and create your own life away from the path of the Lumpen proletariat, you must suffer. As an intelligence professional, you did great or maybe foul deeds for the benefit of others. Only now you seem to want to make your own way in the world. Johnny, I'm also helping *you* achieve greatness."

"You sound like the Fairy Godmother."

Simone laughed. "Maybe that's what I am. The trouble with you men is that pressures below your waist cloud your brains."

"And women don't have sexual drives." Trager was irked by her patronizing. "You admitted earlier you couldn't help yourself with Dankov."

"Maybe because he's feminine."

Trager almost choked. He looked at Simone with astonishment. He had never expected her say something so stupid.

Simone smiled. "Like a woman, he uses sex as a weapon."

"You seem to be an expert on female weaponry. Is this one of your workshops?"

"The arts of the courtesan can be effective. Your suggestion that I might be a practitioner of the arts, was a blow to me. It was a closely guarded secret. I should have acted indignant and put doubt in your mind. Instead, I confirmed it, hoping you'd get out of my way." She shook her head. "Believe it or not, I wish I had your respect."

Trager took her hand and squeezed gently. "I don't understand you, but I do respect you."

She squeezed back. "Like Igor says, you're a great friend. Give me a minute to compose myself."

Simone took four golf-ball-sized Belgian hand grenades out of her shoulder bag and began juggling. "This relaxes me."

Trager watched with amusement. At least she wasn't doing anything funny with the pins.

"Now, about respect and that nasty, cheap comment about this being my workshop. Is that what you think? You think this is a bordello?" She appeared to be talking to the hand grenades. "This is where Igor stays when he is in town. If I spend the night here, he sleeps on the sofa."

Trager's cheeks seemed to burn. Again, he had made a fool of himself. Simone was right about the pressures below the waist. "Where do you live? I don't even have your phone number."

"In a government apartment, and the phones are tapped. It's best we're not seen together."

With a quick movement, Simone added the bottle of scotch to the grenades she was juggling. She sang, "*Sur le pont d'Avignon, on y dance tous au rond.*"

Without warning, she tossed the bottle at Trager.

He caught it with both hands.

"Good reflexes. Johnny, tell me something about yourself, your family." Although she was now looking at him, the grenades kept coming down into her hands and shooting up with automatic precision.

For a moment, Trager dwelt on the memory of a garden, a dog and piano music. "My father was a disabled Korean War veteran. Part of his skull was stainless steel, and he had epileptic fits. My mother was a concert pianist with arthritis. We lived in a New York tenement where the other kids called me 'Son of Frankie'.

"Doesn't sound like a happy childhood."

"It wasn't bad; my parents and I were very close."

"You're lucky. Catch." She tossed the grenades one after the other to Trager, who caught them and dropped them on his lap.

Simone poured herself a glass of wine. "Ever been married?"

"No. My job interfered." Trager returned her grenades. "I don't think mugging you would be a great idea."

"Magic trick." With a loud snap, a black spring-loaded blade materialized in her hand. "I feel quite safe in this town." With another snap the blade vanished. With her palm open, she reached for Trager's ear. Look what you've been hiding in your ear." She showed him a hand grenade.

"Amazing, you're also a prestidigitator."

"I like to show off in front of you."

"Now you really have me amazed." Trager was delighted by her sudden playful mood.

"If I had been a man, would you still have made your mystery tour remark?"

"I like showing off in front of *you*. Had you not been there, Major Kisima would have thought I was a mass of quivering jelly." Trager moved closer, put his hands on her shoulders. Her body yielded to his pull, then her back stiffened. "No, Johnny this is neither the place nor the time."

"Will there ever be a right time?"

She shrugged. "I can't predict the future, but soon my project will be complete."

~

Shortly past midnight, Trager left the Okapi. In the alley, the taxi driver who had taken him to Bond's shack and then to the freight terminal, had been waiting, and drove him back to the villa.

If Longo's men had been searching the house, there was no sign of it. Exhausted, Trager fell into an uneasy sleep.

He groaned when he heard knocking on his bedroom door. He had a slight headache and his mouth was dry.

"*Entrez*," Trager said in bad humor. It wasn't quite seven. Wangohi opened the door. Instead of bringing tea, he stepped aside to let in a corpulent police officer in khaki uniform, Sam Browne belt and a large revolver holstered for a cross draw.

Trager sat on the bed staring in disbelief.

"Monsieur Trager?"

"*Oui,*" Trager said, realizing that his lifelong fear of being woken by the police had come true.

Chapter 26

"I'm Inspector Washira and here is the search warrant." The policeman handed Trager a pink paper.

"Can you wait outside while I dress?"

"We watch while you dress." Washira motioned with his head. Two constables armed with bolt-action Mauser carbines entered the room.

Trager read the warrant. The words *firearms violation* jumped at him. It was unlikely the cops would miss the Glock under the bed. Trager tossed the top sheet aside and reached for his trousers hanging on a chair.

"Would you like some coffee?" Trager asked, desperately trying to think of a way to distract the cop's attention so that he could toss the pistol out the window.

"No thank you, but feel free to have some while my men do their work."

"I need to go to the bathroom."

"Is that it?" The inspector pointed at the bathroom door.

"Yes."

The inspector opened the door. Probably satisfied there was no escape through the barred window, he nodded. "Have your pleasure."

While relieving himself, Trager thought how stupid he had been in thinking he would have time to hide the pistol under the armoire. What little hope he had that the cops wouldn't look under the bed vanished when he came out.

Inspector Washira had his swagger stick through the Glock's trigger guard. "Very nice," he said with admiration. "May I see your firearms permit?"

Trager shook his head.

"Monsieur Trager, you are under arrest, charged with violation of Article 159 of the Criminal Code--that is illegal possession of firearms. And Article 27 of the State Security Act--illegal importation of lethal weapons into the country."

The mention of State Security caused a shiver to run down Trager's spine. "I want to call a lawyer."

"You will get that opportunity later."

At a signal from the inspector, one of the constables produced handcuffs.

"Kindly put your hands behind your back. Be warned that any attempt to resist arrest or flee, authorizes the police to use lethal force."

"Let me put a shirt on."

"You will be adequately supplied with prison clothes."

"Shoes?"

Roughly, the constable slapped a cuff on Trager's wrist, yanked the arm behind his back and slapped the second cuff on.

"Take him away."

The two constables almost lifted Trager by his arms and dragged him out. Another cop stood by the open front door. A Blue Volvo sedan and a paddy wagon with its rear doors open were parked in the driveway.

The cops lifted Trager and threw him into the wagon. He managed to turn his head and not land on his face. Trager's desperation was replaced by blinding pain in his head. The smell of vomit made him gag.

~

When they dragged him out of the wagon, although he wasn't sure, he thought they were in the yard of the central police station, four blocks from the Metropole, on the other side of the park.

The basement of the station echoed a babble of voices and reeked with the sour smell of humanity and the stench of feces. Like a wave gathering force before crashing on the beach, a cheer rose as he was hauled past crowded cells. This sudden show of solidarity by the wretches behind bars gave Trager courage and strength.

Armed with batons, two turnkeys pushed the crowd of one cell back. Someone undid Trager's cuffs and shoved him in.

With a clank, the cell door closed.

A universe of black grinning faces and white eyeballs stared at him. Just like in a crowded bus, there was standing room only. Someone handed him a lit, half-smoked cigarette.

"*Merci.*" Trager took a deep drag and passed the cigarette on.

Trager's toes felt squishy. He looked down. He stood in half an inch of shit. It was difficult, but he had to fight the urge to vomit. Well, this was probably better than being locked up in Longo's place. Trager smiled at his cellmates. There were well over twenty in the six-by-six foot space.

Someone said, "*Bienvenue au Palace Royale.*"

Though he didn't feel like it, Trager pretended to laugh. He was really worried about the diamonds. Wangohi probably found them already in his jacket pocket and was headed for the hills with this new, undreamed of wealth. How would he explain this to Leonora?

"What did you do, murder your wife?"

Trager shook his head.

"The only crime they throw white people into jail for is murder. Who did you kill?"

"Unlicensed gun."

There was silence and a few whispered words for about thirty seconds as his cellmates studied him. Then someone guffawed and the others joined in a roar of laughter and applause.

Trager's eyes adjusted to the dim light. His cellmates were mostly in ragged clothes. The man who spoke French had gray hair and a neatly trimmed moustache.

"What are you here for?"

"Illegal drumming." He gestured to encompass the rest of the prisoners. "We are all here for illegal drumming."

"*Le Roi, le Roi vien.*" The King, the King is coming, a little man with wild eyes shouted.

"We drum for the king. The jails are so full, we will stay in hotels soon."

Trager wished he could sit down.

"Boooo ha, boooo ha," a chant grew in intensity.

There was a sound of rushing water. The rhythmic chant deteriorated into a pandemonium of yelling. Gum-booted guards doused the cells with a fire hose, causing a torrent of muck to run down the gutter-like corridor.

Trager turned around to keep shit from splashing on his face.

The clean up was by no means complete, but breathing became easier.

If a prisoner had no record, he didn't exist. The medieval lack of booking procedure bothered Trager. He could be locked up forever. He had left his watch on the nightstand and didn't know how long he'd been here. It already felt an eternity.

He tried to find hope in something, but in this terrible place, hope was nonexistent. He admired the resilience of his cellmates. Some slept while held up by others.

"How long have you been here?"

"Midnight, they start rounding up."

"Boooo ha, boooo ha." Trager had learned it meant turd.

A megaphone was unable to overpower the voices that turned into a riot of catcalls.

"Good news," the French speaker said. "We are being freed."

Doors clanked and slammed. Slowly, the clanking drew closer. Each time a cell opened, it provoked a wild cheer.

Maybe it was just as well they hadn't booked him. When his cell door opened, Trager surged forward with the other prisoners. As he reached the door, a guard viciously pocked a baton into his solar plexus. His breath knocked out of him, Trager doubled over and fell on his knees. Someone kicked him in the ribs, and Trager rolled on the still-filthy floor.

The pain slowly ebbed and he dragged himself to a corner, where he sat on the floor, his back against the wall. It was good to have a wall to lean against. Most of the cells were cages installed in what apparently was originally designed as an underground garage. After the earlier Dantesque pandemonium, the silence was eerie.

Great people must suffer, Simone had said. But he had done nothing to even strive for greatness. He had been swimming in a swamp he didn't understand, pissing everyone off.

It was afternoon, Trager thought. Boot steps echoed in the cellblock. He got up and tried to look as dignified as possible.

Two guards approached, opened the door. "*Venez.*"

They marched Trager to the end of the corridor and through a side door.

With gratitude, Trager looked at the showers along a wall.

"*Demerdes toi.*"

Trager took his filthy trousers off and rinsed them under the cold shower. There was no soap, but the cleansing effect of the water was wonderful. For a moment, he thought he had lived through the worst of it. He checked himself. Things could get worse, probably would.

With his trousers dripping water on the floor, the guards led him out of what probably were the holding cells into a well-lit corridor with numbered doors.

One of the guards knocked on number seventeen.

"*Entrez.*"

In need of a shave, his khaki tunic sporting sweat stains, Inspector Washira sat behind a small table with a stack of folders on one side. He was writing on a pad of cheap brownish paper. "Have a seat. Cigarette?"

He offered a packet of Cheval Blanc.

Trager was grateful for the politeness and the cigarette. He also warned himself not to fall for the softening-up routine. "Thank you." He took one, forcing his hand to remain steady.

Washira lit it with a match. "There have been additional charges filed against you. Care to explain why you tried to murder a Ministry of Interior official?"

"What?" Trager couldn't believe his ears.

Washira opened a folder and showed Trager a photograph of the Land Rover shot up by Vadim.

Trager smiled. "Upon close inspection, I'm sure you will be able to determine that those bullet holes did not come from a nine-millimeter pistol."

"But you were on the Majidogo road yesterday."

"Yes I was, and I saw that vehicle--after the soldiers who were escorting me captured it."

"*Bien*," Washira sighed. "You have powerful friends who vouch for you. You will make yourself available for questioning while we proceed investigating the Ministry of Interior allegations." He handed Trager a slip of paper. "Here is a receipt for your pistol. You have ten days to pay the fine. If you want your pistol back, apply for a Firearms Permit."

Trager could hardly believe his ordeal was over. Emboldened, he asked, "Why were all those drummers rounded up?"

Washira let out another sigh and shook his head. "A request from the Ministry of the Interior. This Utabu business is getting out of hand. The drummers are preparing for the coming of a mythical king." Washira raised his arms in hopeless gesture. "People are not showing up for work. Drum, drum, drum. The practice of witchcraft is banned in our country. If this thing gets out of hand, there's big trouble ahead." He closed Trager's file. "My driver will take you back."

"Thank you." Trager got up, with a great sense of short-lived relief. As a prisoner, his fate had been out of his hands. Now, he had to worry about the diamonds.

~

Inspector Washira's driver stopped in front of the villa. "Thank you," Trager said and went into the house. He closed the door behind him and froze.

Longo sat in a chair, drinking tea. "Been indulging in a sport?"

"Yes, went for a swim in the sewer. You should try it."

"Don't let my presence bother you." Longo gestured with his hand. "Feel at home."

Wondering what Longo wanted and where Wangohi was, Trager went downstairs. He quickly searched for the diamonds. They were gone. With a feeling of impending doom, he showered, shaved, and put clean clothes on. His legs feeling like chewing gum, he climbed to the living room.

Longo was still there. "May I pour you a cup of tea? You seem tired."

Trager nodded as he took a chair opposite Longo. What did the bastard want now?

"How was your trip to Zamani?" Longo asked while he poured tea.

"Nice, uneventful."

"See anything interesting? Milk, sugar?"

"Yeah, a colorful fellow wearing impressive skins. We ate warthog and drank pombe." Trager tasted the tea, gulped the whole cup. He realized he was incredibly thirsty.

"Who was he?"

"I don't know."

"You don't know? More tea?" Longo's solicitude was starting to get to Trager's already ragged nerves. He accepted another cup.

Longo said. "I find it strange you didn't get a name. That's sloppy work."

"Passing strangers on the road."

"And you didn't take photographs?"

"I did."

Longo's eyes flashed, he emerged from his cocoon of bored politeness. "Where are they?"

Trager leaned back and sipped his tea. Longo, meanwhile seemed to coil like a snake ready to strike.

"I've sent them to be developed."

"Where?"

"Dankov's fort."

"You what?" Longo looked as if he'd been hit in the chops. Trager loved it. He wondered, if Simone told the truth about the film going to Dankov's fort, and if the film was that important, why hadn't Vadim relieved him of it when he had a chance? Was the big man in the sacred grove the future king of Zengawal? Trager's head buzzed with questions, but first, he had to get Longo out of the way and hunt down Wangohi and the missing diamonds.

Longo appeared to calm down. "Where is your houseman?"

Whatever little hope Trager had that Wangohi was skulking in the kitchen or in his quarters vanished. "He's gone to see his mother."

"Where does she live?"

"I don't know. Maybe you can tell me. I need him back."

To Trager's surprise, Longo took a small notebook out of his pocket and wrote in it. "I'll let you know by tomorrow." Writing must have had a positive effect, for Longo smiled. "Douglas Blankenship." He dumped the name as if showing four aces in an unfriendly poker game.

Trager was too experienced a dog to fall for that old trick. "Batmanshit?"

"Blankenship, Douglas E. Maybe you met him in your travels and adventures. He was in Vienna the same time you were and made the acquaintance of our gallant Colonel Dankov."

Longo was a bit too well versed on the Vienna events; on the other hand, Dankov made no secret of that episode. Still, Trager doubted he would have mentioned Blankenship by name. "There was a guy by that name, cultural attaché if I remember right."

Longo nodded. "I was hoping you could give me a little background on the man. He will be heading the American diplomatic mission here. Any reason we should object to this nomination, make him *persona non grata*? Some of my sources say he is actually CIA."

Trager shrugged. "Haven't seen him since Vienna."

Longo got up. "I must remind you your account book with me is getting heavy on the debit side. I trust you will correct that." He strode to the phone, picked it up without dialing. "Buzz my driver." He then turned back to Trager. "Lieutenant Matungi asked me to convey his last farewell." Longo displayed his malevolent smile. "You could save his life by making a deposition to a judge on how you coerced the poor bugger to commit treason."

"I don't know what the hell you're talking about," Trager said in the coldest possible tone, controlling every muscle in his body. To control his brain, he fantasized that if he had a gun he would have taken Longo hostage.

Longo headed out and stopped at the door, holding the doorknob. "The courthouse will be open all night so that you can clear your conscience. The execution is at five forty five."

Chapter 27

He had never killed a man. Trager paced the terrace. The image of Matungi, his wife and children looking into a camera lens, acted as a blindfold. Had he still been with the CIA, the moral choice would have been simple: duty above honor, above conscience. This time, he had recruited someone for his own personal gain. To stay back was cowardly. How could he live with himself knowing he'd been a coward?

Flamingoes in the lake chorused, coward, coward, coward.

If Trager made the deposition, Matungi would have his day in court and not be executed by Longo. Trager would be tried and jailed. One could not run away from one's mistakes.

Having decided, he put a jacket on, made sure he had a pen, and headed out the door. *And Longo will win*, an internal voice said. *Mr. X will win, too. Remember the Piano Man*. Trager stopped under one of the fig trees in the garden. The little internal voice had turned into a chorus joined by the inhuman screams in Longo's basement. The deposition was an admission to defeat, a surrender. *Longo will win*. For a moment, Trager thought he was rationalizing his cowardice. He had the tools to do away with Longo. Matungi had given him confirmation that Tony Bond and Longo were in cahoots. Now it was a matter of nailing the bastard. If he could convince Bamondo . . .

Trager ran back into the house. He took the presidential invitation card out of his desk and dialed the phone number on it. A recording told him he had reached the president's social secretary. He thought of leaving a message, but that was the same as cutting his nuts off. Frustrated, Trager slammed the phone down. The missing diamonds didn't improve his status with the presidential household either.

~

In the morning, Trager called the palace from a payphone. The best he could get from the social secretary was that she would give his Excellency a message to call him.

The thieving Wangohi's family lived in Gambesi, three hundred kilometers of bad road to the north. It wouldn't be easy for him to convert the diamonds into cash. So the diamonds were probably recoverable. All Trager had to do was reach the damn village, find Wangohi, maybe beat the crap out him. Then return to Turako without getting killed. Longo would be curious what Trager was doing. It wouldn't take him long to find out Trager had a fortune on him.

Only Dankov could help, but even if he had a means of contacting him, Trager didn't think it prudent to tell how he ended up with Leonora's diamonds. Simone was also unreachable. Madame Kanzo was Longo's agent. The solution was fairly simple. Travel like the locals.

Trager went to the market, found out that for five-thousand Z-franks, ten bucks, he could have a sitting space on the bus that would take him to Nyuki. Gambesi was twenty kilometers further. The bus left at six and arrived twelve hours later.

Trager thought he could be in Gambesi before Longo realized he had left town. If Wangohi's clan didn't kill him, he would hitchhike back. Africans were good about giving whites a ride.

On his return, he would see Bamondo, convince him that his security chief was a traitor and of the need to set up a little surveillance unit to track Bond's movements and link him to Longo. With luck, he'd have the two bastards in jail before his date with Simone.

Bus ticket in his pocket, Trager went to see Madame Kanzo to make arrangements to meet Simone at the Loldawa Lodge in the Pygmy reserve two weeks from then.

~

Never in his life had Trager had problems with the handling of other people's valuables or money. He wasn't looking forward to seeing Leonora.

Longo's black suits were present outside the Women's League house. The same ladies who greeted him the last time sat at the reception table. Trager bought his ticket and made a donation to the Mobile Clinic Fund.

One of the ladies said, "Madame Bamondo is in her office upstairs. She's expecting you."

With leaden feet, like those of a school kid about to see the principal, Trager made his way up the majestic staircase. Parquet in need of polish covered the floor. The sound of manual typewriters came from an open door with a sign saying Administration. He proceeded to the far end of the corridor, passing the closed doors of the offices of the Zengawal Red Cross, Sports Federation, and Girl Guides of Zengawal. The double door at the end said simply, President.

Trager knocked. Steps sounded on the other side of the doors.

"John, darling, come in." Leonora smiled brightly as she opened the door.

The huge room dwarfed its sparse furnishings. Afraid to look at Leonora, he took in the desk in the middle of the room and a living room set in a corner. An open magazine lay on the floor next to a stuffed chair. He heard a click as Leonora locked the door. Trager took this as a bad sign. "Nice office," he said, testing his own voice. He had never been this nervous in his life.

Her hand on his buttocks almost made him jump. She stepped around him and kissed him deeply.

He pulled his head away. "I've got to tell you something."

"So good to see you." She placed her cheek on his chest. "So good."

"You'll change your mind after what I have to tell you."

Leonora looked up, her face mirrored his worried expression. She took his hand and led him to the sofa. "Sorry I don't have anything to offer, but we'll soon have tea downstairs."

The idea they would be having tea shortly gave him some relief as he sat down.

Leonora picked up the magazine and tossed it on top of the coffee table. She wore s simple beige dress with buttons up the front and a pleated skirt. If she'd buttoned a couple of buttons, she'd look matronly. Trager tried to keep his eyes off the excessive amount of pink bra showing.

"What happened to your face?" she asked as she sat on a chair facing Trager, crossing her legs, and exposing a generous section of thigh.

"I fell flat on my face. That's what I need to talk to you about."

"Don't thank me. It was Judge Ponga who dutifully intervened on your behalf." She smiled as she added, "But I did call him the moment I heard you were in jail."

"Someone stole your diamonds while I was locked up."

Like a shadow, fright crossed her face and was instantly gone. "Stole?"

"I'm afraid so. I'll try to recover them tomorrow."

"Of course it was silly of me to have forgotten them. It was impossibly awkward to return to your house. But I had total confidence in your integrity." She thought for a moment. "They are worth nearly a hundred thousand pounds."

"I'm sorry, I think I know who did it." With bravado he didn't feel, he added. "I'll get them back."

She buttoned her dress to a publicly acceptable level and said in a cold, businesslike tone, "I'll assume you have accepted my offer. Though it is more than what I consider a reasonable advance, it is yours. I'm generous by nature, but I wasn't born yesterday. I won't be taken for a ride twice. You understand, I'm giving you the benefit of the doubt."

Wanting the earth to swallow him, Trager let her vent her fury, disappointment, or whatever she was feeling.

"By having accepted payment, you *owe* me the requested service. Should you fail to produce . . ." she paused as if to think, "let's say in two weeks." A small smile formed on her lips and her eyes stared at him, hard and unblinking. "I have a surgeon who does certain procedures without requiring the agreement of the patient."

"I'll get your diamonds back," Trager said sheepishly.

"At the moment, I'm angry. Very angry. Next time we meet . . . Tuesday at the Club Hipique. Do you ride?"

"No."

A slight pout crossed her mouth. "Pity, but we can talk while I show you my horses. I want a plan." She stood, smiled brightly. "Shall we go downstairs and have tea?"

She took Trager's arm as they went down the stairway.

Wimbo, again at the piano, effortlessly played *Claire de Lune*. Simone sat at a table, chatting with Professor Najua. Trager remembered many of the faces from the previous time.

Leonora said loudly, "Mr. Trager, thank you very much for your kind offer, the orphans will be happy." She shook his hand and went behind the tea bar.

Teacup in hand, Trager headed for Simone's table. She noticed his approach and tapped Najua's hand. Najua's earnest expression changed and he stopped talking. Simone said quickly, "Be a dear. Could you bring some eclairs? They are phenomenal."

Trager went back to the tea table and took his time loading a plate with eclairs. He looked back. Simone no longer leaned forward, Najua laughed at something.

Wimbo broke into Tchaikovsky's *Dance of the Flowers*. On stage, a group of four year-old girls in tutus and wearing hats made of real sunflowers went through a dance routine.

When Trager returned to the table, Simone stood. "Thank you, Professor," she said. Then to Trager, "The sun is behind the trees, let's sit in the garden."

He followed her outside, where tables were set up on the lawn.

Simone took an éclair before he had time to set them down. She looked somehow more vulnerable, younger, with powdered sugar on the tip of her nose.

"You need a napkin," Trager said.

"Did I do it again?" She giggled as she finished the éclair. Trager had never seen her this cheerful. "Johnny, pack your tooth brush, tomorrow we're going on safari."

"Can't do it," Trager said sadly, thinking of the long bus ride to Gambesi and the other things he had to do.

"Why?" Simone looked dismayed.

"The diamonds. Someone stole the diamonds."

Simone broke out laughing. "Is that why you have such a long face?"

"What's so funny?"

"You. Your time in jail must have affected you."

"The diamonds are gone, worth a fortune, I'm in trouble."

Simone shook her head. "Of course they're gone. You wouldn't expect Wangohi to leave them there for anyone to take."

Simone, what are you doing to me? "I thought he stole them."

"He? Never."

"Where are they?" Trager almost expected her to pull the bag out of her purse and dangle it in front of his nose.

"They're safe. The moment *les flics* drove off, Wangohi took the bag, ran into hiding, and sent me a message. I called one of my soldier friends in the palace, and the effort to get you out of jail began."

Trager took a deep, grateful breath.

Simone reached for his cheek. "Did *les flics* do that?"

The soft feel of her hand made the ground wobble. Trager grasped the edge of the table to keep from falling. "I fell. Can I have the stones back?"

"In due time."

Trager's throat went dry. He saw a waiter, waved and asked for a pot. "Are you playing games with me again?"

Simone took her teacup with both hands, lifted it to the level of her eyes, hiding the rest of her face. "Yes. The game is called *chantage*."

Her playfulness was infectious. Trager asked, "What do I have to do?"

"Come with me on safari."

Trager sighed. "Still can't do it."

"Now, what?"

"I have things to do."

"Like what?"

"Business."

"Johnny, you stubborn goat, didn't you book a safari with Madame Kanzo?"

"Yeah, for two weeks from now." Trager poured tea into both cups.

"Good, that's what Longo thinks. We're leaving tomorrow."

"I have a score to settle with that ghoul."

Simone shook her head slowly. "You're crazy, but not as crazy as you think of yourself. Longo will get his comeuppance in due time, but it will

be the result of a team effort. Alone in Turako, you're worse than dead."
She moved the plate with eclairs toward Trager. "Try one, at least."

Trager raised both palms, his stomach revolted at the idea of food.

"You've heard the Americans are reopening their embassy?"

Trager nodded, wondering how come Blankenship was coming.

"*Mon cher*, Longo wants to scuttle this diplomatic overture. He is filing a formal criminal complaint against you on Monday. He wants a trial, a CIA spy scandal. You go on trial and it will look like the USA is trying to subvert the Zengawali government. Nobody, neither Igor nor Pierre, will be able to help you. It will be a great political embarrassment to Pierre." Simone paused and smiled. "To avoid arrest, are you coming on safari?"

"What's this team effort you mentioned?"

"*Sacre bleu*. Igor, you and I. And you'll have some great stories to write."

"Let me have the stones so I can return them."

"To the rightful owner?"

"Of course," Trager said seething with frustration.

Simone shook her head. "He isn't here."

Trager's stomach pushed its way into his chest. "Did she steal them?"

"I think a better term is *borrowed*. Once you leave the country with her they'll become stolen."

"Nice lady. She said if I didn't take her out of the country, she has a friendly doctor--"

"Lukiadis. Most of his patients are referred by Longo. He has a little clinic outside the city, does lobotomies and castrations."

Trager swallowed. He could imagine Longo's goons strapping him to a gurney.

From the playground came the laughter of children ignorant of their parents' evil deeds.

"Don't think badly of her. Leonora is having a rough time. A woman is entitled to a little alimony. And she really likes you."

"I just want to return her stones."

"You will, after we return from safari. I'll show you a few things. You will return a much wiser man than when you left."

Trager was loosing patience. "I want the stones back."

"Like manna from heaven, the stones fell into my hands. I didn't steal them, they just came into my possession. I have a good use for them. A sort of collateral. You're not getting them back until I'm done. If you want to stay in Turako that's fine. I'm going on safari tomorrow. Are you coming?"

"I have to see Leonora on Tuesday."

Simone ate another éclair, getting powder on her nose. "Tell her to bring you cigarettes, visiting hours are two to four. But I think they'll have you incommunicado."

"I'll go to ground."

She leaned forward placing an index finger on the table. "You stubborn goat. Can't you see that's what we're doing?"

Trager wondered what would he achieve by hiding among the Pygmies.

"After we return, we'll fix Longo, I'll sell Schnookie to Leonora and both of you will drive off into the sunset."

"That's not what I want to do."

"What do you want?"

"If I head into the sunset, I want you with me."

Simone shook her head. "We've talked about that, my future lies here."

"Then I'll stay."

"Good, you won't be causing trouble after Doctor Lukiadis has a go at you."

She got up, slung her bag onto her shoulder. "Enjoyed our tea. See you tomorrow at four."

"In the morning?"

She rolled her eyes. "Yes." She bent down as if to kiss his cheek. Her hand on his shoulder sent a pleasurable shiver down his spine. She whispered, "When you get up, don't switch the lights on in front of your house. Longo has it under observation."

Chapter 28

Knowing the significance of the drumming made Trager more aware of the faraway beat coming from the shantytowns. Past midnight after the traffic noise died, the drumming became clearer, louder. Trager tossed in his bed, suspended in a fog of semi-wakefulness. The citywide throb heralded doom. But the night no longer belonged to Longo.

As three o'clock approached, light from a waning moon together with a cool breeze entered through the windows. With the top sheet, Trager wiped sweat off his chest.

He swung out of bed and barefoot, he moved silently to the kitchen and made coffee.

The flamingoes on the lake were silent. On the terrace, Trager sipped his coffee, staring at the presidential palace where only two lights showed on the ground floor. *Leonora, you bitch.* Driving her out of the country would be a one-way ticket to who-knew-where. If he refused, she would convert him into a smiling moron like Mbaya. Trager had no doubt of her vindictiveness.

His gaze moved to the lights beyond the palace. Simone was there, somewhere. No matter what he did, she always got in the way. He had to solve that puzzle. If she had told him the truth, Trager finally understood Longo's game, and why the bastard hadn't killed or jailed him yet. Only Simone's role in all this escaped Trager.

The length of the trip didn't matter. When going on safari, one packed light. He stuffed a few things into a rucksack, including a set of clean clothes for the evenings. What he was wearing now would become his daytime dirty clothes. He wished he had a better weapon than a machete. He attached it to the rucksack so he could unsheath it while backpacking.

The night watchman was nowhere to be seen. A few minutes before four, Trager stood in the shadow of the concrete gatepost. The street was empty. He wondered where Longo had his observation post. If the watchers had listening devices in the house, Trager had been quiet enough not to alert them he was up.

Without lights, Schnookie coasted downhill. With a faint squeal, it stopped in front of the gate. Trager carefully pushed the Land Rover's door handle, tossed the rucksack in the back, and got in.

Simone released the brakes. The car continued its downward rolling. The engine wasn't running. Only when they were a block away from his house did Trager clack the door closed.

"Good morning, Johnny," she said warmly.

"Good morning, Madame blackmailer."

Simone switched the ignition on and smoothly released the clutch.

Trager braced himself for an explosive roar. The engine purred into life. "I'm glad you fixed the muffler."

"One of my palace friends did it using a jerry can. Russians are so brilliant at improvising. They've also put some armor under the floor. Good if you run over a land mine."

"Wonderful, what sort of safari is this?"

Simone turned onto the Lakefront Road. "We'll visit the border area where the Zengawal Liberation Army is massing to attack. Igor will give you a tour." She let out a little chuckle. "As a war correspondent, you'll be able to scoop everyone. Maybe get a Putzer Prize."

Trager laughed. "Putzer is right. In American slang *putz* means a sort of idiot. You probably mean a Pulitzer Prize."

"No, I meant Putzer."

She was a schemer, a thief, and a blackmailer, and he was in deep shit. Why was it he still felt so lighthearted when in her company?"

Past the lake, Trager tensed. White barrels blocked the road. Simone turned her headlights off. A Land Rover with a 105 millimeter antitank gun stood on the side of the road. Beyond the checkpoint, a line of trucks several blocks long waited to be let through. African soldiers inspected the trucks, looking under tarps. A black-painted Russian Trager had seen before appeared to be in charge.

Simone stopped momentarily then was waved through.

"They take things seriously here."

"Trucks from the west. That's where we expect trouble to come from. At daybreak, they'll let them through."

Ahead, headlights blocked the lane. A soldier motioned Simone to go around the blocking vehicle. She climbed the curb and drove past a police truck crammed with people. A police officer gesticulated in apparent frustration and argued loudly with a couple of soldiers.

Simone said, "They've been rounding up drummers again. The soldiers won't let *les flics* pass."

Trager was glad to see someone give the cops a hard time. But conflict between government organizations was often the prelude to civil war.

Passing the offending truck, Simone got back on the street and accelerated. Near the outskirts of the city, the drums grew louder. On a street corner, a mob of people gathered around a bonfire. Drummers pounded away.

Simone slowed. "Maybe they're overdoing it, but I love the way the people are expressing their aspirations."

"For that, they get tossed in jail."

"Longo and his cronies are scared to death. *We*, the people will win." Simone stuck her head out the window. "*Vive le Roi*," she shouted.

"*Vive le Roi*," a number of voices answered. The yell rippled, grew, and exploded into a roar of the mob.

Simone drove off, honking the horn.

"What are you, a rabble rousing Pasionaria?"

Simone didn't answer.

The street became paved highway heading for Maridani. "Light me up, please."

Trager lit her cigar, stretched his legs. In the comfortable silence, while putting distance between himself and Longo, he fell asleep.

Dawn was making good progress when he woke and recognized Maridani's wide, main boulevard. A crowded ambulant market was set up on the square next to City Hall. Simone made a U-turn and parked by the hotel entrance.

A neat looking septuagenarian in a tan safari suit, his throat wrapped in a paisley cravat, stood by the door. He waved a malacca cane. "Bonjour, Simone. How nice to see your radiant beauty. It augurs a perfect day." He removed his Panama hat, exposing neatly cut, wavy, white hair.

"Crethien, you're as incorrigible and handsome as ever. This is John, a correspondent for the *New York Times*."

Trager cringed at Simone's exaggeration.

She gave Crethien a hug then turned to Trager. "Crethien owns the hotel and is the Mayor of Maridani."

The old boy smiled. "Monsieur, it is a privilege to welcome you. I'm just a survivor, was born in this country and managed to stay through the upheavals. This is a nice and prosperous town. Welcome." He glanced to the side. "Ah, here they are."

Two policemen with long, white over-sleeves on their arms stationed themselves on both sides of the boulevard, blew their whistles, and stopped traffic.

"A pleasant good morning to both of you." The mayor of Maridani strode across the street and waved at the trucks that had stopped. Several people spilled out of the crowd in the market and applauded the mayor as he tipped his hat and went up the steps of city hall.

"They have an excellent duck sausage here. It goes well with eggs," Simone said as they went to a verandah at the back of the hotel. She ordered breakfast and told the waiter to fix them a picnic lunch.

In sharp contrast with the conflicting undercurrents of the capital, the atmosphere in Maridani was peaceful. Trager enjoyed the view of the garden and idly watched an attendant scoop leaves floating in the swimming pool. He almost dropped his glass of passion fruit juice when Wangohi appeared bearing a tray. *"Bonjour, Monsieur, Madame."*

Simone spoke quickly in Bassi and was answered even quicker. Trager was going to ask Wangohi what he was doing here. A look from Simone made him keep his mouth shut. Wangohi placed plates with sausage and eggs on the table, bowed and left.

In a confidential tone, Simone said, "He's doing a little undercover assignment while staying out of Longo's reach."

"Someday you'll drive me to commit violence."

"The beans you don't have, you can't spill. Ancient Turkish saying." Simone proceeded to slice her sausage.

~

For the first thirty kilometers west of Maridani, a pall of dust raised by trucks blanketed the road. After a fork, the road narrowed and one could see to the other end of Africa. Simone removed the black scarf she had used as a bandana to keep dust out of her nose. "It will seem to you this road never ends and it leads--"

"To the other end of Africa."

She gave him a quick glance and seemed to chuckle inwardly.

The familiar red soil gave way to yellow. Low scrub, dotted here and there by lone umbrella-looking acacias, replaced the neat plantations. Not ten meters from the road, running in the same direction as the car, a family of warthogs seemed to slide on air, tails sticking straight up like antennas.

"This is the Africa I like," Trager said. "Now that we're at sea, so to speak, will you tell me what's going on with the diamonds?"

"You could get captured."

"Some safari," Trager grumbled.

Though the slope was nearly imperceptible, the road kept going downhill. The air became hotter and more humid. Scrub changed to forest. On the side of the road, a black figure stopped doing something, straightened and darted into the forest. "Chimpanzee," Simone said. "Let's stop and have lunch. Sometimes one can hear them talking."

Trager took the cooler with the picnic lunch out of the car and placed it next to a fallen tree where they could sit in the shade. Simone hauled out a canvas bag that appeared quite heavy. She sat on the log, unzipped the bag and handed Trager a nine-millimeter Makarov pistol and two spare magazines. "If someone asks you for a firearms permit, shoot him with this." Chuckling, she handed him a compact machine pistol.

Trager recognized the Kiparis and weighed the lethal tool in his hand, appreciating the Russian penchant for irony. *Kiparis* was Russian for cypress.

Trager extended his hand like a surgeon to a nurse. "Grenades?"

Simone handed him three miniature grenades, no larger than a golf ball. "These Belgian beauties have three times the explosive power of a conventional grenade."

The grenades fitted nicely into his trouser pockets, the spare thirty-round magazines for the Kiparis in the ample hip pocket of his bush jacket, and the pistol magazines in the right.

"And here is a little present." She handed him a holster for the Makarov. "You'll be more comfortable."

"A correspondent armed to the teeth. I'm pretty sure the Geneva Convention has something to say about that."

Simone turned her head while digging in the cooler. Her lips curled into a slight smile. "And the pen is mightier than the sword. But first you must shoot the enemy so you can live to write about it. Ancient Macedonian saying." She handed Trager a chicken leg. "Enjoy it. The menu for the rest of the safari is tinned corned beef."

After lunch, Simone said, "You drive now. A girl must sleep sometime. Just stay on this road until we get to a small, steep escarpment."

While Trager drove, Simone dug out a small pillow and wedged it between her back and the door. She removed her boots and placed her feet on Trager's lap, causing a tingling sensation in his insides. He couldn't resist taking her toes in his hand and massaging them.

"That feels good, but don't get distracted from the road."

Soon, a wide-brimmed canvas hat over her face, she seemed to be asleep. Trager did his best to avoid potholes. He liked this new level of intimacy and gently rubbed Simone's feet when he wasn't working the gearshift.

The heat in the Land Rover made Trager drowsy; he caught himself nodding off a couple of times. To stay awake, he took one of Simone's cigars and smoked it. It made him wonder how she lived and where. Her father had died. Where was her mother? A princess of the Atlas Mountains had her feet on his lap. Maybe getting chucked out of the Marine Corps wasn't such a bad thing after all. Her shirt was wet with perspiration that made it stick to her stomach. Only the area of the bra remained dry. It accentuated the shapeliness of her breasts. He suppressed a longing to run his hand up her legs.

Nearing four, the harsh sunlight softened to a golden hue. The road began to rise and suddenly descended. Trager brought Schnookie to a halt. Simone removed the hat from her face and blinked, looking sheepish. Strands of wet hair flopped down her forehead.

The escarpment, as Simone had said, wasn't big, maybe a hundred feet or so, but the change in landscape was dramatic. In front lay a vast expanse of golden savanna broken by lines of bluish green brush with clumps of palm trees. Herds of topi with legs that looked as if they wore yellow socks, and stately waterbuck grazed in the distance.

A light breeze smelling of grass gave relief from the heavy, still air of the forest.

The flood plain," Simone said. "The rains will start soon, making it impassable. See that line of forest?"

Trager's gaze settled on a thick line of trees about two miles away.

"The Kuchara River, our border with the Congo. They have to come in the next few days or the rains will keep us safe for another year."

"The Zengawal Army of Liberation?"

Simone nodded. "Made up of Hutu mercenaries and financed by the ASS, Tony Bond's employers."

Trager got out of the car and scanned the border area with binoculars. There weren't any signs of human interference in what looked like the Garden of Eden. A dozen or so elephants moved toward a waterhole.

"This would rival the Serengeti if it wasn't for the security situation."

"I would have expected to see soldiers or something."

"Igor is out there." Simone sighed. "We're meeting him tomorrow." She patted the hood of the car. "Get back in. You're an excellent driver on the road. We'll see how you handle some real driving. If you don't break an axle, you'll be rewarded."

Wondering what she meant by reward, Trager let the Land Rover grind its way slowly down the steep slope. At the bottom, directed by Simone, he turned right and inched his way into tall grass that grew higher than the hood. After about a hundred meters, the right wheel dropped into what could have been a warthog hole. Trager backed out and chose a slightly different route.

"I remember you playing the idiot when we first met. Now I see you're good at most everything you do. Another two hundred meters, just beyond that hummock, you'll see a waterfall. Drive there without getting stuck in the mud."

The place looked like a cove, an indentation in the escarpment where water had bared the underlying rock. A pencil-thin stream of water cascaded into a small pool.

Trager slammed on the brakes as a dark shape jumped from under the grass.

The snotty snout of an old male buffalo was inches from Trager's shoulder. The buff gave a loud snort, turned, and ran away.

"I often wish I had a 458 rifle for self defense, but they're too expensive."

"Not more than the pop guns we have." Trager thought how totally useless a nine-millimeter submachine gun would be against an enraged buffalo, elephant, or hippo."

"These I get free."

Trager got out of the car, stopped at the edge of a sandy beach full of animal tracks. He recognized hyena, and a variety of ungulates as well as good-sized pugmarks left by lion. Simone stood next to him. He put his arm around her waist. It seemed like the most natural thing to do. Soft and warm, her hip rested against his. It almost made his head spin. Still holding her, he turned to face Simone.

She took his nose between thumb and index finger, squeezed and turned his head. "Showers are that way."

"How about my reward?"

"That's your reward."

He kept holding her firmly, enjoying the touch of her breasts. "After the shower, maybe?"

"After the shower, we have tea." She wasn't pushing against him nor pulling away.

Encouraged, Trager tightened his hold to where their thighs touched and her breasts pushed against his chest.

She pulled his nose to where he could see her face. She was smiling. "Let go of me before I decide to break your nose."

"You're cruel."

"You smell like a goat." She released his nose and pushed off with her hand against his chest.

Reluctantly, Trager let go of her. Simone moved away.

"Help me get the things out. Then tea will be ready when we're finished washing up. You can scrub my back, it feels itchy." She took out a folding propane stove, lit it and put a kettle on.

If anything, Simone was more beautiful than the first time he had seen her naked. Trager took a bar of soap out of his shaving kit, unable to take his eyes off as she wiggled out of her trousers.

"No soap for the next few days. You don't want the enemy to smell you," she said. Her breasts swung as she bent to take black panties off.

"No bilhartzia here?"

"The spring is right behind the rock. The snails start over there." Simone pointed downstream of the sandy pool. Bilhatzia was a tiny worm that bored its way through the skin and settled in the liver. The parasite needed man in its cycle to thrive. As the African population exploded, so did the crippling disease hosted by snails that lived in still water.

The rivulet was too small to call a waterfall, but it was a generous and refreshing shower. Simone handed Trager a washcloth. "I need a good rub on my back."

Trager rubbed her back while she held onto a ledge above her head making ooh-and-aah noises. He then massaged her neck and shoulders, trying not to get aroused.

"Will you do something to my back, too?" Trager asked when his arms began to feel tired.

"Sure, turn around." She took the washcloth from his hand.

The washcloth stung as Simone snapped it against his buttocks. "That's for trying to get improper."

~

Feeling clean and refreshed, Trager sat in his undershorts as they had tea. "So we meet Igor tomorrow, then what?"

"If he's found a good target, he'll take you on a raid. You'll be able to write about it, dispel the lies they're telling about us. Refugees, pshaw."

Trager's heart accelerated. He had never seen real combat--though a friendly airplane in Iraq had fired at him during the Gulf War. His partner, Chuck Merrill, got hit and was paralyzed from the waist down. Trager had carried him fifteen kilometers to the LZ, where a helicopter picked them up.

The sun grew in size and looked pear-shaped as it settled into a fine layer of haze that could have been smoke.

"It is so beautiful," Simone said, in a voice filled with awe.

Trager put his arm around her shoulder and she leaned against him. The lower limb of the sun looked flattened as it touched distant hills. Simone's head rested on his shoulder. The sun faded out like a sigh.

Trager felt a slight tremor go through Simone's body.

He squeezed her shoulder and she cooed, "Mmm."

A rustle in the bushes made Simone turn and bring up her submachine gun.

Trager dove for his.

Chapter 29

Simone aimed at the bright brown eyes of the wide-cheeked Syke's monkey peering from behind a bush.

Silently, Trager cursed the damn animal and slid the safety back on. Trying to recapture Simone's tender mood, he reached for her waist. She put her arm out and pushed him away. "Watch those monks come to drink. And we better have a bite to eat before mosquitoes steal our sandwiches."

Seemingly unafraid, a number of monkeys gathered at the head of the waterfall and drank, their rears sticking up.

~

It was almost completely dark when they finished corned beef sandwiches made with thick slabs of dark Russian bread baked in Dankov's bakery. "If anyone has been watching, they'll think we will sleep inside Schnookie. But we'll take my tent and pitch it in that clump of trees. Ancient trick of the Watta people."

Carrying some sort of bedroll and wondering where the old buffalo had gone, Trager followed Simone along a smooth elephant trail.

Inside the clump of trees, it was pitch dark. Trager heard the rustle of Simone assembling her tent.

"*Voilà*," she said in a low voice, and took the roll out of Trager's arms. "It's really meant for one person but we'll manage."

Trager crawled into what was nothing more than a mosquito net with a PVC floor. On it, Simone had laid out a thin mattress. When she got inside and zipped the entrance closed, it was evident they would damn near need to embrace to stay on the mattress. Trager smiled. He took his boots off and placed them under the mattress to act as a pillow.

"Cozy," he said.

Simone wiggled a little, and settled into the crook of his arm.

"Remember, we're tent mates, not lovers."

"I'm available if you change your mind."

"Good night, Johnny."

Trager listened to the buzz of frustrated mosquitoes crowding on the mesh. Like him, they were so close, the flesh so far. From the direction of the spring came a cacophony of frog calls. Somewhat closer, a large animal swished through the grass. The quiet presence of the animal assured Trager no other humans were in the immediate vicinity. A deep rumble heralded the approach of elephant.

Simone seemed to be sleeping through it all.

The hooting of hyena woke him. Warm breath touched his face. Simone had turned. She had her arm around his chest and he felt the warmth of a breast. He touched her forehead with his lips and drifted back to sleep, thinking this was gonna work.

~

Before dawn, Trager woke sensing something had changed. A nightjar was calling with its eerie, creaky voice but the frogs were silent.

Simone was prone on her belly, submachine gun in hand.

Quietly, Trager laced his boots. "Someone is by the waterhole," he whispered.

Simone remained quiet for a while. "They weren't supposed to be here 'til after dawn."

"Who?"

"Igor."

Another minute went by. Trager listened but couldn't detect movement.

"Something is wrong," Simone whispered. "Let's spread out." She quietly unzipped the net.

Trager slowly moved away, while Simone went in the opposite direction. He got under a clump of bushes and waited.

It was so quiet he could hear the soft murmur of the little waterfall.

And someone filling a kettle.

Trager wiped a horde of mosquitoes off his neck, leaving his hand wet with blood.

It was beginning to gray when a voice said, *"Chai gotov."*

A wave of relief swept over Trager, he eased his hold on the machine pistol and stood. *Tea indeed.*

With a rustle of leaves, Simone emerged from the bushes where she had been hiding. "What are you, a comedian?" She sounded indignant.

"I have enough problems without you giving me hell in the morning."

"You're early."

"No, too late."

Trager followed Simone to where they had left Schnookie. With green and black paint on his face, sprawled on the ground, his head leaning against a wheel of the Land Rover, Dankov was unrecognizable. He wore black running shorts and a camouflage tunic. His sour, unwashed smell carried a long way. A folding stock Kalashnikov rested on his lap. "Karibu chai," he said in Swahili.

"Are you alright?" Simone rushed toward him, got on her knees and touched his shoulder.

"Forgive me for not standing up. It feels so good to stretch out." He turned to Trager. "Do you have that short-wave radio with you?"

"Yeah." Trager pointed at Schnookie.

Dankov nodded. "We've been upstaged. It's too late for you to go see the so-called refugee camps. The unspeakable bastards raped and cut the throats of the nuns at Bunaka and massacred the children. No survivors." Dankov paused and sipped from a mug. "Tracks lead across the Zengawal border. Last night, an airplane-load of reporters arrived. It is all nicely organized. The reporters are staying in an old Societe Miniere guest house."

Simone shook her head. "They can't get away with that. Withdraw. Establish deniability. No one in his right mind would believe that god-fearing Cossacks would harm a nun."

Dankov sat up and emitted a bitter chuckle. "Nobody, including many Russians, know that much about Cossacks. The ZAL is ready to move. I have to stop them here."

"You're crazy. That's exactly what they want you to do. If they find you here, no one will believe you didn't kill those nuns. And while you're shooting it out with those Hutu savages, there will be pressure from abroad for Bamondo to get rid of you. Mawingi together with Longo will stage a coup and become heroes in the eyes of the world. Cut off, you'll end up in the Hague answering charges of war crimes. Worse, those ZAL brutes will feast on your heart and liver."

Dankov seemed taken aback by Simone's vehemence.

She turned to Trager. "Let's have some tea while our soldier here thinks of heroic acts he will commit."

Simone took the kettle, poured tea into Trager's mug and extended her free hand to Dankov. "Let me have that mug back."

With a groan, Dankov leaned forward and handed back the borrowed mug.

Simone sat on the sand. For several minutes, not saying a word, she sipped her tea.

Trager tried to digest the information he had heard and wished he had access to a phone or e-mail. It was nearly midnight in New York. With satphones, the news of the massacre would make the early morning radio news and the newspaper late editions. Simone was right. It was the perfect moment for Bamondo's enemies, who had been held in check by Dankov, to make their move.

In the growing light, Dankov looked exhausted. His eyes were closed and he appeared to be dozing.

"Hey, soldier," Simone said. "You can sleep while you hurry back to Turako."

Dankov blinked rapidly then shook his head.

"You'll have to rush to Turako and keep Mawingi in check."

Trager remembered the fat commander of the army festooned with medals.

"That posturing poltroon understands only the power of guns. The students at the university will probably riot."

"You're panicking on an empty stomach," Dankov growled.

"Every Russian officer understands defense in depth. Except *you*--let the ZAL advance. Their trucks will break down. Let those badly disciplined bandits degenerate into a mob. Then, smash them near Turako." Simone hit the palm of her hand with a fist.

"They are promising land to the squatters. Their forces will grow as they advance."

"If Mawingi takes Turako, you won't have anywhere to retreat."

Simone was right. Dankov's position could quickly become untenable. Trager thought about possible avenues of escape. To the west was the Congo. Not much chance there, even if they managed to reach the relative civilization of Kisangani. They wouldn't have enough fuel to reach Chad to the north or Angola to the south.

"When you get to Turako, tell Professor Najua to crowd those drummers into the city. Mawingi will not move the army against the will of the witch doctors. We still have a chance, but you must move fast. Johnny and I will go to Loldawa."

Loldawa? That was Pygmy country. How could Simone still be thinking of going there when war was about to break out?

Dankov stood, undressed and went under the waterfall.

Trager looked at Simone. "Loldawa?"

She gave him her enigmatic smile. "At the moment, it seems like a suicide mission, but you're pretty good in the bush. Together, we'll make it."

Somewhere in the distance, a number of engines rumbled.

"If I'm to be of any help, I should get to the nearest phone and start filing your side of the story."

"There won't be any story to file if I don't get to Loldawa."

"What's so--"

"When you get to Loldawa, you'll know why. In the meanwhile, if we are captured, our story is that we were going to hide among the Pygmies."

Simone took a grenade out of her pocket. "But those animals will not capture me. I'll pull the pin and blow my head off first."

"That feels better." Dankov said. Without drying himself, he put his clothes back on. "My dear Kutuzova." Dankov was comparing Simone with General Kutusov who defeated Napoleon in 1812. "Your strategic thinking is correct. I will use Major Kisima's unit . . ." Dankov turned toward Trager. "I wish it was up to company strength, but we all operate as independent brigades. Kisima's will be the blocking force. He will provide your escort."

Trager remembered the tall, neat African saying, "I'm Major Kisima. At the least sign of resistance, I have orders to shoot."

Dankov picked up his rifle. "I'm off. Join me for breakfast." He left at a run.

Simone blew a kiss after him. "Igor . . ." She then turned to Trager. "Let's pack up and get out of here."

It took Trager less than five minutes to pick up stakes, roll up the sleeping arrangement, and toss everything into the car. Simone had the engine running. The moment Trager got in, she released the clutch and eased the car into the tall grass.

Trager lit a cigarette. It frustrated him not knowing what in the hell Simone was up to. He didn't mind taking risks with her. Actually, he was happy she seemed to trust and respect him. He was also amazed by the way she argued with Dankov, and won him over to her way of thinking. "You seem to have a good handle on Zengawal politics."

"Light me up."

Once she had her cigar going, Simone said, "It's the politics of scorpions. There's a lot of dancing around. Nothing happens 'til someone trips. Mawingi hates Igor because Igor has the respect of his African soldiers. Many of Igor's troops are deserters from Mawingi's army. Give Igor another two years and the new army will be quite capable of defending the country. Mawingi and his corrupt cronies will be history.

"Tony Bond has been successful in organizing the university students, mainly by distributing money and promising jobs. They're the fifth column that is to welcome the arrival of the ZAL."

"Where does Longo fit in?"

Simone shrugged. "For some reason, he won't arrest Bond who has been operating with impunity. My people report secret meetings between Longo and Bond."

Trager almost groaned. "And who are you?"

Simone stopped the car and blew smoke into Trager's face. "I'm the Kingmaker." She put the car in gear, seeming pleased with herself.

"You're as cryptic as ever."

"What we have working in our favor is the witch doctors and their belief in the Utabu."

The car reached the road. Simone turned and continued in low gear up the escarpment.

At the top, two soldiers in dusty camouflage uniforms and black berets stood pointing Kalashnikovs. "*Zimama.*"

Simone gave them the password of the day. "*Kiboko kali.*"

"*Enda mbele kidogo.* The soldiers waved them through.

After a kilometer and a half, trucks covered with camouflage netting stood parked off the road, just inside the forest. A soldier waved them into a cave-like space carved into the underbrush.

Dankov inspected the feet of about thirty soldiers in running shorts, sitting on the ground, their rifles neatly stacked in a row of pyramids.

Simone pointed at a group of men in civilian clothes, who sat in a circle drinking tea. "Those are members of Igor's Advance Reconnaissance Unit."

Trager got out of the car.

Finished with his inspection. Dankov said in Swahili, "You people are disgusting. It's early in the morning and your feet smell like a dead cow."

The soldiers laughed. A sergeant handed out a couple of bottles of warigi, Ugandan firewater. The bottles passed from mouth to mouth, each soldier taking a swig.

Dankov approached Trager and Simone and gestured toward the forest. "Breakfast."

A folding table covered with a crisp white tablecloth stood in a space cleared of brush. Trager was surprised to see wineglasses.

"I'll be right back," Dankov said.

Simone and Trager sat on folding stools. An orderly wearing a white jacket over his uniform poured red wine. "*Kahawa?*" coffee, he asked.

"*Tafadali.*" Please.

"I'm glad Igor has adopted the French Army tradition of wine for breakfast." Simone took a sip. "It tastes phenomenal."

The smell of frying fat wafted through the forest.

A sergeant rushed up. "*Ataman wapi?*"

"*Huko.*" Simone pointed in the direction Dankov had gone.

Dankov was just behind the bushes. Trager could hear what the sergeant said.

"Observation post three reports bird one engine coming this way."

"Contact with Falcon?"

"Informed. Here in thirty minutes."

The sergeant trotted past. A few seconds later, rattlers sounded all over the forest.

"Air raid alarm," Simone explained.

His face washed and shaved, Dankov reappeared wearing camouflage riding breeches and tall riding boots. Gold shoulder boards glinted in the light filtering through the trees.

The orderly poured Dankov a shot of vodka.

"Volunteers?" Dankov asked.

"I'll stick to the wine," Trager said.

Dankov raised his glass. "Life is wonderful when a soldier's table is graced by the presence of a beautiful and intelligent woman. To you, my dear."

The orderly brought Melamite plates with fried eggs and corned beef.

Without ceremony, Dankov dipped dark Russian bread into an egg yolk and began rapidly chewing. He looked like he had been starving. Trager waited until Dankov paused to have a swig of coffee. "In that uniform, you make an excellent target."

"In the business of turning defeat into victory, one must look the part. When I march into the palace this afternoon, it will be either as a conquering hero or a savior," he said brightly. Then, a frown appeared on his brow. "Simone, I have to keep Kisima in Turako until my arrival. The police and the black suits have turned violent against the drummers."

"I won't need him 'til the day after tomorrow."

"Good. Your escort will meet you at Kitanda."

Trager thought maybe Dankov would be more forthcoming with what was going on than Simone. "Maybe you, an old comrade, will explain?"

Dankov shrugged. "I'm just a simple soldier. All I can say is I won't have much of a rear guard to slow a ZAL advance. If they move, you and Simone will end up behind enemy lines."

Part III
Dance of the Scorpions

Chapter 30

"Hey!" Trager said. "If I'm going to get involved, don't you think I'm owed the courtesy of knowing what it is I'm going to do?"

Simone looked up from her food and shook her head slowly. "Igor can take you to Turako and tuck you safely into bed. Sabena stops in Turako tonight. You could be in Europe tomorrow, and comfortably follow events on the news."

Simone had a way of getting to him. He glared at her calm eyes. "That sounds like a good idea." He turned to Dankov. "Do you have a spare seat?"

Simone's face betrayed surprise.

For a few seconds, Dankov's eyes shifted back and forth between Trager and Simone. Finally, he laughed and said to Simone, "Even though out of uniform, he was always one hell of a soldier. I wish he were one of my officers. I trusted him in the past and have no regrets."

Trager heard sincerity in Dankov's words. It made him feel damn good.

"All right, Johnny, if you promise you'll blow yourself up before getting captured."

"I may."

"Tell him," Dankov muttered between his teeth.

Simone sipped her coffee then put her cup down with an air of finality. "The Pygmies have the Utabu."

Dankov added. "They won't release it to a woman or a soldier. Do you still want a seat in one of my trucks?"

"So *you* know where the Utabu is?"

Simone nodded, looking apprehensive.

For a moment, Trager enjoyed the power he held over Simone, and took a sip of wine. "Assuming the Pygmies give us the Utabu, then what?"

"Igor will provide an escort. In Turako, we'll deliver it to the Council of Witch Doctors who will then crown a new king."

"And who will that be?"

"Pierre has the right lineage."

The hum of a light airplane engine drew their attention.

Dankov said, "It sounds like the Societe Miniere's Cessna one-eighty. It has British Registration, G-ZLL. Bastards don't respect our air space. But, even flying low, they'll have trouble seeing us."

"You can't move while those blackguards are snooping," Simone said. "I'll bet they have reporters on board."

"Sokolov will give them a fright." Dankov glanced at his watch.

A soldier with a radio backpack approached. "It's Falcon, Ataman."

Dankov took the proffered handset. "Sokol, Ay Bolit."

Trager couldn't repress a grin on hearing Dankov's call sign. Dr. Ay Bolit was the Russian equivalent of Dr. Dolittle.

"No, don't shoot it down. Maybe scorch his paint with your exhaust."

Somewhere high above, a jet ripped through the sky.

Simone asked, "Well, have you decided?"

"Let's go visit the Pygmies," Trager said with a determination he didn't have.

Simone got up from the table and touched Dankov's epauletted shoulder. "Time to head for the swamps."

Dankov looked up at her and smiled. "We'll be rolling within half an hour." He reached and patted her backside. "Take care of yourself. I'd hate to see that nice derriere fall into the hands of the ZAL."

Not liking the sight of Dankov and Simone touching each other, Trager downed his coffee.

Simone laughed. "Look after your own backside. Your friends in Turako will be wielding daggers."

Dankov stood. "*Lete kitu yango*," he shouted, then took Simone by the shoulders and kissed her mouth.

The orderly arrived with Dankov's blue peaked cap and his Cossack sword.

Dankov turned to the radioman. "To battalion, prepare to move." He put on his cap at a rakish angle and took the sword in his hand.

"Let's go, Johnny," Simone said. "Our Air Force will have scared the pants off Bond's friends."

~

For a hundred and twelve kilometers they drove along the same road they had come down. The forest was beginning to thin when Simone said, "Slow down."

A small yellow metal sign with an arrow marked the intersection. It read:

> *Simwesi 14 Kms*
> *Kitanda 76 Kms*

Trager turned and glanced at his watch. "I guess we'll be in Kitanda by around ten thirty." Even with a bad road, it shouldn't take him over an hour and a half.

"Closer to eleven." Simone answered. She handed him a lit cigarette he didn't ask for. "We'll stop, have a Coke. It will take us the rest of the day to reach the Shikawamba River." She propped her feet against the edge of the glare shield. "It is one of the most beautiful places in Africa," she said as if they were on a tour. "It rivals the Okavango Swamps. I want to set up a permanent camp there. The bird life is prolific; hippo, crock, okapi, buffalo, leopard and elephant are plentiful. With an amphibious plane, tourist access will be easy."

"So in this moment of crisis, we go and see the wildlife."

Simone put her hands behind her neck, making her chest stand out. "I simply love the place."

"Is there another road, a track besides this one?" Trager asked, thinking that if the ZAL didn't wait too long to invade after Dankov's pull out, the junction where they had turned off was less than a three hour drive from the border.

"This is it." Simone gave him a mischievous glance. "Worried we'll get cut off?"

"Yes."

"Those ZAL nitwits won't realize Igor has pulled out for some time, maybe days. We're perfectly safe."

Trager sneered. "If what I gather is right, Tony Bond will be on the radio within minutes of Dankov's arrival in Turako."

"No sense in worrying about it now. If the escort isn't waiting for us at Kitanda the day after tomorrow, we'll have to find another way."

"Like walking?"

"Yes."

"That sounds like fun. We'll spend so much time together you'll end up falling in love with me."

Simone chuckled. "Never let the camel stick her nose into your tent. You'll end up with the whole camel. You wouldn't want that to happen."

"Who else knows the Pygmies have the Utabu?"

"You and Igor."

Trager added the man in the hat and Matungi to the list.

~

Trager didn't like what he was seeing. The forest had been cleared in spots. Miserable looking shacks dotted the landscape of withered crops. "I thought we were heading into the boonies teeming with wildlife."

"Squatters in search of a better life."

"I'd hate to see where these people came from."

"The rains will come in a few days. Fields will turn green. Maize, manioc, cassavas and beans will sprout like magic."

A large village loomed ahead.

"Lean on the horn and *don't* slow down. If we stop, we'll be mobbed. Before you know it, we won't have anything left. These people are desperately poor."

Trager blew the horn. Men dressed in rags stood in the middle of the road waving. A glance at Simone revealed she held her Kiparis at the ready.

Barely missing men who jumped out of the way at the last second, they drove through Simwesi and were out in the open again.

"Nice place."

"We have no police here. The squatters would think we want to evict them."

"Does it get better as we go further?"

"Sure." Simone was again comfortably seated with her feet up. "A few kilometers ahead, we'll be back in the forest, and Kitanda is a nice village. That's where we are developing a tourist center to learn about the Pygmy culture." She spread her arms as if flying. "Once we solve the problem of getting there . . ." She pointed at the side of the road. "We're making progress, the telephone line now reaches Kitanda."

"What keeps the squatters from spreading to Kitanda?"

"Poisoned arrows. We're entering Pygmy territory."

As the terrain dropped, trees grew taller and puddles of muddy water appeared on the road. The humid heat was oppressive.

Trager braked in surprise. After a turn, in front of him was a conglomeration of huts in the shade of a grove of tall trees. A large bright red-and-white sign in English stood at the side of the road.

> *Welcome to Kitanda*
> *Gateway to Loldawa Nature Reserve*
> *Information centre, tourist lodge*
> *Handicraft centre, traditional village cultural exhibit*

"The sign was posted in a moment of optimistic exuberance," Simone said. "But Papa Lal has two rooms for people to stay. And the Lodge is partially completed. The pygmies have already moved into the traditional village. They are such optimists, the dears."

Children poured out into the street and ran behind Schnookie, yelling and laughing. Simone waved at them. "We need a school here."

Trager stopped in front of a building with a corrugated roof and a sign: *Papa Lal's General Supplies*.

Simone took a paper bag and stepped out. The kids mobbed her, she handed each one a candy. She then reached in the back and took an armful of little books and handed them out to a couple of older girls who led the kids away.

An Indian came out on the porch and waved. On seeing who had arrived, he yelled, "Welcome back, Simone," and rushed back inside. A moment later he returned with two glass bottles of Coca-Cola.

Trager accepted one while Simone made introductions. The bottle was warm, but the tingling sensation the Coke gave his palate told him he was drinking the original blend, no longer available in the States or in most of the world.

Lal took a box out of the Land Rover and carried it into the store.

Trager thought, traveling with Simone was the most bizarre experience imaginable. One never knew one's destination. Here he was, drinking a Coke that no longer existed, at the end of a road to a non-existant tourist complex.

Simone looked at her watch. "Johnny, we have a few minutes. Let me show you our project."

She led the way through an alley to the back of the village. A plot of land had been cleared of brush, and trees had been felled to thin out the forest but still provide shade to a group of scattered Rondavels with conical roofs.

Simone made a sweeping gesture. "Imagine a beautiful garden and a swimming pool. The huts will have in-suite bathrooms. There," she pointed at a large thatched roof standing on pylons, "that's the dining room and bar."

"Chamwanamuma."

Trager turned to see two Pygmies holding a plywood sign.

Come visit
Pygmy village

"Oh." Simone made a pained sound then spoke in a language Trager could not understand. The Pygmies came to Trager, shook hands gravely and disappeared into the brush.

"It's heartbreaking," Simone said. "They won't give up waiting for the first tourists to arrive. They lack a sense of time. She again glanced at her watch and started back for the car.

Simone was right, the lodge would be a beautiful place when it was finished. "What's the holdup?"

"Money. Pierre promised funding in next year's budget."

Simone got into the driver's seat and waved at Lal, who now stood on the porch together with a woman in a sari, and two girls between the ages of eight and twelve.

As they left the village, another sign pointed to the beginning of a nature trail. Simone switched into four-wheel drive, steered into a shallow stream, and turned. It was like going through a tunnel. Branches made scratching noises on the Land Rover's roof. "This is the easy part."

Trager stuck his head out the window. Water came up to the wheel hubs. Leaves slapped his face.

A buffalo stuck its head out of the brush and quickly vanished.

"Hang on." Simone accelerated and turned sharply. The car slid sideways as wheels fought for forward traction. Schnookie went up a muddy embankment full with animal tracks. Wheels spun. "We need the winch."

Trager got out and sank nearly to his knees in mud. He unlatched the winch drum and plodded through the muck. He found a tree, looped and hooked the steel cable, and got out of the way.

The engine whined and Simone inched the car up the slope.

Trager inspected the track ahead. It looked like brown soup. He had difficulty walking and fell to his knees a couple of times. He didn't bother to get back to the car, just took the cable and hooked it to the next tree.

~

Three hours later, his every muscle aching, his face, hair, every inch of his body covered in mud, Trager was exhausted. It had taken them three to five minutes to advance thirty meters each time he hooked up the winch. They probably hadn't covered much more than a mile. Ahead, the track rose out of the mud. He could hardly believe his eyes--the track was dry.

Simone winched Schnookie one last time. "Hop aboard, mud-man. We are in what I call Happy Island."

Trager glanced down at himself. He probably looked like a swamp monster. "How much further?"

"About five hundred meters."

"Not to mess up Schnookie, I'll walk."

Simone smiled brightly. "Okay, just follow the track, then the river bank."

Trager watched the Land Rover vanish. With a stick, he tried to remove the ton of mud on his boots. Lurching like Frankenstein with squishy feet, he followed the track. After ten agonizing minutes, he walked out of the forest onto the shore of a wide river with floating islands of reeds. The track disappeared in a thick carpet of creeping grass. A fish eagle screamed in the distance. Closer to Trager, a young buffalo had stopped grazing and looked at him.

"Shit," Trager mumbled. All his stuff was in the car. He didn't even have the pistol to use as noisemaker. If he tried to shoo the animal, the buff would either run away or charge, making Tragerburger. It was a fifty-fifty proposition. Trager looked at the river. He could dive into the water if the buff came for him, but that was probably full of crocks.

Trager took a deep breath and ran screaming toward the buff, flailing his arms.

The buff lowered its ugly head, turned in place and crashed through the bush.

His heart pounding wildly, Trager ran past the spot where the buff had stood and kept going. The grassy shore narrowed and made a sharp turn. Trager realized he was on the tip of a peninsula. As he made the turn, he saw the Land Rover. Simone was still half bent over as she turned to see what was coming. The buffalo was heading straight for her.

"Simone," Trager shouted. The animal was almost on top of her.

She leaped to the side. A useless maneuver, a buff could turn inside the length of a human's leap.

The Land Rover got in the way of the agile brute's turn. The helmeted head crashed into Schnookie, pushing the car forward several feet.

Trager kept running and yelling in an attempt to distract the buff.

Simone was out of sight. The enraged buffalo banged the side of the vehicle, almost tipping it over. Simone crawled from under the car.

Trager was now quite close.

Boom. The buff struck again. Trager thought the teetering car would crush Simone.

"Stay back," Simone yelled. She tossed a grenade and ducked behind the car.

Trager hit the dirt.

The grenade went off with a dry, short bang.

He lifted his head.

The buff, blood running out of his nostrils, was coming for him.

Hooves pounded the ground. He heard the snorting breathing. Displaced air swished by. A white flash of pain. Realization, a hoof had grazed his forehead. Relief, the buff was past, crashing into the brush.

Trager staggered to his feet.

Simone shouted, "Olé." She then took Trager by the arm, steadied him and led him toward the car, where she had started to set up camp. The teakettle on the stove was boiling. "Sit, don't move."

The dizziness was going away but he couldn't see out of one eye.

With a hot washcloth, Simone wiped blood away. "Superficial. It's amazing how little scratches on the head bleed. Hold this against your forehead."

A moment later, she returned. Trager gritted his teeth.

"There," Simone said as she finished taping the dressing.

"It was all my fault--"

"Pshaw. Be quiet and take your clothes off. You're filthy." She began to unbutton his shirt. "You take your own trousers off."

Once he was completely naked, Simone said, "You can't bathe in the lake, bilhartzia." With a washcloth, she began wiping mud off his body. It felt heavenly. Trager tried to think of something else as she got close to his privates.

It didn't help.

Simone said, "Do your own monster."

Trager smiled. "At least you don't consider it a dwarf."

She smiled back. "It all went down there instead of to your brain. Roll over so I can do your back."

Finished cleaning him up, Simone asked, "Do you feel well enough to do my back?"

"Sure."

Trager lit a cigarette while Simone took her clothes off. The more he saw her naked, the more beautiful he found her.

Simone stretched face down on the grass. "Ah, it feels so good."

He poured water from the kettle onto the washcloth and let it cool. He then began rubbing her back. When he reached her waist, he couldn't resist planting a kiss between her shoulder blades.

She didn't say anything.

Trager went between her buttocks and then in between her legs. For a moment, her muscles tightened around his hand, then relaxed. He continued to wash the back of her legs.

"Roll over so I can do your front."

To his surprise, she rolled over.

He hesitated as he considered whether to start at her shoulders or the toes, then decided to carry on where he had left off. As he went beyond her knees, she opened her legs wider. Her eyes were closed.

He again visited the slot between her legs and heard a soft moan. The new moisture that indicated her acceptance filled him with elation and gratitude. He dropped the cloth and his fingers explored gently. Her hips moved ever so slightly. Her hand took his wrist lightly, guiding him in. A shiver went through his spine and his legs shook.

She picked up her knees and wrapped her legs around his neck, pulling him down.

His tongue found the slight bump and made it grow. He had the sensation she was suspended in midair, held by his hands on her buttocks.

First came a ripple and she moaned so he could barely hear it. A tremor, she tightened her hands on his head. Trager stopped. She took bunches of hair. He continued, very gently. A spasm, her hips raised his head like a jack. He held her down with his hands. Her hips wriggled and she said, "Stop."

He continued, she screamed. Her hips rose violently and fell. Both legs stretched, then relaxed and she released the grip on his hair.

Trager raised himself on his elbows. Her flushed face was more beautiful than ever. She looked at peace. Feeling guilty as if he were taking advantage of an exhausted angel, Trager guided himself in. He kissed a nipple. As he got in as far as he could get, she opened her eyes slightly, and, in a dreamy voice said, "Yes."

Her muscles tightened around him and she rose to meet him. Hands pulled and pinched his buttocks. His groans mixed with hers. Trager's body shook and the tremor traveled down his legs. Simone pressed his head against her breasts as she made gasping sounds and went limp.

For a long time they lay on the grass in each other's arms saying nothing. Simone finally broke the silence. "I've been trying to avoid this. It was that stupid buffalo."

"I love you," Trager said, not quite believing he had.

"Nonsense." With her hand, she brushed Trager's hair off his forehead. "Let's call it an accident and pretend it never happened."

"I can't do that. We were so beautiful together."

She gave him a tiny smile. "It was beautiful, and I thank you. Let's have some tea." She let go of him and sprang to her feet.

Trager rose and took her by the shoulders. "That wasn't a fuck and forget."

She shook her head. "No, it wasn't."

"Well?"

"You claim to love me?"

"Yes."

"Then remember me kindly and know that, for a few moments, I loved you, too."

~

The damage the buffalo had done to the Land Rover was impressive. It had bent the rear door badly. At least the thing was jammed closed. Right behind the driver's door, the whole side was bent and the window shattered. The grenade must have caused more damage to the car than the buff. Shrapnel had left hundreds of little nicks and peeled a good part of the paint.

The woman he had won and lost in a matter of minutes was now fully dressed in a pair of baggy army shorts and a clean khaki shirt primly buttoned up.

Trager watched in silence as she sat on the grass drinking tea and smoking a cigar. Confusion, sadness, and longing slapped at him like waves against a rock.

"It's biology," Simone said. "Sometimes it can't be helped."

"I have trouble understanding you."

"We have separate lives, separate paths."

"Sure, very separate. We're tied up like Siamese twins, stuck with each other more tightly than being married. You're holding those diamonds hostage. You've done everything but tie me up to come with you on this jaunt. And still, you won't tell me about the Utabu."

"I hope to find out tomorrow. Hear the drums?"

Trager turned his head in the direction Simone pointed. With the honking of hippo not far off, it was difficult to tell; maybe he did hear the faint sound of drums.

"That's the pygmies announcing our arrival. They should be here in the morning."

"You've changed the subject. We were talking about us."

"It may sound selfish, but I'm talking about me. I have a destination."

"What is it?"

She gave him a wry smile. "Just that you know I have a destination is too much. Only I will know when my journey ends. 'Til then, we can't be lovers."

Trager shook his head with bitter frustration. "You have more secrets than a medieval castle."

She gave him her now familiar enigmatic smile. "Tomorrow, your stubborn perseverance will pay off. You'll know more than you've ever wanted."

Chapter 31

The sun had settled below the horizon. Trager finished helping Simone set up her sleeping shelter and sat by the reeds of the riverbank watching white egrets settle like snowflakes on the top branches of a tree.

He was curious about tomorrow, yet he didn't want to be here. He longed for Simone, yet wanted as much distance between them as possible. For a few brief moments, she had surrendered to him and made him happy. Trager realized he was humiliated by her change.

Mosquitoes started biting, so he unrolled his shirtsleeves.

"Are you coming in, or do you want to feed mozzies and catch black water fever?"

"I'll sleep in the car."

"Wait. I'll put up a sign saying *free meal*."

"That's okay." With all the busted windows, the mozzies would eat him alive. The intensity of the buzz around him was growing.

"I have cognac," she sang in an inviting tone.

Trager flapped his arms about him, and reluctantly headed for the sheltered narrow mattress. A point of red light behind the mosquito net indicated Simone was smoking.

Trager got in and unlaced his boots.

"Don't act so ill tempered. Without me, you'd be in trouble."

"How's that?"

Every time you get angry, you forget your guns."

"Oh." Trager started unzipping the entrance.

"I have them here. Relax, we have nearly twelve hours 'til dawn. Have a cognac, smoke a cigar and be your charming self."

As he stretched next to her, Simone sat up and poured into a mug. "Now put your arm where it belongs--otherwise we won't fit." She handed him the mug and settled in the crook of his arm, lit a cigar and placed it into his mouth. "Comfortable?"

"I suppose," Trager said grumpily and took a sip of cognac.

"I see you're determined to be unpleasant."

"Sorry, I don't feel like talking."

"I'm glad you said sorry, because you're acting like a petulant child."

Too aware of her proximity and milky smell, Trager didn't say anything.

She rolled on her side, a breast rested on his chest. She squeezed his nose with two fingers. Trager said, "Honk."

"That's better. Maybe now we can talk."

"Okay."

"While you sulked, I was thinking." She paused. "He looks so miserable, maybe I should let him screw me all he wants. Would you like that?"

"The way you've put it, it sounds like charity."

"Because it wouldn't cost you one centime. I guess you could call it that. But it's not charity. The next few days might be difficult for us. We'll have to depend on each other. I want to be sure I can count on you no matter what."

Trager felt her hand doing something. He realized she was unbuttoning her shirt.

"Here, kiss it, suck on it." She moved up, her naked breast against his face.

He kissed it. "Button up, I get your point."

She gave him a big wet smooch on the cheek and snuggled closer. "That buffalo nearly killed both of us. You played such a wonderful role of jungle toreador. Then, lying in the grass under the sun, glad to be alive, I let myself go. Please forgive me."

Trager rolled over to face her. Her eyes sparkled in the starlight. They looked so beautiful, his gut tightened. "We shared that moment; there's nothing to forgive." He put his arms around her and she him. They stayed like that for a long time, saying nothing. Feeling her warmth and wondering about her mystery, Trager drifted into sleep.

~

When he woke, they were still locked in an embrace and Simone's eyes, speckled with gold, like those of a lioness, were blinking.

"Good morning, mud-man."

"Good morning, queen of the jungle."

"Get up. Let's make coffee before the Pygmies arrive."

~

Trager shaved using Schnookie's side view mirror and listened to the radio. The Bunaka massacre was at the top of the news. Governments around the world expressed outrage at the barbaric act allegedly committed by mercenaries on the Zengawal payroll. Last night in Turako, a university student protest turned into a riot, and a number of people including policemen were injured.

The government of Zengawal denied its forces were responsible. Commander of the Army, General Mawingi stated none of his units had been out of the barracks.

Trager was surprised to hear that in Turako, the newly arrived American chargé d' affaires had lodged a strong protest.

"The ball of the masked scorpions has started early. Let's hope we're not too late," Simone said.

Trager wiped his face dry. "You have a lot of faith in an object you can't even describe."

She placed a mug of coffee on the hood. "We'll turn the situation around."

"Sure."

With her elbows on top of the hood and displaying her enigmatic smile, Simone said, "Johnny, the nation of Zengawal depends on you. Shortly, the Pygmies will arrive and proclaim themselves your slaves. They will take us to the sacred place where the Utabu is. Tomorrow, we return and, escorted by a military column, you will make a triumphant entrance into Turako."

Trager put his mug down. "You mean to say . . . That . . . Me?"

"You're the chosen one," Simone said solemnly.

"I can't be king!"

Simone burst out laughing, bent over, and slapped the hood of the car. Tears were pouring down her face when she recovered from her fit. "Mud-man, the look on your face, I'll never forget. Drink your coffee, have a cigar. But don't stand there looking stupid."

His head spinning from Simone's shattering new twist, Trager lit a cigarette.

Simone inclined her head to one side. "No, you haven't been chosen to be king, only a humble messenger who will deliver the Utabu. You don't think much of yourself, no?"

"That's better. But why me?"

"It's in the prophecy."

Trager remembered the trip to Zamani, the witch doctor and the Pygmies. "This sounds to me like a bit of staged theater."

Simone lit a cigar. "Just helping history along. The witch doctors found the Utabu, but the white man descendant of the wizards to whom the Utabu could be entrusted, was nowhere to be found until you came along.

"That's why Longo wanted those photographs proving you went to Zamani and there the ghosts of the ancients told you the location of the Utabu."

"But that's a lie. I still don't know what the Utabu is."

"We'll find out today."

"I've been manipulated."

"Manipulated? Look at the story you will have. Think of the Putzer Prize."

"Okay, we pick up the Utabu and take it to Turako. So what *is* the Utabu?"

Simone shrugged. "We'll know when we see it."

A rhythmic chant came from the direction of the river.

"Here they come."

As they stood waiting for the canoes to appear, Simone said, "I will stand behind you and prompt you what to do."

A number of dugout canoes that made Trager think of peanut shells appeared from behind a floating island. The rowers turned toward the riverbank and let their craft slide into the reeds.

An old Pygmy wearing a leopard-skin cape and a black-and-white colubus monkey headdress stepped ashore, his hand raised, brandishing a stick with a bulbous end. He looked at Trager, shouted, "Chamwanamuma."

"Chamwanamuma," answered the fifty or so Pygmy chorus. They all came ashore carrying spears and prostrated themselves on the ground.

"Now take this." Simone handed Trager a palm branch. "Go down the line and touch each one on the head with the branch. Do the chief last."

Trager followed Simone's instructions, not knowing whether to feel foolish or important. When he finished, the chief got on his knees in an attitude of begging and launched himself into a long speech.

"In short, he thanks you for your blessing and begs you to accept him and his worthless people as your slaves, the same way you have accepted the white mama, protectoress of the little people, as your slave. Now I will carry your bag as you get into the chief's canoe. And don't be startled when these people rush and grab you."

The chief finished talking.

With ululating yelling, the Pygmies rushed Trager, lifted him off the ground and raised him above the mob. He floated over a sea of shaved heads. With so many spears around him, Trager was sure he would end up skewered. After carrying him up and down the riverbank in some sort of ceremony, the Pygmies deposited him in a canoe.

Simone handed him his duffel with the guns, said, "Chamwanamuma," and blew him a kiss.

The flotilla headed down the river. A drumbeat tattoo sounded from one of the canoes. The beat was repeated further downstream. Whatever had brought him here, it was as if he had traveled back in time.

A few meters away, only slightly behind, was the canoe carrying Simone. She had attached her long black headscarf as a hatband on her wide- brimmed canvas hat and looked regal.

Trager took his camera out. The sun was still low and the light had that golden glow that gave depth to African photographs. Against the dark green background of jungle, Simone looked fantastic. Trager shot three verticals and three horizontals, changing f/stops. If Simone with her Pygmies, didn't end up gracing the cover of some magazine, he would give up taking photographs.

Today, the egrets sitting on the trees looked like cotton puffs.

Trager took a picture of a cloud of white as they left their overnight perches.

They came to a sharp bend of the river. Hundreds of crocodiles rested on mud banks, their mouths open as if waiting for food to drop out of the sky. Beyond the crocks, a herd of hippo watched the passage of the canoes with curiosity.

Trager was so enthralled with the beauty of the river that for hours he didn't think of his problems with Simone, the riots in Turako, or the possibility of an invasion by the ZAL forces. In some sort of delta, even though he was pretty sure that their general direction of travel was northwest, they made so many twists and turns that he was totally lost.

They entered a narrow channel where the canoes had to go single file. A high, sandy bank rose on one side. Out of the thick growth on top of the bank, crocodiles slid down the sand and splashed into the water.

Drums began to beat a slow rhythm.

A turn in the channel revealed a village under giant fig trees. Like fruit, the sprawling branches were loaded with Pygmies holding bows and arrows.

In a cleared area that looked like a canoe landing, Pygmy women with shaved heads and wearing scant leather loin cloths danced, beating buffalo horns together. A number of elders with leopard-skin capes stood holding sticks with monkey skulls mounted on the tips.

The drumming and dancing stopped as the canoes, one by one, slid to the landing. Trager looked up at the Pygmies in the tree branches and swallowed. The little men stood with their bows and arrows ready to launch, aiming at *him*.

Simone said, "Don't move."

Now what? She had said this before.

She got out of her canoe, faced Trager and pointed at him. She then prostrated herself and shouted, "Chamwanamuma."

The people on the ground followed suit, laying down flat. A deep hush settled over the village. Hippo honked in the distance.

The chief disembarked.

Simone said, "Take your palm branch and prepare to bless the elders and the ceremonial virgins."

Trager looked up. Arrows still aimed at him. His legs tense, he stepped ashore and blessed the elders.

The virgins screeched, jumped up, formed a butt-to-bellybutton line and came down dancing and beating their horns together. As they passed Trager, chanting "oogah-oogah," he touched each with his branch. Simone now stood next to him but slightly behind. "Follow the virgins to the sacred tree."

"How come those guys in the trees are aiming at me?"

"You have to pass the tests. If you're not the real Chamwanamuma, they'll kill you."

"Thanks for warning me."

"I didn't want to scare you. Keep looking straight ahead, ignore the arrows."

It seemed like a thousand ants were running up and down Trager's back.

The sacred tree was a huge fig with roots so large a man would have to clamber over them. Trager saw three seats carved at the base of the trunk.

"You take the center one."

Trager took his seat as Pygmies flooded into what looked like a village square. His attention was drawn by a hut with human skulls neatly stacked against its walls.

The virgins formed a circle and stomped the ground.

The chief sat on Trager's right, Simone on his left. Trager wondered where the bags with the guns were. "How long will this last?"

"All day."

"What if one of their fingers slips?"

"That would be a bad sign. No?"

Women brought out gourds and handed them around.

"Pombe," the chief said.

Trager looked into his gourd. Bees, some still alive, floated in a milk-like frothy liquid. He was grateful for the hollow stick acting as a straw.

The drumming stopped.

"Raise your gourd and toast your slaves."

Trager stood, slowly turned holding the gourd above his head. For the moment, at least, it protected his head from the arrows.

"Chamwanamuma," the crowd roared.

Trager sat and pulled on his straw. The bittersweet drink was just what he needed. "What's this Chamwanamuma?"

Simone, who had maintained the gravity of a high priestess, laughed. "You are."

The chief laughed, too. The crowd roared and the drumming resumed.

By mid-afternoon, the virgins were still stomping. The chief dozed. Trager's gourd was empty and drowsiness was about to best him. Some of the Pygmies in the crowd staggered around, drunk. The Pygmies in the trees continued aiming.

"How much longer," Trager asked.

"'Til the witch doctor comes out of his hut. He is deciding whether or not you are the real Chamwanamuma."

Trager glanced at the hut with the skulls. "He's only now deciding?"

"Yes."

"And what happens if his decision is negative?"

"Your skull will be added to his collection."

"And what happens to you?"

"Nothing." Simone gave him her slight smile. "Don't worry, you're doing very well."

"I'm falling asleep."

"Don't. I think he's watching through a peep hole."

Trager fought to stay awake. The stuff he had drunk was potent. He wondered how Simone would react if they decided to string him up or whatever they did to impostors. He should have stayed in the States and faced the IRS.

~

At sunset, a little hunched-up man, a small drum slung on his shoulder by a leather strap, came to the witch doctor's hut.

The drumming stopped. The tireless virgins left the square.

"This is it. The moment of truth is approaching," Simone said, her tense face covered with beads of perspiration.

For the first time, Trager read fear in Simone's voice.

Chapter 32

The little man began to drum and whirl in a circle before the witch doctor's door. Everyone stood still, watching the drummer, except the Pygmies in the trees, watching Trager. The effect of pombe was wearing off and Trager, who had managed to keep his mind off the arrows pointing at him, again became painfully aware of them.

Gradually, the tempo of the drumming increased, as well as the speed of the drummer's whirling. He appeared to be in a trance.

The virgins returned carrying torches, and formed an aisle in front of the witch doctor's hut.

The drummer went into convulsions and the drumming sounded like a fast-firing machine gun. His hands moved so fast they became almost invisible and seemed to smoke.

Flames erupted on the drum.

The drummer fell backward.

A collective "Ahh" filled the square.

Several Pygmies rushed to the drummer now curled on the ground, pulled the burning drum away, and beat the flames out with strips of leather.

The witch doctor emerged from the door. "Chamwanamuma," he said in a loud, booming voice.

Simone squeezed Trager's hand. "You've made it."

The Pygmies broke into song. "Chamwanamuma . . ."

Trager couldn't believe his ears.

". . . guajira chamwanamuma,"

Lacking were the Spanish words for Guantanamera: *Yo soy un hombre sincero de donde crece la palma.* He glanced at Simone. "Did you teach them that?"

"They needed a song."

Archers no longer aimed at Trager. They had left the trees and danced.

"Chamwanamuma, guajira chamwanamuma, chamwanamumaaaa . . ."

The chief led the procession toward the witch doctor, who wore a necklace of monkey skulls and a colubus monkey cape.

The chief motioned for Trager to follow the witch doctor inside.

"When you enter, get down on your knees and bow," Simone said as she went in behind Trager.

The hut was dark, lit only by two oil lamps made of coconut shells.

Trager got on his knees, bowed to the witch doctor, who tapped his shoulders with the monkey skull, then touched his head.

"So far, so good. You may sit."

The witch doctor's yellow eyes shone in the dim light. He began to talk. Simone translated.

"Chamwanamuma, son of the wizards. You came to save the little people, guardians of the Utabu and rulers of their masters. The wisdom of the moon and the sun and all the stars is in the Utabu."

The witch doctor raised his arms. "*Uatabu ya kabala, ile mtoto yako?*"

"Give him the password."

"What password?" Trager asked, trying to keep panic in check.

"The one you used in Zamani."

Trager remembered. "*Funga da milango.*"

The witch doctor bowed, his head touched the dirt floor. He then reached to his side and picked a bundle wrapped in a colobus monkey skin. He carefully unwrapped it.

Trager watched fascinated as gold glittered.

"Utabu," the witch doctor pronounced gravely.

On top of the unwrapped monkey skin was a golden dome with a heavy band at the bottom. It was a helmet reminiscent of the Toltec heads, Trager had seen in the Yucatan peninsula.

The witch doctor turned the helmet over. Now it looked like a bowl.

"Now comes the ultimate proof," Simone said. Out of her pocket she took out Leonora's bag and poured the sparkling stones into the helmet.

"Zawadi ya Mungo," the witch doctor muttered. He handled the stones and looked at several of them closely. "*Sawa sawa.*"

A bit too quickly, as if afraid the witch doctor would keep them, Simone scooped up the diamonds and returned them to her pocket. "Now pick up the Utabu and march with it to the hut of honor; just follow the virgins."

Trager picked up the Utabu. It was incredibly heavy.

As he stepped out of the hut, holding the Utabu close to his chest, the crowd gave a collective gasp. "Utabu." The whisper rippled through the square.

The drummer who had earlier caused his drum to burst into flames, led the procession, beating a slow cadence on his charred instrument, past prostrated Pygmies. The virgins holding torches formed a path to another hut.

Trager was filled with a strange humility. He was holding an ancient object, supposedly thousands of years old. The similarity of this with the Toltec stone sculptured heads made him think of the links between Egyptian and Mayan pyramids and the possible connections between mysterious and lost civilizations. His legs automatically followed the cadence of the drumbeat.

He almost lost his balance as he stooped to enter the hut.

"Here." Simone spread the colobus skin on top of a bamboo pallet serving as bed.

Trager placed the Utabu on top, and Simone wrapped it in the monkey skin.

Totally exhausted, Trager sat on the pallet and wiped sweat from his brow. Throughout the day, he hadn't had a cigarette; he now wanted one badly. He took the pack out of his shirt pocket and lit one.

Their duffels were in the room. Simone opened hers, took out a bottle of cognac and poured into coconut half-shells.

Outside, it sounded like a party was going on.

Trager sipped his cognac, trying to come out of his state of semi-stupefaction.

Simone said, "Mud-man, you were great."

"Perhaps you can explain this Chamwanamuma business, it seems to me as if I've been used to perpetrate a major swindle on these people."

Simone touched coconut shells and kissed Trager on the cheek. "While working with the Pygmies, I found out about the Utabu and how it would unify the three tribes of the kingdom of Zengawal. According to the witch doctors, the position of the stars was about right for the prophesy to come true. Now it has come true. Everything fits into place as if foreordained by the stars. Even the diamonds from King Solomon's mines." Simone waved the little bag in front of Trager.

King Solomon's mines? Like an idiot, Trager followed the swinging motion of the bag.

"Once we have a strong government and an army powerful enough to protect us, the secret of our discovery will be revealed to the world. Imagine the immense riches just this little bag will represent."

Simone sighed. "For the moment, these diamonds are sold at a fraction of their real value to cover expenses. Dealers in Europe are going crazy trying to figure out who the cutters are. They don't know that the stones were cut thousands of years ago by the wizards of Zamani."

"Is that what Dankov is doing? Protecting King Solomon's treasure?"

Simone nodded. "The only man on earth honest enough not to take off with the loot. And he thinks you're the only man honest enough to be entrusted with the Utabu. We had to keep everything secret even from you because Longo and Bond will stop at nothing to take possession of the Utabu and find the location of King Solomon's treasure."

The sense of unreality increased as Trager tried to absorb the enormity of what Simone said. Even though she dispensed her revelations in small doses, it was still difficult for Trager to come to terms with his situation.

A group of virgins bearing bowls with food and gourds of pombe entered the hut.

Trager realized he was ravenously hungry.

As the virgins laid out the food on a woven mat on the floor, Simone looked into each bowl. "Crocodile tail, warthog, snake, frog--one eats well here, no? With a gesture, she invited Trager to sprawl on the mat.

"As the honored guest, the girls will feed you."

There was a lot of giggling as the sweaty and sour smelling virgins knelt around him and fed him bits of food with their grubby little hands. The sipping of pombe helped a lot. After a few mouthfuls, Trager began to enjoy the bizarre dinner.

He particularly liked crocodile. It vaguely reminded him of lobster. As each girl urged him to eat her food, he ate slowly and accepted a little from each one. After a number of rounds, he was full to the point where it was difficult to move.

Trager crawled up to the pallet as the virgins left.

"A cigar and a good cognac for the digestion. Didn't the dinner surpass your wildest fantasies with women?" Simone placed a cigar in Trager's mouth, lit it with a match.

"I'm too full of new impressions to absorb them all. There's only one more thing I want, but you won't give it to me. Or will you?"

"We're not going to start on that again?"

"I'm an optimist."

"Don't be. Part of the prophesy was that the Chamwanamuma would deposit diamonds into the Mama."

Trager's heart sank. Sadness and anger vied for dominance. Sadness prevailed. "You use men," he said bitterly.

"Despite myself, I'm being honest with you. Doesn't that count for something?"

"I think I'm beginning to hate you."

"That's because you're selfish. A woman gives herself to you and you want to own her. No man will ever own me."

"Do you hate men that much?"

"I only admire men worthy of admiration. Wanting me for my sex is not an admirable quality."

"I told you I love you."

"That's your weakness."

Trager decided his best policy was to remain quiet. Simone did not pursue the conversation, and blew out the lamps.

In the darkness, he felt her getting on the pallet, stretching out next to him without touching. The drums outside mixed with the drumming reverberating inside his head as he drifted into a neverplace where dreams and reality swirled.

The drums were still going strong when Trager realized he had been sleeping. Simone had rolled over and slept with her face on his shoulder and an arm around his chest. Trager stroked her hair and she mumbled something. He placed his cheek against hers.

When he woke again, the drumming had stopped. Light filtered around the sides of the buffalo skin covering the door. Simone was gone.

With a sense of panic, Trager looked for the Utabu and found it under the pallet. The pombe had left a nasty taste in his mouth and his head buzzed. He put on his hat and strapping the pistol on, went outside. The village looked empty. The only noise came from bell-like calls of kingfishers resting on branches above the river.

At the canoe landing, villagers lined up to see Simone who sat next to her medicine box playing Doctor Schweitzer.

When she saw Trager, she waved.

"When are we heading back?"

"First, I have to finish sick-call. It looks like about noon."

Craving a coffee or tea, or anything, Trager returned to the hut and listened to the radio. He swore. The local news broadcast was over. Radio Turako was transmitting a French language lesson. On the BBC, he caught something about Zimbabwe willing to participate in a peacekeeping mission. Trager missed what country it was meant to be in. On Voice of America he heard that the U.S. was sending forensic experts to the Congo. Trager would need to wait until evening. Accidentally, he stumbled unto Radio Kampala's News of the Hour. After quoting the price of coffee and other commodities, the reader said, "Rioting continues in Turako. Throughout the night, police battled masses of rioters in the city center who have been demanding the resignation of President Bamondo. The Belgian Government has dispatched an aircraft to Turako to evacuate Belgian nationals and other European Union citizens. Sources who have requested anonymity stated that foreign mercenaries in the pay of President Bamondo are responsible for the Bunaka massacre.

"In Lumumbashi, a spokesman for the Zengawal Army of Liberation stated that ZAL columns were marching onto Turako finding little resistance. The adoring crowds the Liberation Fighters are meeting at every village they enter, and volunteers who are swelling the ZAL's ranks, cause the main delays. The spokesman added that the campaign so far was reminiscent of President Musoveni's victorious march to Kampala in 1985."

It looked like it was curtains for Dankov, who, if he had any sense, would have left the country by now. Likewise, if Trager had brains, he would do well to stay with the Pygmies until things quieted down, then make his way north to the Sudan, where they would probably castrate him for carrying an American passport. *Thank you, Uncle Sam, for being such a dumb shit and making the world unsafe for Americans.*

And, nice work, Trager. You've been charmed by a crafty woman into doing the most stupid things. Chawanamuma, my ass. Yet, on the banks of the river he had never had such wonderful feeling of oneness with a woman. *Then remember me kindly and know that, for a few moments, I loved you ,too.* Yes, despite her scheming and theater, for a few moments, she had loved him. Of this he was sure. He was also sure that, by allying himself with Simone, he had added more people to the Get Trager Club.

He still craved coffee when Simone returned just before one o'clock.

"We'll be leaving shortly," she said, as she flopped on the pallet and wiped her sweaty face with a towel. "Someday soon, we'll have a clinic and a tourist lodge."

"The ZAL have invaded. There's no resistance."

"Light me up."

She puffed on the cigar, looking thoughtful. After a minute, she pulled her machine pistol out of the bag. Like a suicidal heroine about to sell her life dearly, she slapped a magazine in and let the bolt slam home.

Trager almost laughed at the gravity of her expression.

"Okay, let's get going. *La gloire nous atends.*"

Chapter 33

Nearing dusk, the Pygmies stormed ashore like a bunch of small Marines. Looking a wreck, Schnookie was still there and none of the gear they had left behind had been touched.

After scouring the bush for ten minutes, the Pygmies returned, some of them carrying firewood. The leader spoke to Simone for a minute, while others started a fire and laid a large gutted catfish next to it.

Simone turned to Trager. "There is no danger around us. Tomorrow, we will meet the escort. Everything is going according to plan, no?"

Trager waved at the Pygmies as they set off back to their island. It was time to hear the evening news.

> "This is the Voice of Zengawal News. Michel Bikala at the microphone. The chief of the metropolitan police confirmed that the thousands of participants in illegal witchcraft rites have been released from the Turako National Stadium where they had been detained, some for several days.
>
> "The minister of defense has confirmed that rebels have entered Zengawali national territory from bases in the Congo. In an impromptu news conference for foreign journalists who had just arrived, he stated Zengawal defense forces were deploying and were capable of dealing with the threat. He did confirm that Ugali Township had fallen to rebels marching from the southwest, but that the column was halted and dispersed in a bombardment by the Zengawal Air Force.
>
> "In a radio address this morning, President Bamondo urged calm and national unity at a moment when foreign interests are trying to destabilize the country.
>
> "In other activities of the day, the president held a regularly scheduled cabinet meeting and visited the newly opened supermarket Nyumba ya Mpishi, where he was applauded by the shopping public."

"What do you say to that, you panic monger?" Simone took Trager's nose and squeezed.

"Honk." Trager wanted to say it was all government propaganda or wishful thinking, but he kept quiet.

"Here. Have a cognac while the coals get ready to roast the fish."

Trager accepted the mug and a cigar. He sat down with his back leaning on a fallen tree trunk and watched fireflies begin to sparkle over the river.

Simone sat next to him. "I always feel sad on the last night of a safari. I particularly like the early evenings when it begins to cool off and the excitement of the day is over. It is so peaceful here."

"Yeah." He thought of the ZAL column advancing out of the southwest. The radio hadn't said anything about the west, which appeared to be Dankov's main worry. This would be the column that would cut them off. He remembered the disgruntled squatters at Simwesi village. They looked like prime candidates to join the ZAL when it arrived.

Without realizing he had done it, Trager had placed his arm around Simone's shoulders and she was leaning against him.

"Tomorrow, when we arrive in Turako, the city will come alive with joy when it becomes known the Utabu is there. This time, I look forward to returning to the city."

"Longo will have been going crazy trying to figure out where I've gone. *He'll* be happy to see me."

Simone said airily, "We'll find you a room at the palace. In a few days, you will no longer need to worry about Longo. I think he will play his hand and fall."

Trager wanted to believe her. "I hope you're right, but now we have the fog of war to thicken the mist of politics. Not the best time to be touring the country."

"Mud-Man, you're such a comfort."

~

Simone turned Schnookie onto what looked like a cattle crossing. With wheels spinning, Schnookie climbed up the bank. Its front wheels bit into hard ground. The acceleration gave Trager a sense of relief. Again, he was splattered up to his ears in mud. As they approached the village, he thought of the pleasure of washing the mud off.

The street was empty. Simone rolled up to Lal's store and stopped.

"Where can I wash this muck off?"

"There's a well behind the store. I'll ask Papa Lal." Simone got out of the car.

Trager glanced around. The street was still empty. Where were the children? With an uneasy feeling, he turned and called to Simone as she vanished inside the store.

Trager dug in his duffel, took out the Kiparis. He got out of the car, warily looking around. The village and the surrounding forest were eerily silent.

Simone staggered out of the store, retching.

Trager didn't need to ask what she had seen. He ran through the store, into the back where the buzz of flies was loud.

As his eyes adjusted to the dimness, the full horror of the scene appeared like a movie fade-in. A gruesome tableau of bodies with their throats cut sprawled on a cement floor carpeted with coagulating blood. The bodies of a woman and a twelve-year-old girl were naked. Lal's hands were tied behind his back.

Trager staggered out of the room and controlled his urge to vomit.

Outside, Simone sat on the porch steps covering her face with her hands. Trager touched her shoulder. "Someone will pay for this," he said as outrage replaced horror.

"Here they come, they're late. *Too* damn late." Simone lifted her head as two open Land Rovers loaded with soldiers drove down the street.

The Land Rovers stopped.

Trager's brief sense of relief vanished as soldiers jumped out of the vehicles and pointed rifles at him. Some were barefoot. Others were half-uniformed. Camouflage jackets, black trousers.

Trager recognized one of the would-be muggers from outside the Okapi Bar.

"Drop your weapon," Mugger said.

Simone, as if not accepting the reality of the situation, stood up and demanded, "Where is Major Kisima?"

Mugger, his interest now on Simone, laughed. His men imitated him. "He's bye-bye." Mugger's bloodshot eyes stared at Simone while he licked his lips. "What a nice day we're having. First Hindi, now white meat."

A desperate tingling sensation ran through Trager's body as the men laughed again.

In apparent horrified collapse, Simone slid down a post supporting the porch roof.

Trager surveyed the mob in front of him. He still had the machine pistol in his hand. He couldn't kill the dozen or so men all at once. Probably the kindest thing to do was to shoot Simone.

Mugger's rheumy eyes were back on Trager. "Drop that fucking gun."

Trager could hardly control his growing rage. In front of him stood a gang of rapists and murderers that only a minute ago he had vowed to make them pay. In his impotence, he had trouble unclenching his fingers from around the pistol grip.

With a rifle pointed at Trager's chest, a young African advanced, his eyes shining with malice.

There had to be a way out of this mess. To find it, he had to stay alive. Trager let the Kiparis clatter on the floor.

The man's depraved grin magnified as he reached over and took Trager's pistol out of its holster.

It appeared the goons were blind to the fact Simone sat with a machine pistol on her lap. Maybe they couldn't imagine a woman as being dangerous.

Mugger got out of the Land Rover and sashayed up to Trager, a nasty smile on his face. "We meet again. This time I can kill." He turned to Simone. "First is your turn to watch." He hit Trager with his fist and sent him sprawling against the wall. "How's that, *petite chou*?" He rubbed his fist and laughed. "Where's the Utabu?"

"The what?"

Mugger turned to his men. "She doesn't know."

The men laughed.

Trager looked at his machine pistol behind the young lout's feet, almost within reach.

"Maybe she's hiding it between her legs?" Mugger gesticulated like a stage actor. "Do we have the right tools for a search?"

"Yes." The goons chorused inching their way toward Simone.

"Wait." Mugger pointed. "You two search the car." He then said to Simone, "Colonel Longo is upset. You left without permission. I will punish you." Yellow, foamy spittle ringed the edges of his lips. His eyes turned to Trager. "And you." He chuckled. "You owe me one. Bring my leg."

One of the thugs handed him a piano leg.

"Before fucking, the bull impresses the cow. Isn't that right, *petite chou*?" Mugger nodded at the young man, who grabbed Trager by the front of his jacket and hoisted him up. Trager darted sideways. The piano leg banged against the corrugated metal wall.

Out of the corner of his eye, Trager saw Simone wave. "Igor, you're just in time," she shouted.

As all heads turned, three spindles flew out of Simone's hand and grenades shot straight up into the air, one behind the other.

Simone leapt, hit Piano Man in the face with her machine pistol, and ducked inside the store. Trager followed, diving through the door as grenades burst just above the porch's overhang.

A lethal shower of shrapnel sliced through the goons in the street, most of whom got knocked down with the first explosion. The porch roof crashed down.

The man who had disarmed him hit Trager with the butt of his rifle. With the air knocked out of him, Trager could hardly move. Still, he managed to grab a booted foot and twist. The man fell backward. Desperately, Trager reached out and clawed his fingers into the man's testicles.

The momentum of the howling man's falling body helped Trager get on his feet. He grabbed the man's rifle and stepped outside. Several goons staggered aimlessly on the street. The two men who had been behind Schnookie were bringing rifles to their shoulders. Trager fired from the hip. The men ducked.

He took a grenade out of his pocket, holding it in his fist, pulled the pin with his thumb and rolled the grenade under the car. It exploded just beyond Schnookie. The two bodies flew up and thumped on the dirt.

The carnage the tiny Belgian grenades had created was simply amazing. Trager looked for the Piano Man. The bastard had vanished.

On the far end of the street, crouching men darted from hut to hut.

"Here comes the rest of them," Simone said. "And look what you've done to Schnookie."

The car squatted, both rear tires flat.

Trager jumped on the nearest military Land Rover and swiveled the machinegun aiming to the rear. He fired a short burst at the corner of a hut behind which some men had ducked. Dust flew as bullets went through the wattle walls. A body rolled out from behind the hut.

"Transfer our things to this vehicle."

Simone carefully put the Utabu on top of a folded camouflage net inside the truck bed.

Trager fired at a man running across the street but missed.

The lack of targets told him that the fiends were coming around from behind him. "Hurry."

Simone threw in their bags and several rifles.

"Pour gasoline on the other truck and light a match. Schnookie, too."

"Not Schnookie."

"Do it," Trager yelled.

Simone took a jerry can from a rack and placed it inside the truck. She took the other one and poured gasoline on the other vehicle. She lit a cigar and tossed it at the truck, which erupted in flames. Smoke masked Trager's view, giving cover to the advancing black suits.

A couple of shots rang out behind him. Simone had shot two holes through the radiator and was removing Schnookie's distributor cap.

"Hurry."

Simone got in the driver's seat and made a U turn.

Trager sprayed bullets through the smoke.

As they came out of the smoke, a man stepped from behind a hut and fired from his hip. Simone swerved. The man's terrified face vanished under the hood. There was a bump as a rear wheel rolled over his body.

They drove out of the village. A yellow school bus stood parked next to the welcome sign. Behind the bus lay a line of naked bodies in the ditch at the side of the road.

"Stop." Trager sprayed the bushes around them, and jumped out of the truck. "Here." Simone handed him his Makarov and the Kiparis.

All the men had their hands tied behind their backs and had been shot in the back of the neck. Major Kisima was one of them. Scattered about lay a number of black safari suits Longo's men had discarded. Trager fired a shot at the fuel tank under the bus. A stream of diesel poured out. Trager took a black safari jacket, rolled it up and stuck it briefly under the stream. Stepping away from the bus, he ignited the jacket with his lighter and tossed it under the bus.

Trager turned to get back in the Land Rover and stopped in his tracks.

Simone's chest was covered in blood. She had stuck paper tissues into the nostrils of what now was a swollen purple nose.

"What happened?"

"I don't know. Something hit me."

"Can you drive?"

She nodded.

Trager climbed in.

She drove like a maniac for about five minutes then the truck began to weave. She slowed down. "I don't feel well. You better--"

A blood-coughing spasm racked Simone. She splattered blood on the front panel as she stopped the truck.

My God. With all that blood from her nose, he hadn't noticed . . . Her shirt so splattered in red, it was impossible to tell where else she had been hit.

"Where are--"

Simone coughed again and pulled the tissues out of her nose, releasing a torrent of blood. "That's better." She staggered off her seat and holding onto the truck, came around the passenger side. Trager poured water on his towel and handed it to Simone.

He put the truck in gear and drove. He needed to put some distance between them and that mob of goons before he could take care of Simone.

The truck bounced and swayed as Trager drove fast. Loose articles in the back made a racket that could be heard a mile away. Simone swayed, about to fall off her seat. With his free hand, he held her by the arm to keep her from slumping and hitting her face on the dashboard. He forced himself to slow down. If he broke an axle, that would be it. At about thirty kilometers from Kitanda, Trager stopped.

Simone appeared unconscious.

Trager opened the passenger door, took her into his arms and carried her to a shady spot under some bushes.

"Mud-man," she croaked. "Water."

Trager unbuttoned her sticky shirt, inspected her chest. There were no wounds. She was still bleeding from the nose and had a nasty powder burn on the back of her cheek, neck and ear. He touched her forehead. It was feverish.

Trager rifled through the medical box. He emptied a packet of hydration powder into a mug with water and slowly fed it to Simone then gave her two antibiotic pills. After covering her with a wet towel, he went back to the truck.

The Land Rover was equipped with SSB, FM and VHF radios. He turned the SSB set on, released the folded whip antenna, and pressed the mike button. "Anyone read me on this frequency--over?" he said in French.

Static crackled on the loudspeaker.

He tried again.

The speaker came to life. A faraway voice came in broken. Sta . . . alling . . . nfy . . . crackle.

"This is John, this is John calling Ataman, calling Ataman."

". . . again."

Trager repeated his call.

"Change to crackle three two. I say crackle frequency crackle two."

"You are unreadable say again frequency."

"Crackle crackle crackle, five five crackle."

Trager turned the synthesizer knob to 5532. "This is John calling Ataman."

A voice came in clear but weak. *"Goja kidogo, sisi tafuta."*

The heat of the sun burned right through his shirt as he waited while someone went looking for Dankov. Idly, Trager inspected the mess of loose gear in the back of the open truck. *The Utabu, where was it?* With relief, he pulled the camouflage net to the side and saw the monkey skin next to a machete in a corner, together with a jumble of ammunition drums that had spilled out of a can.

"Juliet, this is Vulture."

Trager breathed a sigh of relief. "Urgent message for Ataman."

"My call sign is Vulture, is Ishtar with you?"

"Affirmative."

"Where is Nubian?"

"If you're talking about escort, they were ambushed, no survivors."

"*Reçu.*"

Trager waited for Dankov to digest the information.

"Your call sign is Ishtar, what is your position?"

"Thirty kilometers south of rendezvous point. Hostiles occupying village, Ishtar wounded." Trager figured Dankov would be more likely to act if he knew Simone was hurt.

"For your information, road is blocked ahead. I'm sending relief column. Can you hold out 'til morning?"

Trager looked around. If they hid the vehicle, they could wait until tomorrow. He worried about Simone, who was probably in shock and needed medical attention. "Can you do better than that, Ishtar needs doctor."

"Expect force Marabou to arrive three hours after sunrise. Report your situation to Tango control on this frequency or two-one-four-five at six-hundred hours. Good luck. Vulture out."

After repeating the instructions, Trager slid the microphone into its spring bracket and switched the radio off. It was nearly three o'clock. He had to wait eighteen hours. Plenty of time for the ambushers to cover the sixty-two kilometers between Kitanda and Simwesi.

With chagrin, Trager looked at the telephone line. He should have cut it as soon as he was out of gun range. The way Dankov had talked, it sounded like Simwesi was occupied by hostiles. The butchers who had killed Papa Lal's family and committed who knows what other atrocities, had plenty of time to communicate with their chums in Simwesi.

He was just about halfway between the two places--six hours leisurely march. At least they wouldn't reach their position until after dark and it would be difficult to spot the tracks where they had gone off the road.

A new noise drew Trager's attention. His heartbeat accelerated. What he had thought as the hum of insects was the drone of an airplane engine.

Chapter 34

It was definitely the sound of a light aircraft engine coming from the south. Trager jumped into the Land Rover, switched the ignition on and slammed the truck into gear while turning the wheel. He accelerated and drove into the thick brush, ducking as branches whipped across the hood and over the folded-down windscreen. The vehicle stalled just short of forest cover.

As the engine noise grew louder, Trager frantically chopped branches with the machete and tossed greenery on top of the truck.

The airplane, a high-wing green-and-white Cessna-180, flew at about three hundred feet, low enough to get a detailed view of the ground, high enough where targets wouldn't flash by. Its registration letters, G-ZLL, were easy to read. Dankov had mentioned the airplane belonged to some mining company in the Congo.

Trager held his breath. Desperately, he hoped they didn't see Simone.

As the engine noise faded, Trager made some quick calculations. The airplane would reach Kitanda in probably less than ten minutes. Pilot and observer would realize they had to look closer. Max twenty minutes before they were back.

Trager went to where he had left Simone.

She was shivering, but her eyes were opened. "Johnny, I thought you left me." She moaned.

Trager took her hand. "I was hiding the truck from that airplane. Get up. We're going in the truck." He lifted Simone to her feet. She held onto his shoulder.

"We need to hide somewhere until Igor's troops arrive tomorrow."

"Where are we?"

"Thirty two kilometers from Kitanda."

"There's an abandoned logging road. Not far. I'm cold."

Worried about Simone's signs of shock, Trager pushed the brush aside and helped Simone in. The truck's engine noise would prevent him from hearing the airplane until it was right on top of them. He backed into the road and drove slowly so as not to raise dust. "Do you recognize the place? How much further?" He asked, urgently aware of minutes ticking by.

Simone didn't answer.

Trager kept looking over his shoulder.

The sight of a stork gracefully gliding on a thermal gave him a jolt. Two more minutes and he would have to pull over the side of the road and hope for the best.

"Slow down," Simone said. "I think it's over there."

They drove past a tree leaning over the road.

"Sorry, I'm confused."

Trager accelerated some. Time was up.

"Here it is. Turn. Go back."

"He put the truck in reverse and went back. After fifteen meters, he saw it--a break in the trees overgrown with brush. In low gear and low range he pushed the truck through the undergrowth. Once he was sure they couldn't be seen from the air, he switched the engine off and listened.

Not hearing the airplane, he went back to the road. With a branch, he erased the tracks leading into the forest. It would fool the airplane, but not people on the ground.

First, it sounded like the buzz of insects then the engine drone grew louder. Trager moved deeper into the shadows. Its flaps partially extended and a nose-high attitude, the airplane flew much lower and slower than on its first pass. There was no question they were working hard to find a hiding hole. A blond man peered out the side window.

The Cessna flew by, apparently not spotting them.

Trager waited for the engine noise to fade and was about to light a cigarette, when something else drew his attention. Banging and rattling came from the south. A vehicle was coming.

Trager squatted and peered through the bushes. A dented bus with rattling bumpers and fenders, belching clouds of black exhaust, worked its way its way down the road. A number of men in ragged clothes, armed with rifles, sat on the rooftop luggage rack. Soldiers in camouflage gear and floppy brimmed hats sat inside.

As the bus drove by, Trager could see the rifles were brand new.

The Zengawal Army of Liberation had arrived, and had recruited new talent. If they could spare the bus to look for them, it meant they didn't have major transport problems for their advance on Turako. Trager thought of the Utabu. He, Simone and the golden helmet were prime targets, quite possibly the reason for the war. Worst of all was the apparent alliance between Longo and the ZAL. The British registration of the Cessna made Trager think of Tony Bond.

~

"Let me have some cognac," Simone said when Trager returned to the truck. He dug in Simone's duffel and found the bottle wrapped in a towel. He let her drink out of the bottle. "That's better," she said. "Deeper into forest, the undergrowth gets lighter. There was a logging camp about two kilometers up the track."

Simone's alertness faded. Tall, green stalks with wide leaves restricted Trager's vision, and rustled as he drove over them. Thousands of white butterflies rose in front of the truck. Trager knew it was a spectacular sight, but, at the moment, it was just white over green, a nuisance.

After nearly two kilometers, the track reached a clearing. What looked like a stone at the edge of a tiny stream turned into a flash of yellow as a leopard sprinted for cover.

Trager turned the Land Rover around and stopped well inside the forest. In the back of the truck, he spread the camouflage net so that it could act as mattress. He kept the head rolled up to make a pillow. "Come here, sweets, we'll put you to bed."

After he had Simone installed, he fed her another mug of hydrating water. "I feel better now, but weak."

"You've lost quite bit of blood."

"I can hear better now." She gave him a faint smile. "Earlier, I thought you left me."

"You were delirious."

"At first, I thought he had shot me. Then I found myself on the floor and alive. I took my pistol out but missed. He hit you with his rifle and I missed again. While he was writhing on the floor, I put the pistol against his temple. Those monsters don't deserve to live. Give me a cigarette."

"Let's get you cleaned up. You're attracting flies."

She shook her head lightly. "Mud-man, we know what happens when you clean me. Go do a reconnaissance or something. Leave me alone for a few minutes." Gingerly, she sat up.

Trager took a rifle and went closer to the road. He wondered if Simone had noticed the butterflies that made this jungle appear like a northern forest in winter. In his mind's eye, he saw two corpses covered with butterflies.

Not far from the road, Trager found a convenient fallen tree trunk and sat on it. For the first time in his life, he had seen combat, had killed several people. Inside, he felt detached from the world, drained of emotion. He also realized the closer one was to death, the less one feared it.

The rattling of the bus drew his attention. He moved closer to the road from where he could see it. It was returning with a lot fewer people than it had come with. It looked like the bastards were beating the bushes on foot.

~

The blizzard of butterflies thinned as he approached the truck.

Trager froze.

A black head in camouflage uniform stood on top of the truck, looking at him. Trager raised his rifle.

The figure waved.

It was Simone.

"How do I look?" she asked, when he got close. She had wrapped her black piece of cloth like a turban around her head with a veil covering her nose.

"As always, you're a fashion leader." Actually, she looked like a terrorist. What had Blankenship suggested? Al Qaeda? "You'll make an excellent cover photo for the *Terrorist Times Weekly*."

"I don't have a Kaliasha. FN rifles are dèclassé."

"Someone mentioned you were Al Qaeda."

She placed her hands on her hips. "Pshaw, just because I received military training doesn't mean I'm an extremist."

Trager stopped worrying about her health.

"Climb on board. I fixed us something to eat."

Once on the bed of the truck, Trager stretched his legs and removed his hat. Simone handed him the top half of a German style mess tin. In it was corned beef mixed with diced onion. Simone lifted her veil to where it exposed her mouth, but kept her nose covered. As he ate, he realized it was getting dark. Night always favored the hunted. Maybe they would live to see sunrise.

An elephant trumpeted in the forest.

Simone said, "Sit next to me so we can comfortably finish this cognac."

She handed him the bottle as he settled next to her. There were about two inches left. Although he would have gladly glugged the whole contents at once, he took a small sip to make the cognac last.

"The nose will be ugly, but I think it is easy to fix. But that powder tattoo on my cheek and neck will leave me marked for life."

"I'm sorry. I really am. Who did it?"

"The piano man shot at me as I hit him."

Then she chuckled. "I shall wear it like a badge of honor."

"What was it the piano man said to you, something about permission?"

"Longo suspected I was getting close to finding the Utabu. That's why I led him to believe you and I would go see the Pygmies later."

Had Trager been already out of the soup and recapping the day's events, he would have laughed. Whether right or wrong, thwarting Longo's plans pleased him immensely. "Too bad the piano man got away, but I'll get him."

"Ah, finally a note of optimism." She took his nose and squeezed.

"Honk."

As it got dark, the chirping and chattering in the forest would have covered a noisy approach by King Kong.

Chapter 35

During the night, Trager and Simone alternated watches every two hours. When off watch, he rested his head on her lap. Her fingers stroking his forehead soothed him into sleep.

Since he had conquered the monsters of the night, dawn was a time for optimism. For Trager, the new day was an opportunity to solve all his problems. At first light, he wiped the dew accumulated on the rifle. Satisfied the weapon was operational, he moved Simone's sleeping head off his lap and wiped the machine gun dry.

At six o'clock, he switched the radio on and listened to the screeches, gargles and whistles of encoded transmissions. A voice came in the clear, "*Ishtar, vous etes la?*"

"*Oui, Ishtar ici, operation normal, pas de perdres.*"

"*Tango Control, reçu, bon courage.*"

A new voice came on the air after Tango signed off. "*Ishtar--Marabou. Kama wesa enda kazkazini, karibu ya towni mbaya. Sisi ta kuja haraka sana. Kama ndege au watu ta sumbuavwewe piga radio Falcon--over.*"

Trager answered, "*Sawa sawa, sisi ta goja wewe ku fanya kazi msuri. Ishtar out.*"

"Well," Simone said. "Mr. Trager speaks Swahili. Any more secrets I should know?"

Hearing Force Marabou was on its way and that he could call for air support if needed, Trager's spirits rose. "Even with that ugly nose, I love you." He took her by the waist, pulled her close, lifted her veil and kissed her lips. Her eyes looked more beautiful than ever. Then she closed them and kissed him back.

"A good way to start the morning," Trager said.

"Next time, brush your teeth first."

"I will." He patted her rear. His hand froze in place as he listened. "Dogs."

Without a word, they jumped into the truck. Trager hit the starter. Click, and nothing happened.

"Battery terminals," Simone said. She jumped off her seat, lifted the cushion, and dug in the tool compartment.

Trager opened the hood.

He didn't need to strain his ear to hear the dogs.

With a wrench, Simone loosened the positive terminal, looked at it, shook her head. "Give me your cigarettes." She emptied the pack, removed the aluminum foil and returned the cigarettes and outer pack. After wrapping aluminum foil on the battery stud, she banged the terminal into place. Try it now."

Trager hit the starter. The engine purred, drowning the barking of the dogs. "You drive, I'll be the gunner."

Simone drove at ten kilometers an hour, Trager looked for targets.

As they approached the road, a mongrel dog came at them, barking.

"Hit it," Trager said.

Simone accelerated. By the time they emerged and bounced over the ditch at the side of the road, she was doing well over twenty klicks.

The truck skidded, the engine roared. A pack of dogs barked, chasing the truck. Two men in front of the truck turned abruptly, raising rifles. Trager fired a burst. The men dove for the bushes. Shots rang out behind.

Swiveling the Dektarev, Trager stepped forward, placed one foot on the passenger seat, the other between Simone's legs. Behind them stood a mob of men, some of them shooting. Trager let go three short bursts. He had trouble hitting anything as Simone zigzagged. Soon, dust created a protective screen.

Simone shouted, "I guess they've unleashed their dogs of war."

"Slow down, we're running out of space. There are baddies ahead, too."

"Airplane."

Trager turned to face forward.

The Cessna was in a shallow dive.

Seconds later, it roared overhead. The same blond looked out the window, a microphone in front of his mouth.

"Call Falcon."

Simone was already on the horn.

Trager heard Falcon say he would be overhead in ten minutes.

The Cessna was coming back, right down the middle of the road, not much above the treetops. There was no need for it's pilot to do that to keep the truck in sight.

Trager yelled, "Stop."

There was no way he could hit the airplane bouncing the way they were.

Simone slammed on the brakes. Trager had to hang on to the pedestal to keep from falling.

The plane roared by. A glass jar tumbled down.

"Grenade, duck!"

Trager dove onto the camouflage net in the back.

There was an explosion in front of the truck. Trager sprang back up.

"A twenty meter miss," Simone said, putting the truck in gear. "I'll go slow and accelerate when they are real close."

This sounded like a good plan. Trager kept his knees loose to stabilize his aim. He would start firing at about four hundred meters or about five seconds before the plane flashed by. At least he should be able to scare the pilot.

The plane was coming in again, lower, vanishing in the dust. Trager fired blindly. Simone stomped on the accelerator. The plane appeared above the dust. Trager fired with no apparent effect. The grenade exploded way ahead of them. "He-he," Trager exclaimed.

Instead of circling for another attack from the rear, the airplane rose and did a wingover.

"Drive fast, stop, and reverse into the dust."

"Hang on."

As the airplane leveled over the road, Simone slammed on the brakes, turned the wheel, skidded the car into a U turn, and roared back in to the dust.

Trager saw the plane at the last minute and the sparkle of several jars. Simone hit the brakes as the airplane roared overhead. Dust, noise, buzz of shrapnel.

"Well done."

"It isn't going to work the second time."

"Where's Falcon?"

Simone turned the car around. "I'll go slow. You shoot him down."

Trager slapped a fresh ammo drum in.

In the light dust, the plane couldn't hide. Trager aimed a little high, to let the plane fly into the stream of bullets, and pressed the trigger, red tracers arched over the plane, straddling it. Trager squatted following his growing target. The airplane roared overhead higher than before. Grenades went into the forest. Trager was pretty sure he had scored some hits.

With dismay, he watched the plane repeat its wingover maneuver.

"Here he comes," Simone yelled.

Trager loaded another drum, hoping not to damage the barrel with another long burst.

"Hit the bastard." Simone waved her fist and stopped the car.

A MIG dove out of the sun and turned behind the Cessna, lining up for another pass.

Trager couldn't believe his eyes. The fighter jet flew below the Cessna's altitude, raising a cloud of dust. It went under the much slower plane and pulled up.

For a moment, the Cessna's shape shimmered and seemed to disembody in the hot exhaust left by the MIG. As it hit the wake turbulence, its wing dipped, touched a tree. The fuselage spun into the forest, the Cessna's wings clattering onto the side of the road.

Falcon's voice came over the speaker. "About five kilometers ahead, Marabou is entering the village."

Simone brought the truck to a stop next to the broken wings

The crash site reeked with the smell of gasoline and fuel gurgled out of ruptured wing tanks. Trager got off the truck and shoved his way through the underbrush.

Whatever hope he had of finding survivors vanished when he reached the fuselage. The plane had hit the ground nose first. Two bodies covered in oil and blood where jammed at the rear of the cabin. One of the doors was open.

Trager managed to squeeze out the corpses' wallets.

~

They left the forest behind and entered the area squatters had cleared. Simone drove at a sedate pace and Trager sat in the passenger seat, his feet resting on the front panel to keep his legs from shaking. The sweat that had soaked his jacket during the Cessna's attack was cooling, causing him to shiver. He was dying for something hot to drink.

Ahead, a puff of smoke blossomed in the air above Simwesi's rooftops. A few seconds later, the bang of the exploding shell reached them.

"Now what?" Simone brought the truck to a stop.

"That's probably our friends urging the rebels to surrender."

Trager picked up the microphone. "Marabou, this is Ishtar, we're two kilometers from the village, is it safe to proceed?"

A string of squawks answered.

"Transmit in the clear, we don't have encoding."

A voice said in French. "Go ahead, we're brewing tea."

~

Guarded by a few soldiers, a large number of men squatted at the edge of the main street. More men were herded to join the squatting group. On the side streets, women looked on apprehensively.

Simone stopped by Genadiy, who studied a pile of assorted rifles. Many of them crude homemade contraptions, with barrels made out of pipe. He looked up and saluted. "I'm glad to see you." He pointed toward the other end of the village. "Go where our vehicles are parked, and have breakfast. I'll be finished here in about an hour."

"Are we at war or what?"

Eyebrows raised, Genadiy shrugged. "I don't know. We've had riots in Turako. General Mawingi sent his army into the streets, supposedly to restore order. He had the palace surrounded. To me, it looked like he was going to attack instead of protect. He demanded I let his troops in. I refused and it got almost ugly." Genadiy grinned. "Then the Ataman arrived. He and a few of our boys were at the head of about a thousand drummers leading them; riding horses borrowed from the Club Hipique. It was impressive to watch the Ataman jump over a steel drum barricade and land in front of Mawingi. I don't know what he said to the fat general, but the troops went back to the barracks.

"I was about to depart for Ugali when the Ataman told me to rush here, put down this insurrection and escort you back to Turako." He pointed at the pile of guns. "Nothing serious here, but we'll see after we question some of these people. I'm interested to know where the assault rifles come from."

"So what's going on in Ugali?"

"Apparently, a ZAL force we didn't know existed came across the border and took the town. Sokolov strafed a roadblock they've set up a few kilometers north east." Genadiy sighed. "If General Mawingi didn't keep us tied up in the capital . . ."

~

Outside the village, soldiers waved from a Land Rover with an antitank recoilless gun sticking out from under greenery that made the vehicle look like a bush. Further down the road, two Isuzu trucks were parked under a grove of acacias.

Simone parked behind one of the Isuzus, next to a squad of sleeping soldiers. A somewhat chubby sergeant greeted them in French. "The commander said to give you a good breakfast." He pointed at a folding table and two folding stools under an acacia. "My name is Antoine. Please allow this bush-chef a few minutes to make an omelet."

As they took their places, Simone poured wine into mugs. Distant explosions sounding like pillows dropped on the floor came from the direction of Simwesi. The rough Algerian rouge tasted better than any vintage wine Trager had ever had.

Antoine arrived with two omelets. "I'm happy to inform you Simwesi has been secured by our company without resistance. But they did find a hoard of ammunition."

~

Nearing noon, Genadiy returned, his troops packed into three Land Rovers. He sat at the table, accepted a mug of coffee from Antoine, and took a sip. "Apparently, there were ZAL forces in the village, but they took off for the forest before we arrived. We found an ammunition cache and two mortars.

"Now I can get back to my mission objective to provide escort." He let out a little chuckle. "A pleasant drive, a bath and a beer at the Metropole. This beats Afghanistan."

Simone said, "I have a couple of things to do, but afterward, we could get together for dinner at the Roof Garden. Make it a celebration." She turned to Trager. "You have to wear a suit."

Trager rolled his eyes. "A suit? I'm trying to think of ways to avoid a date with Longo."

Simone chuckled, shaking her head. "By tonight, that fiend will be history."

Chapter 36

Force Marabou consisted of four Land Rovers, two five-ton trucks, forty African soldiers and NCOs and two Russian sergeants commanded by Captain Genadiy, whose surname Trager didn't know. Armed with seven light machine guns, two sixty-millimeter mortars, five RPG-7 rocket launchers and one one-oh-five antitank canon, the platoon-sized unit could deliver a heavy punch. Genadiy had said they operated as if they were a company.

With such a formidable escort, Trager drove in high spirits. He had one hell of a story to file, one that was sure to get syndicated and open wide the doors of his new career. Dinner and dancing tonight was a great way to end a day shaping toward perfection. Next to him, Simone had a cheerful expression and appeared to be enjoying the drive. A light wind blew dust across the road.

Trager slowed when he saw that the vehicle in front had stopped.

At the junction with the east-west road, Genadiy dismounted and walked around, looking at the ground. The four soldiers in his vehicle spread out into defensive positions.

Trager got out of his truck. It took him only a few seconds to notice the tracks made by Force Marabou when they turned onto the Simwesi road were superimposed by a large number of heavy vehicle tire marks.

"This explains why the police can't contact Maridani," Genadiy said. He looked at Trager, a thin smile on his face. "Welcome to behind enemy lines."

Trager's facial muscles sagged.

"We were just there," Simone said.

Genadiy went to his truck, selected an SSB frequency. "Vulture's Nest, Marabou."

"Marabou, go ahead."

"Confirming column, size unknown, direction unknown, has traveled on highway since we left it last night."

"*Priniata peredacha.*" After a moment of silence, Dankov's voice returned. "New orders. Proceed to Maridani. Make reconnaissance in force. Attack immediately if conditions suitable. End."

Genadiy read back the orders, slammed the mike into its bracket and turned. "What the old man means is, go in with guns blazing." Genadiy took out a packet of American chewing gum and stuck half a piece into his mouth. He signaled for his NCOs to gather.

Trager said, "I was in the military. You could use an extra man."

Genadiy looked at him sharply. "American?"

"Lieutenant in the Corps."

"And you want to fight again?"

"I've never been in combat."

"Pshaw, you should have seen him in Kitanda."

"I have no clue what we'll meet in Maridani, it would be stupid to think we won't be heavily outnumbered. There is a water tower west of the city. If we have an observer there, we'll have a great advantage."

Trager's stomach contracted, his legs felt wobbly. He should have kept his mouth shut.

Grinning widely, Genadiy shook Trager's hand. "Thank you."

"I'd rather be up front."

"An officer on the tower will make the difference." Genadiy turned, took out a map from a case on the floor of the truck and spread it on top of the hood. "Right chaps," he said to his NCOs. "If these people follow the pattern used in Simwesi, they'll start recruiting and handing out weapons." He tapped his finger on the map. "We'll probably find many of them in this school. Another bunch is bound to be in City Hall. The first strong point has to be the sugar mill with the water tower." He glanced over his shoulder.

"Sections four and five, drive down the main boulevard. The moment you receive fire, dismount. Truck retreats firing.

"Sections six and seven, same thing on this street. You take City Hall from the rear. I'll take the school. Section three parallels the boulevard. Your objective is the hotel. We may trap some of their officers.

Section two, after taking the sugar plant, stays in reserve.

"Code name for our observer is 'Babylon'."

"And what will I do?" Simone asked.

"Once we take the sugar factory, you can wait there."

"Wasting a valuable machine gun."

Genadiy thought for a moment. "You're section eight. In reserve with our tank buster. I'll give you three men."

~

Though in a funk, Trager's brain was still working. He couldn't fault Genadiy's plan. It was based on speed and surprise, and in the hope of causing panic. But since they had no idea as of the size of the enemy force, it was also a flight of fancy. He wasn't at all happy with Simone going into combat. He was sure the reserve would be needed almost as soon as they got the feel for enemy's deployment.

Trager corrected himself. The moment *he* made out where the enemy actually was and detected counter-moves.

As they drove toward Maridani, Trager wondered where they would meet the enemy's rear guard that would render Genadiy's plan useless.

At least as far as he knew, no one was chasing after them. But breaking through an enemy force of unknown size did not seem like the brightest idea, especially if it required fighting in an urban environment. To achieve his own aim of reaching the relative safety of Turako, Trager would have opted for bypassing Maridani. He understood Dankov's desperate situation and the need to hit and scatter the enemy before being overwhelmed by sheer numbers. Those had been the tactics of Michael Hoare in suppressing the Simba rebellion in the Congo right after independence. But forty years later, the enemy was well armed. At any rate, Trager was now sure this was a war Dankov couldn't possibly win. And Trager was in the middle of it. His only choice was to act as a soldier and influence the local battle as much in his favor as he could.

Trager drove, keeping his distance from the lead vehicles so as not to be inside the dust cloud. He recognized the road from which he and Dankov had emerged the evening of the diamond shipment. "Be ready to duck," he told Simone. She picked up a rifle and placed it on top of the folded down windshield.

"*Tayeri kwa taka-taka?*" Trager loved the Swahili word for machinegun. Taka-taka was so descriptive.

Tayeri, sisi askari kali." Ready, we're fierce soldiers, the sergeant answered. The other three soldiers laughed, seemingly oblivious of the danger ahead.

The vehicles up front slowed, no longer raising much dust. As Trager looked at the water tower, his stomach tightened, heartbeat accelerated. No one appeared to be on top. The two lead vehicles swung to the right and Trager followed. Machine guns rattled ahead, distracting Trager from his fear of the tower. He accelerated.

Trager slammed on the brakes as he entered the sugar factory's yard. A white Peugeot 505 with all its windows broken had just crashed against a parked truck. Its engine was still running. The driver slumped against the steering wheel. A good sign. Someone had tried to escape.

Two bodies sprawled in the middle of the yard.

A couple of shots rang out inside the office building. One of the soldiers stepped outside and gave the all-clear signal.

Genadiy had already driven out of the east gate and into town. Heavy firing came from the direction of the main boulevard, filling Trager with a sense of urgency.

Simone was already sliding into the driver's seat as Trager jumped out, his eyes fixed on the vertical ladder. "Gung ho, gung ho, gung ho," he yelled, dashing to kill the ladder or anyone that got in the way. If Longo was climbing the ladder, he would chase him and kill him. "Gung ho."

He leapt. His foot hit the fourth rung. He propelled himself upward. *Shoot me, bastards, I make a good target.* Rungs flew past his eyes. *Longo, I'm gonna kill you.* Trager looked up. The opening in the catwalk above was getting closer. He imagined all the firing he was hearing was aimed at him. *I'm the target, you can't hit me. I'm too fast for you.* His hand gripped the inside edge of the catwalk. He pulled himself over and sat on the catwalk, his feet dangling over the edge. His eyes were firmly closed.

"You climb very fast," the sergeant with the tactical radio pack said as he sat next to Trager.

The shooting intensified.

Briefly, Trager opened his eyes and saw a stanchion that held up a safety rail. Gingerly, he slid sideways, gripped the stanchion with both sweaty hands, lifted his leg and straddled it.

The town spread out in an orderly checkerboard pattern. The streets were lined with trees and neat little bungalows. Beyond town the gray, recently re-paved road pointed toward Turako like an arrow. With the sun already low on the horizon, the light worked to their advantage. On the wide, main boulevard, Isuzu trucks were backing up. Soldiers on foot advanced, darting from door to door.

A machine gun fired from the City Hall tower where the clock still showed ten past twelve. Other than that, Trager could not see enemy activity.

Two blocks away from the main drag, the Land Rover with the antitank gun fired several white phosphorous shells into a school. People poured out of the burning building and were met by machinegun fire.

"Ishtar, move forward. Cut retreat." Genadiy's voice said on the radio.

Trager watched Simone's vehicle advance on the southern edge of town. Its machine gun opened up at the people running from the back of the school, across a soccer filed.

They had caught the enemy with their pants down. Trager glanced at his watch. Only seven minutes had elapsed since the first shot was fired.

A cloud of mortar dust blossomed on top of the City Hall tower as a rocket-propelled grenade hit it.

Trager felt pretty useless. He scanned for targets or activity through binoculars. In the hotel garden, a number of bodies lay on the ground. Some floated in the swimming pool. Trager wondered if Wangohi was one of them. Then he saw movement. A figure that looked like an officer gesticulating. Men ran into the building. Trager said into the mike, "Sections four and five, enemy inside the hotel."

Worried about Simone, he looked toward the south. Her machine gunner fired short bursts at men in civilian clothes scattering in a field, in apparent panic.

Heavy firing came from the hotel. The two sections on the main boulevard were pined down.

"Section three entering City Hall from the rear."

A few seconds later, several men ran out of the city hall's front door and got mowed down by the troops on the boulevard.

"*Daktari*, we have wounded in City Hall," an excited voice said.

"Marabou is going into rear of hotel. When free, section two advance on Central Market. Force of irregulars concentrated there."

A Land Rover approached the cottages at the back of the hotel.

The unmistakable blam of an RPG came from the city hall tower. An explosion in the front of the hotel immediately followed. A second rocket hit the hotel.

Men poured out onto the hotel lawn and were mowed down by withering fire from the cottages. The ZAL troops were not very good at covering their rear. Trager let out a sigh of relief. At least the main points of resistance have been subdued.

The sergeant said, "The fight is almost over, those people are drunk."

Out of Trager's vision, sporadic fire came from the east.

The sergeant handed Trager a lit cigarette. "Discipline conquers all, the Ataman says. And the will to pierce your enemy with the bayonet." He spat and watched his spit drop to the ground. "Those people don't know how to fight real soldiers."

The sun had already set. The sergeant looked small waiting for Trager to come down. Trager wiped cold sweat from his eyes, closed them, lay on the catwalk and stretched until he grasped the ladder. Slowly, slowly, he pulled himself. He thought he was going to die as he stuck his feet through the opening. His shaking feet rested on a rung of the ladder. A moan escaped him as he tried to take a deep breath. With his eyes closed he started down. One step at a time.

~

On the main boulevard, policemen who had been hiding now rolled out white painted drums to block the street. A Land Rover was parked in front of the hotel.

Feeling spent, Trager walked past a bullet-scarred villa and the body of a dead ZAL soldier someone had covered with a straw mat.

As he approached the hotel, Simone rolled out of a side street. She waved, and drove on the wrong side of the boulevard. "Need a ride, soldier?"

Trager got in. "Where are the troops you were hauling?"

"I left them in Villeneuf, the shanty town where the hard-core holed up, holding civilians as hostages." She stopped in front of the battle-scarred hotel. "At least we didn't damage the water system. I'm going to have a bath. Feel free to take any room. They've killed Crethien."

After saying that, she lost her composure, grabbed her bag and ran into the hotel.

His earlier perception of this charming town filled him with sadness. Trager's legs began to shake. He leaned on the truck and lit a cigarette to kill the smell of death from the people slain this morning. He tried to think of tomorrow but couldn't. He imagined the terror of the people who came to the market next to City Hall. Across the street, broken stalls and dead bodies told a story he didn't want to read. While on the tower, he was an elated member of a liberating army. Now, he was a witness of the macabre.

"May I help you, Monsieur?" Antoine, dressed in a white shirt with black bow tie, stood by the hotel door. He still wore camouflage trousers tucked into boots and a pistol strapped to his side. The effect was almost comical.

"You wouldn't have something to drink?"

"Mais bien sur, Monsieur." He came down to help as Trager dug for his things out of the mess in the back of the truck. He let Antoine take his rifle and duffel while he hoisted the Utabu.

In the bar, a soldier, rifle slung on his back, swept broken glass. In a corner stood a pile of empty bottles.

"What is your pleasure, Monsieur?" Antoine asked from behind the bar.

"Scotch, anything," Trager said, staring at empty shelves.

"Avec un glaçon?" With an ice cube? Antoine produced a bottle of Dewar's from under the counter. "The pigs hadn't had time to drink it all." He looked at the monkey-skin-wrapped parcel Trager had placed on the bar. "You cut someone's head off?"

The idea that he could be hauling around someone's severed head struck Trager as ridiculously funny and he broke out laughing.

Antoine gave him a questioning look.

Trager realized his laughter sounded hysterical, gulped the scotch and plunked his glass down for a refill. After Antoine poured another, Trager slung his rifle and duffel on his shoulder and placed the Utabu under his arm. Glass in hand, he left the bar and went upstairs where he was greeted by the smell of charred wood.

The door to the first room was open and leaned out, hanging from the bottom hinge. Dismembered body parts littered the blood-splattered room.

A corpse in a pool of blood occupied the second room. Trager went past a room where he heard the sound of water running into a tub. Simone. He checked an impulse to go into her room. He needed time by himself.

He opened another door. Glass littered the floor and the top of the bed. As he kicked the door closed behind him, the Utabu slipped from under his arm. It thumped heavily on the floor and cracked a board. As if guilty of a sacrilege, Trager put his things on the floor, picked up the Utabu, and placed it under the bed.

He then took the bedspread and shook the broken glass off.

To his surprise, there was hot water. Trager luxuriated soaking in the large old-fashioned tub while sipping scotch. War made a mockery of life--a theater of the absurd--but the demented producers of these shows always found actors willing to sacrifice their lives to take part in the lunacy.

~

Isolated shots still rang out in the distance. Rejuvenated, Trager returned to the bar. A table with a starched tablecloth had replaced the stack of empty bottles in the corner. A folding stock Kalashnikov hung from the back of a chair. Genadiy stood by the open window, looking outside. He held his hands clenched into fists, behind his back.

Genadiy turned, the grim expression on his face changing into a sad smile. "At last someone to have a drink with." He nodded to Antoine, who produced a bottle of Stolichnaya.

"*Allah verdih.*" Allah is right, Genadiy pronounced the Russian Imperial Army officer's toast that had originated during the Caucasus wars in the nineteenth century. After downing the shot, he said, "Ach, I needed that. After seeing what I saw today, I'm afraid of drinking alone."

"Worse than Afghanistan?"

A look of disgust appeared on Genadiy's face. "The Afghans aren't cannibals. These brutes killed the mayor and his wife and feasted on their hearts and livers."

Antoine refilled the glasses.

"I thank you for your excellent job. You saved a number of lives with your spotting. To your good health." He placed his glass upside down on the bar. "I'm curious about something. Wasn't it somewhat of a bad time to go on safari in this area?"

"Very bad."

"Didn't the Ataman warn you?"

"Apparently it was the ZSS who ambushed Major Kisima."

Genadiy snorted. "We're surrounded by treachery."

"*Bonsoir*." Simone entered the bar, her face covered with a clean but still-wet black scarf.

Genadiy clicked his heels. "May we offer you a drink?"

"Crethien liked Kirr. I'll have one for him tonight. The Europeans and Indians trusted him, and Africans adored him. Under his guidance, this town represented all that is good in Africa. That's why those barbarians killed him."

Genadiy said to Antoine, "Don't you think you should be cooking dinner? I have a war to attend to."

Antoine beamed and patted the bar. "Tonight, *mon Capitaine*, I'm like *le patron* of Chez Antoine's. We are having duck al'orange."

Three shots rang out less than a block away. Antoine flipped the lights off. Genadiy peered from the side of the window. "It's alright. Some people breaking the curfew, maybe trying to get back home."

The lights came back on.

Somewhat corrupted by the smell of dead bodies, the aroma of roasted duck wafted into the room. Wangohi entered carrying a tray. "Welcome back," he said, grinning. He placed the tray on the table and pulled a chair back for Simone.

As they sat, Wangohi said, "Listen, the drummers are back."

~

During dinner, Genadiy said that by morning he would probably have finished evicting the ZAL holdouts and they would be able to proceed to Turako. Simone picked at her food. Claiming a headache, she excused herself and went upstairs. Shortly after, Genadiy said he had to go join the nightshift to sort out the liver-eating bastards.

Trager was finishing his wine when Wangohi walked in to clear the table. In a conspiratorial tone, he said, "The drummers are saying the Utabu is coming. I know how to read drums."

So far, to Trager, the importance of the Utabu had only a slight personal effect. He had been carrying it with him and someone else wanted it before he got to the goal post. But he hadn't been on anyone's team. Wangohi made him realize the reason he didn't feel part of a team was because the real team playing the game was invisible.

"Thank you for letting me know. Good night."

Trager went upstairs. As he entered his room, the cracked board squeaked, reminding him he had dropped the Utabu. Wondering if he had damaged the ancient treasure, he groped under the bed. He suffered a moment of panic as his hands found nothing. Then off to the side, there it was.

Trager pulled the bundle out and placed it on top of the bed. He undid the knots and unwrapped the monkey skin.

He stared in shocked astonishment.

Chapter 37

Instead of looking at solid gold, Trager's gaze rested on gray lead and flaked gold plating. What had survived for hundreds or maybe thousands of years as Simone claimed, had been ruined in two days of bouncing in the back of a truck. Trager stopped right there. Something that got ruined by bouncing inside a truck could not have lasted hundreds of years unscathed. When he saw it in the witch doctor's hut, the Utabu was perfect.

What he had in front of him was a fake.

Simone, my dear swindling darling. He had been had. The witch doctor was also a victim, or a swindler himself. The ceremony in the Pygmy village had been real. The Pygmies and the drummers were all being razzmatazzed by a fake.

Angry, Trager wrapped the monkey skin around the Utabu and headed across the hallway. He knocked on Simone's door.

There was a movement of bedsprings on the other side. "Who is it?"

"It's John."

"It's late, I'm tired."

"Open up, it's urgent."

Springs squeaked again, a board groaned.

Trager waited, shifting his weight from foot to foot.

The door unlocked.

Vanity seemed to have outweighed modesty. Simone was wrapping her face in the black scarf and wore an unbuttoned shirt that failed to cover her breasts. Trager had never seen her wearing lacy red panties. He entered the room, placed the bundle on top of the slightly rumpled bed, and unwrapped the bundle. "Look."

"Ooh," Simone exclaimed. She placed her hands on her cheeks. Color drained from her face, giving it a translucent, cadaverous quality. Trager took her arm as she began to wobble.

She gulped air as her initial shock turned into a state of agitation. Like claws, her fingers dug into Trager's arms. "We must leave immediately."

"Explain this fake to me."

"We don't have time. We must leave."

"We're not going anywhere. I'm not participating in your swindle."

She let go of him and turned away, clutching her head. She then seemed to calm down, turned and came to him to stand very close. She took his hand and placed it on her breast. "Johnny, I love you," she whispered.

"You lying bitch," Trager spat out.

Shock returned to her face.

Letting out a little cry, she turned away and stepped toward the dresser. She whirled around pointing a pistol at him. "I don't want to kill you, but I will pull the trigger if I must."

The state she was in, Trager had little doubt she would do exactly what she said.

"Turn around."

Considering how to disarm her, Trager stayed frozen. His gaze roved the room.

Simone stepped back, extending her arm, the barrel of her gun pointing between Trager's eyes.

"Turn around." Her voice was firm and commanding,and her hand steady.

Trager turned.

"Hands behind your back."

"No."

There was movement behind him. Trager began to turn. A foot hit him between the shoulder blades and sent him flying against the wall.

He staggered off the wall and turned. A foot caught him under the chin and sent him sprawling to the floor. For a moment, he thought his windpipe was broken. He could breathe, though. His eyes re-focused.

The gun was still pointing between his eyes.

"Get up, turn around, hands behind your back. We're running out of time."

She didn't need a gun to kill him.

As he placed his hands behind his back, she expertly slapped handcuffs on him.

"Lie down on the bed, you'll be more comfortable."

Trager didn't know if she was being sarcastic. He stretched out as told.

Simone straddled the chair and let her pistol hand rest on the back. She looked like something out of a kinky sex magazine.

"Do you know what the most important thing in a person's life is?" She asked in a conversational tone.

Trager wiggled back to get his head on a pillow. "It depends on the person."

She shook her head slowly. "Self esteem and dignity. Without self esteem, you're nothing--a maggot."

Trager wondered where this was leading.

"Are you listening to me?"

"Yes."

"We don't have much time. When I walk out of this room, either you will come along willing to help, or I will mourn you. You're a decent man. I admire you . . ." She looked down at herself and gave out a little, bitter laugh. Her gaze was back on him as she buttoned her shirt with one hand.

"Today, we have reached a crucial point in our lives. I'm going to tell you something no one knows." She bit her lip as if thinking.

Taking a deep breath, she said, "I'm not a princess. I was a maggot, a nobody."

Trager stared at her mouth. It was twisted and her scarf hid what he guessed was a tortured expression.

"My father was Algerian. He cleaned public toilets in Toulouse. My mother cleaned rich people's houses. She was French, and her countrymen despised her for marrying an Algerian. The Arabs despised us all. In high school, I fell in love with the son of a family whose house I helped my mother clean. He was rich and told me we would live in Antibes and he would take me to London and New York."

Trager wondered what this soul baring had to do with their present situation. At least he knew where the story was heading.

"He took my virginity and I was in heaven. One night he took me to a nightclub to meet his friends. I was happy and proud. I put on the best dress I had . . ." Her pistol trembled a little. "He introduced me to his friends and told them what a great lay I was. I was so humiliated. I couldn't get out of bed for a week, maybe longer. It was during that time I became a princess in my own mind. Do I sound crazy to you?"

"No," Trager said, feeling compassion, at the same time wondering if maybe she *was* nuts. Sitting on that chair, her face draped in black, holding a pistol, she really looked demented.

"Don't try to humor me."

"I'm not. Maybe if I had these cuffs off and you weren't pointing that pistol, I'd sound more sincere."

"When the weather was good, on his days off, my father juggled in the streets and spat fire. I passed the hat around. Then we juggled together. The money we earned was put away for my university education.

"I went to the Sorbonne on a partial scholarship. Paris is expensive and I had learned to collect up front. I'm not the first nor last woman to survive through university working on her back. I got my degree. That same summer, war broke out in Bosnia. With some Palestinian friends, we hitchhiked there. So I worked with the Red Crescent in an ambulance saving lives, no?"

She wistfully looked up to the ceiling. Her concentration on Trager seemed to be slipping.

"Don't even think of it," she said, smiling. "I know your eyes so well."

"I'm not very comfortable. The cuffs are biting into my wrists."

"In Zengawal, I did the initial reconnaissance, before Igor came. With Pierre in power, we could do so much. Change the history of Africa. Zengawal would rise out of the misery of ignorance and abuse by the men who had the guns and the stooges of amoral business interests. It would become a country where people of all tribes, races and religions could work together.

"As I learned about the country, I heard the legend of the Utabu. What a wonderful thing it would be if it were true and someone found it. Checking things out with the witch doctors, I found clues and put them together. I knew where the Utabu was."

Simone's eyes shone like those of a mad woman.

"Igor and I went to the old, abandoned fort and found a secret stairway to the dungeons. There, we found proof that King Solomon's mines really did exist. Do you know what we found?"

"No."

"Diamonds--an ark full of diamonds. You've seen some of them. The old fort is built on top of some older ruins. But money alone, not only doesn't buy happiness, it doesn't buy security for a nation. Only a firm cultural base and a powerful symbol buy security for a nation. That's what I, Simone, Princess El Oriot, will give to Zengawal. I will give them a king. For in giving, no one can take from you. What I'm giving is a chance for peace and prosperity to three million people."

She got off her chair. With her free hand, she snapped the elastic of her red panties. "Neither of us looks terribly dignified, to match lofty statements. No?" she said, sounding her normal self.

She picked up the fake Utabu and looked at it. "It's fixable. But I have to get to my workshop and mend it before afternoon. General Mawingi is only waiting to unleash his five thousand men against Igor. For the moment, the drummers are keeping him at bay. Once the Utabu arrives, Mawingi looses control of the Army that will become loyal to their king."

She put her Utabu down. "That's what I've been abasing myself for, to buy materials for this handicraft."

"But you've said you found this diamond treasure."

"It belongs to the people of Zengawal. Igor is keeping it in trust."

"If my hands weren't manacled, I'd start pulling my hair out. Such altruism and honesty don't exist."

"Would you steal the diamonds?"

Trager had to think for a moment. "No, I don't think so."

"So you have the arrogance to consider yourself the only honest person around?"

"You're perpetrating a fraud. That's dishonest. You and Igor are crooks."

She shook her head. "Igor thinks I found the real Utabu. Only you know my secret. We are in a crisis. I'm using a substitute for something that really exists but we haven't found yet. Like the phony diamonds some ladies wear while keeping the real thing in a bank vault. The future of three-million people depend on what happens tonight. Are you with me or with the liver-eaters?"

"Unlock these stupid things so that I can answer honestly." Trager rolled onto his belly. She didn't unlock the cuffs as he had hoped. Instead, he heard Simone pull her trousers on and slip her feet into boots. She went into the bathroom and came back. The sharp ripping noise of the zip on her duffel closing had the sound of finality.

If she were going to shoot him, it would be then.

Chapter 38

The sound of a racked pistol slide made him cringe. This was it. Trager closed his eyes, remembering Simone under him, her warmth and softness. He would die with that thought in his mind.

Not too gently, she picked up his wrists and fumbled with the key. Finally she removed the cuffs. "Good bye, Mud-Man."

The way she said it sounded sad and final. For a moment, Trager lay still. Then, he heard her moving.

Machine pistol slung from her neck, duffel hanging from her shoulder, Simone picked up the Utabu and headed out the door.

At a loss, he stayed on the bed as if frozen, while understanding of Simone's self sacrifice sunk in. "Shit." He jumped off the bed and ran after her.

"Simone, wait," he shouted as her shadow disappeared around the hallway corner. He caught up with her midway down the stairs.

"I knew it was a mistake not to kill you," she said in a defeated tone.

"I'm going with you."

"What for?" There were tears in her eyes.

"To drink cognac and watch you fix the thing. You've been working alone on your project too long."

"And I'll finish it alone." Now she sounded angry.

"It's a dangerous road. The ZAL is bound to have advance elements and scouts up ahead."

"Igor will meet me."

"Igor is up to his ass in crocodiles. He'll want you to hand over the Utabu *maramoja*." Trager used the Swahili word immediately for emphasis. "Can you afford that?"

She shook her head.

"I'll get my bag."

~

An armed man in civilian clothes let Trager out the hotel door. Outside, the sound of distant shooting insulted the cool zephyr floating down the boulevard. The scent of jasmine was corrupted by the stench of death.

Carrying a double-barreled shotgun, Wangohi clambered into the back of the truck. Trager tossed in his duffel and got into the passenger seat. Simone drove away from the hotel. Four blocks down the road, she turned right and stopped by a kiosk lit by a kerosene pressure lamp. Less than a block away, several ramshackle buildings were on fire. The shooting sounded close.

Inside the kiosk, Genadiy sat on a high stool with a radio pack next to him. Seeing Trager and Simone, he said, "Things are under control. Go back to the hotel."

"We're going to Turako," Simone said.

"That's impossible, the road is blocked."

Trager pointed at the map spread on the kiosk counter. "We'll take this road that skirts the sisal plantation and rejoin the highway ten kilometers from here."

Genadiy shook his head. "We won't know what's ahead until Falcon overflies in the morning.

Simone said sharply, "We stopped by to get the password, not to ask permission."

Genadiy looked surprised. "From interrogating prisoners, we know their main force is somewhere over there." He pointed to the east. "They may be preparing for a counter attack or might have said screw it and gone for Turako."

Trager said, "If they have any brains, they'll try to dislodge you and reopen their supply line."

Genadiy pursed his lips. "That's why I'm trying to finish this business as quickly as possible. I'm afraid their main force could overrun us." He sighed. "The challenge is *kitabu*, the answer *mwalimu*. You might be taking the safest course." Chatter on the radio drew his attention. He picked up the mike while looking at his watch. "Time's up, burn the bastards." He turned to Trager. "We're low on grenades and artillery shells. We're using Molotovs. Go with God."

As they left the kiosk, Trager fiddled with the grenades in his pocket, feeling guilty he didn't leave a couple with Genadiy.

Trager climbed in the back to man the machine gun. Without switching headlights on, Simone made a U-turn and headed north. When they got to the edge of town, she turned onto a dirt road.

She slowed as they approached the last houses.

A shadow stepped out from behind a tree.

"*Sisi rafiki*," we are friends, Simone said.

"*Kitabu*."

"*Mwalimu*."

"*Endelea salama*," go in peace. The shadow waved them through.

The new moon had already set. Trager inhaled deeply the fresh air of the countryside. The sky above was an explosion of stars. Reflected lights from Turako formed a pink cupola over the eastern horizon. The road was barely discernable as a ribbon lighter than the sisal plants on both sides. Dankov had mentioned this was good terrain for planting mines. Trager hoped no one had had bright ideas.

On reaching the eastern boundary of the plantation, Simone stopped. The main road was less than a kilometer to the south, and if the baddies were around, that was the most likely place to find them. Trager checked to see his flashlight was in his pocket and picked up the rifle.

He hadn't gone a hundred meters when a nightjar sitting on the road flew off shrieking. Trager stood still and listened.

He reached the road and lay down. Wishing he had night vision glasses, he scanned the road in both directions with binoculars. Nothing.

Across the road stood a group of shacks. If anyone was watching the junction, it would be from there. For several minutes, Trager scrutinized the area, looking for movement. Not really long enough, but they were in a hurry.

He crouched, waited for someone to react, and ran across the road. A dog started barking. After walking around the huts, Trager decided the junction was clear. He went back across the road. Once inside the plantation, keeping his eyes closed, he signaled with his flashlight. In the distance, three short flashes answered.

The Land Rover arrived, and Trager got back in.

On the asphalt road, Simone accelerated to forty kilometers an hour, twenty five miles. "We'll be in Turako in an hour," she said.

"If we don't meet any liberators," Trager couldn't resist saying.

Twenty minutes later, the truck began to climb the rise to the Kipali police post.

The candy-striped barrier was raised.

The cops had either taken off or were taken out. Bad sign.

Simone stopped.

From the rise, some of Turako's lights could be seen.

Trager scanned the road ahead, but couldn't see anything moving. "Maybe we should give Igor a call on the radio."

"No," Simone said. "If the ZAL were this close to the city, there would be fighting." She put the truck in gear and drove on.

Trager was sure there were enemies ahead. "I don't think we should continue."

"Pshaw, we're almost there."

The road turned and the city lights disappeared behind the last hill before reaching the suburbs. Dark shadows, a line of trucks, stood on the side of the road. Trager's pulse rate increased. "Don't stop now, drive slowly."

The trucks faced in the direction of Turako. The faint hope they were friendly vanished.

They went past one, two, three trucks. No one challenged them. Hopefully, the ZAL would take them for one of their own. Five, six, seven trucks. Three armored vehicles with big guns, looked like old French Panhards.

Shit. Ahead, a group of soldiers milled about in the middle of the road.

Simone brought the truck to a halt. "*Mission des Nations Unies. Lesez passer,*" she said.

There was whispering among the soldiers in floppy hats. A tall, lean man in a beret came forward. "Ah, a United Nations lady," he said in the thick accent of southern France. "A rare pleasure. Delighted to meet you. I haven't had white pussy in some time--take her off the truck."

Trager stuck his hand into his pocket and jumped off the truck trying to remember the name on the Belgian passport Dankov had showed him. "*Imbecile. Nous avons l'autorisation du Comandant Payot.*" He held the grenade in his fist. With his thumb, he pulled the pin out.

"And who in the hell are you?"

Hoping in the darkness his move would not be noticed, with an underhand toss, Trager threw the grenade under a truck.

The tall man came to Trager and grabbed him by the front of his jacket.

The grenade exploded.

The man let go of Trager.

Wangohi stuck his shotgun across the truck and blasted the head off a soldier pulling Simone from her seat.

In the pandemonium, Trager's pistol-shot was hardly heard. The Frenchman staggered and fell.

Trager jumped back on the truck as Simone drove off the road and bounced across the drainage ditch.

An artillery shell ripped nearby. Trager lobbed a grenade behind the truck at no particular target. He was trying to create maximum confusion.

Another shell ripped very close. A truck went up in flames.

Clear of the convoy, Simone bumped back on the road.

"Turn on your lights."

"You're crazy."

"You don't want to be shot by friendlies."

Simone turned on the headlights, while Trager waved his flashlight. He glanced back. In the light of two burning trucks, the convoy was pulling back.

Nearing the top of the hill, they came to a barrier made of rails and razor wire.

"Get off with your hands up," a voice shouted.

"*Kitabu*," Trager said.

"*Iko rafiki*," friends, the voice shouted.

The shadow of a large man appeared from behind the switch in the road. From the way he walked, Trager recognized the elderly sergeant with the Nagant revolver he had seen in Dankov's fort.

Dobroy vecher, Kuzma," Simone said in Russian.

Several soldiers grunted as they moved the barrier aside. Simone drove over the ridgeline and stopped on the protected side of the hill. In the glow of the city lights that began a couple of kilometers from the hill, Trager could see that Kuzma still wore his ancient revolver as he came huffing behind them. "How did you get through?"

Simone got off the truck and hugged the giant. "We were lucky, but those people aren't very good at protecting their rear."

"The Ataman wants to see you right away. He's in the palace."

"Tell him we'll see him in the morning."

The sergeant shrugged. "I gave you the message. Now, could you tell how many troops are down there?"

Trager said, "At least a battalion with armored vehicles."

"I have *one* antitank gun, fifty cadets, a few soldiers and a witch doctor. Tell the Ataman we'll be overrun if I don't get reinforcements."

"You have a radio," Simone said as she climbed back into the truck.

~

Trager thought that, on reaching the city, he would feel relieved. Instead, his apprehension grew. The town was quiet. Policemen armed with old bolt-action rifles manned barricades at some intersections but let them pass unchallenged. A wall of sandbags blocked the road on the north side of the lake that led past the palace. It appeared Turako was a city going through the motions of offering resistance to the army at its gates but had already surrendered to its fate.

Simone detoured, and soon they crossed Avenue de la Liberté. On a parallel street, she stopped at the parking lot gate of a tall building. On seeing the military Land Rover, two policemen opened the gate.

Simone said, "We call this building Cutthroat Tower. When Mbaya took over the country, he ordered most of the civil servants living here killed. This is where I live."

Wangohi stayed behind to watch the vehicle. Carrying the Utabu, Trager followed Simone up the stairs to the fifth floor. She put her bag down and unlocked the door. Then, holding her machine pistol ready, she kicked the door open. Seconds later, she turned the light on, and said, "Come in."

Trager stood dumfounded. He had expected a modest but nice apartment. He found himself in a small room divided by a partly drawn curtain hanging from a laundry line. The entrance side of the room had a small table hugging the wall with a two-burner propane stove on top and two cheap chairs. On the other side of the curtain was a single bed and a dresser topped by a pile of books. Pictures of animals cut out of a calendar and tacked to the walls did little to match the elegant woman with the almost squalid abode.

Simone went into the bathroom, and came back with a kettle. "Make coffee while I have a shower." She pointed at a shelf of tin cans covered with plastic lids.

Trager lit the stove, found coffee and sugar. He heard the shower running and Simone singing. On a shelf, he spotted the only luxury in the place, a half-full bottle of cognac. He poured a shot into a plastic mug. His legs were leaden as he sat down. He Inspected the dingy room. It didn't look like the place of a high-class call girl. Maybe Simone had been bullshitting him when she said she charged a thousand bucks. She had been lying about everything else.

Simone came out wrapped in a towel and her face uncovered. Trager winced at the sight of her swollen purple nose. She dug in a dresser drawer, pulled out a red piece of cloth and wrapped her face with it. "You like it?" With a hand on her hip, she turned to face Trager.

"*Tres chic.*" Trager said, hoping she would peel the towel off and invite him to bed. But she turned again and opened another drawer, tossed a camouflage uniform on the bed, and slipped into lavender panties.

After the water boiled, Trager made coffee.

"It smells good. Today we'll be living on coffee and raw nerves." She took the mug Trager offered. "By sunrise, the whole city will know we have returned. Igor will be going crazy trying to find us. I suspect Longo has been going crazy for days. Tony Bond will also scour every nook and cranny to get his hands on the Utabu." Simone gulped some coffee and sat down. "Mud-Man, now I believe you will help me. After I fix the Utabu, we'll have to run the gauntlet."

Chapter 39

Picking up his gear, Trager followed Simone out of her apartment, down the corridor, and up one flight of stairs. She stopped in front of a door above her apartment, and went through the same entering procedure as she had done earlier.

"This is my safehouse," she said, double locking the door.

Trager was struck by the dark soot on the walls. The bleak room had a folding chair and a cot. Trager smiled at the vase with paper flowers on top of a safe that stood in a corner. He placed the Utabu on a metal table next to industrial-size propane burners mounted on a metal frame.

"Go and have a shower. You can sleep on the cot."

While Trager undressed, Simone opened the safe and took out two small lead ingots, three of gold. She fired up one of the burners that filled the room with a roar. She also switched on a fan mounted on the window with white-painted glass panes.

In the tiny bathroom, Trager inspected his face in the small mirror. Aside from needing a shave, his face didn't look too bad. Only a slightly bluish bruise on his chin. The cut on his forehead was healing nicely.

After a refreshing shower, Trager toweled himself dry and stepped out.

Despite the exhaust fan, the room was full of smoke. Wearing a thick apron and goggles over her head wrap, Simone had the appearance of a cook from hell. She stirred a pot thickly covered with lead.

"Well, we finally see the witch at work."

"Go to bed and be quiet."

Trager shrugged and sat on the bed, which was below the level of thick smoke. His eyelids grew heavy. He stretched out and was immediately asleep.

He must have slept a couple of hours, for it was daylight when he woke. The smoke had subsided. On top of the metal table, the Utabu stood on a stand. It looked like an uneven golden mess. Simone slept in the chair. A radio played African music. Trager looked at his watch. Five to seven.

He got up and peered into the safe. There were a few lead ingots left but no more gold. The thought of Simone peddling her ass to buy the gold angered him for a moment. His anger turned to admiration for her determination to be somebody and make a difference. A woman working alone and in secret to change the political system of an entire country.

The short beeps preceding the long one indicating the top of the hour, drew his attention to the radio and he checked his watch. Beeeep. It was three seconds fast.

"*Ici La Voix du Zengawal* . . .

Simone woke up and listened.

> "In a communiqué, the ministry of defense stated government forces have retaken Maridani suffering minimal losses. The main invading mercenary force is now cut off.
>
> "In a pre-dawn press conference at Army headquarters, commander of the Army, General Mawingi stated his army was ready to crush the rebels."

Simone groaned. "I'm inspired by his modesty."

> "In other news, President Bamondo will be receiving the American envoy to Zengawal, Mr. Douglas Blankenship, who will be presenting credentials in Flamingo House this morning.
>
> "The National Folkloric Ballet will be performing tonight at the Majestic Theater . . ."

Simone lit a cigar. "At the moment, things look alright. As long as Mawingi doesn't try a coup today." She pointed at the Utabu. "I'll be finished polishing it this afternoon. And we'll deliver it to the Babaku."

"Who's the Babaku?"

"Oh, you've met him. He's the witch doctor you saw in Zamani."

~

Once Simone judged the overhauled Utabu was cold enough, she began polishing it with an electric tool. Outside, drumming grew louder throughout the morning. From the half-opened window, Trager could see the streets around Cutthroat Tower were teeming with people.

About ten o'clock, a telephone he had not noticed rang on a shelf under Simone's workbench.

"Answer it, tell whoever it is I'm not in."

Trager picked up the receiver of the rotary dial instrument. "Allo?"

"Is that you, Johnny?" Dankov asked. "Let me speak to Simone."

"She isn't here."

"Where in the fuck did she go?" He sounded angry.

"She tells me nothing."

Dankov switched to Russian. "You better get out of there right away. I suspect they have a live monitor on her phone. Shit. Don't move, I'll be there in ten minutes. Damn, with these crowds, twenty minutes."

Trager hung up. "Igor is on his way."

"Okay, Mud-Man, go downstairs to meet him. Nobody knows about this place. The phone is an extension."

Trager took the keys and went downstairs, wondering who would arrive first.

He was in the apartment hardly ten minutes when there was a knock on the door. Trager opened and was pushed aside by two Uzi-totting black suits.

Longo walked in.

He appeared familiar with the place, opened the bathroom door, peered inside and closed it. "Where is she?"

Trager shrugged. "I don't know, she left early."

Longo approached Trager, a menacing expression on his face. "Don't play games with me."

"She doesn't tell me anything."

"She doesn't?" Longo presented his crooked smile. "The piano man wants to get intimately reacquainted with both of you. Where's the Utabu?"

"I don't have a clue."

"Of course." He raised his hand as if to slap Trager.

Trager had enough of being bullied. "You hit me and you're dead meat."

Shock registered on Longo's face.

"Well." Longo smiled and looked at his men aiming their submachine guns at Trager. "We are getting cheeky around here."

Trager smiled in return. "Your credibility is gone."

"What do you mean?"

"You're nothing but a sold-out agent of Tony Bond's."

For a moment, Longo stood with his mouth agape. He gestured with his head. "Take him--"

He was interrupted by a knock on the door.

The fury expressed on Longo's face turned to a sadistic smile. *"Ah, la princesse."* He opened the door.

Dankov in camouflage uniform barged in. "Put those guns down-- Outside," he bellowed at the black suits. The men looked at Longo, who, to Trager's surprise, nodded.

Once Longo's men were out and the door closed, Dankov asked Longo, "What are you doing here?"

Longo grinned. "Checking on the welfare of our illustrious guest."

Dankov shook hands with Longo. "He looks fine to me. I didn't expect to see you 'til this afternoon."

"Yes, this afternoon." Longo turned to Trager. "It's always a pleasure seeing you. We shall meet again soon." Having said it, Longo walked out.

"Not a pleasant man," Trager said.

Dankov sat on one of the chairs, looked around. "I can't understand why she lives like this," he said, shaking his head. "What is Simone up to? She has the whole country in an uproar, then disappears."

"Do you have your pocket flask? My nerves."

Dankov pulled the flask out of his back pocket and tossed it to Trager. "Tell me about the Kitanda ambush."

"Longo's men did it. Major Kisima fell for some sort of ruse. He and his men were executed."

"You're sure they were Longo's?"

"One hundred percent."

"Do you have proof?"

"Only what I've seen."

Dankov took the flask back and pocketed it. "That's too bad. Bamondo won't act against Longo without evidence that will stand in court. Maybe you should talk to him anyway."

Trager noticed the red armband on Dankov's rolled up sleeve. Written with black laundry marker, it said: Peace Force.

"I'm short of people. The Ugandan army is concentrating troops near our border, just waiting for an excuse to intervene. And what am I doing? I have to use a sizeable force to discourage Mawingi from ordering troops out of the barracks again. He damn near succeeded in a coup attempt the other day." Dankov chuckled. "I told him I had a sniper aiming at his head. If I took my cap off, the sniper would pull the trigger. As my fingers touched my visor, fatso ordered his troops to return to barracks." Dankov's expression returned to serious. "Americans are sending airplanes to airlift a Zimbabwean peace keeping contingent, and the Brits have sent a squadron of Harriers to Nairobi."

"It looks like time to leave."

"Imagine Wellington at Waterloo. He also thought the battle was lost before he ordered the last, desperate assault on Quatre Bras. Our situation here is precarious but not desperate. If this afternoon at the cabinet meeting Bamondo agrees to transfer the Simba Guards regiment to me, I'll be able to drive back and destroy the ZAL force waiting outside of town."

"How's Genadiy doing?"

"We air-dropped him a hundred rifles so that he can organize a militia. With luck, the ZAL will find themselves between hammer and anvil."

"It seems to me the problem would be solved if Mawingi was fired."

"No. The Army is made up of Wussis who will not take orders from a Bassi. So I rather have that incompetent in command. Only the Simba guards are integrated. I have several instructors there. Where in the hell is Simone?"

Dankov stood, removed his beret and scratched his head. "Without an escort, Longo will grab you and Simone the moment I'm out of sight. The best thing for you to do is join my force. Longo won't dare move against one of my uniformed officers commissioned by Bamondo."

Trager was aware of the American law prohibiting its citizens from serving in any capacity for a foreign government. He hesitated for a moment, but if Longo wouldn't touch him, Simone was safe.

He put his heels together and stretched to his full height. "At your orders, *gospodin Polkovnik.*"

Dankov opened the door and bellowed, "Abdallah."

A wiry African soldier walked in carrying a camouflage uniform on a hanger and a green duffel. Two Kalashnikovs were slung over his shoulder.

"Here's your commission." Dankov pulled out a folded paper. Sign both copies. You can resign anytime with twenty-four hours notice. You'll

note it's backdated so that no one can prosecute you for the Kitanda shootout."

"That was self defense."

"If you're right about those people being Longo's men, you could be charged with resisting arrest and killing security personnel. I also know he has done something unusual for him. He has obtained a warrant for your arrest."

"You could have told me that sooner."

Dankov chuckled. "I didn't want to pressure you too much, Major. After all, we are a volunteer force." He turned to Abdallah. "Wait outside."

Trager looked into the green duffel that contained webbing, a Makarov pistol, a personal radio, a pair of gleaming paratrooper boots, and a flack jacket. His uniform already had the red Peace Force armband pinned to a sleeve. "What's this Peace Force?"

"It creates confusion with the foreign correspondents who have flocked into Turako. We're out of the closet now. The presence of a few white soldiers has prevented a panic exodus of Europeans."

~

Simone had half the Utabu gleaming like a mirror when Trager returned to her safehouse. She glanced at him and continued polishing. "You look better in uniform."

Above the whine of the polisher, Trager heard a commotion outside. He opened the window and looked toward the park. People were running away from teargas grenades and a line of police in riot gear. He decided to go downstairs and test Dankov's theory that Longo wouldn't dare arrest him. "If I don't return in fifteen minutes, call Dankov." He had to repeat himself above the noise of the polisher.

Simone nodded. "Be careful."

To increase his authority, Trager slung the Kiparis machine pistol on his shoulder.

Sure enough, two black suits loitered outside the main door. At first they didn't recognize Trager, then started for him.

"Get out of here," Trager said, "before I have you thrown out. Tell Colonel Longo I will see him at the palace later. Understood?"

The two men looked at each other.

Trager yelled at the two policemen by the gate. "Open the gate so these gentlemen can leave."

A number of people milling about the front lawn gave Trager looks of approval.

Not looking happy, the black suits left.

With mounting self-confidence, Trager watched them cross the street and vanish behind a procession of women marching, banging on pots and pans. He went to Wangohi, who, wearing a wide-brimmed straw hat, sat in the truck with his shotgun across his lap.

"What's going on out on the street?"

"They are protesting the police have dispersed the drummers."

A fire engine came behind the women and sprayed them with water cannon, knocking many off their feet, and triggering Trager's sense of outrage. Other than making a lot of noise, the women were behaving in an orderly manner. The water cannon was excessive force.

Trager rushed outside, gestured for the fire truck to halt.

The women cheered and hooted and resumed their march.

That's was when Trager realized Longo's men were standing in doorways across the streets surrounded Cutthroat Tower. Another batch of them sat inside a parked bus. Maybe Longo wouldn't touch him while in uniform, but nothing would stop him if the uniform also had the Utabu.

Chapter 40

Bluffs worked only if the delivery and timing were perfect. Mindful of this, Dankov stepped out of the borrowed presidential pool Mercedes and returned the guard's salute. Sergeant Renko was waiting inside the palace door with the soft leather briefcase and Dankov's blue peaked cap. Dankov exchanged his beret for the cap and they marched toward the Cabinet Room. Without looking at his watch, Dankov knew he was three minutes early. The Emergency Defense Committee consisted of Defense Minister Tongo, Chief of the National Police Kimodo, General Mawingi, the Minister of Education Najua, Longo and Dankov. If Dankov had his way, he would have had Tongo, Mawingi and Longo shot. Now he had to listen to them while pretending everyone was civilized. The problem was, Bamondo actually listened to their arguments. In committees, one needed allies. Dankov didn't have any.

The anteroom was full of military and police aides smoking cigarettes and talking in agitated tones. Dankov glanced at them, making sure they were unarmed, and strode into the Cabinet Room.

Everyone in the committee was already there and their conversation stopped.

"Good afternoon, gentlemen." Dankov removed his cap and took a seat near the foot of the table. With a flourish, Sergeant Renko placed the briefcase in front of Dankov and left the room.

Hostile eyes stared at him; all except Najua, who, as usual, seemed to be enjoying a private joke, and the chief of police absorbed in some papers before him.

Dankov said, "Gentlemen, before the President arrives, you might be interested in this briefcase. During World War II, it was presented to my father by Marshall Konev." Dankov smiled. "But what makes it interesting today are its contents. Colonel Longo, you will be particularly interested as it involves matters of internal security. You know that airplane the British accuse us of shooting down? A patrol reached the crash site and found interesting documents." Dankov heard the hubbub in the anteroom subside.

"The airplane carried a report from an agent in Turako naming specific individuals in this government as being in the payroll of MI-6."

With satisfaction, Dankov watched Longo's eyes shift. "I can do . . ." He delayed, waiting for Bamondo to come in.

Longo said, "In that case, you should hand those documents to me."

"Of course, I--"

"Gentlemen, good afternoon." Followed by his aide de camp and private secretary, Bamondo entered the room.

Softly, Dankov let his breath out with relief.

With a scraping of chairs, everyone stood. Now that Dankov had a threat hanging over Longo, he might get his backing when he asked for the Simba Guards to be transferred to his command.

Bamondo sat motioning the rest to do the same. "Considering the situation, let's get right down to business. I have read everyone's noon reports. Anything to add?"

The chief of police raised his hand. "We had to break up fighting between Bassis and Wussis in the park. Persons unknown, lobbing cans filled with cement at a group of drummers sparked it. The same type of projectiles were used to attack drummers in the Lipanga precinct."

Bamondo nodded. "Thank you. I see the situation has improved since you stopped breaking up the drummings.

Mawingi said. "The drummers interfere with the Army's movements."

"Use the side streets. Are you still planning to attack that ZAL column tonight?"

"Yes, Excellency, we will deploy during the night, and deliver a fatal attack at daybreak."

Dankov wondered *whom* Mawingi would attack. "Excellency, may I suggest the Simba Guards be incorporated into the special operations group. That will in effect create a strong new mechanized brigade to support General Mawingi."

"Excellent idea," Mawingi said, "but it should be done the other way around. The Special Operations Group should reinforce the Simbas, then our whole army will operate under a unified command."

Dankov said, "The Simbas' new communications equipment is not compatible with that of the rest of the army."

Najua took his unlit pipe out of his mouth. "The Special Operations group has been doing a splendid job. The Simbas would benefit by being attached to it."

Dankov caught Longo's eye and patted the top of the briefcase.

Longo probably understood that if Dankov got the Simbas, the whole nature of the war would change. In a few days, his highly mobile Cossacks, supported by the Simbas, could scatter the ZAL and still keep Mawingi in check.

Dankov stared at Longo, who responded with furtive glances. "The Simbas have almost completed their training. Their tactics are more compatible with the Special Operations Group. The regular army would lose less than ten percent of its manpower." *And fifty percent of its effectivness.* "But I see this is a difficult decision. If you will allow me, Excellency, I will move to a different subject for a moment."

Mawingi grinned. Longo appeared relieved. Dankov opened the briefcase and removed the two wallets Trager had given him. "These are the wallets of the two occupants of the British aircraft that crashed yesterday. The garrison commander in Maridani has Polaroid photos that prove the plane was not shot down but crashed." Dankov took out some papers and showed them to Longo, gesturing with his head that he was about to pass them to Bamondo.

Longo moved his eyes, indicating a negative. He said, "While we examine the contents of the wallets, I think it's a good idea to incorporate the Simbas to Special Operations."

Looking at some of the photographs from a wallet, almost absentmindedly, Bamondo said. "I'm glad the majority agrees." He slid the wallets to Kimondo. "I guess these should go to the Swiss embassy." He then addressed everyone. "Well, we had time to consider our military advisor's suggestion on the Simba Guards. It seems the majority agrees with Colonel Dankov."

A neutral expression on his face, Mawingi nodded.

"By presidential decree, the Simba Guards regiment is transferred to the Special Operations Group," Bamondo said with finality.

The Simbas were a regiment in name only. It was really a small battalion short of officers. But the troops were well disciplined and indoctrinated. Now Dankov had a fighting chance. He glanced at Mawingi, who held his swagger stick as if he wanted to break it.

～

The crowd gathered outside the old ambassador's residence was still eerily quiet. Blankenship handed the report he had just finished to the State Department code clerk; then went to the foyer from where he could see the street side.

Dressed in almost unserviceable trousers and a faded sport shirt, the NCOIC of the Marine detachment, Gunnery Sergeant Parsons, stood in the foyer. Chewing on a toothbrush stick, he looked like a local African.

"Gunny, I see you're back."

Parsons nodded. *"Ndio Bwana."*

Blankenship peered through the glass panes of the front door. The number of signs the crowd held had increased. *Peace, Love, No troop,* mixed with *Yankee go home* and *Welcome to Zengawal.*

Two cops stationed outside had no trouble keeping the crowd off the sidewalk.

"Hey, Gunny, what do you make of it?"

"The best I can tell, they're just gawking." Parsons grinned. "Maybe you should come out on the balcony and wave."

"What do you hear in town?"

"Everybody is talking about the Utabu, and that foreigners want to steal it. They are also speculating who the next king will be. Some say he will march in tonight with the ZAL."

"The ZAL still just outside town?"

"From what I could tell, there are a few white mercs holding a roadblock with a handful of Africans. Nothing else to stop them. I don't know what the ZAL is waiting for."

"No sign of Trager?"

"Corporal Jones was to his house again. No answer. He saw a carload of ZSS people hanging out nearby."

"Something tells me that boy's got his ass deep in alligators."

"Over here, it's crocodiles, sir."

Chapter 41

Simone produced a little silk pillow. "Now we add a pad for the comfort of the wearer," she said studying the newly polished Utabu. "I guess practice makes perfect. It looks better than it did before."

"Yeah," Trager said. "But we'll need Igor to provide a heavy escort to get out of here."

"No. We can't use soldiers."

"You haven't seen the gorillas Longo has around the building."

The telephone rang. Trager was sure it was Dankov calling again. "Really, we do need an escort."

"No."

Trager picked up the phone. "No, she isn't back yet."

"In that case, you'd better come to the palace. I'm holding an officer's briefing in one hour."

Trager glanced at Simone. "Maybe I should wait a bit longer."

"You've wasted enough time. I need every single body tonight."

"Okay." Trager hung up, knowing that soon Dankov would be very pissed at him.

Simone said, "Now, I have to use the phone."

"Longo will know you are here and storm the building."

"Mud-Man quit worrying me."

She picked up the phone and dialed. "Mr. Singh? . . . Oh, so sorry, wrong number." She hung up and dialed again. "Hello, Mr. Singh, this is Simone. I'm sorry but I think we'll need to cancel next week's French lessons." She listened for a bit, said goodbye and hung up. She turned to Trager. "The first call was to alert our people that the Utabu is here. The second was to a real person to throw Longo off." She looked at her watch. "The show starts in twenty minutes." She turned off the light and opened the window.

The drumming in the park began to die down. Within ten minutes, only a far-away siren broke the silence, as the crowd in the park became hushed. Trager thought this akin to being in the eye of a hurricane. The crowds thinned as people drifted out of the park.

A lone drummer began a different beat--a rapid staccato followed by a deep boom.

Simone had exchanged her sweaty red face cloth for a black one. She handed Trager a black dress. "Put this on. I wore it to a costume ball as a fat lady." She chuckled. "Longo won't recognize you."

"I think he likes to haul women into his dungeon." Trager put the dress on. Simone produced a tube of grease paint and painted Trager's face black. Outside, the pandemonium increased.

Simone looked at her watch, then she placed a pink shower cap on Trager's head. "I think everything is ready."

Trager, Kalashnikov around his neck, picked up the gunnysack containing the Utabu, and stepped into the ill-lit corridor.

They descended the stairs and went out by a side door.

A huge mob rioted outside the building, and the ZSS bus was on fire.

Dressed in leopard skins and tall cylindrical white caps, Wangohi and two other men stood next to the Land Rover, which was completely covered with palm fronds. Pointing straight up, the machine gun looked like a little palm tree. A truck full of drummers stood parked by the gate.

"Looks like carnival time," Trager said.

"Good execution of plan, no?"

Trager followed Simone, feeling ridiculous in a dress and combat boots. Never mind the rifle hanging from his neck.

Simone climbed into the driver's seat. Trager stood by the machine gun, secured in the upward position by twine that would easily snap should he need to use it.

The night air smelled of teargas, and made Trager's eyes burn.

The drummers on the truck began drumming and the policemen opened the gate. Simone followed the truck that slowly opened the way through the crowd. Trager searched for Longo's men. Isolated shots rang out nearby. On reaching the intersection, Trager saw an island of black suits on the steps of the courthouse, battling a howling mob armed with sticks. It looked like a revolution in progress.

Screams came from the direction of the park. Supported by two fire engines, a line of riot police charged the mob. A block away from Cutthroat Tower, the crowd began to thin, and the little convoy gathered speed.

Simone said, "First stage of plan almost complete. Next, I'll change vehicles. You tell Igor I will see him and Pierre in the morning."

Now what? "I'm your escort, remember?"

"Don't mess up the plan, go to the palace."

They drove past Hell's basement, which appeared to be closed. At the next intersection, Simone turned right while the drummer's truck kept going straight. She pulled up behind a parked taxi and got out. "I'll see you at the palace tomorrow."

Wangohi, still carrying his shotgun, took the gunnysack. The two other leopard skins got out, too. Trager watched them all get into the taxi and drive off. His first reaction was to jump into the driver's seat and follow, but he saw the wisdom in using the anonymity of a taxi. He watched the lights disappear as the taxi turned a corner.

Worried about Simone's safety, Trager used empty back streets to reach the palace.

Two sand-bagged machinegun nests flanked the back gate. Trager brought his vehicle to a stop and switched off the headlights. "It's Major Trager."

Suspicious eyes peered over the sandbags.

A Russian came out of the gate. "*Kto vi?*"

"*Mayor* Trager *predstavliayus kak prikazono,*" Major Trager reporting as ordered.

Trager wondered what was so funny as the Russian almost doubled up laughing and waved him through. He parked on the side of the driveway as guards looked at him strangely.

The giant sergeant Kuzma came out of the palace door followed by several other Russians, who began to laugh.

Trager removed his pink shower cap.

Dankov came out of the door laughing. "Stop," he bellowed. "Put that cap back on and come with me."

Hurriedly, Dankov led the way down the corridor toward the front of the palace, past the front door, that was now sandbagged, and into the presidential offices wing. He entered a reception office where a Zengawali major with ADC aguilletes sat behind a desk. Seeing Dankov, he jumped to his feet and stood at attention.

"Tell his Excellency I need to see him right away."

The ADC picked up a phone.

"You may go in, sir."

Wearing a sweat-stained safari suit, Bamondo was on the phone. He abruptly finished the conversation, looking puzzled.

"Excellency, I would like to introduce Major Trager, acting commandant of the palace guard."

What?

Bamondo said, "Is that you?"

Trager felt like a nitwit. "Yes, your Excellency. Pardon my dress . . ."

"Well, Igor, for a moment I was appalled at this buffoonery. I'm afraid you have embarrassed our friend. Have a seat, gentlemen."

"Would you mind if I undress a little?" Trager asked

Bamondo nodded, almost snickered. "I needed this moment of humor. A drink?"

A steward appeared and took drink orders as Trager pulled the dress off.

Dankov sat on a sofa and said to Trager, "You may as well tell us what's going on in town."

"The mob turned against a group of ZSS agents and burned one of their buses."

"They did?" Bamondo looked amazed. He glanced at Dankov. "It looks like we have an insurrection on our hands."

"We will have one, if Mawingi's troops try to restore order," Dankov said. Then he asked Trager, "Any news from Simone?"

"She's safe, hiding somewhere."

"Thank God," Bamondo said. "We were worried."

The steward brought the drinks.

Bamondo sipped his Cinzano and soda. He asked Trager, "You've traveled quite a bit lately, what's your take on the situation?"

"The best I can call it is chaotic. There doesn't seem to be any resentment against the government, but the people fear the ZAL, who are recruiting in the occupied areas. From what I've seen, the ZAL has a hardcore, but in general there is no strong will to fight."

Dankov said, "The best intelligence we have on the ZAL has been gathered by Major Trager. I'm going to smash them tonight."

"Sometimes I think you're over confident."

Dankov finished sipping his beer, wiped foam from his moustache and grinned. "I didn't want to reveal this during our meeting this afternoon, but thanks to my friend here, the ZAL column outside the city has lost its leader, a capable French mercenary by the name of Poletti. My advance reconnaissance people have been mingling with the ZAL. They report there is talk of pulling out tonight. This will be difficult for them. Captain Kolzov is in a blocking position in Maridani."

Bamondo shook his head. "You're always pulling surprises."

"That's because I don't trust your people."

"I wish you would. They might like you better if you did."

"I don't care if they like me or not." Dankov shook his head. "In this country, racial harmony works among the masses, but most of the cabinet resents my presence. Everything indicates that some people in this government are secretly allied with the ZAL. The ZAL column that's waiting outside of town could have overrun us last night, and Major Trager reports that people of *our* security service ambushed him in an attempt to gain possession of the Utabu. Had they succeeded, the ZAL could have marched right into town with the new king at its head."

Bamondo shook his head. "That damn Utabu." He looked sharply at Trager. "You mean John has actually seen the Utabu?"

"Tell him."

"The Pygmies who had the Utabu entrusted Simone and me with it. She is handing it over to the witch doctors right now."

Bamondo shrank behind his desk. "Where is she?"

"I don't know. She and Babaku took off."

"So the Utabu really exists."

Trager nodded, aware of the enormity of the hoax and the awful consequences for him and Simone if the hoax was uncovered.

Bamondo said, "Although I never believed in the Utabu's existence. I ordered Colonel Longo to investigate, and if it did exist, to bring it to the palace." He smiled wryly. "It would look good in the museum."

Dankov stood. "It's time for me to go, and John needs to familiarize himself with the security arrangements."

Bamondo rose, came around his desk and shook Dankov's hand. "I wish you the best of luck and success in battle. I can't express the gratitude I feel for your efforts to save this country." He then turned to Trager. "I'm grateful to you, too. You have also proven yourself a trusted friend."

~

Finished giving Trager a quick tour of the palace defenses and descending down the service stairway, Dankov said, "I expect to be back in the morning. Sergeant Kuzma will keep you out of trouble here. I'll radio progress of the battle. You keep the president advised. If he sleeps at all, it will be in his office." He opened the back door.

A formation of about twenty African soldiers came to attention and Sergeant Kuzma saluted.

Dankov bellowed, "Attention to orders. As of this moment, I'm passing command of the palace guard to Major Trager, who will remain in command until properly relieved."

"Present arms," Kuzma ordered.

Trager returned Dankov's salute and they shook hands. Then Trager commanded, "Order arms." At least for the moment, being again a soldier felt damn good. "Dismiss."

He returned Kuzma's salute and remembered to make an about face to the left instead of the American way to the right.

As he entered the guardroom, an African corporal said, "Telephone call for you, sir."

The commandant's office, crammed with a desk, two guest chairs, a sofa and a coffee table was claustrophobic. Trager picked up the receiver. "Commander of the guard."

"Congratulations." He recognized Leonora's voice. "Come and see me right away," she said in a commanding tone.

That was the last thing he wanted to do, but at least he would be able to return her diamonds. "Are you in your apartment?"

"Yes. I'm waiting."

Trager took his new handheld radio and marched out of the guardroom that was actually a suite that included a bunkroom and armory.

The guards outside the presidential apartment wore camouflage dress without embellishments. Trager returned their salute and rang the doorbell. The same maid he had seen before opened the door and led him past the dimly-lit sitting and dining rooms then down a corridor. She opened a door and stepped aside.

Trager stood at the threshold, taking in the visual clash of images. A bright chandelier lit a white space splashed with gold and burgundy. Dwarfed by the size of the room, a set of burgundy chairs and sofa stood on one side by the outer wall. On top of a piano-shaped peninsula with steps perched a canopied bed that made Trager think of the main altar of Saint Peter's Basilica in Rome. From somewhere came the gurgling of water.

His amazed gaze roamed the room until he found Leonora reclining on a Roman type couchette in a corner. Wearing gold silk pajamas, she motioned him to take a seat in a chair with curved scissors-like legs. "My wayward boy, where have you been?"

Trager extended his hand with the bag of diamonds in it. "Getting these back."

She took the bag and smiled. "I never doubted your honesty." She gestured toward the large draped windows. "It's bad out there, isn't it?"

"It could be much worse."

"That's what I'm afraid of."

"By tomorrow, we'll see improvement."

She curled up. "And I believe in fairy tales. This place is doomed and I'm still here." In a sudden motion, she stretched and sat up placing her bare feet on the floor. "Now that you're the hired help, where do your loyalties lie?"

That was a good question Trager hadn't asked himself. "The palace. That's what I'm doing here, protecting this property."

"That makes me feel better. The gallant John Trager playing a starring role in Flamingo House Massacre III. This time it'll be worse than when

Mbaya took over. You and Igor are heroes who will die outside my doors. That's very lofty, but you will depart for the pantheon of the gods." She gestured toward the bed, "and leave me to be raped. What am I to do, welcome them with open legs or commit suicide?"

"The picture is not--"

"I need to get out of here. You must help me."

"I can't--"

"Listen to me. I'm not asking for anything big. That moment has passed." She reached under a cushion and took out an envelope. "I can't trust anyone else. Please deliver this, tonight."

"I'm on duty."

"It's not far, just the Metropole. I'm desperate." She reached over and put her hand on his knee. "My promise to you is still good. This letter will bring a rescue helicopter. You can come with me, or, if you stay and survive, I'll meet you in Europe."

Delivering a letter a couple of blocks away didn't seem like too big of a deal. If this desperate woman wanted to leave her house, who was he to prevent her from doing so? He was a guardian, not a jailer. "Alright, who do I give this letter to?"

"Tony Bond. If you can't find him, give it to Katharina, she's the violinist. They are playing at the hotel now."

"Bond, Tony Bond?"

Looking terrified, she bit her lip and nodded.

He took out a pack of cigarettes. "May I?"

She nodded again.

For a moment, Trager's mind refused to accept what he was thinking. *She couldn't, yes she could. She wouldn't, yes she would.* He had considered the possibility of the CIA recruiting her. It appeared that someone else had already done it. This was his opportunity to find out more about Bond. "Who does Bond work for?"

"I don't know."

Trager waved the letter in front of her. "It's your choice: wait here with open legs or get out. If you want me to deliver this letter, tell me everything from the beginning." He placed the letter on her lap and stood.

She wrapped her arms around his legs. "I beg you."

"What is Bond?"

"He . . . is the ASS representative."

"And you pass information to him."

She nodded.

"Like placing your reports into the piano at the women's league."

Her eyes grew bigger.

"Did you tell him Simone was going to see the Pygmies?"

Leonora answered with another nod.

"You may as well let go of my legs. It wouldn't look good if your husband came in."

"He won't be in tonight." She let go and placed her hands on her lap.

Trager sat down.

"Before I first arrived, did Bond tell you I was coming? And told you about my background?"

"Yes. He said that you were a friend of Igor's and to inform him if you came to the palace."

"So you knew of my existence before that soiree?"

She nodded while looking at her toes. Then she looked up. "I tried to warn you. Remember when I asked you if you had learned to tango in Buenos Aires?"

"Yes. How often do you meet Bond?"

"About once a month."

"Where?"

"In his villa."

Trager raised an eyebrow. This was hard to believe. "How do you get away with that?"

"Longo's men take me there."

This confirmed it. Bond and Longo were in cahoots. "So you had a good communications set up. How come you need me to deliver this letter?"

"The courier hasn't been able to come in since Igor tightened security."

"And why did you ask me to take you out of the country?"

She looked at him for a while and shook her head. "Do you know what it is to live a lie for six years? It was all fine when we lived on the yacht."

"You've been spying on Pierre that long?"

"The ASS rigged the Miss Belgium contest so that I would win. They knew Pierre's weaknesses. The moment I won the title, he was after me. We were married two months later. The ASS wanted to install him as president and were delighted when he and Igor met. I was instructed to encourage Igor to come along. But when Pierre came here, he kept Igor and he would no longer obey the ASS."

She gave him a bitter smile. "I was happy, because I, too, told them to *fuck off*. But I wasn't free. Dear Tony has tapes of phone conversations. Pierre would kill me."

"Do you understand the stress?"

"And you believe Bond will take you out now?"

"Yes. It's over. Pierre is finished and so is my job. Longo, backed by Mawingi and the ZAL, will overthrow Pierre any day now. Longo is the chosen next president. And I am scared. The way he looks at me . . . scares me."

"I'll deliver the letter," Trager said, as a sensation of sadness enveloped him. He felt sorry for Bamondo and wondered why anyone would ever want to be a head of state. It was the surest way to surround oneself with enemies. As far as Trager could tell, besides Igor and Simone, Bamondo didn't have a single friend in this world.

Chapter 42

Just in case, Trager took two African soldiers with him and carried a Kaliasha with a round in the chamber. From the palace front gate, the Metropole was only a block away. Police barricades stood in the distance and this part of the park was empty of people.

At the hotel door, two Russian soldiers stood wearing their Peace Force armbands. Trager told his men to wait outside, returned the Russians' salute and entered the hotel. Sure enough, the Bosnian refugees were scratching away, this time an African tune, *Malaika*. The terrace bar was crowded with people. By their dress, Trager could see they were mostly journalists. They stood two deep by the bar and every table was occupied.

"You look rather martial, old chap."

Startled, Trager didn't know from where Bond had appeared. "It's the latest fashion."

"Up in the roof garden, it's quieter. That's where I was 'til I saw you crossing the street. Recognized you by your walk. Come, I'll stand you a drink."

While they were in the elevator, Trager handed Bond Leonora's envelope. "She wants to be exfiltrated."

"Going back to the palace?"

"After you buy me that drink."

"Tell her to be on the lawn by the lake thirty minutes after she hears a police siren sound three times. It will be sometime tomorrow night."

If Bond knew about the intended coup, it meant nothing would happen tomorrow--unless Bond was tossing red herrings.

The elevator door opened and they stepped out onto a terrace with lots of potted plants. Bond pointed to the west. "Best place to watch the war."

In the distance, several parachute flares drifted down leaving trails of golden smoke.

Trager sat at a table. "I'll have a Jumbo."

"I hear your wild Russian friend got command of the Simba Guards and is terrorizing the populace."

"I don't know a thing."

"Your friend Blankenship is in town."

"So I've heard."

"You want passage out?"

"No thanks." If he had an ounce of brains, he'd go out with Leonora. Instead, he wondered how Simone was doing. "How's your friend Longo?"

"Pretty busy, I would imagine. Did you get a good look at the Utabu?"

"What's that?"

Bond smiled. "It had never occurred to me that the delightful Mademoiselle would be involved in the recovery of that priceless artifact. Longo didn't appreciate what you did to his men in Kitanda. I would really recommend you reserve a seat in that helicopter. When the balloon goes up, there will be no quarter given, and these chappies are notorious for settling debts."

Trager pulled at his beer. The faint booming of artillery told him Dankov was messing up Bond's calculations. "Tony, I think you're betting on the wrong horses."

Bond leaned back entwining his fingers over his stomach. "Betting is one thing, *riding* the wrong horse is what kills you. This is the final straightway. Longo is riding hard." Bond chuckled. "The good colonel is going bonkers trying to find the Utabu tonight. He has raided a number of places, so far no luck. But the night's still young and there are just so many places the witch doctors can hide."

Trager gave Bond the wicked smile that made people nervous. "Don't get overly optimistic."

Bond grinned back. "It must be the phase of the moon, and the prospect of seeing the lovely Leonora would make any man's heart soar." He leaned over the table and said in a confidential tone, "I love her tits."

The sound of shooting came from the direction of the Central Market. Trager's body tensed as he thought of Longo combing the town.

~

This time, Leonora answered the door and let Trager in. She now wore a long silk robe the same color as her pajamas. "Have a seat," she said as they entered the little sitting room. She no longer appeared upset and had removed her makeup. Her face shone from a heavy dose of cream.

"I like it here. This used to be one room. I had it converted into an apartment, a place I feel comfortable in. Mbaya who, had airline stewardesses brought in for him, built that fornicatorium next door. Sometimes he'd have a whole crew of girls. The ASS wanted him removed because his lavish spending was creating unrest."

"They sound difficult to please."

She smiled coquettishly. "Not as difficult as you are. Did you see him?"

"Yes." Trager explained about the signal and the helicopter.

"It sounds almost too easy."

"Not so easy if the palace guards start shooting."

"Oh." She bit her lip. "Are you coming with me?"

"I couldn't leave my friends behind." He thought of Simone when he had posed a similar question. "But thanks for asking."

"I like you. You're a loyal friend. And I was sincere with my invitation to meet in Europe."

"Thanks." Trager stood and Leonora accompanied him to the door. As he reached for the doorknob, she took his arm and pulled hard, turning him into an embrace. "You stubborn man, remember my promise." She kissed him, her body pushed into his, her hips rotated.

Next thing he knew, she had her hand on his stiffening member and was pulling him down on the floor. There was nothing under her robe but the most gorgeous female body he had ever seen. She undid his zipper, pulled him out. Trager remembered to keep his feet against the door. That would at least give him some protection if someone tried to open it. She adjusted her position and guided him into her moist warmness.

He was aware of her heavy breathing, her aggressive answer to his thrusts. His boots thumped against the door as a violent shiver went through him. She let out a sigh.

~

With a general unease, Trager returned the soldier's salute as he left the presidential chambers. The guards must have heard his thumping feet on the door. He hurried down the corridor. On the landing before the formal stairway, he looked at the park and wondered where Simone was. Leonora's sticky wetness on his penis made him feel guilty, and he was afraid the soldiers in the guardroom would notice the smell of woman on him.

Before entering the guardroom, he lit a cigarette and went straight into the bathroom, which had two shower stalls.

The ritual cleansing didn't do much for him. By succumbing to Leonora's charms, he had become as treasonous as everyone else in this wretched country.

When he came out of the shower, a Russian soldier waiting for him handed him a message. "From the Ataman."

Trager read it:

> Enemy engaged and routed. 3 armored cars destroyed. Many prisoners.
> Friendly losses: 1 vehicle destroyed, 8 Vulture Force KIA, 10 Simba Guards KIA. WIA 4 VF 15 Simba
> Vulture

Trager hurried to Bamondo's office. The ADC dozed at his desk. Trager said, "The ZAL has been routed."

The ADC jumped to his feet and pushed the intercom button. "Commander of the guard to see you, Excellency." He nodded for Trager to go in.

Bamondo must have been sleeping on the sofa. He yawned.

Trager handed him the message slip.

"Well, at last some good news. This will put me in a stronger negotiating position." He shook his head and tapped the message with the back of his fingers. "That's an awful lot of casualties. Colonel Dankov lost nearly a third of his men."

"The enemy had light armor."

"We should have used our tanks, our army has enough of them . . . It seems the Simbas fought well. That was an unknown quantity. Our army has nev--."

A number of shots rang outside the palace, followed by the screech of metal and the sound of broken glass. Trager leapt and switched off the only lamp illuminating the room.

He peered out the window.

A taxi had crashed into the main gate.

An alarm Klaxon hooted. Trager ran out of the office unholstering his pistol.

When he reached the front door, several black suits had surrounded the taxi and dragged someone out of the back seat. Trager recognized Simone's voice screaming.

The guards inside the gate stood watching.

Running toward the Palace's front entrance, Trager yelled, "Open the gate."

The black suits had Simone out and were bundling her into a black Mercedes. A guard fiddled with the lock of a side door.

Trager dropped his pistol and let it hang from its lanyard, then grabbed a rifle from a guard's hands.

Simone disappeared inside the black car.

Trager fired through the wrought iron fence at the car's tires.

"*Arretez!*" he screamed in desperation.

The guard swung the door open. Trager ran through.

One of the black suits turned with a submachine gun in his hands.

"Drop it," Trager yelled.

Palace guards poured out and surrounded the Mercedes.

Simone stumbled out of the car into Trager's arms. She pointed at the cab driver, who stood by the steaming hood of his taxi. "He needs protection, too."

A black suit came up to Trager. "That woman is under arrest. Here is the warrant."

Trager could hardly restrain himself from hitting the man with the stock of the rifle. "Tell Colonel Longo if he comes up with any more trumped up charges, I will personally castrate him."

The black suit smiled. "I will tell him. Your name Monsieur?"

"Major Trager."

"Nice to meet you, Major. I wish to inform you that this is a country of laws. We are not *les cowboys*."

"I'll remember that."

Trager turned and addressed his soldiers. "Push that cab out of the way and place the driver in one of the detention cells."

He was relieved to see Simone inside the fence, bumming a cigarette from one of the guards.

Trager came up to her. "Let's go inside."

"I must see Pierre."

"He's in his office now, probably watching your dramatic arrival."

"They almost caught me. Thank you, Mud-Man."

"What were you doing?"

"You'll hear when I tell Pierre."

~

"What was that all about?" Bamondo demanded when they entered the room. He glared at Trager. "You shot at *my* security service people. I can't have that. Consider yourself under arrest."

Trager felt blood leave his face. Bamondo was a blind fool.

"Pierre."

"Don't Pierre me, young lady." Bamondo picked up the phone. "Have the palace guard second in command report to me immediately."

"Don't get carried away with your temper," Simone said.

Trager touched his pistol, then forced his hand away from the holster.

Bamondo pointed his finger at Simone. "Don't interfere."

"Very well, I was going to tell you who was going to be crowned king tomorrow. Does that interest you?"

Bamondo's fury seemed to abate. "Crowning a king tomorrow?"

"Yes, that's what's going to happen. I just came from the council of witch doctors."

"They are an illegal body, they have no right--"

"*Merde alors*," Simone shouted.

His face expressing shock, Bamondo stepped back half a pace.

Placing her hands on her hips, Simone stepped forward. "Those Longo louts wanted to take me so that I would tell them where the Utabu is. You live in a palace of dreams. Longo and his men are the biggest lawbreakers in this country. And you want to arrest one of the few people you can depend on? Arrest me too. I'll join the rest of the women being raped tonight in the ZSS basement."

"You exaggerate."

"Ask John, he's been locked up."

"Is it true Major?"

"I only heard the screams."

The door opened. Kuzma entered and clacked his heels.

"Sorry to have bothered you. I don't think I need you," Bamondo said.

"At your orders." Kuzma left.

Bamondo rotated his arms like windmills as if not knowing what to do next. "Alright, let's sit down." He pointed at some thermoses on top of a credenza. "Have some tea, coffee, cocoa."

Simone opened the credenza and took out a bottle of cognac and a cigar.

Trager poured himself tea and sat down.

Simone arranged herself on a sofa and took a big swig out of her glass. "The council of witch doctors, that unfortunately is still outlawed, has decided. You will be crowned King of Zengawal. Harm will befall whoever oppose this decision."

"I can't believe this."

"The witch doctors have the Utabu, they feel you are a wise and deserving ruler. The only condition is that you have to abolish the colonial law that prohibits the council. You can do that by presidential decree and announce it on the radio in the morning." Simone smiled. "Another little condition is to get funds to complete Stage One of the Pygmy tourist project. After all, it is the little dears who guarded the Utabu."

Yeah, for a couple of days. Trager was amazed at Simone's gall.

"As for myself, once you get used to being a monarch of a united and happy kingdom, maybe you would see fit to elevate the Tourism Board to Cabinet level and make me minister."

"You'll have to become a Zengawali citizen."

"I'll file the paperwork day after tomorrow."

"So the rumor is true. And all tribes will accept me as their king?"

Simone nodded. "Peace is at hand."

Bamondo shook his head. "I can hardly believe it." His preoccupied expression slowly changed to a grin. "This is beyond my wildest expectations. It is better than winning an election."

"If this was an election . . ." Simone raised her glass. "You would win by something like seventy-five percent. With the Utabu, it would be closer to ninety."

"I think I need a drink." Bamondo looked jubilant.

"A small one," Simone said. "I'll tell your ADC to wake up staff. They have a lot of work to do for tomorrow's coronation." Without waiting for a reply, she opened the door and spoke to the ADC.

Bamondo said to Trager, "I apologize for my outburst at you. When I become king, I'll be able to award knighthoods. Join me with a little drink."

"Thank you, your future majesty."

Bamondo laughed. "I promise it won't go to my head."

After suppressing a yawn, Simone said, "And I am very tired." She turned to Trager. "Can I have a bunk in the guardroom?"

Bamondo said, "Use one of the guest rooms."

"Thanks, Pierre. Tonight, I want to sleep enjoying the security I feel when I smell sweaty soldiers."

~

His eyelids heavy and reluctant to open, Trager yawned and stretched on the sofa. A steward placed a tea tray on the coffee table.

"What time is it?" Trager asked as his eyes failed to focus on his watch.

"Seven o'clock, sir."

"Thank you." Trager rolled over and reached for the teapot. From the guardroom came the sound of voices, the smell of oil, and the noise of weapon's mechanisms being checked.

Sergeant Kuzma entered. "Good morning, Major," he said in Russian. "Builders are waiting outside the front gate to rig up bleachers and the distinguished guest platform for the coronation. Foreign television crews want to rig a tower. I have detailed ten additional guards to watch the workers. If it is alright with the Major, I will start frisking and letting them in."

"Go ahead. Any news from the Ataman?"

"The ZAL force has scattered. It will take some time to round up all those armed bandits. But I expect the Ataman to be back sometime this morning." Kuzma grinned and gestured as if introducing someone. "Captain Kolzov reports Maridani is secured. He has organized a two-hundred-man militia and will be arming them with captured weapons. He has become a real warlord. We're gaining strength not by the day but by the hour."

The tea and a cigarette were clearing Trager's mind. Even though from the windowless office one couldn't tell what was going on outside, the mood in the guardroom was cheerful. It appeared the crisis was over. He guessed Simone was right. She had brought peace back to the country.

~

After shaving and changing into a fresh uniform, Trager went down to the basement where the aroma of fresh bread and coffee wafted from the guard's mess. His stomach almost hurt from hunger. He forced himself to keep going into the communications room.

On the secure radio channel, Trager brought Dankov up to date on the situation in the capital. That there would be a parade as the witch doctors brought the Utabu to the palace.

He also needed troops to provide security for the Utabu, which Simone had told him was hidden in the Jumbo brewery, almost across the street from Longo's headquarters.

Dankov's slightly disembodied voice came back. "Get the senior cadets from the military school. I'll send five of my people to beef them up."

"How many cadets is that?"

"About seventy, plus four of my instructors."

Trager thought that this force could keep Longo at bay, but who knew about General Mawingi, who had five thousand men.

Finished with Dankov, Trager studied the city map then called Mawingi on the telephone.

"General, this is the officer in charge of organizing the military part of the parade. Together with the President, you will receive the parade, which will be headed by the first infantry regiment. No heavy weapons are to leave the barracks. Ammunition is to be issued only to officers and NCOS. A messenger will bring out the orders signed by the President."

"I am always happy to obey the President's orders." Mawingi hung up.

Trager wished Dankov would hurry and come back. The apprehension he felt by being responsible for security with only a handful of men made him almost sick. During the parade, the palace would be extremely vulnerable. He thought of the parade in which President Sadat of Egypt was murdered. It was a pity that the three hundred Simba Guards were busy rounding up what was left of the ZAL.

Chapter 43

A soldier entered the room and clacked his heels. "Breakfast is ready for you in the garden, sir."

"Thank you." Trager hurried outside. The last meal he had had was two days earlier in Maridani.

Wearing a print dress a little too large for her and a black Robin Hood hat with a veil covering her nose, Simone sat at a table set up on the lawn under a large fig tree. The sight of her, and the spectacular view of the shimmering lake bordered by flamingoes, dissipated Trager's somber thoughts of what could go wrong today.

As he approached, Simone said, "I ordered a big English breakfast. The chef tends to go overboard, but I think you need food, too."

Trager bent down to give her a kiss. Up close, he could see the bandage covering her nose. She offered her mouth. He tasted her toothpaste and felt her soft lips. After about two seconds, she pulled away, laughing. "Breakfast is on the *table*."

The immaculate white starched tablecloth and napkins, heavy silverware and fine crystal, and the beautiful Simone looking like a film star of the nineteen forties, gave him a sensation of happy unreality.

Trager helped himself to scrambled eggs, lamb kidneys, sautéed mushrooms and a croissant.

Simone said, "Imagine a photograph of us with flamingoes in the background on a travel poster. People from all over the world won't be able to resist the temptation and will flock to Zengawal."

Simone's upbeat tone enhanced Trager's sense of relief and he laughed. He was surrounded by beauty. Like Kuzma had said, they were growing stronger by the hour. After the Army swore allegiance to its new king, peace would be assured. "I'll provide the photographs."

"This last week has shown we work well together. I'll make you PR director at the ministry."

She extended her hand. "Deal?"

He took her hand and brought it to his lips. "A very happy deal."

"Mud-Man, you're incorrigible. But this is a happy day. If you kiss my hand again, I'll tell you something.

He kissed her hand again.

Leaning forward, she rested her chin on a slightly open fist. "With my minister's salary, I'll be able to rent a villa next to yours, and we'll see each other often after work."

"And on weekends we'll stay in bed late."

"And you'll telephone me when you're ready to get up, and we'll have breakfast together."

"No, I'll whisper into your ear."

She chuckled and gave him a warm smile. "And we'll travel to the ITB in Berlin to promote tourism. Separate rooms, of course."

"But adjoining."

"With a connecting door."

"That you will keep unlocked."

"Hmm, most of the time."

"And we'll go camping by that pool where I first saw your outer beauty."

"As long as you promise not to sneak tamarind pods into my tea."

Trager's cheeks burned. He had forgotten about his plan to give Simone the runs. "That was--"

Laughing, Simone patted his hand. "You're so lovable when you blush." She got up. "Now I must go," she said, looking serious.

Trager's facial muscles sagged. "Where are you going?" he asked, the feeling of alarm returning.

"Upstairs, second floor. From the service stairs straight ahead, third door on the right. Meet me there in five minutes."

What the hell is she up to now? Trager watched her hurry across the lawn and disappear into the staff entrance door.

Trager finished his breakfast and went into the palace.

He counted doors in the hotel-like corridor and knocked.

"*Entrez.*"

Trager walked into a large bedroom furnished in Provençal style. Smoked polarized glass on the French doors softened the glare from the lake. Simone stood in the middle of the room, her hands inside the pockets of a white terrycloth robe. She no longer wore a hat. The veil just covered her nose.

"Don't move," she said as if holding a gun in her pocket.

"Now what?"

She smiled. "A little quiz."

"About what?"

"During breakfast, it seems we have agreed on our future modus vivendi, no?"

"Yes."

"Together, but independent?"

"Yes."

"We'll see each other frequently, but not every day?"

"Yes."

"You won't object when I travel by myself?"

"No."

"We'll exchange keys to our villas?"

"Yes."

She shrugged. "No more questions. Lock the door."

Simone spread her hands, opening the robe and let it slide off her shoulders. She then clasped her hands in front of her, in mock modesty.

Trager swallowed.

She said, "Don't just stand there, we're no longer just tent mates, no?"

"The only thing missing in this ceremony is witnesses."

"I'll witness you." She came to him laughing, wrapped her arms around his neck and legs around his waist. "Take me to bed."

He deposited her on the bed and took his pistol belt off.

Simone jumped off the bed. "Let Ishtar undress the warrior." She took his jacket off and undid his trousers. "Damn boots," she said as she pulled his trousers down. "And no underwear? I thought only women in thin, tight dresses did that."

"All my stuff is dirty."

"With your pants down, you can't escape. Now I can pounce on the object of my immediate desire." She pushed him onto the bed and jumped on top of him. "Trapped." Making playful growling noises, she bit his chest and with her teeth pulled on his nipples.

Trager's arousal was intense. His mind totally focused on the physical sensations as teeth, lips, tongue alternated on a voyage to where all his force was concentrated.

His radio beeped.

"Shit." He rolled over to reach the handheld on the floor. Simone bit his buttock.

"Au. Go ahead."

"The American ambassador is at the back gate to see you, sir."

Simone rolled him back over and had him in her mouth.

"Me?"

"He's asking for you by name."

Trager looked at Simone, astride and descending.

"I'll receive him in the garden shortly."

He dropped the radio, closed his eyes and felt only Simone around him.

~

A black Marine Corps gunnery sergeant in tropical uniform stood by a black Lincoln Continental parked under the rear entrance canopy.

"Good morning, Gunny," Trager said, returning the sergeant's salute.

Wearing a beige suit and a Panama hat with a flamboyant flowery headband, Blankenship sat on a bench near the spot where the breakfast table had stood. He shook his head as Trager approached.

Trager said, "Welcome to Zengawal, jewel of Central Africa."

"You're a jewel in deep shit, *amigo*. I couldn't believe my eyes," Blankenship said, pointing across the lake, "when I saw you through the telescope." He groaned. "I was watching this beautiful mystery lady, and suddenly, here comes AC Shoe dressed in a soldier suit. You've ruined my breakfast. And you better get into civvies, *pronto*. Or they're gonna nail your ass as an enemy combatant."

"There is no combat against the United States."

"There will be tomorrow."

"Huh?" Trager's heart accelerated.

"The peacekeeping force is landing tomorrow. Zimbabwean soldiers flown in by American pilots. If there's one shot fired, you're fucked. Remember the American Taliban?"

Trager sang, "Taliban, Taliban, tally me bananas."

"And your *compadre* Dankov is heading for The Hague, where he'll be tried for crimes against humanity."

The happy mood that had enveloped Trager since meeting Simone this morning vanished. "What have you been smoking?"

"I've gone to the trouble of coming here, in breach of protocol and who knows what else, to warn you. While I'm here, I may as well get some information."

"See the foreign minister."

"If you give me info, you can wear your soldier suit and they'll give you a medal for infiltrating the enemy."

"I can tell you one thing. Dankov was not responsible for the Bunaka massacre."

"He'll get his chance to tell the court."

"You've been manipulated. A Mr. Cruizet, who owns half of Belgium and a good chunk of Europe, controls the CASC. Through the CASC he gets the White House all excited."

Blankenship shrugged. "The U.S. gets a payoff. We get to build an airbase here."

"If you want an airbase, ask Bamondo. He'll lease you the land for a buck a day."

"Bamondo represents all that's evil in this continent. At least that's what the President said in his speech yesterday. You can't have an enemy without a bad guy. That's the essence of keeping the American masses entertained and rallied behind the flag-waving president. With Europe skittish about us going against Sadam Hussein, we need an air route not under European control. So this is the place where our airplanes will be able to refuel. Playing mercenary against what the U.S. wants to do will cost you plenty. You'll be arraigned before a secret court where everyone but you will have a top-secret clearance. You won't even be allowed to see the evidence against you, nor hear witness testimony. It will be classified. For people like you, USA may as well stand for United Stalinist America."

"You do have a way of pissing me off."

"I'm the last friend you've got. I can give you asylum at the residence."

"By tomorrow, if not sooner . . ." Trager gestured around them. "Look, its quiet, the riots are over. The ZAL has been routed. The excuse for military intervention is gone."

Blankenship shook his head. "Reality and political reality are two different things. The lady you had breakfast with is a terrorist."

"Because she attended a training camp financed by the CIA?"

"We financed Bin Ladin for a while. Now, he's a bad guy. She'll end up in Guantanamo."

Guantanamo?

Blankenship must have noticed the shock on Trager's face. He reached over and touched Trager's shoulder. "There will be an evacuation of foreign nationals. You and she can get on one of those planes. No one will spend much if any time looking for you."

Trager felt sorry for Blankenship. Political reality was a swamp in which the U.S. had lost its bearings since the end of the cold war. Now it staggered through the quagmire flaying its arms like a blind giant. Though never virtuous, the old goat did have a sense of honor. "I've had similar offers by lesser people." Trager glanced beyond the palace fence. The sidewalks of the lakefront road were thick with throngs cheerfully heading downtown. The big show was only a few hours away. "This is a nice place, the future Switzerland of Africa."

Blankenship growled.

Back in her dowdy dress and Robin Hood hat, Simone approached.

Blankenship stood and removed his Panama. "*Enchanté Mademoiselle.*"

"It's a beautiful morning, Mr. Ambassador."

"I'm just a chargé."

"And a voyeur. He was watching you through a telescope."

Simone cocked her head to one side. "Here?"

Trager nodded.

"One of my lesser sins." It was the first time Trager had seen Blankenship blush.

Simone laughed. "Too bad I was unaware of your admiration. I could have opened the window and given you a show."

"My life is full of missed opportunities." Blankenship groaned as he returned to his seat.

~

A Land Rover packed with soldiers drove across the lawn and stopped near the bench. Dankov jumped out. "Well, well, Uncle Duggie."

Blankenship said, "I see you've been fighting again."

Dankov's face and uniform were covered in dust and powder residue. He removed his beret and sat down. A diagonal line divided the dusty and clean parts of his forehead. "Are you here to pave the way for the Zimbabwean invasion?"

"They're peacekeepers."

"They'll suffer heavy casualties. I found some Zimbabweans on active duty in their army among the ZAL prisoners. I heard on the BBC that American C-130s have refueled in Entebbe while en route to Harare. You should inform your government we have an effective army that has routed the mercenary so called rebels. We don't need peacekeepers."

Trager was sure Dankov's information did not come from listening to the BBC.

"I've been reduced to the status of messenger boy. What do you have? Fifty, a hundred men to defy the most powerful nation the world has ever known?"

Dankov seemed amused. "Not only do I have more men than the handful that stopped the Germans at Brest-Litovsk, but I also have my honor."

"Capitulating to *force majeure* is considered honorable."

Dankov grinned. "Show me your imperial forces."

Blankenship's face became somber. He shrugged, stood and bowed. "*Mademoisele, gospoda ofizery, au revoir.*"

Chapter 44

As Blankenship drove off, Simone shook her head. "And I was dreaming of peace."

"When the glacier growls, there will be an avalanche," Dankov said.

Trager sighed. What had started as the most wonderful day of his life lay in ruins. He took Simone's hand. She squeezed back.

Dankov gave them a curious look. "I have to report to the President. Anything you can add from your talk with Fatso?"

Trager told them what Blankenship had said, while Simone kept shaking her head.

"We'll talk about this later. Combat dress for the coronation. After seeing Bamondo, I'm having a shower and a nap." Dankov began to turn then stopped. "What do we have here, a couple of love birds?"

"None of your business, Igor," Simone snapped.

Starting at eleven o'clock, every hour on the hour a jet fighter made several passes over Turako, rattling windows with sonic booms. According to Sokolov, the fighters had British markings and the flights appeared to originate in Uganda. Dankov's intelligence source reported that an RAF Tornado squadron had arrived at an airbase outside Kampala.

By three o'clock, both sides of Avenue de la Liberté and the park were jammed with a well-behaved crowd. A block away from the palace, the Second Infantry Regiment's thousand or so men stood in neat formation. The front gates of the palace remained open after all invited guests had arrived and were installed either in the presidential reviewing stand or on the bleachers on the sides.

Martial music grew louder. People craned their necks as the Army Band approached. Both on the street and among the invited guests, the mood was festive. Balloons and little paper flags added color to the crowds.

Dankov and Trager stood at the back of the presidential stand. Dankov said, "Let's go."

Trager worked his way around on one side of the reviewing stand, while Dankov came from the other. General Mawingi sat in the front row together with ministers next to the still-empty presidential chairs. As if sensing someone's approach, he turned and gave Trager a dirty look.

Dankov came from Mawingi's blind side. "Good afternoon, sir."

Mawingi turned, looking surprised then smiled.

"A word in private, sir?"

Holding his sword in one hand, Mawingi drew closer.

"This is to remind you, sir, that any false move by your troops and you will be the first to die."

Mawingi stared for a moment then said, "Am I to consider myself a hostage of foreign mercenaries?"

"We're living an interesting moment, General. I hope that, during the reception, we'll drink from the cup of peace."

Mawingi's face turned jovial. "Colonel, I congratulate you on last night's victory. We will drink to that, too."

A trumpet fanfare sounded and everyone stood. The guests applauded as Bamondo with Tissu at his side and followed by his ADC entered the reviewing stand. He wore tails and a white tie. The bulletproof vest he wore underneath made him look a little more corpulent than usual.

Dankov and Trager hurried to the back of the stand. With Simone's moment of triumph approaching fast, Trager brimmed with exuberance. Simone sat in the back row together with Leonora. Trager winked at Simone. She smiled back, gave him a happy nod.

The sound of the military band grew distinct and powerful. A weapons carrier bearing the Army colors turned the corner. The color guard wore white tunics and kepis. A Land Rover with the commander of the Turako garrison followed.

Upon reaching the front gate, the garrison commander got off, unsheathed his sword, marched to the presidential stand, and saluted. The music stopped.

"The Army of Zengawal is ready. Request permission to march past."

Mawingi returned the salute, asked the president something, and then bellowed, "Pass in review."

Playing Colonel Bogey's March, the band turned the corner and formed a box facing the palace.

Trager fingered the butt of his pistol and glanced at his Kalashnikov lying under Simone's seat.

The First Regiment appeared. The white parade dress tunics made them look unthreatening. The officers in front of each company saluted the reviewing stand with their swords. As the last company marched past, and turned the corner going toward the Metropole, Trager sighed with relief. The band marched off and the martial music was replaced by the thunder of drums.

Drummers dressed in animal skins whirled into view. Behind the drummers came a truck decorated with palm branches. Two lines of cadets in blue uniforms, carrying their rifles at the port across their chests, marched on both sides of it. The glittering reflection from the Utabu was almost blinding. It rested on a stand at the front of the truck. Behind the Utabu stood a solemn group of men in tall leopard skin caps. Wangohi was at the back also dressed in full witch doctor regalia.

The truck stopped where the band had stood. Trager was pleased to see the cadets who had now doubled the size of the palace guard. Everything was going to come all right. Trager glanced at Simone, who wiped at tears under her veil.

Groups of dancers, sports clubs, boy scouts, marching choirs and more drummers went by in endless procession. No one paid attention to the sonic booms overhead.

The Army band was back and stood to one side of the palace. The drumming died. The witch doctors, who overnight had become Elders of the Nation, descended from their truck.

The band broke into the Olympic fanfare.

The fanfare over, it seemed the whole city held its breath.

Headed by Babaku carrying the Utabu, the Elders crossed the street in stately procession toward the palace.

For Trager, this was a moment of strong emotion and drama. It was difficult to believe Simone had orchestrated this birth of a nation. She was a genius. It was her moment. Trager wanted to go to her and squeeze her shoulder, but he remained on the side of the stand, watchful for possible assassins.

It occurred to him that Longo wasn't around. Nor was Tony Bond.

Standing in front of Bamondo, Babaku made a speech. Something about the deserving son of Zengawal.

Holding the Utabu high over his head, Babaku climbed the four steps to where Bamondo stood. "Kneel, humble son of Zengawal."

Bamondo kneeled.

"If it fits, may the ancient spirits of the wizards of Zamani guide you."

Babaku lowered the Utabu and placed it on Bamondo's head.

There was a collective gasp.

The Utabu slid down Bamondo's face until it covered his nose.

"The pillow," Simone exclaimed as she jumped up.

"It doesn't fit," Babaku said in his booming voice.

Like the sound of a swarm of bees, a whisper traveled down the park.

Trager noticed Dankov now held a rifle in his hands.

Babaku removed the Utabu from Bamondo's head.

Trager saw a flash of blue as one of the Elders slipped Simone's pillow into the helmet.

Babaku placed the helmet on his own head. "By the wisdom of the ancients, I am *le Roi*."

"*Vive le Roi*," the Elders shouted.

"*Vive le Roi*," a roar answered from the street.

The band broke into the Zengawali national anthem.

Mawingi helped a shaken and pale Bamondo back on his feet as the elders marched away.

Dazed, Trager couldn't believe what he was seeing.

Dankov ran in front of the Elders and aimed his rifle at them. "Stop, thieves."

The strains of the national anthem died in discordant fading agony.

Time appeared to freeze as the procession stopped.

The noise from the crowd hushed.

Hundreds of stunned guests held their breath.

Bamondo's voice thundered, "Come back here, Colonel."

"You can't let them get away with this. It's treason." Dankov's voice echoed in the deathly silence.

"I order you to put that rifle down."

"Obey the President," Mawingi shouted.

Dankov stood aside. He turned toward the street and bellowed. "Cadet company, march to the rear of the palace."

As the Elders resumed their stately exit, Dankov disappeared from Trager's view. He then reappeared behind the stand and hurled his rifle to the ground. The weapon bounced and clattered on cobblestones, causing the heads of the stunned guests to turn.

Now without escort, the Elders climbed back on the truck.

Drumming broke the silence and the truck pulled away. The crowd roared, "*Vive le Roi*."

Simone came to Trager and buried her face in his chest. "I can't believe this. All the sacrifice, all the sacrifice." She looked up at him, shook her head and broke down into uncontrollable sobs.

Guests drifted away.

Trager's body stiffened as he heard machinegun fire.

Screams came from the park.

"Close the gates," Dankov yelled.

Letting go of Simone, Trager grabbed his rifle and ran up front.

In an effort to close the gates, palace guards shoved people aside. People who had left the palace were pushing to get back in. Others wanted to get out.

The staccato of more machineguns joined in the barking. The firing seemed to be coming from the top of a building by the Metropole, where the ZSS had its downtown offices.

The park was a scene of total panic. Balloons drifted skyward as a stampeded mob trampled women and children.

"Step aside, step aside." Trager tried to clear the way for the gates to close. He had to hurry. The stampede was threatening to engulf the palace grounds. He had to lend a shoulder to shove the gates closed as a sea of humanity reached the fence.

The shooting ceased.

"Assassins, assassins." Initially a murmur, the chant turned into a war cry of a mob gone berserk.

Hit by a cement-filled can, one of the guards went down next to Trager.

Like banners, bits of bloody clothing perched on top of sticks floated over the mob.

"Assassins, assassins." Angry faces pressed against the fence bars. A man who had climbed on the shoulders of others was about to go over the top. A guard shot him.

There was the sound of glass breaking behind him. "Get the tear gas," Trager yelled at a corporal. He could have saved his breath. Gas mask on, Kuzma led a squad of soldiers who began lobbing tear gas canisters over the fence.

Trager looked down at the man who had been shot and had fallen inside. Fortunately, he was only wounded in the shoulder. Despite the extreme burning of his eyes, nose and skin, Trager picked up the wounded man and staggered with him inside the crowded foyer, where he deposited him on a settee.

Dankov stood on the grand staircase, blocking access to the panicked guests, and talked into his handheld radio. Two palace servants closed the front doors. Trager summoned them and told them to take the wounded man to the dispensary in the back.

Someone opened the doors to the ballroom. From another world, Piano strains of *Claire de Lune* drifted into the foyer. It sounded like Wimbo playing.

Sirens blared outside as riot police supported by fire trucks with water cannon made a baton charge.

Trager searched for Simone as the several hundred people crowding the foyer calmed down.

The majordomo, armed with a bullhorn, climbed a few steps of the staircase. Once he got the people's attention, except for coughing and retching, the crowd grew silent.

"*Mesdames et Monsieurs*, on behalf of the president, it gives me honor to welcome you to Flamingo House. It is my pleasure to invite you to step into the ballroom where refreshments are being served. The President will join us shortly."

The little speech had a calming effect on the crowd. Ladies took compacts out of their purses and began wiping mascara streaks, straightening up turbans and hats.

Outside the palace grounds, several inert bodies sprawled. Some wounded staggered about. A man sat on the curb clutching his head.

Saying, "*Pardon, pardon,*" Trager pushed his way through the crowd and reached Dankov.

Dankov said, "They killed most, if not all, the Elders. My men at the Metropole report that the firing came from the Biashara building next door. I'm recalling the Simbas and the troops in Maridani. Have you seen Mawingi?"

There was the rattling of windows from a sonic boom.

"No." Trager scanned the crowd now pouring into the ballroom. Military uniforms were conspicuously absent.

"I'm afraid he will move against the palace. If the Simbas don't arrive in time, we don't stand a chance."

"Where is Simone?"

"She and Leonora went to the presidential quarters."

A waiter came up the steps. "Major Trager? There is an urgent telephone call for you, a Mr. Bond."

Trager and Dankov exchanged glances.

"Go see what he wants."

Mystified, Trager followed the waiter into the vestibule of the men's room.

Over a bad connection, Bond said. "It looks like you should be able to make it across the street. We need to talk."

"Talk about what?"

"You're the only one in Flamingo House who's got the sense to listen. Let's see if we can stop this bloody bloodshed. Forget the bloody, old chap."

"Where are you?"

"The last place we met."

After hanging up, Trager went to the foyer and looked out the window. The riot had been pushed well back. Several ambulances stood parked near the Metropole. This was not the time for considering personal safety. Trager knew Bond wouldn't have called if it wasn't a matter of extreme urgency.

Chapter 45

Amid the litter and trampled bodies, the smell of teargas lingered in the park. In the distance, the mob still chanted, "assassins, assassins." The desolation left behind the riot was nothing compared to the bleakness inside Trager's chest. He briskly cut diagonally across the park with his finger next to the rifle's trigger.

The truck the Elders took their last ride in stood in the middle of the street resembling a bloody colander. The dead driver still sat in the cab. A dense patch of dead bodies covered the lawn where people had stood to watch the parade and got mowed down together with the Elders. With faint hope, Trager looked inside the truck. The Utabu was gone.

Dankov's "peacekeepers" were still at the hotel door. Trager went inside and into the empty Terrace Bar. Tony Bond sat at the bar talking to a lone bartender.

"Beer?"

Trager nodded and sat at a table far enough from the bar where the bartender could not overhear their conversation.

Bond arrived with two bottles of Jumbo. "No glasses today, old chap."

He flopped down and lit a cigarette. Bit of a balls-up, what?"

"A fucking mess. Who killed the Elders?"

Bond shrugged. "People think Bamondo ordered the killing. They'll lynch him." He touched Trager's bottle with the neck of his. "You're well placed to do the world a favor and prevent further bloodshed. Tell Bamondo a helicopter will pick him up and his entourage tonight at ten and take him to a safe location outside the country."

Trager took a swig of beer that eased the burning in his throat. "You better give me a more convincing argument."

Bond frowned. "Very well. At this very moment, Longo is at the Cutthroat Tower demanding allegiance of the civil servants. He's planning a modest thanksgiving service at the Presbyterian cathedral tomorrow. Once that's over, Mawingi'll crown him outside on the cathedral steps. Meanwhile tonight, Mawingi is getting a load of hydraulic fluid for the recoil mechanisms for his tank guns to make them serviceable again."

"You mean Mawingi will attack tonight?" Trager admired Dankov's finesse in de-fanging Mawingi, but it couldn't last forever. Smuggling a few drums of hydraulic fluid would have been relatively easy. "Did you provide Mawingi the oil?"

Bond shrugged. "He is so afraid of your Russian friend, he plans to reduce the Evil Palace to rubble before sending in the infantry. Pity, it's such a nice building." He sighed. "The whole situation is out of control. The shooters thought they were killing Bamondo. With the Wussis thinking Bamondo killed Babaku, there will be civil war. When Longo gets crowned the Bassis will rebel." Bond took a deep breath and shook his head. "The peacekeepers won't have a chance. They'll need over thirty thousand troops to maintain order. The moment the Wussi tanks are out on the street, the Bassi police will leave town and head for the hills."

"What are you going to do?"

"I'm out on that helicopter with or without Bamondo. Tell Dankov I wish him good luck. Do you want a seat?"

"No, thanks."

"How about the lovely mademoiselle?"

"Yes, take her out."

Bond nodded and handed Trager a card. "My UK address. It's been a pleasure."

~

His watch showed five past seven when Trager left the Metropole. Outside, it was already dark. A lone policeman tried to chase dogs away from the massacre scene. The palace was illuminated as usual. As he crossed the park, Trager stopped. A dog chewed on one of the scattered corpses.

Trager shot the dog.

Entering the palace was like crossing a time warp.

The sound of music and animated conversation almost shocked Trager as he entered the foyer. A party was in full swing in the ballroom. He peered inside. Overlooking an archipelago of diners, Bamondo, flanked by Najua and the chief of police, sat at a long, elevated head table. At first glance, it appeared that no one had given importance to the events of the day. But Leonora's smile was fixed on her face as she sat neither talking nor eating. Bamondo, too, sat like a statue. The animated conversation that filled the room lacked the jovial tones of a social gathering. Maybe it was more like the rumble of voices one heard at a busy airport after it was announced that fog had closed it down.

Trager told the majordomo that he needed to see Bamondo.

Still dressed in tails and white tie, Bamondo came out, lighting a cigarette. Trager briefed him on the situation and gave him Bond's evacuation offer.

"When does he need an answer?"

"It isn't necessary. The helicopter lands and takes off with or without your Excellency aboard."

Bamondo smiled and placed a hand on Trager's shoulder. "You better stop calling me Excellency. Bond is right, the country will be ungovernable for some time." He closed his eyes. "I'm running like a dog." He looked around as if considering what to do, dropped his cigarette on the floor and crushed it with his patent leather shoe.

~

The swelling on Simone's nose had gone down considerably and she covered it with only a patch gauze secured by surgical tape. She sat next to Dankov at the long table in the officers' dining room and had traded her dress for a camouflage uniform.

"Have a seat," Dankov said, and poured champagne into a flute glass.

Trager walked up to Simone. She turned and gave him a quick, sad smile. "I was worried about you." He kissed her lips then sat next to her. She handed him the glass Dankov had poured.

After Trager had recounted his conversation with Bond, Dankov rubbed his chin. "Mmm, *da*. His thinking is similar to mine. If Bamondo goes, our job is finished. I have activated our emergency escape plan. Two helicopters and a support plane should be leaving Russia within hours. They'll be here in a couple of days."

"Will Mawingi give us two days?"

Dankov snorted. "Of course not."

It looked like their proverbial goose was cooked. Trager waited for Dankov to reveal some hare brained scheme.

"Once we tuck Bamondo, Leonora, and Simone and whoever else fits into Bond's *vertafliushka*--"

"I'm staying and I don't want to hear any arguments," Simone said.

Dankov looked at the ceiling. "Then we go to my fort and comfortably wait for our *vertafliushki* to arrive." He grinned. "Should I reserve a room for you two?"

"Adjoining rooms with a connecting door," Trager said.

"If you are concerned about appearances, Father Alexey can marry you."

"Oh, shut up."

Dankov shook his head and said to Trager, "You see what sort of hellion you've won yourself? Tonight, we'll have to maintain order. There will be panic once it becomes known Bamondo is abandoning his flock."

Dankov took a deep breath. "Then I will have to pay our African soldiers and say good bye. It's sad we can't take them with us."

~

Just before nine o'clock, the Simba Regiment arrived. Tired soldiers in dusty uniforms took positions outside the palace security perimeter. Shortly after, Genadiy rolled in together with an assortment of civilian trucks and several buses loaded with his ragtag militia armed with captured ZAL weapons and wearing red armbands in lieu of uniforms.

Trager and Dankov watched them from a second floor balcony.

Dankov said, "It is ironic that, in this moment of defeat, I have more troops than ever before. If Bamondo had a soldier's guts, we would now be disarming Mawingi's troops and tomorrow would have revealed a country at peace. Instead, we're seeing the eve of civil war. For me, that's a bitter legacy to leave."

He put his arm around Trager's shoulders. "Imagine this, we could go in, make a bit of noise and arrest Mawingi, clean up Longo's hell-hole and install our own king."

"Let's do it," Trager said. "Give me a couple RPGs and the cadets. I know the layout. I'll take Longo's joint."

Dankov shook his head. "As of midnight our employment is over. A man of honor obeys the constituted authority. It's a messed up world. After midnight we're nothing more than an armed band."

Then he looked at his watch. "It's time."

~

The Simbas had deployed to the residential neighborhoods, declaring Flamingo Heights, Lakeshore Estates and Turako Park safe for the moment. The Maridani Militia secured the city center. As hundreds of Europeans headed for the airport, part of Force Marabou kept the airport road open.

At the front gates of the palace, a line of chauffeured cars lined up, picking up guests. There were even a few taxis. The city was now quiet. Only occasionally, a shot or burst of automatic fire broke the illusion of calm. The police had vanished.

On hearing the sound of rotor blades coming from the east, Trager stopped watching the orderly exodus of guests and hurried to the back of the palace.

In the garden, where the lawn met the lake, a strobe light flashed. The helicopter flew overhead, not showing lights. It sounded like a large Sikorsky.

Illuminated by the eerie flashes stood a line of men: Dankov, the chief of police, the palace majordomo and a few others Trager didn't recognize. A few yards away, another group seemed to be in a huddle. Trager knew it was Bamondo, Leonora, Tissu, Bamondo's private secretary, Najua and his wife and kids. Simone was saying good bye to them.

The helicopter noise drew closer as it turned over the lake.

Blinding landing lights came on. The pitch of the blades changed and the helicopter settled.

Dankov saluted as people ran to the helicopter and were helped into the door. Trager recognized Bond, who jumped out and helped lift Najua's children through the chopper's door.

Machinegun fire came from the hill. The guns at the gate answered it.

The helicopter lifted, banked sharply and climbed over the lake.

A wail rose from near the staff entrance, where a group of palace staff stood embracing each other.

Dankov strode up the lawn and removed his Zengawal Army beret. His orderly handed him his Cossack peaked cap.

Sergeant Kuzma came up to Dankov, saluted and said, "The charges are ready and the basement's clear."

"Detonate."

A muffled sound of three explosions in rapid succession came from the building as the communications equipment was destroyed.

A radioman said, "Observation post Alpha reports tank engines starting."

"Thank you. All units begin phase one of withdrawal."

A red and a green rocket flew off the palace roof.

"This is it?" Simone asked, as she approached Trager, wiping tears from her eyes. Her walk unsteady, she appeared physically diminished. Trager put an arm around her shoulder, wishing he could lessen her personal tragedy.

$$\sim$$

The ominous squeals of tank treads came from the direction of the park. The Simba Regiment and the cadets stood in formation along the lakeshore road. They presented arms as the first Land Rover drove out of the palace grounds. Dankov stood in his vehicle and saluted. The Simbas removed their caps and roared three cheers.

A knot formed in Trager's throat as he drove past the troops that had defeated the ZAL.

"*Au revoir, mes amis,*" Simone said almost to herself.

The convoy circled the lake and took the back streets. The sporadic shooting increased into a steady exchange. The glow of several fires flared over the city center.

Near the market, a group of policemen stopped looting a store and scattered as the convoy approached.

Just outside of town, Force Marabou augmented by a blue Land Rover joined the column. Simone waved. "That's Sokolov, our one man air force."

~

It was nearing dawn when they approached the Majidogo River. Several huts on the Wussi side of the river were burning. With his siren blaring, Dankov sped into the village while his soldiers fired into the air.

It took fifteen minutes to clear barricades erected on both sides of the bridge.

The police on the Bassi side waved and cheered as the convoy went by.

The sun was already high when they drove past the drift where so long ago Simone stopped and led Trager to the pool. Simone said, "I guess we won't be camping there."

"For us, the world is getting smaller and smaller," Trager answered.

"What are you going to do once we're out of here?"

"I don't know. I haven't though about it." Trager didn't like the way Simone had phrased the question.

Chapter 46

The fort was as Trager remembered it, except that trenches, sandbag bunkers and barbed wire entanglements now surrounded it. On the level ground in front of the fort, five Russian soldiers and about forty Africans stood in formation and presented arms as the convoy arrived.

Trager and the others waited inside their vehicles while Dankov dismounted and inspected the troop. He gave them a brief speech, thanking the Africans for their service, and ordered them dismissed.

The Russian sergeant in charge said, "They request permission to keep their weapons."

"Granted."

"Urrah, urrah, urrah." The troop cheered.

Dankov saluted as they marched off down the hill

~

To his disappointment, Trager was back in his old room. Simone had opted for a room by herself. After a quick wash, he went to the officers' mess for lunch.

Genadiy, Vadim and Sokolov were about to belt down a shot of vodka when Trager walked in.

"Join us," one of them said.

Trager poured himself a shot.

"Death to the Ugandans who will attack us tomorrow."

"Death," Trager chorused with the others. It sounded like a primeval pagan rite. "Are they coming?"

Genadiy said, "A brigade with artillery and tanks is massed on the other side of the hill. They've set up camp four kilometers from the border."

"You always have such good news," Trager said.

The others laughed.

"We can always retreat to La Porte and join our black comrades," Vadim said.

"They will be fighting for a long time." Genadiy added. "Let's have another one. All my life, I dreamed of dying a heroic death defending a fort."

"To the last man," Vadim offered.

"And woman, too." Simone entered the room, followed by Dankov.

The second vodka went down better than the first shot. Trager's inner ache eased a little. He thought that, if Zengawal hadn't meant so much to Simone, he'd probably be as cheerful as the young Russian officers appeared to be--but of course, this was all outward bravado. Who knew what they felt inside?

Dankov said, "I apologize for discussing business in the mess. The rescue aircraft are delayed. The Turks won't authorize overflight. So they have to fly trough Iraq. If the Saudis don't cause problems, they will refuel in Sanaa and Asmara with a flight plan for Mozambique. Actually, they will land in Tanzania; in Kigoma to be precise. The *vertafliushki* will have to make two trips to get us all out. The first flight will arrive two hours after dusk, the second flight five hours later. So it has to be the day after tomorrow."

~

Two-hunderd-fifty miles southeast of Jacksonville, Florida.

Major Rodney Espinoza guided the old B-52 bomber into position behind the KC-135 tanker. This was the first of two midair refuelings his mission required. The top-up would allow him to reach launch point over the Gulf of Guinea and launch the two missiles. His next rendezvous would be in mid-Atlantic on the way back. He had no idea where the missiles were targeted, but a good guess was somewhere in Africa. He chuckled as his intake connected with the fueling boom. *Somewhere in Africa. The place is big enough you can't miss.*

~

Fort Chaipangani, Zengawal.

Trager leaned on the crenellated parapet and put his arm around Simone's waist. The forest looked unreal, like an old vacation picture.

Simone took a drag of the cigarette. "These things are awful. With all that was going on, I forgot to loot Pierre's humidor."

"With my private income and a bit of journalism, we'll be able to afford cigars."

"Where?"

"Spain, southern France . . ."

"No, Johnny. It won't be the same. We did great things together. Even before you came, I was happy here. I had something important to do and I could see us living close on Flamingo Heights, going on safari, even attending boring diplomatic receptions. Still building a country, leading close parallel lives."

"We could go to another African country." Trager thought he heard a strange noise.

She shook her head. "It wouldn't be the same."

"From one day to another, nothing stays the same. That's what makes life."

"Trager, you stubborn oaf, Europe is back to ground zero--"

"Alarm," a muffled shout came from downstairs.

Trager shot down the ladders. Below, boots pounded on stairs. He ducked into his room, grabbed his Kaliasha. A machinegun rattled somewhere as he ran out of the fort.

Dankov was yelling, "Two vehicles with me. You keep the bastards pinned down."

The machinegun fire came from the bunker perched above the fort.

Trager jumped on one of the trucks tearing off.

The radio crackled. "They're surrendering."

The vehicles reached the road at the bottom of the valley and turned right. In a minute, Trager saw a number of Dankov's soldiers on foot coming down the hill with the agility of goats.

On the road stood an olive drab Land Rover. Three men in Ugandan Army gumboots, their rifles on the ground, waved tee shirts.

From the direction of the fort, an anti-tank gun fired.

Trager couldn't see where, but the shell exploded about half a mile up the road.

The radio crackled. "We've got a Sherman tank."

A Ugandan captain was telling Dankov. "But we're not supposed to have opposition from your army."

"Tell your commander he's got it wrong. We're the British Army, and this border is under *our* protection. Get your column out of here before I call an airstrike."

Trager couldn't help but grin at Dankov's gall.

Leaving their weapons behind, the Ugandans turned their vehicle around and drove back. Dankov inspected one of the worn out Kalashnikovs. "It's a crime to send out boys armed with this third-hand junk."

"They are pulling back," someone reported on the radio.

Dankov said to Vadim, "Go set the charges inside." He then turned to Trager. "Get your *schmat* out of the fort. We'll sleep in the trenches."

~

Even though they were wiring to blow up the fort, Trager took a bath. Once he was ready, he went into the cellar, put some wine bottles in his bag, and a couple of bottles of Armenian brandy.

Simone came down and stuffed a bag with booze, too. "Mud-Man, come here. I'll show you something." She took out a flashlight. "Have you ever seen a secret door?"

"No."

She grinned like a little girl. "Watch." She gave a stone in the wall a hefty push. "Give me a hand."

Trager pushed the stone with both hands and the stone began to sink. There was noise inside the wall.

It's unlocked now." Simone pointed to the side. "Go ahead, push."

Trager pushed the wall and opened what had been an invisible hinged door.

Simone led down some stone steps. At the bottom, she shone the light around a medium-sized room with some worm-eaten wooden shelves along the walls. "Here is where we found the cut diamonds."

"The secret of Zengawal," Trager said in awe. "You should write a book."

"Pshaw, and have all the Longos in the world wanting to kidnap and torture me?" She bummed a cigarette and held Trager's hand while he lit it. "Here we are in a chamber that predates known history. A mystery that now will never be solved. I was looking forward to starting an archeological dig here. Instead, we have trenches. I'll have to inspect them to see if those gun-toting heroes have uncovered something of interest."

~

Next to the horseshoe machinegun nest he occupied, Trager dug a shallow sleeping trench wide enough for two. He tried to pass the time away by reading a lousy Russian detective story he had found in the fort's guardroom.

Simone had been inspecting all the trenches, looking at strata layers and unearthed stones.

The sun had just set. A soldier was lowering the British union jack that had been flying above the fort for the benefit of the Ugandans halted at the top of the pass.

Black smoke still floated over the spot where the old Sherman tank had been knocked out.

"Take a look," Ivan, who had introduced himself as a machinegun virtuoso, said.

Trager looked over the ledge. Hundreds of black shapes were coming out of the forest. It was the largest buffalo herd Trager had ever seen. It amazed him how quietly the animals moved. The buffaloes were probably slipping away from Ugandans infiltrating the forest.

Simone came over and handed Trager a Billy can full of stew. She sat with her feet inside the sleeping trench and covered her shoulders with a blanket. "I have found what looks like an old wall. It almost proves that, when the Arabs arrived here in the thirteenth century, this flat ledge already existed."

Trager uncorked a bottle of Chateauneuff du Pape he had rescued from the cellar.

By the time they finished eating, it was completely dark. The scream of a jet engine echoed in the valley. An airplane was coming low, very low-- too damn low!

"Missile," Trager yelled.

He grabbed Simone, threw her into the machinegun nest and dove after her.

The scream grew louder. The earth shook. Trager covered his ears. The missile had hit close but missed the fort and the trenches. A second scream approached. The ground swayed, searing hot air blasted over the deep nest.

Debris pounded the ground.

Then it grew quiet. Trager peered over the side. Isolated fires illuminated a scene of dusty fog.

The silence around the fort was complete, as if the forest had died. Coughs mixed with the crackling of burning timbers.

"Roll call," Someone yelled.

"Post one, all here."

By the time roll call was over, it was evident five men were missing.

"Father Alexey and the guys in the kitchen," Simone said.

As the dust cleared, pictures after the collapse of the World Trade Center came to Trager's mind. More than half the fort was gone. Only a corner remained standing. It didn't seem possible anyone inside could have survived. Nevertheless, soon, a party was searching the rubble. Trager desperately hoped no more missiles were underway. The kitchen area was completely blown away. Somehow, Dankov's office on the second floor, though missing a wall, was still there.

Dankov grumbled. "They should have waited for us to do the job. It would have been much neater."

Trager saw Simone disappear under a chunk of leaning wall. "Hey, don't go there, it can collapse," he shouted, knowing it was a useless warning. She always did what she wanted.

He lifted a piece of coral concrete and found a large boot with a bloody foot still in it. Only one man had feet that big--the giant Kuzma.

Ten or fifteen minutes later, his heart squeezed as he heard Simone's muffled voice call urgently, "Igor, John, come help me."

Trager rushed under the leaning wall and found a jumble of slabs. Simone's voice came from somewhere under the rubble. A light showed through spaces in the debris. "Are you alright?"

"Of course I am. See the hole?"

A shaft of light disclosed an opening. Trager stuck his feet in and wiggled his way down with Dankov right behind him.

Alcohol fumes mixed with the smell of dust. Trager found himself in what had been the cellar. Its walls still held, but the floor had collapsed.

"Follow me," Simone said, and led the way down the pile of rubble that had poured down the cellar and the secret chamber underneath. Trager realized that the secret chamber's floor had collapsed, too. Simone kept descending then stopped. "Turn your lights off and listen."

Trager could only hear her agitated breathing.

"Hello," she shouted.

Hello, hello, hello, her voice echoed several times.

Trager was amazed. They were inside a huge space.

"Turn on your lights and follow my beam."

The three lights together showed a slope of rubble. As they swept sideways, a stone wall appeared into view. Then a thick stone column and then another, a broken table.

"Come, *mes gars*."

They descended to the stone floor of the huge vaulted chamber.

Simone directed her beam to the left.

Trager's heart almost seized with fright.

Chapter 47

The man staring at him with unblinking eyes stood in a deep stone niche. It took Trager a few seconds to process the sight into comprehension. He was staring at a life-size dusty woodcarving of a man.

Simone approached it, swished off dust with a handkerchief. The sheen of gold appeared on the figure's head.

"The Utabu," Trager muttered.

Simone finished wiping the pointed helmet with a leaf-like crown bordering its base. As she continued dusting, a cape of golden chain mail came into view.

Simone turned and said, "Igor, I don't want you to ask any questions. Just keep your mouth shut." She then opened the cape, laughed and stood aside revealing a large, erect penis.

"Gentlemen, that does it. I'm keeping him. We'll have to build a crate." She walked off to one side. "Follow me."

She approached and opened an arched gate with barred doors. "The entrance. The entrance to what--King Solomon's mines?"

Beyond the gates, a long tunnel led downhill.

Dankov said. "Someday, we'll come back and find out. In the meantime, we'll take your ideal man with us and seal the entrance."

Trager went back to the statue. At its feet there was a small chest. He opened it and saw it was half full with large uncut diamonds.

"Simone, don't forget to take this with you."

She looked into the chest. "This belongs to Zengawal."

Dankov said, "Then give it to Mawingi. And how come the man doesn't belong to Zengawal?"

"I told you not to ask questions. I happen to like his penis. Give me that box--neither Mawingi nor Longo are getting it."

She then smiled at Trager. "You aren't the jealous type, are you?"

"No."

"Good. I'll live with my ancient man until it's time to return him to this country. You can live next door if you want to."

Trager's heart made a wild leap. "Turn your lights off."

In the total darkness, Trager pulled Simone to him. She came without resistance and wrapped her arms around his neck. They kissed.

~

It took a good part of the night to find boards, hammer a crate together and haul the heavy Utabu Man out of the subterranean chamber. Then Dankov placed several explosive charges and blew the opening closed.

The roar of colubus monkeys woke Trager shortly after dawn.

Simone slept still, clinging to him. During the night, the nearness of her body helped him forget the nightmarish situation they were in. With the long-range communications equipment in the fort gone, contact with Dankov's outside world was lost. Now they had no way of staying abreast on the progress or lack of it of the rescue flight. The smell of coffee drifted across the debris-strewn little plateau as soldiers brewed their morning drink in Billycans. Trager reached over and lit the Sterno. He had everything ready so that he could have coffee in bed.

Simone pulled his neck down. "Hmm, Mud-Man, give me a kiss. We've spent the night together. I should get something for that."

After he kissed her, she squeezed his nose.

"Honk." He kissed her again.

"Okay, coffee's ready." Trager glanced at the coffin-like crate with the Utabu Man lying under a small tree not far from where they were.

They listened to the BBC news while passing the coffee back and forth. In Turako, the situation was described as chaotic. Army and police clashed with each other. There had been an uprising in the barracks. Looting was widespread. Zimbabwean troops had control of the airport. Snipers prevented their advance into town. Europeans, Indians and Arabs were streaming for shelter at the airport. Belgium was sending paratroopers to protect its citizens. Unconfirmed reports said that the Army had massacred more than two hundred people at the cathedral.

Simone shook her head slowly. "I think it's all my fault."

Trager took her hand. "No, big trouble was brewing. You tried to prevent it."

"Had we found the Utabu Man earlier, paraded him on the streets, and then placed him on display on the palace foyer, would that have brought a different result?"

Trager thought for a moment.

"Yes. Then, the Utabu would have become a national symbol of unity, not the symbol of one man's power."

Simone gave a little smile. "A wooden king."

~

High, wispy mare-tail clouds drifted across the sky heralding the much delayed rains were about to arrive. Trager wondered who would get there first, the rescuers or the rain. For the moment, he decided to say nothing. There was no need to increase everyone else's anxiety level.

He returned to reading his novel, trying not to think that the Ugandans could appear any moment.

"*Vertolet!*" helicopter.

For a brief moment, Trager was elated, but, as soldiers took cover, aimed machine guns and RPGs in the direction of the approaching helicopter, he realized the chopper couldn't possibly be their savior.

He searched and found the dot descending over forested slope across the valley. At least it was only one. Through binoculars, he saw it was a civilian machine, white with a red stripe.

"Hold your fire," Dankov bellowed.

The helicopter hovered, descended and landed on the road below the fort.

Trager could now read American registration numbers.

Two soldiers scampered down the slope. A minute later, they were talking to someone through the open door. Finished with the conversation, they stepped away from under the idling rotor and one of them spoke into a walky-talkie.

"Mr. Blankenship of the American embassy wants to speak to Major Trager."

After the cruise missile attack, Trager was quite sure the American government's intentions weren't friendly. Blankenship probably came to assess damage. Trager stood and waved at Dankov who waved back with approval. To Simone, Trager said, "I'll be right back."

She looked worried. "Don't go."

"It's only Blanky. I'll be right back."

"Be careful."

Trager went over the ledge, worked his way around wire entanglements.

Blankenship came out of the helicopter, walked away a comfortable distance, and sat on the grass on the side of the road. He wore a green polo shirt, chinos and a shoulder holster with his old 1911 model Colt .45 automatic he had lugged around since his days in the Marine Corps.

"What brings you out to Dankov's Shangri La?"

"Concern over one American citizen. I'm glad you survived the night. I was sure you and Dankov were destined to die together."

"Thanks for the impressive display of American power. I guess they used the coordinates supplied by me to target the missiles?"

"They probably availed themselves of satellite photography. Today, at the Pentagon, they're pissed. Most of you guys survived--especially you."

"An elderly sergeant died along with a good cook and a priest."

"Sit down and listen carefully."

By the tone of Blankenship's voice, it was obvious he didn't bear jolly news. Trager sat next to him.

"The Antonov-12 and the two helicopters are now in Baghdad. They have refueled and are awaiting clearance to overfly Saudi airspace."

On hearing this news, the tightness in Trager's chest eased.

"The Russian government denies knowledge of the existence of these aircraft and has no objections if our Air Force shoots them down as they enter the southern no fly zone."

Trager took a clump of dirt, crushed it in his fist and watched the dust pour down between his feet.

Blankenship grunted and wiped sweat from his forehead. "I've made a deal with a certain government official--You, John Dalton Trager, surrender into the custody of the FBI to answer charges of sedition, treason, bearing arms against Americans, conspiracy to kill Americans . . . There's more that I haven't had time or inclination to read. You surrender and we allow the plane and helicopters to proceed."

"That's all a bunch of crap," was all Trager could muster to say. Like his life, the dust coming out of his fist was now a tiny trickle. Everything was ending.

"The Brits are pissed off, too. But I can hold the Ugandan Army back just long enough . . ."

If what Blankenship said was true, Simone, Dankov and about fifty Russians would die, and so would he.

Trager looked up the slope from an attacker's perspective. Yeah, they could probably hold out for several days, even against a determined enemy. Eventually, the ammo would run out. Without the rescue flight, they were doomed.

"Make up your mind. The FBI is waiting inside the chopper."

"You wouldn't shoot down unarmed planes on a mission of mercy."

Blankenship nodded slightly. "Saudi Arabia, Egypt and Muscat won't let them pass unless we give the okay. Belgian paratroopers are supposed to arrive in Turako today. There's furor over the Bunaka massacre, and they're coming after Dankov to haul him and his accomplices to The Hague. The U.S. government doesn't want the precedent of one of its citizens tried in the world court. We're willing to let Dankov slip out, as long as you surrender to the FBI."

If the lives of Simone, Dankov and his soldiers could be spared, the prospect of jail was easier to bear. Trager had no illusions of getting a fair trial.

"I'll get my things."

"No, you come with me now or the deal is off."

"They'll shoot you down."

"Call them on your radio."

Trager weighted the radio in his palm, took a deep breath. "Vulture, the rescue planes are on their way." He hesitated and said abruptly, "I'm leaving now. Good luck."

He placed his rifle and radio in the middle of the road.

As he walked toward the helicopter, he kept his gaze to the ground. He would never see Simone again.

~

Soldiers no longer hunkered in their holes but stood outside the trenches watching the helicopter lift. Trager recognized Dankov standing in the middle of the plateau, Simone next to him.

No one waved.

The pilot lowered the nose and the helicopter accelerated, heading toward La Porte. Trager pressed his cheek against the window to see back. People were no longer visible. The ruin of Dankov's fort looked like a gray accusing finger pointing at the sky.

Faintly in Trager's mind played a tune of hope.

> *We'll meet again*
> *Don't know where*
> *Don't know when*
> *But I know we'll meet again some sunny day.*

Hope however faint, however false, was the essence of survival.

Epilogue

Four years passed and his release on parole had been denied. The time he had spent in solitary awaiting trial had steeled Trager for what was to come. After sentencing, it had taken him two weeks to realize he would survive the eight years in prison.

Everything in life was relative. In Fort Knox he wasn't exposed to the riffraff and dregs of society that populate most prisons. He considered himself lucky. He wasn't allowed to write his memoirs, but he did work on the prison's newspaper and gave French and Russian lessons to other inmates. During these lessons, he got a perverse pleasure from sneaking in lessons on tax evasion and money laundering.

"If you master the verbs *avoir* and *etre*, you pretty much have it made," Trager said to his class that consisted of two former CFOs and a former Enron vice president.

A guard came in and said, "Trager, you have a visitor."

Trager went to the visitors' hall where he saw Blankenship twice a year. Since retiring, the old goat had lost quite a bit of weight and had launched into a career of trying to obtain Trager's release.

In a loose suit, fitting like a collapsed tent, Blankenship looked the picture of a failed lawyer. After a few minutes of chitchat, he handed Trager an envelope. "This has completely fucked up your chances of parole, but I thought you'd want to see it anyway. You can read it once I leave. The good news is I managed to get your name on the list for presidential pardons. So I hope to have you out by Christmas."

Back in his cell, Trager read the letter.

> *Dearest Mud-Man,*
>
> *Even with Igor's contacts, it took some time to find out what happened to you and to realize your leaving us was an act of selfless heroism.*
>
> *It was raining when the helicopters arrived, but we guided them in by setting vehicles on fire.*
>
> *I did not write earlier for reasons I will describe below.*
>
> *Igor now lives outside Ostrogorsk, where he has a horse farm. Leonora is divorced and lives with Tony Bond in England. Pierre says conditions are favorable for his return to Zengawal. He has asked Igor to go back with him. Igor has gracefully declined.*

I have opened two art galleries, one in Saint Petersburg and one in Moscow. Both are doing well. I plan to open another one in Paris next year. I also have a farm two hours by horse from Igor's place. There are two houses on the property. In the summer I live in one of them with The Man.

Presently, in Saint Petersburg, I have a photo exhibition called Secret Africa. Mud-Man, your photographs are selling, and selling and selling. I don't exhibit your Venus in Paradise. An enlargement hangs in the bedroom in my Ostrogorsk dacha. By the way, I got a nose job and it is now as good as new.

Blankenship telephoned a few days ago saying a presidential pardon is a sure thing and said it was okay to write. Before, a letter from any of us would have reduced your chance of parole because you are considered a flight risk. With a pardon, you may come and live in the other house on the farm. It is a five-minute walk from where Venus in Paradise hangs, so you'll be able to see it frequently, if that is what you wish to do.

In Saint Petersburg, it's difficult to find a place, but I have a bed larger than the sleeping trench at Fort Chaipangani.

I have opened a dollar account in your name. The proceeds from your photographs are at the moment slightly more than thirty-two-thousand dollars. The exhibit has been labeled by the press as photos taken by an American prisoner of conscience. I don't know if you have a conscience or not. Over here, it's good marketing. No?

Stay well and come to see me if you wish.
Ishtar

The End